The Traitor's Wife

THE WOMAN BEHIND BENEDICT ARNOLD AND THE PLAN TO BETRAY AMERICA

A Novel

ALLISON PATAKI

"If you read one book this year, make it Allison Pataki's *The Traitor's Wife*."
—**MICHELLE MORAN**, international bestselling author of *Madame Tussaud*

Praise for *The Traitor's Wife*

"Historical fiction lovers will look forward to more from this promising new novelist."

—*Publishers Weekly*

"I consider this to be the debut of a major writer of historical fiction."

—Mary Higgins Clark

"If you read one book this year, make it Allison Pataki's *The Traitor's Wife*. Few authors have taken on America's Revolutionary War so convincingly, and this story of Benedict Arnold's wife will appeal to lovers of historical fiction everywhere. Highly, highly recommended!"

—Michelle Moran, international bestselling author of *Madame Tussaud*

"Allison Pataki's captivating debut novel examines history's most famous tale of treachery through a woman's eyes. Meticulously written and well-researched, this story will transport you back to the American Revolution and keep you turning pages with both its intrigue and love story. *The Traitor's Wife* is a well-told tale."

—Lee Woodruff, author, blogger, and television personality

"*The Traitor's Wife* is a gripping novel steeped in compelling historical detail. Pataki writes lyrically and succeeds in bringing to life, and humanizing, notorious characters from our nation's past. Ultimately a story about honor and heart, readers will have a hard time putting this book down."

—Aidan Donnelly Rowley, author of *Life After Yes*

"Allison Pataki has given us a great gift: a powerful story of love and betrayal, drawn straight from the swiftly beating heart of the American Revolution. Replete with compelling characters, richly realized settings, a sweeping plot, and a heroine who comes to feel like a dear, familiar friend, *The Traitor's Wife* is sure to delight readers of romance and lovers of history alike."

—Karen Halvorsen Schreck, author of *Sing for Me*

THE TRAITOR'S WIFE

A Novel

THE WOMAN BEHIND BENEDICT ARNOLD AND THE PLAN TO BETRAY AMERICA

ALLISON PATAKI

HOWARD BOOKS
A Division of Simon & Schuster, Inc.
New York Nashville London Toronto Sydney New Delhi

Howard Books
A Division of Simon & Schuster, Inc.
1230 Avenue of the Americas
New York, NY 10020

First Howard Books trade paperback edition February 2014

HOWARD and colophon are trademarks of Simon & Schuster, Inc.

For information about special discounts for bulk purchases, please contact Simon & Schuster Special Sales at 1-866-506-1949 or business@simonandschuster.com

The Simon & Schuster Speakers Bureau can bring authors to your live event. For more information or to book an event contact the Simon & Schuster Speakers Bureau at 1-866-248-3049 or visit our website at www.simonspeakers.com.

Interior design by Davina Mock-Maniscalco

Manufactured in the United States of America

1 3 5 7 9 10 8 6 4 2

Library of Congress Cataloging-in-Publication Data

Pataki, Allison.
The Traitor's Wife : A Novel—The woman behind Benedict Arnold and the plan to betray America / Allison Pataki.—First Howard Books trade paperback edition.
pages cm
1. Arnold, Margaret Shippen, 1760–1804—Fiction.
2. Arnold, Benedict, 1741–1801—Fiction. I. Title.
PS3616.A8664T73 2014
813'.6—dc23
2013023625

ISBN 978-1-4767-3860-4
ISBN 978-1-4767-3862-8 (ebook)

To my grandmothers,
Peggy and Monique

"To beguile the time, look like the time;
Bear welcome in your eye, your hand, your tongue:
Look like the innocent flower,
But be the serpent under it."

—Lady Macbeth,
William Shakespeare's *Macbeth*

*"Love to my country actuates my present conduct,
however it may appear inconsistent to the world,
who very seldom judge right of any man's actions."*

—Excerpt of a letter from Benedict Arnold to
George Washington, September 24, 1780

CONTENTS

PROLOGUE

"All Is Lost"

September 24, 1780
West Point Fort, New York

THE TALL ONE, General George Washington, sent word that he would be late to breakfast. I wonder—is this the first fraying border of a carefully stitched plan about to unravel? Or, is it simply a straightforward message: The colonial commander is running behind schedule, have your cook and your lady plan accordingly. *I thank the messenger, a dark-haired favorite of the general, a Mr. Alexander Hamilton, and return to the pantry. But this change to the schedule seems to portend a larger inevitability. My insides twist as the suspicion takes root, taunting me—my mistress is going to fail.*

"What's he up to, postponing the whole breakfast?" Mrs. Quigley sulks under a cloud of flour but keeps kneading the dough. "Now the loaf will burn, the tea will oversteep, and the peaches will attract flies."

"He's the commander of the Continental Army. I suspect that General Washington has faced more formidable foes than a few flies in his peaches." Mr. Quigley, my master's butler, fidgets with the pewter buttons of his coat as he scrutinizes his reflection in the silver teapot.

"He'll think us a bunch of uncivilized country bumpkins!" Mrs. Quigley snaps back at her husband. The white curls that escape her bun are now even lighter as wayward wisps of baking flour settle in them, like one of Mistress's powdered wigs.

"There, there, Constance." The old man pats a hand on her back. "All will be well. I'll go inform Master Arnold of the delay." Mr. Quigley exits the smoky kitchen, and I follow in his trail. I do not have it in me to tell the old man how wrong he is.

The disruption to the schedule does not upset my mistress, who awoke this morning in fine spirits.

"How could I be anything but cheery today?" She yawns as I draw the curtains aside, letting in the gentle sunlight of a warm September morning, ripe with the aroma of the swollen peaches that hang heavy in her orchard below. She and her husband, at last, are just days away from attaining their dreams. The prestige and wealth that have so long evaded them, dancing like a seductive mistress only to recede back behind her veil, are finally within reach. No, nothing will ruin my lady's merry mood today.

When the second messenger arrives on horseback, Mistress hears the frenzied pace of the horse hooves, throbbing like the Native's drumbeat, outside her open window.

"Another rider? Goodness, we must be the busiest home on the Hudson River this morning." Mistress chuckles, tugging at the loose sleeves of her white linen nightdress. "Don't they know we are set to receive Washington and his party for breakfast this morning? You'd think they could withhold these errands for at least one day." She sighs, her features fresh from rest, beautiful beneath the frame of loose blond curls. "Better go see what they want." She directs me with a nod and I leave her room, making my way down the narrow wooden staircase.

"Scoot, pup." I edge the dog aside from the door. From my perch on the front step, I shield my eyes and stare up the shaded post road. The rider emerges from the dappled cover of the thick trees into the stark early-morning light. My heart lurches involuntarily at the memory of another morning, when another rider had trotted up this trail. How that soldier had been here to see me. But I cannot allow myself to grow hazy in daydreaming, not today.

I notice that this man is not liveried in the General's crest, and therefore does not come from Washington's camp. He approaches the house at alarming speed, urging his weary horse forward with the ruthless spurs of his dusty boots. He halts just feet from me, his horse breathless, the rider looming over me like one of St. John's horsemen come to warn us of the end of the world. I straighten up to my full height as the man alights from the horse, landing in a cloud of churned-up dirt, uniform filthy, hair matted with sweat.

"Can I help you?" I stand, sentry-like, before the front door of the farmhouse.

"I need to speak with Major General Benedict Arnold." The man, still gasping for air, careens toward the house, dust surrounding him like a shroud. "Water my horse, miss. I must speak to the General!" The man hands me the bridle and staggers toward the front door without another word.

I hear the commotion in the front of the house as this lone rider calls out the master's name: "Where is General Benedict Arnold? Urgent message for Benedict Arnold from the south Hudson."

I tie this man's horse to the post out front and glide noiselessly back into the house, positioning myself out of sight at the top of the stairway. I hear my master approach the messenger in the drawing room. His telltale plodding on the wooden floor—lopsided, uneven—due to the war wound that has forever crippled him and rendered his left leg useless. Muffled sounds as the master of the house greets the messenger, his voice like gravel as he chides his subordinate.

"What is your aim, man? Barging in on us like this on the morning we are to receive His Excellency George Washington, and with the lady of the house not yet arisen and dressed?"

The messenger answers through uneven breath. "I assure you, Major General, you will pardon my abruptness when you see the message I'm delivering. I was ordered to deliver it posthaste."

"Good heavens, from where are you coming?" My master's voice now betrays his alarm.

"North Castle Fort, down the Hudson. A full day's ride, sir."

"Give it here, then." I hear papers being ruffled as they change hands. Silence follows, with just the sound of the morning birdsong to accompany the scene unfolding inside the farmhouse.

Then the master's gait, again lopsided, but with an urgency I haven't heard in years. He soon reaches the stairs, causing me to flee back into my mistress's room.

"What is it?" Her eyes widen as I dash across the threshold of her sunlit chamber.

"Master's coming!" is all I have time to say. We hear his rapid approach; using his impressive upper body strength, he's pulling himself up the stairs. The floorboards groan beneath his boots as he climbs. I look to my lady, and her features are horror-struck as we understand each other. No words are needed between us after all these years.

"But surely it's not . . . it can't be?" Mrs. Arnold fidgets with the bedcovers, deliberating whether to rise or remain abed.

"Peggy." Arnold bounds through the door, his hulking frame atremble in the doorway. Struggling to breathe, he gasps, "They've found us out! All is lost, all is lost. We're unearthed." His face tells me that he

struggles just as much as my lady does to make sense of the words, even as his lips utter them. And then, as quickly as he entered, General Arnold exits back out my lady's doorway. And I am left alone, in this room, with nothing but my lady and her shrill wails.

"BENEDICT!" she cries after him. "BENEDICT ARNOLD!"

CHAPTER ONE

"Never Anger Miss Peggy"

May, 1778
Philadelphia, PA

CLARA KNOCKED on the front door once, twice. She checked the address scrolled on the worn piece of parchment again. Her grandmother's familiar handwriting directed Clara to arrive at the Shippen mansion on the corner of Fourth and Walnut Streets, deep in the district that housed the city's wealthiest residents.

A crack of a coachman's whip drew Clara's attention away from the Shippens' door, and she gazed over her shoulder toward the street—a noisy thoroughfare of horse hooves, carriage wheels, and the deafening drum of marching British soldiers. A servant leaned out of a window several houses down and emptied a series of chamber pots onto the cobblestone street before disappearing once more into the home. The closeness of the noise and stink was unlike anything Clara had ever experienced on the farm.

The Shippen mansion, like its adjacent structures, was composed of red brick and built with an orderly symmetry: the sort of architectural purposefulness she'd heard about since George Washington and Thomas Jefferson had built their homes in this style.

The tight row of brick society homes lining Fourth Street resembled one another but for the shutter shades; some houses had green shutters, some light blue, some dark blue, some white. The Shippens had elected to paint their shutters black.

The Shippen mansion sat back from the street, flanked in front by a small patch of grass and two cherry trees in the full bloom of late spring. The entryway, a wide wooden door, stood above three short steps and below a triangular pediment. A top row of arched dormer windows poked out from the sloping roof, with two rows of shuttered panes below. The windows—built not only for allowing in light, but also for their decorative appeal—testified to their owner's wealth; a passerby on the street might be so lucky as to catch a glimpse of the famous Judge Edward Shippen studying his books, or spy one of his beautiful daughters as she flitted through the vast parlor on her way to receive a gentleman caller.

This must be the right home. Clara knocked at the imposing front entrance again. The door opened, and Clara was greeted by the lined face of a woman past her youth.

"Good afternoon." The woman had soft features framed by a graying bun, which peeked out around the edges of a clean, white-linen mobcap. She greeted Clara with an appraising smile.

"Is it Clara Bell, come at last?" The aged woman opened the door wider to reveal a fine appearance—an indigo petticoat made of linen to accommodate the warmer weather, draped by a clean linen apron. On top she wore faded gray stays over a crisply pressed white blouse. A fichu was tied around her neck to ensure the modesty required for service in such a fine home. She rolled back her cuffed sleeves and waved Clara inside.

"Thank you, ma'am." Clara entered through the open door, clutching her tarpaulin sack as she stepped over the threshold. The woman closed the front door behind her, shutting out the noise and stink of the street and allowing Clara to ease into the airy interior of the home. Its soundless tranquility was a welcome relief after the hustle of Fourth Street.

"Well, Clara Bell, we've been awaiting your arrival all day." The older woman smiled, taking Clara's sack from her arms. "Was it a tiring journey from the country?"

"It was fine, ma'am," Clara answered, even as she was certain her haggard features betrayed her fatigue.

"You took a post carriage?"

"Aye, ma'am."

"That must have cost you a small fortune."

"I'm grateful to have the employment, ma'am." Clara managed a timid smile, finding words evasive in the grand hallway in which she'd suddenly found herself. She felt as though she'd awoken into this buffed and varnished grandeur without a clear recollection of the circumstances that had brought her to Philadelphia. Clara blinked, remembering. The abandoned farmhouse. Oma dying. In her last moments, her old grandmother penning a letter to a friend from years ago. Oma urging Clara to leave the Hartley farm, as the Hartleys themselves had done, fleeing the approach of the British and the Iroquois.

"I am Mrs. Quigley, housekeeper for the Shippens."

"Very nice to meet you, Mrs. Quigley."

"Yes, well . . ." The housekeeper's reply faded to a sigh as she surveyed Clara's appearance. Clara stood still, feeling her cheeks grow warm; her warm-weather petticoat of linen was creased and dusty from the trip, but it was the only one she possessed of its kind. She'd only rotate it out of her wardrobe when the weather changed and the crisp autumn air required her wool petticoat. Unlike this housekeeper, Clara's clothes were not bought in a store, but were homespun, sewed by Oma. Clara wore her petticoat and stays in the cotton ticking pattern, off-white fabric with blue stripes. Her apron, once white, had been laundered so many times that it now bore a yellowish tint.

"Follow me, Clara." Mrs. Quigley turned and crossed the room in several brisk strides. Clara followed, hurrying to take in the surroundings as she kept apace. The Shippens' front hall was well lit by a wall of broad, clean windows. The focal point at the center of the hall was the expansive staircase, which drew the eyes up in a languid arc until it reached the second floor. Removed from the entrance was a maple fireplace. A fire crackled even on this warm spring afternoon, filling the front hall with its welcoming aroma, which mingled with the distinct scents of furniture polish and ladies' perfume.

"Quite a bit grander here than it was at the farmhouse, I imagine." Mrs. Quigley turned just in time to catch Clara, eyes rapt, examining a feather-light shawl of creamy robin's egg blue. It was store-bought and fine, its border embroidered with yellow silken flowers, its colors as bright as a springtime morning. It had been left, haphazardly discarded over the back of an upholstered armchair, as if its owner could be reckless with an item so fine.

"Miss Peggy's shawl. We better put it back in her closet where it belongs or we'll never hear the end of it." Mrs. Quigley scooped up the expensive item. "All right, then, follow me, child." Clara trailed the housekeeper through an open doorway into an ample drawing room. The Shippens' furniture seemed designed to impress the eyes with ornate decoration as much as to entice the body into its plush comfort. The chairs of the drawing room were carved out of smooth mahogany, their slender curves varnished to a glossy sheen. Clara's legs suddenly felt leaden with fatigue; how she longed to sink for just one moment into one of these chairs.

"You look like you've never been inside a drawing room before, girl," Mrs. Quigley remarked, fluffing a silk pillow on a nearby settee.

"Not one like this, ma'am, I haven't." Clara's eyes roved hungrily over every detail of the quiet room, the only sound issuing from an encased clock, taller than Clara herself, that occupied a far corner. Oil paintings in bronze frames adorned the walls. A soft splash of May sunlight streamed in through the windows, mingling with the dancing shadows cast by the fresh white candles in their sconces. How fine they must be, the people who frequent these spaces, Clara thought. At night, when the sunlight vanished and only candlelight remained, how easy it must be for them to slip into a corner and whisper a piece of gossip or listen to a verse of an admirer's poetry.

"Enough of your daydreaming. What do you think, girl?"

"It's . . . it's lovely here," Clara stammered, looking around with ill-disguised awe.

"It's nice, isn't it? Course, you'll hear every day how the money's gone and the furniture is growing outdated, but I think it's just fine." Mrs. Quigley smiled, the skin around her serious eyes creasing into a soft, worn pattern. "Well, Clara, you've had a long trip from the countryside; let's have you come in and catch your breath." Mrs. Quigley led Clara through the drawing room past a smaller, smartly decorated parlor with salmon-colored walls, shelves of books, and a silk sofa across from a card table.

"Books for the judge, cards for the ladies. That's how they'll spend their evenings. Course, Miss Peggy won't be contented with either activity—she wants to be out dancing every night." Mrs. Quigley kept a brisk pace as she crossed the room. Once through the parlor, a doorway allowed entry into a separate wing, which could be closed off from the front of the house. The two women proceeded now down this long, narrow passageway. No light shone here except for that which pierced the small windows of the rooms on either side of the corridor, and there was no ornamentation on the clean white walls. Clara stole quick glances into the rooms as she followed the housekeeper. Some rooms appeared occupied, others abandoned. This wing, she realized, housed the Shippen family's servants.

Clara peeked into the empty rooms she passed—most held just bedframes and unused chamber pots, but they looked comfortable and of a good size. "Mrs. Quigley, if you please, why are all of these rooms empty?"

Mrs. Quigley sighed, jingling a set of brass keys as she led Clara farther down the hall. The old woman appeared unsure how to answer the question. "Just a few years back we were at full capacity, with two servants in each of these rooms. But we've had to let so many folks go, most of the rooms are empty now."

"On account of the war?" Clara asked.

"You're a curious one, aren't you?" Mrs. Quigley glanced back over her shoulder at Clara, studying her for a moment before answering in a hushed tone. "You'll have heard that Judge Shippen has refused to take a side—either Tory or Rebel."

Clara nodded. The Shippens were one of the city's most prominent families. The news had traveled as far as Hartley Farm when Doctor William Shippen, the judge's brother, had come out strongly for the colonials. That's when his brother, Clara's new employer, had cut all business dealings to avoid appearing partial to either army.

Mrs. Quigley continued in a muted tone. "Without much coming in, we run a lean operation now that the war is on."

Clara wondered why it was that they were bringing her into the household under these circumstances. Mrs. Quigley must have guessed at her thoughts.

"But Mistress Peggy fought hard to fill your post; she insisted to her father that we had need for a lady's maid in the household. What with me, well, I'm busy enough running the home that I barely have time to tend to the missus, let alone her two daughters."

"What are they like?" Clara asked.

"The Shippen ladies?"

"Aye," Clara nodded.

Mrs Quigley considered the question. "You shall see for yourself, soon enough." The old woman halted at the end of the corridor. "Here we are, Clara. After you."

Clara hesitated, standing still.

"Your bedroom, child," the housekeeper said. "Go on."

Clara passed the housekeeper, her eyes lowered. Her bedroom? It would be the first room she'd ever had to herself. At the farm, she'd always slept on a straw pallet beside the kitchen fire, Oma's snoring frame curled up beside her. But here she had a bedframe. And a door that could shut, offering an entirely new privilege: privacy.

Of course, when compared to the front of the Shippen house—with tables serving no purpose other than to host card games, and silver bowls serving no purpose other than to hold flowers—these quarters were dull. But Clara could barely contain a giggle over the thought of having her own room.

"Nothing fancy, I'm afraid. Will it suit you?" Mrs. Quigley fidgeted with her brass keys, apparently in a rush to get to her next chore.

"Suit me? Why, a room to myself . . ." Clara looked around her new domain. There was a single straw mattress on a rusted iron frame. A simple dresser of dark walnut stood against the opposite wall, and a thin desk and stool occupied the corner. The window, small but bright, faced out the back of the house. Clara crossed the room and peeked out the window. She spied the formal garden, done in the Continental style with tightly clipped shrubs, pruned rose bushes, and a tidy carpet of green lawn. Beyond that was a small orchard, its trees appearing to hold the first signs of apples. Cherry blossoms bloomed in the May warmth, forming neat columns of shady pathways. The manicured grass, so unlike the wild fields of the farm, was intersected by meandering pebbled walkways, where her ladies must tread when receiving finely dressed visitors. Birdsong pierced the blue sky, as did the aroma of fresh-petaled flowers. It was an Eden in the midst of the colonies' busiest city.

Behind the garden stood a rectangular stable, where Clara spied a young man sitting between the large doors. Clara watched this figure as he plucked out a simple melody on a handmade guitar, as if entertaining himself while awaiting the arrival of some riders. Suddenly aware that he was being surveyed, the stableboy paused his singing, looking up in time to catch Clara's gaze. She ducked her head back behind the window, blushing.

"Oh, so you've seen Caleb." Mrs. Quigley was beside her at the window, swinging it open to allow in the fresh spring air.

"Who is he, ma'am?"

"The resident troublemaker." Mrs. Quigley smirked, wiping the dust from the windowsill.

Clara glanced back outside and noticed that the young man named Caleb was no longer sitting at his post. She inhaled, taking in the heady scent of fresh flowers. "Mrs. Quigley, have you grown accustomed to all of this?"

"Aye, it's a beautiful old home, all right, but don't let it seduce you. There's plenty to be seen in this house that ain't so beautiful." Mrs. Quigley's eyebrows arced a moment before her face softened. "Clara, I hope you don't mind my saying so, especially after I've only just met you, but you look just like your grandmother did. Course, when she was a lot younger."

Clara lowered her eyes, her focus blurring at the mention of her Oma.

Mrs. Quigley continued. "She was a dear friend of mine, and I was happy to have the opportunity to help her."

"Thank you, ma'am."

"I know you'll miss her."

"Indeed." Clara's eyes stung with the threat of tears, but she did not wish to weep before her new employer. Still, it seemed strange, illogical, to refer to her grandmother as someone from her past.

"When she wrote, asking me to find a post for you in the Shippen household, I was eager to help. Anything to make her final rest a bit easier." Mrs. Quigley sighed, and Clara bit her lip, hesitant to respond in case her voice cracked.

"But enough of that business. Where were we? You think you shall be comfortable here?"

"Very." Clara straightened her posture, grateful to change topics.

"Good." Mrs. Quigley slapped the mattress once, producing a cloud of dust. "You'll get one fresh candle a week, and not more, so mind you how you use your nighttime lighting. Quills and ink you'll have to request on a need-by-need basis."

Clara thought about this: she had no one to write.

"Judge Shippen tries to be generous, but there's only so much he can manage, especially with trying to keep Betsy and Peggy in the latest fashions." Clara could tell from the housekeeper's terse manner that this was a topic she'd discussed before.

"Now, Clara, I suppose you'll want to change before you meet Mistresses Peggy and Betsy?"

"Change?" Clara looked for the second time with disapproving eyes over her own appearance. "Oh, ma'am, I've got just the one other petticoat in my sack, a wool one."

"*One* other petticoat? Did they not give you clothing on that farm?" Mrs. Quigley was a kind woman, but she could barely conceal her dismay.

"Only what Oma and I had time to sew. Sorry, ma'am."

"Oh, don't be sorry, child." Mrs. Quigley sighed. "I'll talk to my husband. He's the judge's valet and the foreman of the servants. We'll see what we can arrange. Perhaps we can advance you a little bit of your wages to get you some fresh clothes. You're a lady's maid to the Shippens now, and we will want you to look the part. Now,"—the housekeeper paused, girding herself with a long, slow inhale—"let's go meet the Misses Shippens."

Clara followed Mrs. Quigley up the staircase that connected the servants' quarters to the second floor. "This is our passage, so that we can travel up and down without disturbing the family." Mrs. Quigley's breath grew uneven as she climbed upward. Clara noticed a short, round woman with orange hair descending the staircase toward them, weighed down by an armful of linens.

"Oh, hello, Brigitte, you've changed the beds?"

"Aye, Mrs. Quigley."

Mrs. Quigley paused, looking at the woman. "Clara, this is Brigitte, the chambermaid. Brigitte, meet Clara, the new maid to Miss Peggy and Miss Betsy."

"Nice to meet you, Brigitte." Clara curtsied to the older woman.

Brigitte nodded a wordless greeting in their general direction before continuing past them down the stairs.

"We'll have time for introductions to the rest of the servants later. For now, it's important that you meet your ladies." Mrs. Quigley's voice grew quieter as Clara followed her farther up the steep, narrow flight of stairs. "The ladies should be back from riding any moment, so first we'll return this shawl to Miss Peggy's bedchamber. We'll meet Miss Peggy first, and you must try to make a good impression. You'll see very quickly that Miss Peggy is the favorite of the judge."

"Does the judge have just the two girls?" Clara asked.

"The judge and Mrs. Shippen had four children. Miss Elizabeth—they call her Betsy—is the eldest. She's to be married soon, which will be a tremendous relief for his Judgeship. Betsy is followed by Miss Margaret—Peggy they call her. And then two boys, both of whom died." Mrs. Quigley sighed. "Such sweet boys, such a shame to lose them so young."

Clara nodded her silent reply.

"So now it's just Miss Betsy and Miss Peggy. As far as I was told, you are to wait on both Miss Betsy *and* Miss Peggy, but we'll see how they do about sharing. Miss Betsy does not seem to need her own maid, especially since she and Mrs. Shippen are so preoccupied these days with the coming wedding." The housekeeper cocked her head. "Once Miss Betsy marries Mr. Burd, it'll be just Miss Peggy in the house. She shall probably be the one who demands most of your time and attention."

"Are they close, the Misses Shippens?" Clara paused atop the stairs.

"Well . . ." Mrs. Quigley weighed her next words. "They are very different. I don't think I've ever had a cross word from Miss Betsy. Miss Peggy . . ." The housekeeper looked down at her young mistress's light blue shawl, musing on its unseen owner. When she continued, her tone was barely a whisper. "I'm sure you've read about Miss Peggy—in the society pages?"

"No, ma'am. We servants didn't get much chance to read the society pages at Hartley Farm," Clara answered.

"Miss Peggy is"—the old woman paused—"quite pretty. A favorite of the young British officers in Philadelphia. Smart. And . . . strong-willed."

Clara tried to imagine her new mistress sitting in the formal drawing room downstairs, holding forth amidst a group of admiring officers, but she suddenly found it hard to conjure the image; none of the girls at the Hartley farm had inhabited the same world as Peggy Shippen.

"It's best you don't ever keep Miss Peggy waiting. And under no circumstances should you ever argue with her. Try not to arouse her temper." Mrs. Quigley eyed Clara in the dark stairwell with—what was it—pity? "Of course, you'll learn all this for yourself, in time. That is, if you last."

And with those final words, Mrs. Quigley pushed open the door to move from the servants' stairwell into the second-floor corridor. Here, even in daylight, the candles on the walls were lit, producing a pale, amber light that danced off the framed oil paintings. How was it possible, Clara wondered, to own this many paintings? Clara scanned the quiet hall, covered by finely stitched red carpet, no doubt bought from a London carpet maker. She tried to step softly, but the wood of the floor creaked below her boots and made her feel as graceful as an ox. This hall, the quiet inner realm of the Shippen family, felt like a private space in which she had no business treading. Did Miss Peggy realize how lovely her home was? Clara wondered. Or was this corridor just another hallway to her?

Mrs. Quigley led Clara past an open doorway that peeked into a grand bedroom, its windows as tall as the ceiling, its bedframe draped in ivory-colored curtains. Clara glanced in but did not pause until they reached the next doorway.

"Miss Peggy's suite." The housekeeper hovered on the threshold, looking once more over Clara's humble appearance. "Are you ready?"

"Aye." Clara nodded, but all this pomp had succeeded in thoroughly wracking her nerves. When they stepped in, Clara gasped, her gaze flying upward to the high ceiling. Opposite her, floor-to-ceiling French windows offered a view over the same gardens Clara had just admired. From somewhere below, horses clipped by, the sound of hooves on the cobblestones reaching them in an even serenade. Miss Peggy's four-poster bed soared high off the ground, and looked like it could easily fit four people under its creamy silk canopy. On top of the bed, in addition to a heap of satin-covered feather pillows, there were several silk dresses, any one of them costing more than Clara's monthly wages. They lay in wrinkled and unceremonious disarray, cast aside after a past revelry now complete, like leftover dishes at a formal feast forgotten once the guests move on to dessert.

"How about some fresh air, what do you say?" Mrs. Quigley crossed the room with her authoritative stride, pulling roughly at the French windows, as if she felt no need to tiptoe through this space. "Well, don't just stand there like a sack of flour, Clara. Help me open these windows." Mrs. Quigley looked at her new hire with a mixture of bemusement and frustration.

"Miss Peggy has been riding all afternoon with her sister, Miss Betsy, and Miss Betsy's suitor, Mr. Edward Burd."

"Does Miss Betsy sleep in here too?" Clara looked at the oversized maple bed, thinking that perhaps there were two who occupied the space.

"Share a room? Ha! You think the Shippen girls would ever *share* a bedroom?"

"It's certainly big enough for two."

"This house itself isn't big enough for those two at times.

They'd last one day before Miss Peggy shredded her sister like a wildcat. No, Miss Betsy is in the bedroom next door, the one we just passed."

"Oh. What a grand room to have all to one's self," Clara said. Back at the Hartley farm, five people would have lived in this space. "Are all the rooms in the house this big?"

"You think her room is something, you should see her wardrobe." The housekeeper pointed toward the corner of the room, where an imposing structure of varnished pine stood. Mrs. Quigley walked toward the armoire, folding the blue silk scarf neatly and tucking it into a drawer. "Course she frets and complains that they are all outdated dresses, but I think they look very fine. With the war, it's a wonder she gets new dresses at all."

In the distance across the garden, figures moved toward the stable. Clara watched from the window and saw the same young man—Mrs. Quigley had called him Caleb—whom she'd noticed earlier. He'd put his guitar away and was leading a broad-chested horse of a rich chestnut hue by the bridle. Clara's heart leapt; did this mean her new mistresses had returned home from their ride?

"Come away from the window, child, and listen to me," Mrs. Quigley snapped, her pose suddenly rigid. "After a day of riding, the ladies will want to change out of their riding habits. Best you help Miss Peggy first, just so that there's no unpleasantness. Miss Betsy has no problem dressing herself. The misses have got a social event to attend tonight, so Miss Peggy will select one of her fancier gowns. She'll probably complain to you that she has nothing new to wear. That girl never lets her poor father forget that she wants new clothing."

Clara nodded, feeling her nerves tighten.

"And you'll need to do her hair for dinner. Can you do hair?" Mrs. Quigley asked.

"I can. I did Mrs. Hartley's hair sometimes." Clara answered, relieved that she would be up to the job in at least one way.

"It'll probably be a different fashion for Miss Peggy, but that's all right, just do what she tells you." Mrs. Quigley crossed her hands in front of her waist.

From downstairs, a door opened and shut. The front hall filled with the sound of female laughter. "I hear them, they are back. Quick, Clara, stand up straight."

Clara felt a growing sense of discomfort as she tried to calm her unsteady nerves. It didn't help that the old woman now appeared tense as well. How had she allowed herself to think she, Clara Bell, belonged in a house such as this one? She patted down her skirt and adjusted her cap.

"Don't fidget, child. Just be still." Mrs. Quigley's snappy order did little to soothe Clara's worry.

Footsteps ascended the grand spiraling staircase, the click of a lady's heels on the wood. Then the heeled tapping grew muffled as Peggy paraded down the carpeted corridor. Clara's eyes were fixed on the door, so that she saw it opening wider. Clara took a deep breath and put on the mask of a polite smile as a slight, trim figure appeared in the doorway. The young lady, who appeared to be the same age as Clara, fixed her clear blue eyes on the two figures by her bedside.

"Ah!" Peggy Shippen screeched, recoiling in the doorway. "Oh, Mrs. Quigley." She said the name like a censure, clutching her bosom with a small, gloved hand. "You gave me such a fright."

"Please, I beg your pardon, Mistress Peggy." Mrs. Quigley nodded submissively, and Clara mimicked her. "We should have warned you we were in your bedroom."

"Yes, indeed, I thought I had seen a ghost." Peggy looked from the housekeeper to the unknown girl beside her. Clara longed to fidget, to make sure her hair was tucked neatly into her white mob-cap, but then she remembered Mrs. Quigley's instructions to be still. "And who is this with you?" Peggy crossed the room, tossing her horsewhip haphazardly onto the ground as she approached the two servants.

"Miss Peggy, this is Clara Bell. Our new maid. She will be attending to you and your sister." Mrs. Quigley stepped forward, gesturing toward Clara.

"I see." Peggy nodded, narrowing her eyes on Clara. "So you are to be my new maid?" Peggy ran the length of Clara's height with her eyes, circling her as she would examine a horse on the auction block. Having a girl like Peggy Shippen this close to her was a sensation entirely new to Clara; Peggy's presence seemed to loom larger than her petite frame, spreading throughout the room like the scent of her rosewater-steeped skin.

If Peggy Shippen thought her own appearance looked plain or out of fashion, what must she think of her maid's apparel? Clara wondered. Peggy was short and thin, with her elaborate dress fitted to draw attention to her narrow waist. She wore a silk riding jacket of a rich forest green with a black velvet collar and matching cuffs. The buttons down the front were closed so that the jacket fit snugly, tailored perfectly to her frame. The accompanying skirt draped over a wide-waisted pannier so that her trim waist expanded into an alluring, hourglass shape. On her head Peggy wore a small bonnet of the same green silk, which rested neatly on the blond curls she had clipped back above her neck.

"Mrs. Quigley"—Peggy turned back to her housekeeper—"thank you for bringing her to me. You may leave us now."

Mrs. Quigley curtsied, and then, with a fleeting glance in Clara's direction, left the bedroom. Clara, aware that etiquette dictated that she should not speak first, kept her gaze fixed on the wooden floor.

"The new maid." Peggy was opposite Clara now. Even in her heeled, leather riding boots, she stood several inches shorter than Clara. "Look at me."

Clara obeyed, lifting her focus from the floor into a pair of bright, round eyes.

"What did you say your name was?" Peggy walked toward her new maid, shocking Clara by taking her hand in her own.

"Clara Bell, ma'am."

"And what do you expect you shall be doing in my room for me?"

"I was told to help you and Miss Betsy dress for supper, Miss Peggy."

"Never mind helping Betsy," Peggy said. "She's downstairs teasing her fiancé, giving him hope he might get a goodbye kiss. Poor Neddy, he might as well be wooing a nun."

Clara felt her cheeks redden as she lowered her eyes to the floorboards.

"You shall help me dress, Clara." Peggy paused a moment before smiling. "It's not right that you should split your time between me and my sister. Why, Betsy's already got herself a fiancé."

"As you wish, ma'am." Clara balled her fists, twisting the cotton cloth of her skirts in her fingers. Best stay quiet, best not to have an opinion on this sisterly struggle, she told herself.

Peggy continued. "I think you and I shall be great friends." With that, Peggy lifted her skirt, offering a sudden view of her bloomers, as she loosened the laces of her heeled boots. "Feels good to take these boots off."

Clara nodded, stretching her arms forward to receive the boots from her mistress. In stocking-clad feet now, Peggy crossed the room and sat at her vanity table before a broad, clean mirror. "I had too much wine this afternoon." Peggy yawned, unclipping her riding cap and shaking her blond curls loose. "I just get so enthralled by the good wine, the French wine, like what we used to drink before the war. Father doesn't buy it anymore." Peggy ran her fingers through her hair, still yawning. "Besides, wine is the only way to pass the time with the two of them, they're so dull."

"Perhaps you have time for a nap, my lady?" Clara suggested timidly, not sure what else to say.

"No," Peg answered absentmindedly, as she leaned closer to the mirror to scrutinize her face. "I must dress. After dinner Betsy and I have a big evening—dancing and card games at Lord Rawdon's."

"I see." Clara nodded.

"Well, what are you waiting for?" Peggy turned, staring at her maid. "Dress me!"

"Oh, yes, of course." Clara fidgeted, shifting her weight from one foot to the other.

"Well? What is it?" Thinly veiled frustration permeated Peggy's voice now, and Clara remembered the advice of the old housekeeper: never anger Peggy.

"My lady, I will be happy to help you dress. It's just . . ." Clara held forth her hands—her nails caked in grime, her palms stained from the dusty road. "Perhaps I might wash my hands first?"

Clara's spirits sunk with the look of irritation that crossed her new mistress's face. "Very well. Come here." Peggy offered her basin of fresh water. While Clara dipped her hands into the cool bowl, sending the floating flower petals aflutter, Peggy watched. "How did you get this job, Clara? Where did you work before this?"

"If you please, my lady, I worked at Hartley's farm in Lancaster." Clara dried her hands on her apron. "Right next to your own family's farm, where you lived for two years at the outbreak of the war."

"I know where Lancaster is." Peggy narrowed her eyes, her tone suddenly chilly. "Do not mention that farm again, understood?" Peggy shook her head, blinking her eyelids as if to tamp out the recollection Clara had summoned to her mind. When she spoke again, her voice had regained its composure. "There are things that happened there that . . . that I do not wish to remember."

"I do apologize." Clara cringed. This was not going well at all, and Mrs. Quigley's warning suddenly seemed prophetic: she wouldn't last here. It had been foolish to think that she, Clara Bell, a servant from Hartley's Farm, would be up to the task of serving a lady like Miss Peggy Shippen.

Clara detected the sound of footsteps ascending the staircase. "Peggy?" a woman's voice called out.

"It's Betsy." Peggy turned to the maid. "Quick, run behind my closet, out of sight. Go!" Peggy practically pushed Clara away from her, and Clara obeyed, heart racing as she dashed behind the hulking piece of furniture.

"Peggy." A timorous voice now drifted in from the doorway of the bedroom. From her spot, Clara could see Miss Peggy but not the elder sister.

"Oh, Betsy, hello. Well, did you let Mr. Neddy Burd see an inch of flesh? Perhaps a kiss, if only on the cheek?" Peggy's voice was cool and taunting as she turned from her seat before the mirror.

"Stop teasing, Peggy."

"Poor man looks wound up tighter than a spring. Won't you at least let him see a glimpse of your ankle, Bets? He may be patient, but even saints have their limits."

"Peggy, quit being vile or I shall tell Papa."

"Oh, what do you want, Bets?" Peggy cocked her head to the side.

"Mrs. Quigley tells me our new maid is here."

"Is she?" Peggy sounded bored.

"Yes. Mrs. Quigley said she was with you."

Peggy raised her hands as if to ask, where? Clara receded farther behind the armoire, feeling as guilty as a thief.

"But . . . Mrs. Quigley just told me."

"Bets, you see perfectly well that I am here and this so-called maid is not. What would you like me to say?"

Betsy paused, quiet. "Where did she go?"

"I do not know, Bets, I have yet to lay eyes on her."

"Oh," Betsy said. "Well, if she turns up, will you send her my way? I'd like help dressing."

"Of course," Peggy agreed, her tone obliging.

"But do you promise, Peggy?"

"I shall send her your way, I promise. Now, Bets, I'm about to dress myself. Be a dear and close the door?"

Betsy left without a word, quietly closing the door behind her.

"Come here." Peggy wheeled back around, so that her gaze now fixed on her maid through the mirror. She waved her hand. "I said come here." Her face was encouraging, even sweet. Clara treaded forward, keeping her eyes down.

"Thank you." Peggy took Clara's hand in hers and gave it a soft, conspiratorial squeeze. Clara felt uncomfortable, ill at ease over unwittingly taking part in a lie to one of her new ladies.

"Lean down beside me, Clara." Peggy urged her maid closer, her voice suddenly silky, and this sweet tone did more to put Clara on edge than any previous iciness had. "You know, Clara, you are not *ugly*. In fact, I'd say you're quite pretty. For a farm girl." Clara looked into the glass before them, staring at the two faces. Hers was stained an unattractive, rosy pink after her long journey in the sun from Lancaster, while Peggy's was creamy and unlined, like freshly pressed lace. Their complexions were similar—both fair, with light eyes—but Peggy's hair was silky, the texture of freshly spun gold, while Clara's appeared more like dried straw at the end of the harvest. Clara thought her eyes looked dull and colorless, while Peggy's shone blue under shaped eyebrows and long eyelashes. Peggy's gaze was alert, her features active, as though they were perceiving things, understanding things, which Clara herself had not even noticed.

"You flatter me, Miss Peggy." Clara pulled her face back from the mirror, retreating behind her mistress.

"No, I don't flatter people," Peggy answered matter-of-factly, powdering the tip of her nose. "They flatter me. Go fetch my rose-colored silk dress."

"Yes, ma'am."

"And I'll need my white satin gloves, my white heels, my widest pannier hoopskirt, and any of the ribbons—either white or pink—that you think would be agreeable with the rose silk of the gown." Peggy pointed Clara in the direction of her wardrobe, and Clara crossed the room to retrieve the requested items.

"Tonight shall be very festive. Of course, every night is festive now that the British officers are in Philadelphia," Peggy chattered, coating her lips in pink lard to tint them a bright hue. Clara stared into the vast abyss of Peggy's crowded armoire. A rose-colored gown. But there must have been twenty pink dresses in the wardrobe. She saw silks in shades of pink that mirrored nature's softest petals: cherry blossom, tulip, begonia, hydrangea. How would she ever determine which one her mistress had meant by "rose"?

"Well?" Peggy was still at her vanity, applying rouge to her cheeks.

"Rose, rose, rose," Clara muttered as she fingered the parade of gowns. How lucky the girl who possessed just one of these gowns, and her mistress owned them all. Clara settled on what she determined to be the correct one, removing it gently from its hook and carrying it toward her mistress. When Clara advanced toward her mistress, she saw that Peggy had stripped down to her shift and stays, prompting Clara to blush and lower her eyes. She supposed a lady need not be modest with her maid, but Peggy didn't seem self-conscious of her near nakedness at all.

"Oh, you're as bashful as a nun. Or worse, my sister." Peggy giggled. "I want you to re-fasten my stays to make them tighter." Peggy turned around so that her backside was to Clara. Fixing her grip to one of the posters of the bed, Peggy braced herself for the assault on her waistline.

Clara untied the existing knot and pulled on the laces. The hourglass shape ensured by a lady's bone stays looked much less comfortable than the cotton stays worn by servants like herself, and Clara felt a moment's appreciation for her less-constricting wardrobe.

"Tighter, I can manage a bit tighter," Peggy urged her maid, even as she appeared to struggle for breath. "I'm to have the smallest waist at the party tonight."

Clara nodded, pitying her mistress but obeying her orders as she redoubled her efforts and pulled anew on the stays. The top of Peggy's corset fanned out to add to the appearance of a full bosom and also to ensure that a woman was forced to hold her upper arms out, like a ballet dancer. With elbows bent and hands clasped together in front of her waist, she'd be in the position considered most ladylike.

"That's enough." Peggy winced, closing her eyes for a moment. Clara tied off the laces and awaited her next order. With her corset tightened and waist pulled in, Peggy leaned on Clara as she slid into her ample pannier hoopskirt.

"Goodness." Peggy closed her eyes and reached tenderly toward her abdomen, still adjusting to her constricted breathing. "Always takes a minute to adjust."

"I can loosen them." Clara reached for the laces, regretting that perhaps she'd tied the stays too firmly.

"No, no." Peggy shook her head, her breathing still labored. "All the gents like to imagine that they take my breath away. If they only knew it was the corset." Peggy opened her eyes and smiled at her maid. "Now, the pièce de résistance." Peggy pointed at the gown that was fanned out on the bed, its skirt taking up the entire width of the bedframe. "I do love this one." Peggy stroked the rosy silk affectionately. "And so does he."

Clara, interest piqued, nevertheless let the comment drift aside like the breeze streaming through the open windows. She held the dress wide to help Peggy slip into it.

"Even loyalty to the British crown has its limits, I suppose." Peggy giggled.

"Pardon me, miss?" Clara wrinkled her brow, unsure of the meaning.

"My dress," Peggy said. "It's *à la française.*"

Clara nodded. "Oh, of course." But still she had little idea of her lady's meaning, and Miss Peggy's smirk indicated that she suspected as much.

Peggy pointed down at her dress. "The tight stomacher visible in front, it's the highest fashion of the French court. And now the British."

"It's certainly very fine," Clara replied, admiring her mistress's figure. The bodice of the gown, with its white silk stomacher, hugged Peggy's curves before the expansive skirt spilled over the side hoops and cascaded to the floor in its rich, silky splendor. The creamy white skin of Peggy's arms peeked out under ruched sleeves of lace. The neckline came low to show the hint of Peggy's bosom, decorated by a thin strand of pearls.

Dressing Peggy Shippen was an art form, Clara realized, and her mistress had more adornments in mind for this one evening than Clara possessed in her entire travel sack. After the gown was fastened snugly around the contours of her diminutive figure, there were the accessories to be put in place: stockings gartered above the knees, white satin shoes over her feet, pearl earrings that looked like large raindrops.

"You look like a doll, if you don't mind my saying so, miss." Clara marveled, her nerves softening under the comforting tonic of her lady's increasingly ebullient mood. Each time Peggy caught a glimpse of herself in the mirror, her features seemed slightly more alight.

"We must hurry or we'll be tardy for dinner, and we wouldn't want Father to complain," Peggy chirped, lowering herself carefully onto her cushioned seat before the looking glass. "Well, what are you waiting for, Clara?" She looked at her maid.

Clara stared back, baffled; what more could be done to tune Miss Peggy's appearance? Was it not time that she leave and go assist Miss Betsy?

"I know what you're thinking. Forget Betsy, come fashion my hair," Peggy ordered, her tone dry.

"Aye, Miss Peggy," Clara answered, sidling up behind her mistress. So perhaps she would not have time to make Miss Betsy's acquaintance before dinner. "How shall we do it?"

"Continental fashion, like that French queen," Peggy replied, as she smeared more color across her lips. "The higher, the better." Clara had seen the occasional images of the French queen in the newspapers; she knew how Louis XVI's bride had made the *pouf* the height of fashion.

"Did the girls on your farm dress this fine?" Peggy flashed a dazzling smile at Clara through her reflection in the mirror.

"Not at all, ma'am." Clara pulled Peggy's hair through her fingers. "I don't think Mrs. Hartley ever asked me to fashion her hair like that of a queen." She smiled, surprised but flattered by the interest Miss Peggy was taking in her.

"Well, you had better get used to it. Since the British seized the city from the . . . rebels"—Peggy could barely hide the contempt in her voice as it tripped over the word—"the hair must be higher, the corsets tighter. And the *dresses*! Before they got here, it was all homespun. But now the shops are open once more, and we get fresh silk, ribbons, lace." She lined the lids of her eyes with charcoal as Clara wrapped strands of her blond hair around the iron, releasing them into buoyant curls.

Clara considered this, hesitating. Her mistress sounded as if she enjoyed the company of the British soldiers. Clara herself still nurtured a secret allegiance to the rebel cause. How could she admit this to her mistress? She could not, not if she hoped to keep Miss Peggy's good favor.

"Everything has been *so* much more fun since the British got here! I think I've enjoyed myself more in six months than most girls do in an entire lifetime." Peggy sighed, staring at a pair of silhouettes cut out of paper and leaning against her mirror. The lady looked just like Peggy in profile, drawn to the collar of an ornate dress, with her hair *à la française*. The man wore the British regimentals and tricornered hat, and his features were handsome, slightly delicate even. The silhouettes were arranged so the two figures appeared locked in each other's gaze, immutable.

"Is that you, my lady?" Clara asked, studying the cut-paper silhouettes.

"Oh, yes. It's me and Johnny." Peggy's forefinger reached for the paper and tenderly stroked the would-be cheek of the gentleman. "He made it for me—he promised that I'm the only one he made a silhouette for."

Clara let that comment hover in the air, without response, as she continued her diligent styling of Miss Peggy's hair. When her *pouf* was sufficiently high and her cheeks sufficiently rouged, Peggy sprayed her hair with the powder pump to infuse the faintest hint of white into her locks. She dabbed her wrists, neck, and bosom with floral-scented perfume, and stood to admire herself before the full-length looking glass. "Well." She completed a twirl, the skirt of her gown and the smell of her perfume fanning out around her. "How do I look, Clara?"

Clara had never seen her equal. "I can't imagine there will be a single gentleman in all of Philadelphia who will not want to stand beside you, Miss Peggy."

"I'm sure Meg Chew will be dressed just as nicely," Peggy retorted, her features turning sour for a moment. "But Johnny told me he's looking forward to seeing *me* tonight, not Meg Chew."

Clara, not sure of how else to answer, nodded. "Of course he is." As Clara gazed once more in the mirror to admire her mistress, she caught sight of her own reflection, and couldn't help but feel fresh embarrassment over her own plain, homespun figure.

The kitchen in the Shippen home was a hive of activity—filled with harried servants, fragrant aromas, and serving dishes being jostled from hand to hand. Clara watched in awe as food traveled from the hearth and somehow melded into the tantalizing presentations on the china platters. At the center of the kitchen around a long wooden table stood several servants, arranging the various ingredients into tidy, savory-looking dishes.

"Clara, there you are! How did it go with the Miss Shippens?" Mrs. Quigley looked over from where she was sorting a set of silver wineglasses. "You look lost child, come here and tell me how it went."

"I hope it went well. I did Miss Peggy's hair, and I helped her dress." Clara gazed around, still distracted by the largest, noisiest kitchen she'd ever seen.

"And Miss Betsy? You've met her as well?"

"No, ma'am," Clara answered, feeling guilty, as if it had been her own fault. She told the housekeeper about the exchange between the Shippen sisters and her orders to hide behind the wardrobe.

"Sounds about right." Mrs. Quigley's shoulders sagged as she listened. "Well, not your fault, Clara. And speaking of wardrobe"—Mrs. Quigley settled the final glass and then reached for a wine decanter—"I've spoken with Mr. Quigley, and we agree that you'll need to spruce up your wardrobe a bit now that you're a maid in the Shippen household." The housekeeper looked over Clara's attire disapprovingly again. "We shall be able to help you."

"Thank you, ma'am." Clara could not help but smile—she could not remember the last time she'd had new clothes.

"It's nothing, child. Now don't just stand there completely useless." The housekeeper took Clara by the arm and escorted her through the two rooms that abutted the kitchen. "The scullery is back here."

"The . . . what, Mrs. Quigley?"

"I keep forgetting you've just come from a farm." Mrs. Quigley sighed. "The scullery. It's where the dishes are scrubbed, washed, and dried after the meals. You'll help with that. And here"—the housekeeper moved fluidly to the next small room—"is the larder. The pantry?"

Clara nodded. That one she knew.

"Who's this?" A wide-hipped, middle-aged woman with strong features and an accent Clara immediately recognized as German appeared from out of a nook in the pantry, her thick arms cradling a crate of peaches.

"Hannah, hello," Mrs. Quigley said. "Meet the Miss Shippens' new maid, Clara."

"Ah," Hannah shifted her cargo to her hip and wiped her hands on her dirty apron, reaching forward for a handshake. "The name's Hannah Breunig. Cook for the Shippens." She introduced herself with the same clipped diction as Oma.

"Clara Bell," Clara answered politely. "It's a pleasure to meet you, Mrs. Breunig."

"It's Hannah. But I'm sorry to say I don't think anything's a pleasure right now, not when this dessert still needs baking. But just stay out of my way and we won't have a problem." Hannah turned back to the kitchen and both Clara and Mrs. Quigley followed her.

"Ah, so this is the young lady who needs the new wardrobe?" Clara turned to see a man with thinning hair the same gray hue as Mrs. Quigley's.

"Oh good, you're here, Arthur." Mrs. Quigley nodded at the man, who wore a formal white collared shirt with a tailored black jacket, cropped breeches, and buckled shoes. His thinning hair was combed back neatly. Clara noticed the servants in the kitchen stopping their harried work to curtsy as he passed them. "Hello, Clara Bell. My name's Arthur Quigley. My first claim to notoriety is that

I'm married to Mrs. Quigley. My second title is that I'm the butler and valet for Judge Shippen."

"Mr. Quigley, it's a pleasure." Clara curtsied.

"Arthur, I've just told Clara that we've made arrangements to assist her with the . . . deficiencies . . . of her wardrobe." Mrs. Quigley addressed her husband formally, though Clara noticed the way her stern eyes had softened.

"We shall be happy to help." Mr. Quigley nodded. "Can you cook, Clara? In a pinch?"

"No, sir. I'm sorry to say I'm not much use with cooking," Clara answered.

Mrs. Quigley leaned over the table and handed her husband the tray of neatly arranged wine goblets. "I would think with a grandmother such as yours it'd be the first thing you'd learn."

"Quite the opposite, I'm afraid," Clara answered. "Oma always did all the cooking, never wanted anyone else to ruin her food. I learned all the ladies' arts. Hair styling, sewing, mending."

"Well, Miss Peggy will certainly have you laboring at each of those tasks night and day," Mr. Quigley answered, taking the wine decanter from his wife. "And have you met Miss Betsy as well?"

Mrs. Quigley interjected, answering for Clara. "It seems that Miss Peggy required Clara entirely for herself this afternoon." The housekeeper's eyes rounded out the message, and Mr. Quigley nodded.

"I see." He turned back to Clara. "Best not to get involved in any territorial disputes, Clara. We've got enough men fighting a territorial battle across this continent, without starting another war in the Shippen household. You just keep your head down and do as you're told, and if it gets too out of hand, you come to Mrs. Quigley or myself. Understood?"

"Understood, sir." Clara nodded.

"You shall meet Miss Betsy at supper." Mr. Quigley fidgeted with the collar of his shirt, as if to render its stiff creases even more crisp.

"Who is this? There's a face I don't recognize."

Clara turned in the direction of a new voice in the crowded kitchen and found herself staring into a broad, smiling face. Like her, this man was younger than the other servants in the kitchen, with light brown hair and hazel eyes. He looked familiar. Yes, from his brown wool breeches and loosely fitted linen shirt, Clara could tell this was the guitar-playing groom she'd spotted outside the stables.

"I think I saw you earlier," the young man spoke first, grinning at her. "The name's Little, Caleb Little."

"Nice to meet you." Clara curtsied, lowering her eyes.

"I saw you looking through the window," he continued. She felt her cheeks grow warm.

"And you are?" He raised his eyebrows.

"Oh, right, I'm Clara Bell. The new lady's maid for the Miss Shippens."

"Ah, Clara Bell, that's an enviable post you have," Caleb answered, cracking a lopsided grin. "I'm the stable groom."

"And the footman, don't forget, so wash your hands and get ready to serve dinner, Caleb," Mrs. Quigley said, interrupting them.

"That's right, I'm the footman now as well." Caleb Little rolled up his sleeves and crossed the kitchen toward the washbasin. "Double duty since they sacked all the rest of the servants." Caleb's accent was more rough, more American, than the proper Quigleys or the German cook.

"And lucky to have the job, so I better not be hearing a complaint." Mrs. Quigley raised a finger.

"Of course not, ma'am," Caleb answered, leaning over to wash his hands and splash his face. Clara's eyes lingered as he rubbed the back of his tanned neck with a wet rag.

"You're going to be with Caleb at dinner tonight, Clara," Mr. Quigley explained. "Watch how he serves, and you'll fill in for him on occasion."

Clara peeled her eyes from Caleb, turning toward the valet. "I've never served dinner for a family like the Shippens."

"It's not too hard, Miss Bell." Caleb winked as he turned back to face her, toweling off his wet face. "As long as you keep Miss Peggy's wineglass full, you should have nothing to worry about."

"It *is* hard, and she *should* worry about it," Mrs. Quigley snapped at Caleb. "And you could stand to worry a bit more too. Now start getting these dishes out on the table."

"Sorry, Auntie." Caleb nodded his head respectfully toward Mrs. Quigley before flashing Clara a mischievous grin. With that, the housekeeper handed her nephew the tray of wineglasses and pushed him through the door, ordering Clara to follow behind.

"DINNER IS ready to be served," Mr. Quigley announced to the kitchen. His voice set off a fresh round of errands among the staff.

"The family is seated—go, go!" Mrs. Quigley kept Clara and Caleb running to and from the kitchen to the dining room, carrying tray after tray of hot food. Hannah had the Shippens starting with trays of meat: miniature game hens, a rabbit pie, and fresh sturgeon. Accompanying the meat were heaping bowls of rosemary potatoes, carrots from the garden, steamed fiddleheads, spinach, and roasted beets.

"My aunt acts like we are serving the royal family, but really you just have to make sure you don't spill and you don't trip. As long as you manage that, they'll never even notice you're in the room. All they're looking at is the food and one another's clothing," Caleb whispered to Clara at the threshold of the dining room, but Clara wasn't listening to the footman beside her. Her eyes were feasting on the scene before her, a tableau unlike the family meals she'd known at the Hartleys. The Shippens sat around a table of walnut, with ornately carved chairs showing the ornamental flair once again popular in Europe. The table was spread with a damask tablecloth, every inch festooned with the freshly polished silver and china plates wreathed in a floral pattern. "Ready?" Caleb paused beside her, weighed down by the plates of meat he carried.

"Caleb, I can't. Let me watch you this first time," Clara pleaded, placing her bowl of potatoes down on the buffet in the hallway. "I'll drop something, or do something incorrectly, I just know it."

"What's the matter, Clara Bell? 'Fraid of a few Shippens just because they wear fancy clothes and pump powder into their hair?" Caleb smiled, his hazel eyes lit up with teasing.

"Let me see how you do it first. Please?" Clara pleaded.

"All right, just this once, then you're helping me serve." Caleb winked. "Here I go." He straightened his posture, shrugging off the casual affability he'd displayed just moments ago in the servants' quarters and marching into the dining room with sudden and impressive poise. Clara lurked in the hallway outside the dining room, watching the family from a concealed corner where they didn't suspect her presence. She spotted her mistress first, the brightest spot in the dark, wood-paneled room. The candlelight danced playfully off her features, and the sight of Peggy Shippen made Clara freshly nervous. She stared on, admiring Peggy's genteel features, her soaring hair, her perfect attire.

Caleb distributed the plates of meat evenly along the table and

Clara watched, studying his graceful movements, the way he served the family members without getting in their way as they sipped their wine. Judge Shippen was greeted reverentially by each member of the family as he took his spot at the head of the table and led the group in a short prayer of thanks.

Beside the judge sat a man with a very similar likeness and a heavier frame. "That's Doctor William Shippen." Caleb was back by Clara's side, whispering into her ear as they watched the family. "Doctor William is the judge's brother." Judge Edward was like his brother, Doctor William, in many ways, but seemingly more of a deflated version—as if there was less flesh on his bones and a wearier spirit shining through his eyes.

"Doctor William, unlike his brother, is known to be supporting the colonies," Caleb explained.

Clara nodded. This was a well-known piece of gossip. "But Miss Peggy seems to have openly loyalist tendencies," Clara whispered, thinking back to the conversation she'd had earlier with her new mistress.

Caleb considered this, his features folding into a casual, cockeyed grin. "Well, how many colonial men do you see in Philadelphia wearing store-bought suits, ready to serve her Champagne and caviar?" He stepped away to deliver a platter of sturgeon to the table.

Across from Doctor William, occupying the middle of the table, sat the Shippen girls, Peggy and the other young lady whom Clara knew to be Betsy. She was a less striking version of her younger sister. Like Peggy, she dressed *à la française,* wearing a silk gown of light lavender with a yellow stomacher. Her hair was fixed in a low bun that seemed simple beside Peggy's elaborate *pouf*. Her eyes were the same blue as her younger sister's, but less alert, and as Clara observed their body language she determined that Betsy took her cues from her sister, as if Peggy were the elder of the two.

At the opposite end of the table from the judge sat the lady of the house, dressed in a simpler style than her two young daughters. "That's Mrs. Margaret Shippen," Caleb said, returning from the table, "the judge's wife." She wore a plain gown of plum-colored silk with no ornamentation, her neck covered by a white linen neckerchief that seemed all the more modest beside her daughters' exposed bosoms. Mrs. Shippen had graying hair and wore nothing on her face except a tense expression, but she listened attentively as her husband spoke.

"The French may be clamoring to enter into the war on the side of the colonies." The judge took a slow, deliberate sip of wine, his lean fingers clutching the silver cup tightly. "But I tell you, brother, they will not. They can't afford another war."

"Brother." Doctor William's voice boomed in comparison to the judge's meek tones. "You have the kind and timid nature that assumes, I believe incorrectly, that monarchs arrive at their decisions by determining what is right and prudent, not by what is beneficial to their Empire. A chance to remove the British threat from this continent and ensure his hold over Canada? Of course Louis will join the war. The French have made that apparent after the colonial victory at Saratoga." Doctor William paused. "Edward, am I expected to eat this meat by itself?"

Caleb picked up the bowl of potatoes that Clara had not yet delivered, placing them in her hands. "Your turn, Clara Bell, they're asking for the potatoes."

Clara hesitated. "Must I go in?"

"You lived in the countryside swarming with Iroquois and you're afraid to serve some potatoes?" Caleb teased her. "Follow me." Caleb picked up a bowl of cranberry relish and led her into the dining room.

The eyes of the judge and Mrs. Shippen turned upon Clara,

and she froze near the threshold of the dining room. Silence filled the room. The only noise was a pop from the hearth, where a log collapsed. When the judge did not speak first, Doctor William addressed Clara.

"Well? Are those potatoes for us, then?" he asked, a good-natured smile lighting his ruddy features.

"Who is this? Is this her?" Betsy turned to her sister, speaking about the unknown face.

"Oh," Peggy piped up. "Everybody, this is the new maid, Clara."

"You're the girl that Mrs. Quigley sent for?" Judge Shippen asked.

"Indeed, sir, Excellency, Judge," Clara answered.

"Any one of those three titles shall do, but not all three at once." The judge laughed.

"Nice to meet you, Clara," Doctor William answered. "Now bring those potatoes here. I happen to be starving."

"Yes, sir." Clara obeyed, depositing the potatoes in front of Doctor William.

"Clara helped me dress for dinner." Peggy sipped her wine, turning to her sister.

Betsy's spoon clamored to her plate. "She did? But you promised you would . . ." Seeing her younger sister's smirk, Betsy did not finish, but crossed her arms in front of her body.

"Calm yourself, Betsy. I had her fashion my hair for Lord Rawdon's soiree tonight. You hardly needed help managing a hairdo like the one you're modeling."

At this second insult, Betsy's pout threatened to turn to genuine tears. "Well, why did she not help me?" Betsy turned from her sister to her father. "Papa, you told Peggy that we were to share the new girl, but Peggy's kept her all to herself."

"But Papa, Betsy doesn't need a maid, she already has a fiancé.

I don't see why she needs help getting ready for parties when all she does is sit in the corner and sulk that Neddy wasn't invited."

"Girls, if you are going to quarrel, there shall be no new maid at all." Mrs. Shippen's features were pinched, and Clara noticed that she barely nibbled on her food. For her part, Clara wished to finish serving the potatoes and disappear from this room.

"Mama, I am not quarreling. I just don't think it's fair that Peggy always gets—"

"Enough, Elizabeth," Mrs. Shippen snapped at her elder daughter, rubbing her temples in a slow, rhythmic gesture. "I have a headache. I cannot bear another row tonight."

"You always have a headache," Peggy muttered to herself, sipping her wine.

Betsy, having lost the round to her sister, changed tracks. "Fine. Then I'm not going with you to Lord Rawdon's tonight, Peggy." Betsy uncrossed her arms and took a forceful stab at the bowl of potatoes offered by Clara. Clara braced herself, struggling to keep the dish steady.

"I don't care." Peggy shrugged her shoulders and leaned to help herself to the same dish.

"But you can't go either, then." Betsy tugged on the bowl of potatoes, so that Clara was pulled back toward the elder sister.

"Why is that?" Peggy stared down her sister, challenging her.

"Because you aren't allowed to go out alone, remember? Mama? Papa? Remember you told Peggy that she comes home too late and spends too much money and she shan't be allowed out alone anymore?"

"We did agree to that, Edward." Mrs. Shippen threw a weary look to her husband, already fatigued by the coming spat.

"Nonsense!" Peggy cocked her head. "All the girls go out alone. You don't see Meg Chew or Becky Redman with a chaperone. Papa, don't listen to this spoilsport."

"But not all the girls find themselves the subject of ridicule, Margaret." Mrs. Shippen turned a mirthless expression on her daughter. "It has already been agreed upon. If your sister will not accompany you, you shall not go."

"Ridicule? How have I been made the subject of ridicule?" Peggy's eyes smoldered as she turned from her sister to her mother.

"Well, you lost your entire purse at cards the other night, for one thing." Now Betsy appeared to have the upper hand, and Clara noted genuine concern in Peggy's eyes; her evening plans might in fact be thwarted.

"When your purse contains nothing more than a shilling, that's not a difficult accomplishment," Peggy said.

"Any money gambled is money wasted," Mrs. Shippen retorted.

Peggy turned wild eyes to her father, and when he cocked his head, she saw that she might in fact be kept at home. "Papa, this is unfair. You must let me go. Betsy is just being petty. I planned on this long ago. Please tell me I may go."

"We did tell you, my dear Peggy, that you would need accompaniment from now on." The judge avoided his daughter's eyes, keeping his attention on his plate.

Peggy glanced from her father to her mother, her lips pursing as she watched her chances recede. She avoided her sister, who smirked beside her. Then, glancing up at her new maid, Peggy showed a flash of inspiration. "Fine. I'll take Clara with me."

Mrs. Shippen answered quickly. "We know nothing of Clara." Looking up at Clara, Mrs. Shippen spoke quietly, almost inaudibly. "I apologize, Clara, I am sure you are a young woman of impeccable character, but it takes time to build trust."

Clara nodded, wondering if they were done with the potatoes so that she might retreat into the other room.

"Once Clara has been here several months and Mrs. Quigley vouches for her character, then perhaps she may become a companion." Mrs. Shippen finished.

"Mrs. Quigley!" Peggy repeated the name. "Mrs. Quigley too. Send them both. Send the whole servants' quarters, for all I care. Papa, how about if Mrs. Quigley and Clara accompany me?"

Judge Shippen deliberated and his wife watched with a strained expression. Judge Shippen threw his brother a look as if to congratulate him on not having daughters.

"Dear, sweet Papa, please do not make me suffer. Please tell me that I may go."

"All right, Peggy my dear." The judge's posture sagged as he agreed. "Take Mrs. Quigley and this new girl. And try not to spend money at cards, please."

"Anything for you, Papa." Peggy bounced up from her chair and flew to her father, whom she showered in enthusiastic kisses. Smiling at Clara, Peggy nodded.

"Whose soiree is this?" Judge Shippen asked.

"Lord Rawdon's. It's at his home," Peggy answered her father as Clara slipped out of the room, determining that the potatoes were no longer of interest to the family.

"There, you survived." Caleb greeted Clara at the serving buffet. "Though your presence certainly caused quite a stir."

Clara sighed, fearing that the judge might regret having brought her into his household.

"And you've managed to get yourself an invitation to a soiree tonight." Caleb smirked.

"About that." Clara winced. The thought of such a party filled Clara with dread: a home full of young women just like Peggy, and in addition, English officers!

"There now, don't look so fretful, Clara Bell. You'll have Mrs.

Quigley with you. And I'll be driving you over in the coach." For some reason that Clara could not explain, Caleb's words and his presence served to quell her nerves.

She smiled, relieved to be in this quiet corridor with him and away from the Shippens. "I seem to have set off a feud among the sisters."

"Nothing new." Caleb shrugged. "Mrs. Shippen complains of headaches every day—but how could she not have a headache with that chorus to listen to? Now, these meat pies need serving. How about you help me?"

When they reentered the dining room, the family conversation had shifted away from their own battles back to that of the war between the colonies and the British. Clara tiptoed in behind Caleb, offering a meat pie to Judge Shippen.

"Why did the Battle of Saratoga make the difference?" Mrs. Shippen fed herself a small bite of fish, looking to her husband. Her brother-in-law answered first.

"It's simple, Margaret. Benedict Arnold, in winning at Saratoga, has proven to the French that the Americans can actually win this war. Arnold provided the proof that those reluctant Frenchmen needed. Not to mention, he's rallied the entire populace, a fact very much appreciated by our General George Washington."

"But brother"—Judge Shippen served himself a sliver of the meat pie, which Clara held before him—"I still believe that it is in the best interest of the colonies to renounce violence and mend the relationship with the mother country. It baffles me that you don't see it that way. Why must we sever our ties with a country that shares our religion, our history, our sensibilities, even our blood?"

Before Doctor William could answer his brother's question, Peggy interjected. "My father, like all of us, is still hoping that the Continental Congress will accept the peace measures put forward by the crown." Peggy spoke confidently, summoning Clara toward her so that she might herself be served a slice of the meat pie. "King George has proven himself both forgiving and benevolent."

"Ah." Doctor William turned to Peggy, impressed. "So my niece has an inclination toward politics?"

"I do." Peggy cocked her head and drained her wineglass. "I am in close acquaintance with a great number of British officers, and follow the updates of the war with great interest. I was very disappointed to read of Benedict Arnold's victory in Saratoga and the ensuing hints by the French that they would align themselves with Washington and the rest of the rebels."

"Brother, your youngest has beauty and brains, even if I do not agree with her politics," Doctor William said, seemingly charmed by his young niece. "Well, dearest Peggy, in spite of your and your father's aspirations for peace and unity, which come from pure hearts I'm sure, the Continental Congress will never reattach itself to King George and England," William answered authoritatively, leaning back to make room for his full belly. "They have declared themselves a free people, and are willing to fight until that dream of liberty is realized. And they will fight now, I believe, with French assistance."

"But, brother." The judge reentered the discussion, his voice quiet. "I hope that you don't speak these dangerous thoughts outside of these walls. Such language could get you in trouble."

"The British won't hold Philadelphia much longer." Doctor William shrugged, taking a swig of wine.

Now Peggy answered. "I think you underestimate the strength of the crown. I have the chance to mingle with members of the British officers quite often, and—"

"Mingle, is that what you call it?" Betsy simpered.

Peggy ignored the comment from her sister. "And the British

feel no such insecurity in their hold over Philadelphia. Or the colonies as a whole."

"My dear niece Peggy." William took another hearty bite of meat, enjoying the debate. "The Redcoats are barely beating us when we are nothing but a ragtag bunch of volunteers. How shall they defeat us once we have the purse of Versailles backing us?"

"France cannot afford this war." Peggy pushed on, impressing Clara with her knowledge of politics and economics. "Louis has enough trouble keeping that Austrian-born wife of his under control. I think he'd better subdue Marie Antoinette and do battle with her profligate spending before engaging against foreign enemies."

Clara slipped out of the room and stood just outside the threshold of the dining room, where she could continue to listen to this family discussion. The judge, shifting in his seat, seemed less enthused by the topic. "How was your recent trip to Virginia, William?"

"Oh ho, trying to change the topic, are you, Eddy?" William's voice boomed.

"Papa," Peggy interjected, smiling at her father, "as interesting as this has been, may I be excused? I must prepare to depart for Lord Rawdon's." Peggy made to rise from the table but her mother's stern voice stopped her.

"Peggy, we have not finished our meal. You will stay and eat with us."

Peggy turned from her mother to her father. "Please, Papa, I shall be late, and they'll begin the card games without me."

"Cards?" Mrs. Shippen's interest was suddenly keen. "We just told you: no more gambling at cards. Edward, I think this is a mistake. I think Margaret should do as her sister plans to do, stay home tonight and do something to feed her mind." Mrs. Shippen rubbed her temples once more, shutting her eyes.

Judge Shippen eyed his daughter and wife wearily.

Peggy made a face. "But we already agreed I could attend."

"Would you not like a night at home with your parents?" Mrs. Shippen opened her eyes, still massaging her forehead.

"Do you think I dressed like this for a night of reading with my parents?" Peggy laughed. "Papa, you already promised that I could go." She directed her focus toward her father, her expression growing taut.

"Peggy, my dear, I did not realize that it was cards again . . ."

"Papa!" Peggy widened her eyes, interrupting her father. "I shall refrain from the card games, I promise." Peggy paused. "And besides, a night spent mingling with the finest, most well-educated officers of the British Army is certainly a night spent enriching the mind."

"Is that so?" Betsy sniggered, exchanging a meaningful glance with her mother.

"Well, they are certainly a lot more interesting than your boring old Mr. Burd." Peggy turned, snarling at her sister.

"All right, all right, enough of this quarreling. Peggy, you may go to Lord Rawdon's," her father acquiesced. "But not until we've finished supper. Your mother has ordered a peach tart for dessert."

"But Edward . . ." Mrs. Shippen clenched her jaw.

"Margaret, please." The judge held up his hand, silencing his wife. "And Peggy, please do not stay out as late. I'd like you home by midnight." Judge Shippen looked at his daughter dotingly, while Mrs. Shippen sighed in frustration, dropping her silverware down on her plate. Peggy tossed a smirk in her mother's direction.

"Ready, Miss Bell?" Caleb was beside Clara, pulling her from her observation of this family drama.

"Will you please stop calling me 'Miss'? You've been here longer than I have. Please, call me Clara."

"Only if you'll agree to call me Cal."

"All right, all right." Clara nodded.

"Well, congratulations, Clara Bell. You survived your first Shippen dinner. All that remains is dessert." Caleb put the peach tart in her hands and smiled at her as she once more entered the dining room.

After the dinner, the judge and Doctor William retreated to the study while Peggy excused herself. Clara remained in the dining room to clear the table. The elderly woman she'd seen earlier, in the stairwell, emerged as if from the air.

"Caleb, that is Brigitte, right?"

"Call me Cal."

"Sorry, Cal. Is that Brigitte?" Clara asked.

"Oh, yes. Brigitte is Hannah's sister. She doesn't talk much, except to Hannah. She cleans the dishes, strips the bedding, dumps the chamber pots. All the sorts of jobs that allow her to avoid speaking to anyone. But you better go to Miss Peggy—she's probably in a hurry to get to this soiree. Especially if André will be there."

"Who's André?" Clara remembered back to the cut-out silhouette that Peggy had attached to her mirror, the face of the handsome British officer. "Miss Peggy mentioned someone named 'Johnny'?"

"The very same. John André is the man who is about to make your life very difficult."

"HOW VERY predictable that Betsy would pass on this soiree, when General Howe himself will be there. Does she not know that wherever the general goes, the best officers are sure to follow?" Peggy stood in front of Clara, adjusting her gloves as the carriage rolled to a halt before her. "But then, she's as averse to fun as Mother is."

"Good evening, Miss Peggy." Caleb hopped down from his perch and with one fluid gesture opened the coach door and extended his hand toward Miss Peggy.

Peggy let her eyes slide sideways toward her maid. "At least I have you here with me to help me . . . what was it . . . *behave*?" Peggy flashed her dazzling smile—that look that appeared sweet and yet had the effect of putting Clara more on edge—before taking Cal's outstretched hand and hoisting herself and her full skirt through the carriage door.

Clara entered the carriage behind her mistress, receiving a teasing grin from Cal as she did so. Mrs. Quigley entered last, complaining that she did not have the luxury of taking a night off to attend a soiree, not when there was silver to be polished, china to be scrubbed, table linens to be pressed and sorted. But, Clara noticed, the old woman had changed into a clean, fresh dress of green and purple calico and had pulled her hair back tightly, giving her a more formal appearance than she'd modeled earlier in the day.

The carriage carried them west past the bustle of Market Street, just as the shop owners were shuttering their windows and wishing one another a pleasant night. As the last rays of daytime poured down, the Shippen carriage sped forward on an increasingly rural road toward the Schuylkill River.

"We are getting you new clothes, Clara." Mrs. Quigley rested her hands in her lap, twisting a kerchief in tight knots. "It is not acceptable for you to be attending a *soiree* at Lord Rawdon's looking like a farm hand."

Clara, tired from the day, wished to reply that she would have happily stayed home, that she would have preferred to retreat to her private, quiet bedroom and have an evening of peace, but Oma's stern face remained in the fore of her mind, so she simply smiled politely and answered, "Yes, ma'am, thank you."

As Caleb urged the horses to speed ever quicker toward the Schuylkill, Peggy's mood soared. She did not look at her maid or her housekeeper, but rather kept her gaze fixed firmly out the window, staring at the sun-streaked river, which appeared as if engulfed in flames, and the darkening evening into which she could not wait to be set loose.

Caleb slowed the carriage as they approached a mansion, large and well-lit, perched on the hill above the river. In the indigo pall of twilight, a large British flag was visible where it hung at the front of the mansion. Peggy spotted their destination and pinched her cheeks, drawing a rosy blush from her ivory skin.

"Is this Lord Rawdon's home?" Clara regretted the question the instant she saw Mrs. Quigley's stern expression: servants were not supposed to break the silence. Peggy, however, seemed all too happy to reply.

"The British seized this house from a prominent rebel when he was forced to flee." Peggy tugged on a loose wisp of golden hair, pulling the curl taut before allowing it to spring back into its coil. "How very fortunate for us. It makes a perfect spot for a summer fête."

The horses pulled the Shippen carriage under a porte cochere and they were greeted by an entourage of wigged footmen. Peggy alighted from the carriage, clapping in delight at the military band that stood on hand to serenade the arriving guests. *"Music!"* Peggy exclaimed.

"Miss Shippen, welcome." A middle-aged man in the bright red jacket of a British officer appeared, bowing opposite Peggy in a low curtsy. "You are a vision, Miss Shippen, as always." Clara watched the greeting as Caleb helped her exit the carriage.

"Lord Rawdon, this is magical." Peggy cocked her head, sending her strands of blond curls dancing around her cheeks. Had she practiced that perfectly coy mannerism before the mirror of her bedroom? Clara wondered.

"Miss Shippen, I hope you will do me the honor of allowing me to sit beside you at the card table this evening?" Lord Rawdon, though nearly twice Peggy's age and seasoned in battle, appeared cowed before his dainty gowned guest.

"But of course, Lord Rawdon. It would be my honor to be seated beside the host." Peggy smiled, but turned her attention to the crowd of guests assembling farther down the hill. "Well, Lord Rawdon, I would not wish to monopolize your time. A host is in high demand at his own party."

"Please, Miss Shippen, the others are gathering under the tent on the lawn. Once my guests have arrived and we are a full company, I will meet you there for cards and Champagne."

"Thank you, Lord Rawdon." That was all the permission Peggy needed to take her leave. Peggy curtsied once more, perfectly polite, before lifting her skirts up and walking briskly across the lawn.

"Better follow." Cal directed Clara's gaze toward the retreating figure of Miss Peggy and Mrs. Quigley, who labored to keep apace.

"Will you not join us?" Clara asked, her gaze darting between the familiar sight of Cal and the large crowd of elegantly dressed revelers down the hill.

"I'll have to take care of them first." Caleb cocked his head toward the Shippen horses. "Good luck, Clara Bell." He leaned close and whispered in her ear. "Don't let them take your money at cards . . . these Redcoats are good at parting us simple Americans from our purses."

Clara laughed. "Thanks for the warning, Cal."

Cal led the carriage toward the stables to water the horses as Clara's eyes traveled down the lawn toward the tent. A canopy hung against the velvety blue of the early evening sky, and a trellis draped in ivy welcomed the guests inside. Small, circular tables for parties of six were arranged throughout the tent, covered in white damask tablecloths and crystal Champagne flutes. Throughout the tent, arrangements of freshly clipped wildflowers spilled out of vases, their perfume mixing with the fragrances dabbed on women's wrists to give the air a fresh, springtime aroma. Chandeliers of tiered candles hung overhead, and the light not only danced on the faces of the revelers but on the glasslike surface of the nearby Schuylkill River.

Clara trotted toward the figures of Mrs. Quigley and Miss Peggy and reached them just as they stepped inside the tent. Mrs. Quigley was pulled immediately into the task of fetching Champagne by a servant, and Clara stood alone beside her mistress before the assembly.

"Oh my," Clara sighed.

"What is it?" Peggy cocked her head toward her maid.

Clara, who had not realized she had uttered her thoughts aloud, stammered, "It's enchanting, that's all." Her eyes traveled to the far corner of the tent, where a string quartet played a languid waltz that could barely be heard over the sounds of laughter, flirtatious compliments, and the occasional bawdy joke.

"Oh, yes of course." Peggy waved a gloved hand, less interested in the décor and the music; Clara noticed her lady's eyes darting from face to smiling face, seeking out one smile in particular.

"Hello, Peg." A man, dressed in a suit of pale robin's egg blue, waved as he crossed the tent toward Peggy.

"Joseph Stansbury." Peggy leaned in and kissed the man, who appeared to have spent longer dressing than even Peggy herself. His cheeks were bulbous, cherry-colored orbs stained in blush, below a heavily powdered wig of tight curls. His heeled shoes looked as though they could have been chosen from Peggy's wardrobe.

"I love this rose shade on you." Joseph studied Peggy's dress with interest, speaking in a distinctly British accent.

"Thank you." Peggy performed a playful twirl. "I like the blue on you, Stansbury."

"Yes, the blue would complement you nicely, with your eyes," the man agreed, cupping his chin in his slender fingers, a ring on his middle finger catching a glint of candlelight.

"I'll have to order a gown in that color. How is your store?" Peggy asked.

"Business is good now that the British are back in charge."

"I shall toast to that." Peggy smiled.

"We got some new dishes today, straight from London. You're going to love them." He turned his sharp eyes on Clara. "And who is this?"

"Oh, this? This is nobody." Peggy shook her head. "Just my new lady's maid." Peggy waved her hand perfunctorily in the direction of Clara. "You know how my parents are suddenly so concerned with protecting my virtue."

"So they send this poor creature out to protect your honor?" Stansbury's eyed narrowed on Clara—her homespun clothing, her dusty boots, her weary posture. Clara balled her fists but bit her lip to prevent the utterance of an impolite retort.

"Well, I'll say this much: you know you're a lady, Peggy Shippen, when you get your own lady's maid."

"Haven't I always been a lady?" Peggy teased.

"Well, does she have a name?"

"Of course, Clara is her name. Clara, this is Joseph Stansbury, the china merchant on Market Street. We'll pay a visit to his store soon."

"A pleasure." Clara curtsied, as she'd seen her mistress do, before the china merchant.

"Shall we go get some Champagne?" Joseph Stansbury offered a thin arm to Peggy.

"In a minute. I'll come find you inside, Stansbury."

"Are you shooing me away?" The merchant pouted, crossing his arms.

"Please, Stansbury, just go, quick!" Peggy waved the man away as she turned toward a figure in a red coat gliding toward her.

"Miss Shippen." The dark-haired officer approached in several smooth strides, the sword at his waist swinging back and forth as his heels clicked confidently on the ground.

This man, Clara realized, was John André. She could see the resemblance to the cut-out paper silhouette in the bedroom, but he was more arresting in person. Major André's body was tall and lean, adorned in a stiff red coat and tight-fitting breeches, with the glossy leather boots of the British officer. He wore his dark hair pulled back, a ribbon tied loosely at the nape of his neck.

"Major André," Peggy answered, her voice suddenly faint.

"You look ravishing, as usual, my dear." André took Peggy's hand and gave it a soft kiss. He was close enough now that Clara detected the faint, sweet scent of Champagne on his breath. As she stood beside her mistress, Clara felt the smoldering intensity of his brown-eyed gaze.

"Major André, I—" Peggy said, not taking her hand away from his lips.

"What is this formality, *ma chérie*? I prefer 'Johnny,' you know that."

"Johnny . . ." Peggy allowed both of her hands to be scooped up in his—her skin even more white against his dark, olive coloring.

"Johnny." Peggy inched her body closer to his, so that she was looking up into his face. "I wore the rose gown. It's your favorite, right?"

Her hands in his, he lifted her arms wide so that he might stare, unabashedly, at her figure. Clara cringed at how bare and vulnerable her mistress suddenly appeared: her exposed shoulders and collarbone, her tiny waist, the broad cascading skirt. *"Magnifique."* André winked at Peggy, and his approval was met with several exaggerated blinks of Peggy's eyelashes. "Though I must say, whatever dress you put on immediately becomes my favorite."

Peggy demurred, a sheepish blush, and Clara realized that this was the first time since she'd met Peggy that her mistress had very little to say.

"Shall we?" Major André wove his arm through Peggy's, *"Entrons-nous?"*

Leaving Clara near the tent's entrance, Peggy allowed herself to be escorted under the twinkling chandelier and deeper into the tent. "Oh, Johnny, I'm so glad that Lord Rawdon has arranged for the string quartet tonight. Your military bands—your drums and your fifes—are all fine for your marches and battles, but for cards and Champagne, I just want the violins." Peggy's voice was like warm honey as she tilted her head sideways, looking up at her escort and gliding farther away from Clara.

"That girl." Mrs. Quigley was back at Clara's side, muttering under her breath with clear disapproval.

"You're back." Clara's frame slackened with relief as she caught sight of the old woman.

"Not for long, I fear. Apparently I left my work behind at the

Shippen home only to work at another person's home." Mrs. Quigley clasped her hands together in front of her skirt, turning toward the receding figure of Miss Peggy. "And I return to find her already scooped up by the most notorious flirt of the bunch." Mrs. Quigley stared at André with mistrust. "Had Miss Peggy not been born to a high family like the Shippens, well, I don't like to think what might have become of her . . ."

But Clara's eyes wandered back to the figure of Miss Peggy, whose entrance into the tent seemed to have attracted dozens of watchers. Miss Peggy floated flawlessly through the crowd, turning heads as she passed, greeting her fellow guests but never entering into conversation long enough to cede Major André's attentions. Her movements, so honed and subtle in their natural elegance, reminded Clara of a willow branch lilting in the breeze.

"Now what happens, Mrs. Quigley?" Clara took in the scene as if it were some play she was attending for the first time.

"Easy, Clara, you're not the swooning type as well, are you? We've got enough on our hands with Miss Peggy." Mrs. Quigley frowned at Clara, who made a sudden effort to throw back her shoulders and not appear so entirely rapt with the surroundings.

Mrs. Quigley sighed, clasping her hands together behind her back. "Now they'll play cards and sip Champagne for the next few hours, and we'll stand here and look on as the night grows chilly. Once they've had just enough to loosen their morals, they will grow sleepy and we'll carry our mistress home, where we will deposit her safely into bed." Mrs. Quigley nodded her chin, staring crossly once more at Major André.

"Do we stand here the whole time, watching?"

"Yes, we do, and now you know why I see this as a waste of a night." Mrs. Quigley snapped, suddenly ornery. Clara decided against telling the old woman how excited she was by the idea of watching this evening unfold.

Mrs. Quigley jerked her chin toward Peggy. "But it was wise of the judge and Mrs. Shippen to make sure Miss Peggy was not unaccompanied. I don't like to repeat gossip, mind you, but I've known the folks in this town long enough to catch wind of the tales that are being spread about. And lots of folks have been talking about the . . . *friendship* . . . between our Miss Peggy and that officer of late."

Clara turned toward Miss Peggy just in time to see her deliver the final line of a joke that caused Major André to erupt in hearty laughter.

"Course, I haven't got the faintest idea why Miss Peggy requested that *you* join her tonight, saving for the fact that she wanted to lay her claim on you over Miss Betsy." Mrs. Quigley looked at Clara, her eyes serious. Clara could not help but smart at the comment—it did in fact seem as though Miss Peggy sought her companionship at least, if not friendship. And why should she not?

"Just you be careful, Clara. That's all I'll say."

Clara nodded, obedient, but in her mind she was thinking about how delightful it would be to have a young woman as fine and sought-after as Miss Peggy to call a friend. If only Oma could see her tonight, at a grand soiree hosted by a lord!

"Oh there you are, Quigley, thank heavens!"

"Oh, bother, what now?" Mrs. Quigley and Clara turned to see a large woman, breathless, hovering outside the threshold of the tent. Like Mrs. Quigley, she wore calico print and a linen cap, and carried herself with an air of determined—if not a bit harried—authority. "Quigley!"

"Hello, Lottie. Splendid night you've arranged here." Mrs. Quigley turned toward the woman and slid out of the tent, with Clara following behind.

"Splendid, my foot!" The woman crossed her thick arms. "Our cook has taken sick before finishing the fruit tarts. If Lord Rawdon finds out that his cook has chosen tonight, of all times, to get sick, he'll sack her immediately." The woman's eyes were wide with panic. "Is this your new maid?" The frantic housekeeper eyed Clara. "Can you lend her to me? Just for tonight?" Before receiving permission, the woman clasped Clara's arm in her hard, bracing grip and began to tug her toward the house. "We need someone to help finish these tarts."

"She can't cook, Lottie," Mrs. Quigley answered, her voice thick with irritation about this fact. "Oh, for heaven's sake, I'll come." Mrs. Quigley turned to Clara with a stern expression. "Right, I'm going to run up to the kitchen to help them for a bit. You"—she raised a finger in Clara's face—"you, Clara, do *not* let Miss Peggy out of your sight for one minute. You hear me?"

Clara nodded, looking through the entrance into the tent to locate her mistress. "Aye, Mrs. Quigley." The housekeeper still looked reluctant to leave Clara, or, more likely, Miss Peggy. She cast a nervous glance toward her young mistress and saw that Major André was squeezing her waist. "Not for a *second*!"

Clara nodded. "Yes, ma'am, I understand." The two older women hustled away from the tent toward the house, arguing with each other as they crossed the lawn. Clara, alone outside the tent, pulled her neckerchief closer around her shoulders and turned back toward the party, fixing her gaze on her mistress. Lord Rawdon had once again found Peggy, and he'd succeeded in momentarily separating her from Major André.

Clara leaned in, too timid to enter the tent on her own, and instead paused at the threshold and strained her ears to pick up the strands of their quiet conversation. "My lady, Miss Shippen, that this land could produce beauty like you, it makes all thirteen colonies worth fighting for." Lord Rawdon made these declarations with the unseasoned awkwardness of a man more skilled in battle than in the ballroom.

"You are too generous with your words, Lord Rawdon." Peggy smiled under her host's praise, but she edged away. She glanced over her shoulder, in the direction of Major André. He stood beside the musicians in the corner, his attention occupied with another gowned beauty. This lady was arresting in a manner entirely different than Peggy Shippen. While Peggy was petite in stature, with golden hair and a fair complexion, this woman was tall and full-figured, with glossy brunette locks and a warm skin tone. She was dressed in a silk gown of a rich scarlet red. Her hair, like Peggy's, was pulled high up off her neck, and she wore a ruby necklace, which fell on her bosom and invited admiring stares from the officers who passed. Standing opposite Major André, she was his perfect complement.

"Admiring the cast of characters?" Clara jumped at the sound of a man's voice, and she turned to see an unfamiliar face beside her under the trellis.

"Oh, I'm sorry, I did not mean to startle you, Miss . . . ?"

"Miss Bell. Clara Bell." She shifted her weight. This man did not wear the uniform, as most of the men in the tent did, but he looked more dapper than a servant in his black wool coat, starched white linen top, and matching black breeches. Around his neck he wore a maroon cravat, and he held his black tricornered hat in his hand.

"Fascinating, isn't it?" He inched his way closer to Clara, peering over her shoulder into the tent.

"I suppose," Clara answered, shifting away from this brazen man.

"Which one are you here with?" The man asked, turning his gaze on Clara.

Clara straightened her posture. "I'm the lady's maid to Miss Peggy Shippen."

"Aha! Is that so?" This man, with neatly combed dark hair and light eyes, spoke with an accent that gave him away as British.

"Yes." Clara looked at him, hoping he would now leave her in peace to watch the party and supervise her mistress. And where was Cal? she wondered.

"An enviable post, being lady's maid to Miss Margaret Shippen. How did you manage to get that position?"

Courtesy required that she answer his question, though Clara did not wish to engage in continued conversation with this forward stranger, not while she was to be watching her mistress. She answered him, keeping her eyes fixed inside the tent. "My grandmother, before she died, was an old friend of the Shippens' housekeeper."

"Mrs. Quigley," he answered. "But I thought the Shippens had cut their waitstaff?"

"That's right." Clara turned to him. How did this stranger know so much about the Shippen family's situation?

"Go on—you were telling me about your grandmother?"

Clara looked into this man's face. She had to admit he was handsome, even if she found his manners a bit uncouth. "When the Shippen family relocated to their farm in Lancaster at the start of the war, they were near the farm where I lived. My grandmother helped the Shippen family and their servants stay fed that first winter."

"Ah, so you saved the Shippens, and now they've hired you. One favor returned for another favor?"

"I don't know that I like being referred to as a favor, sir." Clara bristled. "I intend to work hard and earn my keep. I'm no charity case."

"Indeed you are not, Miss Bell. I meant no offense. Besides, it's to you we owe our thanks for Miss Peggy Shippen's presence tonight."

Clara chuckled in spite of herself. "Nothing that dramatic, I'm afraid."

"Mrs. Quigley is a fine lady," the man added. Clara turned to him.

"And how is it that you consider yourself so knowledgeable about the Shippen home?"

The man smiled. "I spend enough time there, I ought to know a thing or two."

"Is that so?" Clara's eyebrows arched.

"I am the secretary to Major John André. The name's Robert Balmor. Major André and I, we spend quite a lot of time with the younger Miss Shippen." Robert smirked.

"I know that Major André is a favorite of my mistress." Clara peered into the tent and saw that Miss Peggy was still embroiled in conversation with Lord Rawdon.

"And Peggy Shippen is a favorite of Major André's as well," Robert answered.

Clara did not like the way he spoke of Miss Peggy with such familiarity.

"Have you met that gentleman yet?" Robert pointed toward the man in the pale blue suit.

"Why yes, that's Joseph Stansbury," Clara said, feeling a surge of pride at knowing something as well. "He runs the china shop on Market Street. Miss Peggy introduced me to him when we first arrived."

"Ah, yes. The illustrious china merchant from London." Robert nodded. "He's a good friend of Peggy Shippen's. And, I suspect, the only man in the tent who is more interested in Miss Shippen's ball gown than in what lies beneath it."

Clara blushed and shifted her weight. How brazen the men were at this gathering! Seeking to divert the conversation, she pointed toward Major André and the brunette beauty at his side. "And who's that lady? Major André has barely left her side since we arrived." Clara knew her mistress would not be pleased about that.

"Ah, that's Meg Chew," Robert answered, a hint of reverence in his voice. "Not too difficult on the eyes, is she?"

"Miss Peggy mentioned a Meg Chew," Clara said, remembering their conversation in her mistress's bedroom.

"Yes, Meg Chew is a rival of Peggy Shippen's. Her only rival, really." Robert's gaze flitted between the two women as they would between two pastries of equal allure. And he was not alone; Clara noticed that most of the men in the tent seemed to be angling to speak with one or the other.

Meg still had André's attention, yet Peggy made no move toward him. She simply watched from the far side of the tent, smiling as if Lord Rawdon were the most charming man at the soiree. Clara couldn't decide which of the two rivals was more enchanting. Peggy had a girlish vitality, a mischievous glimmer in her eye, while Meg Chew seemed haughty, supremely confident, even regal.

"Your master is an artist?" Clara asked, thinking back to the silhouette in Peggy's possession.

"Yes, he's constantly drawing sketches, cutting out paper silhouettes, even writing poetry."

Clara nodded. "He gave one such silhouette to Miss Peggy."

"And another to Miss Chew." Robert cocked his head.

"That seems cruel," Clara answered.

"He's a great favorite of the ladies. Something about him—he writes a poem about them, speaks a little French, or draws their likeness, and they fall for him. His good looks don't hurt, I suppose."

Her mistress could tame him, Clara thought. She'd only known Peggy Shippen a few hours, but already she was certain of that.

"Problem is, the major can't seem to make up his mind as to which one he wants," Robert continued. "One week we are spending every afternoon in Judge Shippen's parlor as André paints Peggy. The next week, he is strolling the gardens at the Chew mansion, composing a poem with Meg."

Robert and Clara stopped speaking as Lord Rawdon crossed to the center of the tent and encouraged his guests to take their seats for card games. Wigged footmen descended on the tables immediately, distributing cards and bowls of pistachios, and filling flutes with French Champagne. Clara watched as Lord Rawdon seated Peggy beside himself. Opposite them sat Meg Chew and Major André.

Well, at least she was at his table, Clara thought. "Who are the remaining guests at their table?" she asked, watching the seats fill.

"Joseph Stansbury you already know." Robert pointed at the merchant who sat on Peggy's other side. "And that other lady is Christianne Amile, another Tory belle."

Clara watched as Major André clinked his glass against Meg Chew's, saying something to make the brunette toss her rich curls back in laughter. Across the table, Peggy was chatting with an officer who had approached her to pay his respects.

"That's Captain Hammond, coming to talk with Peggy now," Robert said. "Another admirer." Clara could sense Peggy's frustration—it was evident in the slightly tense manner her gestures had assumed, even as she attempted to flirt with this other admirer. "Every man is paying his respects except your master, who seems to be entirely ignoring her."

Robert weighed this, but did not reply.

"Why is he jilting her, spending the whole night with Meg

Chew?" It wasn't right, flaunting his courtship in front of Peggy's face when he knew she cared for him.

"Well, I do believe he prefers Peggy Shippen," Robert said thoughtfully. "But Major André is a smart man. The Chews are a much wealthier family. The Shippen money is old money, which is respectable, and there once was a lot of it. But since the colonies rebelled, Judge Shippen has halted all his business dealings. He's afraid to trade with either the British or the rebels. It's hard to believe how quickly their money has been sapped up."

Clara looked at the yards of fine silk adorning her mistress's figure, the string of pearls around her neck and in her vaulted hairdo. She thought back to the elegant coach in which they'd ridden to the party. "Not that hard to believe," Clara mumbled.

Robert looked over his shoulder. "I could really use a glass of ale. Or better yet, Champagne."

Clara stared at him, eyes wide.

"What? Just because we are attendants, we can't enjoy the party too?" The keen way Robert looked at her put Clara on edge, and she angled her body away from his to look back into the tent.

"I am certain that I should not be drinking Lord Rawdon's Champagne," she answered.

"Tut, tut, aren't you a proud one?" Balmor teased her.

"I must behave properly, in a manner befitting the Shippen household," Clara answered, certain that her reply would have garnered Mrs Quigley's approval; but now it seemed to garner Robert's scorn.

"And you don't think Miss Peggy is drinking Champagne in that tent?"

This point silenced Clara.

"We British don't believe in being so stiff, Clara. War can be fun, can't it?" Robert whispered in her ear, speaking so close that his breath landed on her neck, causing a few soft hairs to stand on end.

The string quartet struck up a minuet and the entire tent grew excited with the upbeat tempo. In the hustle of couples rising to dance, Major André got up from the table and slid beside Peggy. He extended a hand and lifted Peggy to dance.

"Ah, look who just asked Peggy to dance. Should we not mimic our very proper, very elegant employers?" Robert extended his hand toward Clara as he gave an exaggerated bow. "May I have this dance, my lady?"

"Oh, no, I can't dance," Clara answered quickly. The thought alone made her uncomfortable. Oma had never let her learn.

"All you have to do is follow my lead." Before she could protest, Robert had stepped toward Clara and wrapped one arm around her waist. Clara resisted. She'd never had such intimate contact with a man.

"I cannot." She shook her head.

"I won't bite, I promise." Robert's smile served to calm her, somewhat. He took her other hand in his own, and he began to sway opposite her, leading her across a small patch of the dark lawn. Over his shoulder, Clara caught glimpses of her mistress, who was floating across the dance floor, her eyes fixed on Major André.

"Is this so torturous, Miss Bell?" Robert stared at her, his head falling sideways.

"I suppose not, Mr. Balmor." Clara suppressed the flush that rose to her cheeks.

The music came to an abrupt halt and Robert dropped her hands. Clara noticed, with surprise, that she felt disappointment when he pulled away.

Before Clara understood what was happening, the men in the

tent had left their partners in the middle of the dance. They stood, arms heavy at their sides, gazes fixed straight forward. From somewhere, a drumroll started.

"What is going on?" Clara looked around the crowd, confused, and noticed that a column of British flags had appeared in the tent, marched forward by smartly dressed soldiers.

"There he is." Robert strained forward to see a small figure, just entering the tent. He was older than the rest of the men, and flanked on both sides by officers, aides, and attendants. The shoulders of his red jacket were weighted down with oversized silk epaulets, and he wore a scarlet sash across his narrow chest. On top of his head rested a white wig of tightly wound curls. He looked throughout the tent scrupulously, his eyes fixating on each officer, who, in turn, seemed to stand a little more erect under his gaze. Clara turned to Robert, curious.

"That is General Howe," Robert whispered. "General William Howe, Commander of the British troops in America." The military drums pounded out a rhythmic roll until the men, in perfectly rehearsed unison, saluted him.

With a wave of his hand, the general told his men to resume their dancing, and he took a seat at a table with two of his aides-de-camp. At this point, Lord Rawdon's attendants paraded into the tent with dishes of fruit tarts and silver pots of coffee.

"I see Mrs. Quigley helped them finish the desserts," Clara said, pointing at the sweets being deposited on the tables.

Robert glanced around the tent, noticing how all the officers were suddenly consumed with the arrival of General Howe. "Now's our chance," he whispered. "I'm going to steal us a bottle of Champagne. Come help me."

"I certainly shall not."

"You act so offended, Clara." Robert smirked. "But I bet that when I return, I shall be able to convince you to have a glass with me. Have you ever had French Champagne before?"

"I have not." Clara crossed her arms.

"Well, it's one thing the French got right. I'll be back and you'll see for yourself." Robert was off, gliding undetected toward a vacated table on the outer edge of the tent. The officers, still jostling to approach the general, did not notice as he swiped a full bottle.

"Now I must just find us two glasses!" Robert smiled at her, holding up the frosty bottle. "I'll be right back." With a wink, Robert disappeared farther into the crowded tent.

Clara looked on—appalled, yet somehow amused. What would Oma say about such a brazen young man? But Clara was the maid to a lady as grand as Peggy Shippen now. Was she not allowed to share just a bit of the fun being enjoyed by the rest of the partygoers? And Robert had turned out to be perfectly polite to her. And hadn't she spotted servants taking clandestine sips of Champagne all night outside of the tent? The mood inside the tent was too merry, the evening too pleasant, the music too cheerful for her to decline a small glass of Champagne.

Clara turned her gaze back to the dance floor, looking for Peggy. She scanned the dancing bodies, looking for that bright spot of pink silk. But where had her mistress gone? At the tables, where couples had resumed card games, there was no pink. Clara checked near the band, in the queue of guests lined up to meet the general, but her mistress was nowhere in the tent. Clara's heart quickened. In the excitement of the general's entrance, she had lost sight of her mistress and had allowed her to slip away, unnoticed.

"Oh, no." Clara felt as if she might cry. Her first night and she'd already failed at her job. Mrs. Quigley would dismiss her for sure. She stepped away and hurried along the perimeter of the tent, wondering if perhaps Miss Peggy had stepped outside to get some air. But it was so dark, she'd never be able to see. And then Clara detected a sound, a faint giggling, coming from down the sloping hill by the bank of the river. Clara squinted, willing her eyes to see in the darkness.

"Johnny!" More laughter. The voice by the river was, without a doubt, Peggy's.

Clara focused in on the sounds. A blurred outline slowly took shape as Clara's eyes adjusted to the night. Two figures. Peggy and Major André, sitting beside each other near the river.

"I thought I'd never be able to steal you away from our gracious host, the esteemed Lord Rawdon." Major André's genteel British accent was easily detectable now that Clara had located them.

"Fortunately General Howe provided sufficient distraction," Peggy answered, leaning toward her companion. They clinked glasses and then Peggy drained her Champagne. Clara noticed, with horror, that André did not sip from his own glass, but instead offered his drink to Peggy as well. She drank it.

"If I were Lord Rawdon, I'd have never let you out of my sight, not for one minute. Not when every other gentleman in that tent is just waiting on his opportunity to pounce on you." Major André leaned in toward Peggy playfully—was he tickling her?—prompting her to erupt in laughter.

"Oh, Johnny, I'm so glad it was you who pounced first." Peggy hiccupped, and the two of them leaned toward each other.

Clara watched, shocked, as Major André took Peggy's chin in his hand and pulled her face to his. Before Clara could protest, Major André was kissing Peggy. These were not the tame kisses a gentleman placed on a lady's hand or a lady's cheek—these were brazen kisses, kisses that ought to offend a lady's sense of decorum. Clara wanted to run in between them, to intervene, but she noticed with horror that her mistress was happily returning the kisses. But then, to her relief, Peggy pulled her lips away.

"I am not sure I shall allow you to kiss me any longer." Peggy edged her body away from André's, staring back toward the tent as if she might leave him alone by the river. She still had the hiccups.

"Why not, my darling? Why would you torture me?" André reached his arms toward Peggy, but she swatted them away, crossing her arms like a petulant child.

"You certainly spent enough time talking to *her* tonight," Peggy said with a pout, and Clara knew instantly to whom her mistress referred.

"My darling." André's shoulders sagged, his body entirely willing to play the part of the penitent lover. "I was merely being polite. I can't outright reject her when she speaks to me. You know that Meg means nothing compared to . . ."

"Don't say her name," Peggy answered, her tone icy.

"Fine." André threw his hands up in defeat. "I shall not."

"Do you prefer her?" Peggy turned on him, and even in the dark, Clara could sense how intently she stared at him.

"Not at all, my darling. How many times must I tell you?" Yes, but did he not say the same thing to Meg Chew? Clara wondered.

André's hands inched closer to Peggy's body, and this time she did not swat them away. She did, however, turn her face when he tried to kiss her.

"Tell me," she said.

"Tell you what?"

"Tell me that I'm your favorite, Johnny."

André was consumed by his desire, Clara could tell; he would say whatever he needed to say in order to resume kissing her. "You are my favorite, Peggy."

"And you love me, and me alone?"

"You know I do, my darling Peggy."

"Then tell me. Say it."

"Why must you torture me?"

"Say that you love me!"

"I love you, Peggy Shippen."

"Fine, you may kiss me now."

"I think you like to see me suffer, my darling." André leaned toward her, placing a long, slow kiss on the side of Peggy's neck. And then it was whispers Clara could not fully detect, soft kisses, a giggle. And then suddenly, in the middle of the dark, inconspicuous night, Major André and Peggy were lying down beside each other, spread out in the grass. Clara strained her ears and detected more whispers, a sigh. When Johnny's hands stroked Peggy's bare neck, threatening to rove even lower, Clara was certain that her mistress would at last remember her virtue and protest. But to her shock, the only protest issued from Peggy's mouth was a sigh. Clara could have fainted in shock.

To think of the proper young woman she'd watched at dinner just a few hours ago, discussing politics with her uncle and father—a doctor and a judge! What would Peggy's father think if he knew about his daughter's scandalous behavior? He'd be devastated.

Major André was removing his coat now, prompting Clara to stagger backward with fresh horror, as her mind flashed back to scenes she'd accidentally witnessed on the farm, scenes she'd unwittingly walked into in the hay loft or the rear stall of the dairy barn. She was reminded of what she had heard about how she herself had been conceived—the disgraceful act that Clara's own mother had performed out of wedlock, the act that had ultimately taken her mother's life. No, she didn't survive the childbirth, Oma had told Clara, because of the cardinal sin that she'd participated in to create Clara's life.

And now her mistress, the well-bred, highborn Miss Margaret Shippen, was sprawled in the grass with a man who was not her husband, while all of Philadelphia society reveled just feet from her! Such a thing, if discovered, would ruin Miss Peggy. Clara had to intervene, before this went so far as to be irreparable to her lady's reputation. Perhaps Miss Peggy didn't know what her kissing would lead to, what that man was capable of doing to rob her of her virtue.

"Miss Peggy." Clara edged down the hill toward her mistress, her voice shrill.

Her mistress did not respond, but rather kept running her fingers through John André's black hair, now loose of its ribbon. Clara experienced fresh horror as she saw, through the feeble light of the moon's reflection, that Major André was allowing his hand to wander toward the hem of Miss Peggy's skirt. Why did her mistress not protest?

"My lady, Miss Peggy!"

This time both Peggy and Major André looked up.

"You're wanted, my darling." Major André kissed Peggy's bare neck, sounding irritated by the distraction.

"Oh, it's just my maid," Peggy answered him. "Clara, go away." Peggy shooed her maid with her hand and refocused her attention on wrapping her arms around Major André's waist.

Clara turned toward the tent, desperate. Fortunately, no one in the tent was looking in their direction; they were too consumed by their Champagne and dancing. But then her situation went from desperate to dire when she spotted the familiar figure of Mrs. Quigley. The housekeeper was standing at the entrance of the tent, scanning the crowd for some sign of Miss Peggy. Just a matter of minutes now before they were discovered, and Clara would be tossed out of the Shippen home before she'd even spent a night there.

A fresh giggle, followed by a prolonged sigh, told Clara that Miss Peggy had no intention of rebuffing her companion's roving hands.

"*Mon Dieu,* Peggy Shippen," André spoke in a low, husky voice.

Clara turned back now toward the couple. "Miss *PEGGY*! Please!" Clara was astounded that she had found herself in this position.

"There you are." A familiar voice. Robert was beside her, carrying two flutes brimming with Champagne. "I've brought some refreshments for us. What are you doing down here by the river?"

"Robert." Clara felt weak with relief. "Thank goodness you're back."

"Did you miss me?" Robert grinned, his features delighted at her reaction. "I'm sorry if I've kept you waiting." He was moving toward her. Was Clara imagining it, or did he appear like he might try to kiss her? Were all the men at this party completely mad?

"Robert, please." She stepped away from him and shook her head, diverting his attention. "Look, down there!" She pointed at the two figures reclined on the lawn. "My lady and Major André are down there acting *very* indiscreetly. And Mrs. Quigley is going to see. She will most likely embarrass my mistress and most definitely dismiss me."

"Where am I looking?" Robert narrowed his eyes in concentration.

"*There!* At Major André and Miss Peggy." Clara pointed.

"Oh, I see." Robert looked from the housekeeper back to the couple down by the river. "Yes, that's a problem, you're certainly right about that." He took a few steps closer to Peggy and the major.

"Major André." Robert cupped his hands and called in their direction, his voice much more assertive than Clara's had been. "Major, the old woman is coming back." Then, under his breath, "So you might want to remove your hand from under Miss Shippen's hoopskirt."

When Clara saw the two figures separate at that warning, she was so relieved she could have kissed Robert.

"Oh, thank goodness," she sighed. "Thank you, Robert. Thank you."

"Maybe's it's not an enviable post you have here after all." Robert smirked, still standing too close.

Clara did not have time for this man's flirtation, but rather kept her eyes pointed on her mistress as Major André wished Peggy good night, whispering some salacious secret into her ear before rising. Peggy stayed on the lawn, adjusting her jewelry, ensuring that her dress was in place and her hair had not gone lopsided, while André rose and strode toward his secretary. "Balmor, let's go. I've had enough of this party."

"Well, Miss Clara Bell, it's been a pleasure. Don't blame yourself for tonight getting sort of... out of hand." Robert placed his hat on his head. "This Philadelphia society may be genteel, but it's not tame. In fact, sometimes it makes the French court at Versailles seem like a nunnery in comparison." Robert tipped his hat once with a small bow, and then he disappeared into the night with his master, who was muttering something about a tavern.

Silently, Clara approached her mistress. Peggy was looking out over the river, her pale skin glowing in the light of the moon reflected off the water's calm surface. She stirred when she heard Clara beside her.

"Oh, Clara," Peggy spoke calmly, as if she had not just mortified her new maid. "Hello, Clara." Peggy's voice was soft, girlish. "Sit beside me."

Confounded, Clara obeyed, sitting down slowly on the grass as the river lapped the shore. She was furious with her mistress, having just been forced to witness such a scene of her indiscretion.

Peggy turned her face so that she was just inches from her maid. Clara observed that the *pouf* of her hair had deflated, so that the curls now hung around her face. Her eyes were ablaze, her cheeks flushed, giving her a sort of mad, savage look. Clara decided in that moment that she'd never seen anyone more beautiful. "Oh"— Peggy leaned her head slowly on her maid's shoulder, exhaling a slow, serene sigh. Clara stiffened, but tried not to show how nervous such a gesture made her. "Clara, now you know. I am so in love."

II.

"All is lost." Peggy repeats the words into the abandoned bedroom, as if through repetition she will find their sense, a meaning. "But I don't understand."

I turn and leave her alone in the bedroom as I make my way down the steps. I find Benedict Arnold in the cramped drawing room with the bewildered messenger.

"Did they say with whom this spy had conducted his rendezvous? Did this spy, this British fellow, offer up the name of his fellow traitor?" Arnold asks. The messenger, confused, shakes his head.

"I know nothing of the matter, sir, simply that I was to deliver this letter with haste."

"But did you hear anything else, man?" Arnold towers over him. "The letter says the spy was apprehended with secret documents. Documents intended to give over the fort at West Point, and the body of our Commander Washington. Who gave him these documents?" Arnold waves the letter in the messenger's face, his voice thundering down at the man from the deep recesses of his stocky frame.

"I do not think they know yet, General Arnold," the messenger answers, apologetic. But this answer satisfies my master, convinces him that high command has not yet pieced it together. Has not yet discerned his own central role in the plot.

Perhaps there is still time. Perhaps he can avoid the hangman's gallows after all. But Washington rides toward him this very instant, expected at the farm for breakfast. Expecting a casual breakfast with Benedict Arnold, one of his favorite generals, and Arnold's pretty wife. He must be quick. I know what he is wondering: should he take his wife with him or leave her behind? To leave her would be risky for her. And yet Peggy Arnold can take care of herself. She can play the role of siren; laughing, and flirting, and dancing until she's clouded the judgment of every man in the room.

No one will suspect a flower of such beautiful bloom to conceal a serpent underneath. She can manage it. She can manage anything.

CHAPTER TWO

"Delicious Little Heathen"

May 1778
Philadelphia, PA

CLARA WAS summoned to Peggy's room shortly after breakfast, and she found her mistress buried under a mountain of white silk, hoopskirts, gauze, stockings, and feathers. Clara's shoulders dropped. She had hoped to dress Miss Peggy quickly so that she might report promptly to Miss Betsy for dressing; she had no interest in setting off another family spat this morning.

"Oh! There you are!" Peggy, who seemed in no hurry to dress, rose and took her maid by the hand, pulling her down onto the fabric-strewn floor beside her. She was still in her white-linen sleeping shift, her loose hair tumbling around her shoulders. Her face looked fresh and cheerful. "Did you have fun at Lord Rawdon's?"

Clara hesitated. Oma had told her to always tell the truth, but she wavered; were maids honest to their ladies, or did they choose the answer that was most polite?

Peggy didn't await a reply, but rather retrieved a letter from her pocket and waved it before Clara. "Johnny sent a letter first thing this morning. He said his secretary, Robert Balmor, enjoyed speaking with you."

"Oh, well, I don't know about that, Miss Peggy."

"Oh, now I believe I see my modest maid blushing," Peggy teased. "Something is different about you today, Clara." Peggy studied her maid, her eyes roving freely over Clara's figure. "You have new clothes."

Clara couldn't help but allow a sheepish smile. That morning during the servants' breakfast, Mrs. Quigley and Caleb had entered the kitchen with a large pile of women's clothing.

"Special delivery for Miss Clara Bell." Caleb unloaded an armful of fabric onto the table: shifts, wide-sleeved blouses, gowns and petticoats in wool and cotton calico, fichu neckcloths, muslin and lace mobcaps, aprons, and even one formal gown—very basic to be sure—of midnight blue silk. Surely they couldn't mean that *all* those clothes were for her—the pile was far too fine and far too plentiful.

"Mrs. Quigley." Clara looked to the housekeeper, placing her teacup down so as not to spill a drop near the clothing. "I'd have to work six months without wages in order to pay for half of this."

"Nonsense, girl." Mrs. Quigley poured herself a cup of tea and sat beside Clara. "They were just sitting in the closet collecting dust. All the maids who have passed through here over the years have left clothes behind. Of course, they might not all fit."

Just then Clara lifted a petticoat of white and yellow ticking that appeared easily twice her size. "But you're a seamstress, or so you claim to be. You can alter them." Mrs. Quigley took a sip of her tea. "Besides, it'll be good practice, since you'll be mending the family's clothing. Miss Betsy's and Miss Peggy's especially."

"But I can't keep all of these." Clara unfolded a calico petticoat with the pattern of small cherry blossoms and examined the fine stitching. "Surely we must donate some of these to the poor?"

"Clara, you're as poor as they come."

Clara could not help but laugh at the old woman's candor.

"Now put that dress down and finish your tea before it gets cold."

"Consider it your uniform, Clara." Mr. Quigley entered the kitchen, looking smart in a black suit of lightweight wool and white knee-high stockings. "During the day you'll wear just a basic dress and the apron and linen cap. And then at night, you'll need something respectable to go calling with Miss Shippen."

"I was telling my husband how well you held up last night, being thrown into modern-day Sodom and Gomorrah like that." Mrs. Quigley stared at her new employee appraisingly, betraying what appeared to be grudging admiration. "When I returned from the kitchens and did not see Miss Peggy in the tent, I panicked. Thought maybe she had escaped with that Major André! But then when I found the two of you, simply sitting side by side down on the bank of the river, I was so relieved." Clara felt a pang of guilt at the praise. If only the old woman had witnessed the preceding scene as Clara had. "She seems to have taken quite a shine to you, Clara."

"Now, I don't know about that, ma'am." Clara averted her eyes.

"Well, she didn't bite your head off on the first night. That's more than we all expected for you." The housekeeper chuckled, looking at her husband with a knowing grin.

"Just keep up the good work, Clara Bell. When Miss Peggy is happy, peace reigns in the Shippen household." Mr. Quigley poured himself a cup of tea, and the kitchen of servants erupted in good-natured laughter.

"Clara." Peggy was now digging through the pile of silk on

her bedroom floor. "Do you know about the Meshianza Masque?" Peggy's eyes roiled with that same intensity that Clara had seen in them last night at her first sighting of John André.

"No, my lady. What is that?"

"Read this." Peggy held out the daily paper, pointing at the front page. "It's going to be a party, such a *grand* party, the likes of which Philadelphia has never seen." Peggy turned her gaze to the article. "Read it aloud, Clara."

Clara turned to the journal and began reading: "'*The Meshianza is a Masquerade hosted in the honor of General William Howe, who is departing Philadelphia to return to London.*'"

"You must have seen the general at Lord Rawdon's?" Peggy interrupted. "The short little man? I was so irritated when they stopped playing the music because he entered the tent."

Clara nodded, reading on at a quick pace; this chore was taking entirely too long. "'*General Howe's men, laboring hard to organize a fête in their leader's honor, have confiscated the mansion of rebel millionaire Joseph Wharton and intend to transform the space into a Turkish court and harem.*'"

"Did you hear that? A Turkish court and harem!" Peggy interrupted, clapping.

"It sounds like quite the evening." Clara offered the paper back. "Now, Miss Peggy, shall we get you dressed?"

"Not yet, read on, it gets even better."

"'*Howe's men shall dress to resemble the grand knights of the crusades who defended the Holy Land under King Henry IV. They will be divided into two camps for a jousting tournament, adorned as the Knights of the Blended Rose versus the Knights of the Burning Mountain.*'"

Peggy grabbed her wrist. "You're coming to the part about *me*!"

"'*Before a jousting tournament begins between the two armies, the knights will pause to receive favors from their ladies—twelve of Philadelphia's favorite belles, admired not only for their beauty and virtue, but their steadfast affection for the British crown. These lovely maidens will be dressed* à la Turque, *in full Turkish garb like that which would have been witnessed in the harems of ancient Constantinople.'"*

Was Miss Betsy going to come in and find the new maid, who was supposed to be dressing both sisters, sitting on the floor reading the newspaper with Miss Peggy?

"Why did you stop reading, Clara? Keep going."

"*'Each maiden will remove favors from her turban, which she shall bestow on her Knight before the joust. Once the tournament is complete, the entire party will retire into the mansion for dinner and dancing. The evening will be concluded with a fireworks display.'"*

Clara lowered the paper to the sound of Peggy's clapping. "This was all Johnny's idea, having us dress up as the ladies of the Turkish harem while they dress as Knights."

Clara wondered if her mistress had bothered to read the article immediately below the piece on the Meshianza Masque; the report outlining how the French had announced their alliance with the American rebel troops, and how, at this very moment, Washington's Continental Army was nearby, preparing to descend on Philadelphia and drive the British troops north.

"Guess who *my* knight is." Peggy's blue eyes sparkled. "Guess who has asked to escort me."

Clara needed only one guess. "Major John André."

"That's right." Peggy picked up a strand of gauze and twirled it overhead, as if preparing for her role as a harem dancer. "That should knock the haughty smile right off Meg Chew's face. Johnny chose *me*."

A knock at the door filled Clara with dread: she must have kept

Miss Betsy waiting too long. But she was relieved to see Mrs. Quigley appear. "Miss Peggy, you have visitors. A Mr. Joseph Stansbury and a tailor from the clothing shop Coffin and Anderson."

"Send them in." Peggy rose from the floor.

"Your dressing gown, ma'am." Clara stood up and retrieved her lady's most conservative robe. Then she began to edge toward the door and Miss Betsy's bedchamber; she certainly wouldn't be dressing Miss Peggy in front of these two men.

"No, Clara, you stay with me, wait until you see what they're bringing." Peggy tossed the dressing gown onto the bed. "Send them in at once, Mrs. Quigley." Peggy clapped excitedly, dancing in her flimsy shift.

"But my lady." Mrs. Quigley looked as scandalized as Clara felt. "You're not wearing anything but your nightclothes! Hadn't you better put on a dress first?"

"Yes, Mrs. Quigley," Peggy said, unruffled by the old woman's modesty, "but they are coming *with* my dress. Send them in."

The two men entered, carrying with them a splash of color that seemed to brighten the entire room. The china merchant, Joseph Stansbury, paraded in wearing a tightly tailored suit of canary yellow, with an ornamental neckerchief and a chalky white wig. Behind him walked the tailor, his figure slumped under what appeared to be fifty pounds of white and scarlet silk.

"There it is." Peggy marveled, outstretching her hand to her friend, the merchant. Clara's eyes took in the mountain of bright scarlet and cream-colored silk that had been fashioned into this gown.

"My dear lady." Stansbury kissed Peggy's hand solicitously. "*Voilà*, it's the gown of the season."

"Miss Shippen?" The tailor looked from the calico-clad maid to the nearly nude lady in her shift, apparently unsure of which lady was the intended recipient of the delivery.

"Me," Peggy replied. Turning to Stansbury, she grumbled, "Does he really not know my face?" The merchant shrugged.

The two men, aided by Clara, helped Peggy step into her layers of costume. The dress was of white silk with long sleeves, with a rich scarlet sash tied around the waist to match the color of her knight's garb.

When it came time to fit the turban onto her head, they had difficulty, as Peggy was adamant that her blond curls must remain visible. After several attempts, the tailor withdrew in silence to the corner of the bedroom, crossing his arms as if to observe the scuffle from a safe distance. Clara appeased her mistress by tugging loose several ringlets of hair to frame her face. When Peggy was satisfied, she glided to the full mirror, admiring the effects of her costume.

"I look like quite the Turk, don't I?" She turned to Stansbury, her face teeming with excitement.

"I'm not sure there were many Turks with blue eyes and blond hair," the merchant answered, adjusting one of her feathers. "But you look *divine*!" He winked, and Peggy erupted in laughter.

"Divine—or devilish?" Peggy cocked her head, her turban tilting to the side.

"Can't you be both, Peg?" Stansbury asked.

"Father is going to faint when he sees me. And Mother, oh, I don't even want her to know I'm wearing this."

Just then, the door to the bedroom swung open and Betsy appeared. "I've waited long enough, and now I wish for Clara to help *me* dress!" Betsy stopped midstride, gasping at the sight of her younger sister. "Oh, Peggy."

"Betsy!" Peggy performed a theatrical twirl for her sister, all merriment and good cheer this morning. "What do you think, am I quite ready to dance the night away *à la Turque*?" Peggy turned to Stansbury. "Betsy is going too, but since she's engaged to Neddy Burd, they didn't invite her to be one of the Turkish maidens."

"I wish I could wear one of the costumes." Betsy stared at her younger sister, not attempting to conceal her envy.

"Well, you should not have taken yourself off the market at the height of the social season." Peggy shrugged her shoulders, turning back to her reflection in the mirror.

Another knock on the door and a weary-looking Mrs. Quigley appeared. "My lady, Major André is here to see you, accompanied by his secretary."

"Perfect timing," Peggy said. "We'll ask him what he thinks of my costume!" Betsy, Stansbury, and the tailor excused themselves so that Peggy could take the visit with the major. Clara was preparing to follow them through the door—perhaps she could finally tend to the forgotten Miss Betsy—when Peggy stopped her. "Clara, you stay, I'm sure *Robert Balmor* is eager to see you."

Clara felt her face growing warm under the observant eyes of the housekeeper, still standing in the doorway.

"Would you like to welcome the gentlemen in the parlor downstairs?" Mrs. Quigley's question sounded more like a suggestion.

"No, in here," Peggy answered. Clara wasn't sure whether Peggy was oblivious or simply indifferent to the distress her words caused her poor old housekeeper.

"In your *bedroom*?" Mrs. Quigley did not attempt to mask her horror. "My lady, I must insist—"

"I am *not* going downstairs dressed like this. Mother will wail in horror and Father will complain about the cost of all of this silk. Send them up here."

There was a silent standoff as the housekeeper, staring at the young lady she'd served since her days in diapers, hovered outside the bedroom.

"For heaven's sake, Clara is in here with me. What do you think we're going to do, run straight to bed?" Peggy scoffed at the old woman, causing her to stammer in wordless horror before quitting the room, defeated.

A minute later, Major André appeared in the doorway, accompanied by his secretary, who smiled the instant he spotted Clara. Thinking back to how they had danced the night before, and how he had offered her a glass of Champagne, Clara felt fresh shyness in the sober light of day. She made herself busy with fluffing Miss Peggy's skirt, positioning herself so that she was partially concealed behind the massive hoopskirt.

"Ladies, hello." Major André glided into the room, bowing before taking his sword from his hip and placing it casually on Peggy's bed. "Look at what we have here." He approached Peggy, kissing her outstretched hand as she stood before the mirror. "What a delicious little heathen you shall make tomorrow night." André leaned in close, pausing by Peggy's ear to whisper, "I hope you'll behave like one too."

Clara knew in that instant that she would be unable to contain her mistress—she would have to refuse acting as Miss Peggy's companion to the Masque, not unless Mrs. Quigley or some other servant accompanied her. If left alone with Miss Peggy, Clara could not be sure what sort of trouble her lady might find.

As Peggy and André began giggling, Clara was sure to avoid Robert Balmor's eyes. Mr. Quigley rapped on the door. "Fresh flowers for the lady, from Lord Rawdon." The butler entered carrying a bouquet of white and pink lilies.

"Thank you, Mr. Quigley," Peggy answered. "Just place them on the end table."

"So I have competition?" André eyed the flowers, helping himself to the note that Peggy's admirer had tucked into the petals.

"Does that come as such a shock?" Peggy asked.

"Rawdon certainly seems quite taken with you, Miss Shippen."

Peggy smirked before turning her attention back to her new dress. "A beautiful bloom does not invite the attention of the bees, and yet they buzz around it; is that not so, Major André?"

Aye, and a rotting carcass does not invite the attention of the flies, and yet they buzz around it, Clara thought to herself, but she bit her tongue. She alarmed herself with how much she sounded like her Oma.

"Well, what do you think?" Peggy's tone was teasing.

"You don't want to know what I'm thinking. Not appropriate in the presence of ladies." André and his secretary exchanged a laugh, which Clara found supremely unsuitable.

"Coffin has done a nice job." André turned his focus back to the gown, the sash, and the jewels with an inspecting gaze, circling Peggy with a slow, lithe stride.

"Do you like it, Johnny?" Peggy stood fixed, awaiting his approval.

"I shall wear the sword, but *you* shall pierce the heart of every man present, as usual." André winked at Peggy. Clara turned her gaze from Major André to his secretary and noticed that she had caught Robert staring at her. She averted her eyes.

"And what else shall you wear?" Peggy asked, adjusting the turban on her head to ensure that her blond hair fell in a flattering arrangement.

"I am going to wear a white satin vest with scarlet sleeves to match you. Wide harem pants, a hat of red satin, and large peacock plumes." He approached her now. Clara noticed Mr. Quigley glowering at André, but Peggy only giggled in delight.

"Johnny! It'll be the first time I'll see you out of your officer's uniform."

"That's not *entirely* true, my dear." André winked and both he and Peggy erupted in laughter. Clara felt nauseous, and she decided in that moment that she despised Major John André; she hated André and the frivolous, reckless behavior he never failed to solicit from her mistress.

Mr. Quigley, who seemed to be taking much longer than necessary to deposit the vase of flowers, probably on orders from his wife, cleared his throat from the corner, and André pulled himself away from Peggy back to a respectable distance.

"You will be such a dashing knight, Johnny." Peggy turned from the mirror to André, reaching her hands out to him. "Will you have a shield for the jousting? I couldn't bear it if you were hurt."

"Yes, of course. I've painted my shield with our crest, featuring two cocks fighting."

"Delightful. And what will our motto be?" Peggy asked. "I have an idea." She pulled him close and whispered something only André could hear.

He laughed. "Why, you *are* quite the little heathen, aren't you, Miss Shippen? No, no, so as to avoid offending some of the more genteel members of the party, our motto shall be: No Rival."

"Oh, all right. That sounds very fine." Peggy nodded approvingly. "I'll be sure to tell Meg Chew."

"You are devilish." André laughed. "So, my darling, I've brought you something."

"A present?" Peggy asked.

André nodded. "For you to wear tomorrow night." André retrieved a small box from Robert's outstretched hand and placed it into Peggy's grip. She slowly untied the ribbon and slid the box cover loose. *"Oh!"* she squealed in delight.

"Clara, come look at these." Clara looked into the box to see two combs bedecked in claret jewels the color of the scarlet satin. "You'll have to figure out the best way to style these in my hair."

"They will look delightful beneath your turban, my dear," André said, sticking one of the combs into a loose wave of Peggy's hair.

"Is a gentleman supposed to know what a lady is wearing beneath her turban?" Peggy's eyes glanced up at André's suggestively. With his face poised just inches from hers, Clara worried that André intended to kiss Peggy, right there in front of all the other company present.

"When you wear that costume you are no longer a lady, my darling, nor should you act like one."

"WAKE UP, Clara! Your mistress is calling for you!" Mrs. Quigley's stern voice shook Clara from her deep slumber. Her dark bedroom was pierced only by the hint of a feeble, predawn light.

"Is it time to rise?" Clara looked up groggily. She'd never had the luxury of lying in bed past dawn with Oma on the farm, but this felt even earlier than her usual waking hour.

"It's time to rise whenever Miss Peggy wants you," Mrs. Quigley answered, sighing. "Tonight is the Masque—she probably didn't sleep a wink last night in her excitement."

Clara dressed quickly in the dark. She slid into a simple dress, feeling its well-tailored tightness around her body. The sleeves fit her arms, the midsection fit her waist—there was a precision, a snugness, which Oma's homemade wools and linens had never achieved. The dress smelled of firewood and beeswax, vestiges of the previous, unnamed owner who had worn this through the Shippen home. But it was all hers.

Clara found Peggy sitting upright in bed. The curtains were opened to let in the violet hues of dawn, and Peggy stared out the window as if willing the sun to rise faster.

"Clara!" Peggy turned to her maid, her hair tousled from sleep. "Thank goodness you're here. I was too eager this morning and I'm afraid I tore my dress." Peggy rose from her bed and ran to the spot where her costume lay draped over a chair. "You must fix it." Peggy pointed to a tear that ran parallel to the back row of buttons.

"Can it be done?" Peggy's face creased in anxiety.

"I will do my best, Miss Peggy," Clara answered, already weary, and she hurried to fetch her sewing kit. Back in Miss Peggy's room, she installed herself on the window seat, working on the dress while Peggy washed, all the while chatting merrily about the coming evening.

"I hope this day goes quickly. I just want it to be evening already!"

They asked Hannah to send breakfast up to Peggy's bedchamber so that Peggy could sort her ribbons and Clara could finish her sewing. When the dress had been mended, Peggy stepped into her costume once more to examine Clara's stitching.

Both Clara and Peggy noticed the figure hovering near the doorway of the bedchamber.

"Betsy, do you intend to sulk on my threshold like some ghost deciding whether or not to haunt? Either come in or continue walking."

"I was just looking." Betsy lowered her eyes, embarrassed.

"You can see better up close. Come in," Peggy said. Betsy obeyed. The elder sister examined the trim of pearls that cascaded down the skirt.

"What do you think?" Peggy threw her shoulders back, her chest forward.

"Do you think I might borrow it some time?" Betsy asked, arms folded in front of her own plain skirt.

Peggy laughed. "For what?"

"I don't know. Anything. A future ball, perhaps?"

Peggy turned her eyes from her sister back to the mirror, fluffing her hair under the turban. Quietly, she answered, "If you refrain from cream and pastries for a bit. Otherwise I don't see how you shall squeeze into it."

Betsy's hopeful face wilted.

Peggy sensed her sister's hurt and walked toward her, taking Betsy's hand in her own. "Bets, you know as well as I do that we are not the same size."

"I'm taller." Betsy lifted her chin, defiant. Clara noticed, with relief, that Peggy let the comment go unanswered.

"Come here, Bets, you must see the hair combs André gave me to wear!" Peggy flitted about her room, locating the combs and slipping them into her hair.

"How do you think I should wear them?" Peggy asked, cocking her head left and right to scrutinize her appearance from several angles. Her brow furrowed as she scrutinized her reflection.

"Clara, I don't like this right here, I can still see the tear." Peggy shed the dress and handed it back to her maid. Turning to her sister, Peggy asked, "What are you going to wear tonight, Bets?"

"I do not know." Betsy stared longingly at her sister's gown. "Some dress in my wardrobe, I suppose. But I should like Clara to help me dress."

"Yes, of course." Peggy shrugged her shoulders, not removing her eyes from her own reflection. "As long as I don't need her."

When at last the tear in the dress had been repaired, Clara handed the dress over to her mistress and plopped down on the sofa, taking a moment's respite. Peggy Shippen kept a fast pace all day, Clara was learning. Would she have time to steal away for a quick nap before the evening?

"Clara, what are you doing? Get up, next we must wash my hair so it has time to dry before we style it." Peggy showed no signs of fatigue, and Clara realized that there would be no rest before the evening.

"Perhaps I should bring us up some lunch first," Clara suggested, observing the clock that told her it was midday.

"I'm not hungry." Peggy shook her head. "But I'll take some wine." Peggy stared into the mirror, holding the gown out before her.

"Yes, my lady." Clara rose from her seat beside the window, looking out over the street as she stood. There, on the cobblestoned lane, a small group approached the Shippen home. Clara studied the assembly—a cluster of half a dozen men, dressed plainly in clothes of gray and black.

"Goodness," Clara sighed. If Peggy had suitors visiting in groups this large, Clara would have to enlist reinforcements. But these men were older, and certainly not dressed like British officers. The leader of the group knocked on the Shippens' door.

"Miss Peggy, I don't know how you have the energy to do this every day, taking calls from so many admirers."

"What else should a girl of eighteen be doing to occupy her time, Clara? Sitting at home knitting with her bore of a mother? I can guarantee you, Meg Chew is doing nothing of the sort!"

"Who is it this time?" Clara asked, studying the men below. They looked nothing like Peggy's other suitors. Peggy approached the window and peeked down to the street.

"Oh, they are *not* for me!" Peggy stated, her tone derisive. "They are for Mother."

"Your mother has suitors?" It seemed highly irregular.

"No!" Peggy replied. "You are such a laugh, Clara. You really *did* come from a farm."

Clara nodded.

"It's the Quakers," Peggy explained.

"The . . . who?" Clara leaned once more beside her mistress at the window.

"Quakers. A religious society. William Penn was one. No doubt they are here to lament the erosion of our morals or some such boring business. So, what do you say, bring me some wine and then we shall figure out which stockings I should wear."

WHEN THE Quakers departed, Judge Shippen sent word to his daughters that they were to meet him in his study downstairs. Clara was towel-drying Peggy's hair, which she had just finished washing with lemon and verbena soap. "I am sopping wet!" Peggy grumbled to Mr. Quigley when he delivered the summons. She had planned to go out in the garden to lie in the sun and allow her locks to dry before curling them.

"I am simply a humble messenger, Miss Peggy, delivering the message from your father." Mr. Quigley put his hands up defensively. "Judge Shippen awaits you and Miss Betsy in the study."

But Betsy was already down there, as evident by the shrill protests Clara heard as she descended the staircase behind Peggy. "But I do not intend to dress like a concubine—you cannot prevent *me* from going!" Betsy whined. "Papa, please let me go to the Masque!"

Clara paused outside the study, meeting Mrs. Quigley at the threshold.

"Best if you wait here with me, Clara." The old woman folded her arms and leaned against the doorway. "We need play no part in this."

"What is this?" Peggy breezed into the study, passing her sister to approach her father, who was seated behind his broad, walnut desk. Mrs. Shippen entered the room and stood over her husband's shoulder. "What is *she* doing in here?" Peggy stared at her mother.

"Girls, sit, please." Judge Shippen was fidgeting with his plume, dipping it in the inkwell only to draw a series of straight lines on the parchment in front of him. Peggy and Betsy sat beside each other on the chairs opposite their father's desk.

"Girls, your mother and I have just been visited from a few prominent members of the Society of Friends."

"The Quakers," Peggy said sourly.

"Yes. They've educated us a bit more on this ball which you planned to attend this evening. They've told us some . . . *details* . . . which you seem to have neglected to share with us." From her spot in the doorway Clara saw the judge look at his younger daughter with a rare sternness.

"So what?" Peggy answered him with a bored shrug of her shoulders. A puddle was collecting on the floor beneath her wet hair.

"Is it true," the judge said, "that you, Margaret, are to attend the party dressed like a pagan member of a Turkish harem?" The judge's cheeks flushed while he posed the question.

"Father, when you put it like that, it sounds much worse than it is. It's a ball in honor of General Howe. We must show our support for him before he departs for England."

"Answer the question, Margaret," her mother interjected.

"What question, Mother?" Peggy asked with exaggerated sweetness.

"Are you to attend dressed like a Turkish harem member?" Mrs. Shippen repeated.

"That's one way to look at it. It's all for entertainment. Perfectly harmless. The men will be the Knights of the Crusades and we shall be the maidens of Constantinople."

"So it *is* true." Judge Shippen appeared wounded. "When the Quakers told me this, I didn't want to believe it, Margaret."

"It is not so vulgar as you would have it seem. Johnny, er, Major André and the rest of Howe's men have been working diligently for weeks—on sets, costumes, a jousting pavilion. It's nothing more than an elaborate play, Papa." Peggy rose from her seat as if to approach him behind the desk.

"Sit down, Margaret," the judge spoke, his tone fortified by momentary resolve.

"Papa." Peggy didn't obey, but rather glided toward him.

"Your father told you to SIT *DOWN*!" Mrs. Shippen's voice seemed to rattle the books on the shelves, and it served to sufficiently cow Peggy, who slinked back to her seat.

"Since you see nothing wrong with the sacrilegious and indecent content of the evening's costumes and entertainment, I shall change my line of questioning." Judge Shippen still fiddled with his plume. "Do you believe it is appropriate to be prancing around like a harem girl of the Far East while your countrymen are spilling their blood mere miles away? When there might be a battle in Philadelphia by the end of the month? Are you so absorbed in your world of silk, and lace, and British officers, that you are not offended by this debauched evening?" Judge Shippen folded his hands in his lap, appearing bolstered by the completion of his soliloquy. "An evening in which you will not take part, Margaret."

From their spot in the doorway, Mrs. Quigley turned to whisper, "Never in all my years have I heard the judge speak so forcefully." Clara nodded.

"But I cannot cancel my appearance now, Papa." Peggy's voice had a shrill edge about it, as if she realized she might actually be thwarted. "Not when they've planned on me being there. I've ordered my dress. André and I have planned our costumes accordingly. It would be discourteous."

"And how much did that dress cost?" Mrs. Shippen leaned over her husband's desk.

"It did not cost you a cent, Mother. André and the Crown paid for it."

"Even more insupportable."

"Enough." The judge raised his arm, silencing his wife and causing Clara to flinch where she stood outside the room. "Margaret," the judge spoke in a slow, measured tone, "I am resolute on this matter. I'm afraid I must forbid you from attending."

"What, Papa?" Peggy looked to her sister, incredulous. "No! You can't! You can't listen to the counsel of some craven old Quakers! I *will* go, do you hear me? I will go!"

"You will not go," her mother replied.

"André will not allow this! He will not allow you to embarrass General Howe and all the men who have planned on my attendance."

"André already knows. He's made other plans." Her mother's tone stayed cool.

"WHAT DO YOU MEAN?" Peggy was in a fury, tears tracing straight, determined lines down her cheeks. "Papa! What does Mother mean?" Peggy scurried behind the desk and knelt at her father's feet.

"Judge." Mr. Quigley poked his head into the study. "Judge Shippen, they have arrived."

"Who has arrived?" Peggy asked, looking from her father to the butler.

A voice sounded from the front of the house, followed by the thunder of dozens of buckled boots falling on the creaky wooden floor. Clara turned where she stood; she'd been so absorbed in the argument she had not yet noticed the group entering the hall.

"Greetings to the Honorable Judge Shippen and his family! We are here on an errand from Major André." The Shippens hurried from the study, Clara among them, to the front hall. A dozen men in matching white wigs stood in a neat line, wearing the red jackets that usually so excited Peggy.

"Where is Major André?" Peggy asked, passing each of the men. "Where is he? Why are you all here?"

"Message for Miss Margaret Shippen from Major John André." The front man in the column broke the formation only to extend his hand to Peggy with a note. Clara approached her mistress's side. Peggy tore the letter open, looking frantically at the familiar cursive that usually caused her heart to jig so happily.

I understand that you will be unable to attend the Meshianza Masque with me this evening, a fact which brings me great sadness. Do not let your heart be troubled that you have left me without a maiden to offer me a favor before the jousting tournament. I was desperate, you must understand, so I've asked Meg Chew to come with me, and she has taken pity on a jilted squire whose fair lady is otherwise occupied.

Your wounded knight,
J. André
Postscript: Meg will need to borrow your costume, as she has not had time to order her own gown. My men will retrieve it.

Then, as if on cue, Mr. Quigley descended the broad staircase, the white and scarlet gown, along with the turban and all the accoutrements, folded neatly in his arms. Without looking at Peggy, or responding to her hysterical proclamations, the butler handed the folded costume to the head of André's livery, and the soldiers turned on their heels to depart.

They left in their wake a frantic Peggy. Her father's face grew distressed as he watched his daughter pounding on the door, threatening to run after them and reclaim her gown. Caleb emerged from the pantry and held the sobbing girl back as she tried to open the front door and charge out onto the street. Even as Betsy tried to soothe her, Peggy could not be consoled.

"I will *never* forgive you!" Peggy hissed, looking at her mother with bitter accusation in her eyes. "You can't stomach the idea of anything fun, can you? What's the matter, Mother? Were you never asked to a dance when you were young?"

"Please, my dear Margaret, remember yourself. This is your mother to whom you speak." Judge Shippen looked as though his fortitude might give way.

"Just let her rail, Edward." Mrs. Shippen was unfazed, but her reaction only seemed to further infuriate Peggy.

"You can never let me enjoy myself. And now Johnny will take that horrid Meg Chew, and she will probably seduce him!" Peggy rushed at her father, either to assault him or to collapse at his feet in desperate supplication, but Mr. Quigley stepped in between the two and held her arms.

"Caleb, some help!" The butler struggled to contain the thrashing arms of his young mistress. All the servants poked their heads in from where they had gathered to witness the scene. Clara had been warned of her lady's temper, but the sight was still staggering; Peggy resisted until she was carried up, with much kicking and clawing and ranting, by Caleb to her bedroom, with Clara following close behind.

"If you don't calm down we will lock you in your bedroom for the rest of the day and night," Mrs. Shippen called up the stairs, while the rest of the family and household staff stood in stony silence in the front hall, aghast at the events they had just witnessed.

"I DESPISE YOU!" Peggy screamed back, before Clara and Caleb managed to shut her bedroom door. Once in her room, with no route to escape, Peggy collapsed onto her bed, where she proceeded to vent her anger in the furious beating of her feather pillows. "I'm ruined!" Peggy wailed, over and over again. *Or you are saved*, Clara thought, but she dared not utter it.

THE SHIPPEN gardens at dusk were a welcome refuge after the chaos of the house, and so Clara accepted a tray of food from Hannah and sought a solitary place to eat her supper. From the stone bench under the cool shade of the arbor, Clara glanced up and saw that Peggy's windows were ajar, but she heard no sound issuing from the bedchamber. Miss Peggy seemed to have cried herself to sleep, at last. How a girl could sob so passionately and for as long as Peggy had, Clara did not know.

Sunset. The hour that they were meant to depart for the Meshianza Masque. Clara had to admit to herself, even if it would have been a glorious spectacle to see the tournament, she felt undeniable relief at Peggy's being forbidden to attend. She could not deny that she had had a heavy sense of doom about it all.

Clara finished her stew, using the stale brown bread to sop up the remainders in the bowl, and rose from the bench. The gardens were tranquil and protected from the din of the city streets, but they were entirely different from the farm at dusk. Clara sighed, imagining the scene unfolding at this hour on the farm, as it used to be. Mr. Hartley and the boys would be back from the fields, dust-caked and weary, sitting down to a supper spread forth by Oma. She and her grandmother would wait until the family's dinner had been cleared before themselves sitting down beside the hearth and finishing the remaining food. Oma had always been sure to cook enough so that Clara went to bed with a full belly.

How much a few days had done to change her life, Clara thought, as she looked out over the manicured shrubs and tightly clipped cherry blossoms—so different from the unruly apple trees and mazy paths of newly sown dirt she had always known. Though her bedroom afforded a view of these gardens, Clara had not yet been to explore these paths. Clara decided that before she returned to the dimly lit distress of her mistress's bedroom, she'd walk a bit, and perhaps even make her way over to the stables.

The horses at Hartley farm had always been a comfort in their reliable simplicity—their earthy aroma, their slow movements, their appreciative gazes as you stroked their noses. The smell of the stable would be familiar, even if nothing else here was. Clara followed the pebbly footpath across the lawn and meandered toward the large, rectangular building.

Clara pushed the heavy sliding door over and peeked into the barn. "Anybody in here?"

From somewhere distant, she heard the muffled notes of a guitar. Probably Caleb playing in some hidden spot of the orchard. Clara inhaled, breathing in the familiar scent: a mixture of horse sweat, hay, and leather saddles. A large brown head peeked out from the front stall. Clara looked at the large horse and laughed.

"Oh, hello! I didn't mean to disturb you." Clara slid the door open wider, allowing the sideways rays of dusky sunlight to spill into the stables. She approached slowly, as Oma had taught her to do, and extended her hand, allowing the horse to become familiar with her scent. "Hello there, handsome fellow." The horse was a rich chestnut color, with a white diamond above its nose, and she knew it immediately to be Miss Peggy's. "Why, you and I work for the same lady, don't we? Yes, we do." The horse leaned closer to Clara, welcoming her affectionate strokes. "Yes we do, we work for the same lady."

"You've only been with her two days and you're already talking to animals? Didn't take her long to drive you mad." Caleb's voice startled Clara, and she jumped back, alarming the horse as she did so.

"Didn't mean to spook you." Caleb walked toward her, his arms raised apologetically, from the back of the darkening barn.

"Pardon me, I didn't realize there was anyone else in here," Clara answered, embarrassed.

"Just taking a moment away from that crowded kitchen." Caleb grinned. "Looks like you're doing the same."

"Aye." Clara nodded.

"I actually stay out here during the warm months. Up there." Caleb pointed toward the hayloft.

"Really?"

Caleb nodded.

"Why do you live out here when there are all those empty bedrooms in the servants' quarters?" Clara edged back toward the horse and resumed her petting of its coarse, short hair.

"I like having my own space, getting away from that house at least once a day. Otherwise, I'd go wild." Caleb paused beside her, a piece of straw dangling from his mouth. "That, and I prefer the company of the horses to the Shippens. Find 'em to be more polite." Caleb leaned his elbows on the door of the stall, standing beside Clara as they both stroked the horse.

"Right, Hick? This is Hickory," Caleb said.

"Nice to meet you, Hickory."

"Miss Peggy's horse."

"I had guessed that." Clara stroked the horse's long nose, blushing when her hand accidentally brushed against Caleb's fingers.

"What do you say, Hickory, you think Miss Peggy goes easier on you or on Clara?"

"Well, she has yet to use the crop on me," Clara answered. "How about you, Hickory?"

"Just a matter of time," Caleb quipped, and they both laughed. After several moments of comfortable silence, Caleb continued. "How are you doing, Clara? With everything? I imagine it's quite different here than at a farm in the countryside."

Clara nodded. "I was just thinking the same thing. How different it is here."

"So then, how are you managing?"

"I'm not sure," Clara answered. "I think she likes me. I hope so."

"No, I mean, how are *you* doing?"

Clara shrugged her shoulders. "I guess I don't really think that it matters how I'm doing."

"Course it does. You've got feelings, just like everyone else. Just like Hickory here, right, Hick?"

"Well, I am doing all right."

"Just all right?" Caleb arched his eyebrows.

"I was raised not to complain," Clara admitted.

"Suppose it's not complaining? Suppose you're just answering a friend's question?" Caleb nudged her gently.

"Well, it's just that"—Clara wavered—"it's hard to keep Miss Peggy happy." She stared through the open stable door, watching as night settled over the grounds, extinguishing the last glints of golden daylight.

"I think we'd all agree with you, Clara Bell. Damned near impossible, in fact."

"Her moods change so suddenly."

"As we all witnessed this afternoon," Caleb agreed.

"But I don't mean to sound ungrateful. Being in a grand house like this . . . with gardens, and stables. And I have enough food to eat, and a bedroom to myself. If my Oma saw me living like this, attending parties with British officers, she'd think I'd climbed a few stations in life."

"Who's Oma?"

"My gram," Clara explained. "It was just me and her back at the Hartley farm. My mother died when I was . . . young."

"And your father?" Caleb asked.

Clara shrugged her shoulders. "Never knew him." She should be embarrassed to admit that she was a bastard, unwanted, but Caleb listened attentively. Offered no judgment.

"My Oma was sick for a while. Right before she passed, she got me this position. I'm grateful to have it."

"Now is not the time to be without family and without work."

"I'm not really sure what would have happened to me had Oma not gotten me this post. Not after the Hartleys left." And suddenly, without realizing why she was doing it, Clara found herself opening up about a past she had never shared. "The Hartleys were supporters of the colonial cause, you see. They were tired of the British raids and didn't want to swear a loyalty oath to the crown. They moved up north, and couldn't take us with them. Oma and I stayed back because she was too sick to travel by that point. She died a few weeks later."

Caleb looked at her, his eyes earnest. "That's quite the story you have, Clara Bell."

"Reminds me," Clara continued. "My first day here, I mentioned the Hartley farm as well as the Shippen farm and Miss Peggy scolded me. Told me never to mention it again. What happened there to cause such a reaction?"

"Oh." Caleb nodded. "Right when the war broke out, the judge relocated us all to the countryside, to his farm in Lancaster. To think, we were neighbors." He paused.

"And we never met." Clara smiled back as Caleb continued.

"The judge thought it would be safer there than in the city, on account of the fighting here. We spent just shy of a year there."

"And why was it so terrible for Miss Peggy? What happened to her?" Clara asked.

"It was no more terrible for her than for anyone living in the countryside at the outbreak of the war," Caleb explained. "There were raiding parties throughout the area, and you heard stories of nearby farms burning and Iroquois attacks."

Clara nodded. She had lived that life for all seventeen of her years: the smell of smoke after dark caused panic, the sound of hoofbeats awoke terror until you could be certain that the riders did not pause outside your door.

"But as far as Miss Peggy suffering any particular tragedy?" Caleb leaned toward Clara. "All she suffered from was boredom. She complained every day about the country. Hated it." He removed the long piece of straw from between his lips, holding it aloft like a pipe. "Said she was missing out on all the excitement in the city. She was sixteen at the time, and she missed her debut. She was convinced her life was over."

"Ah, she said the same thing today." Clara nodded.

"Indeed." Caleb agreed. "Finally, the Lobsterbacks took the city and established British rule, and the judge decided that we weren't any safer out there than we would be here. So, he refused to take the oath to Washington and the new nation, and moved us all back here to the British-held city. As you can imagine, Peggy supported his decision."

"I am sure." Clara nodded. "Have you taken it, Cal?"

"What?" he asked.

"The oath to Washington." Clara said, speaking quietly in the darkened barn.

Caleb looked over his shoulder, making certain that they were alone. "I did take it. I consider myself to be a free man," he whispered. "But keep that between us."

"I did too," Clara admitted.

They stood for a moment in companionable silence, the only noise between them the steady breathing of Hickory and the distant din of carriages rattling up Fourth Street.

Clara turned to Caleb. "What about you, Caleb Little?"

"What about me?"

"What's your story? You say the Quigleys are your aunt and uncle?"

"Mrs. Quigley is—was—my mother's sister. They protected me when Judge Shippen let everyone go a few years back."

"And where are your parents?" Clara asked.

"Dead."

"Both of them?"

"The yellow fever. Summer of '70. Swept through the city like a wildfire," Caleb answered, sliding the piece of straw back between his teeth.

Clara thought about this, realizing she was not the only person in this house to have suffered loss. "Look at us, then, Caleb. A pair of orphans."

"That we are." Caleb grinned at her, a sad, honest grin. "And how are you finding the help here at the Shippen mansion, Clara Bell? Are we as difficult as the Shippens themselves?"

"Oh, even worse," Clara quipped, and they both laughed. "No, I'm finding everyone very agreeable. Mrs. Quigley is always looking out for me. Mr. Quigley is a generous man. Hannah is always helpful when I need her. Brigitte, well, I haven't heard Brigitte say two words together, now that I think about it."

"Didn't I tell you that would happen?"

"You did." Clara nodded.

"And the footman who doubles as stableboy? You know, the mysterious one with hazel eyes who sleeps in the barn?" Caleb asked, teasingly.

"Oh, you mean the one with the horsey smell?"

"So that's what you think!" Caleb laughed. "Hickory, this rough farm girl is hurting my feelings."

"I didn't take you for the type." Clara studied his face, feeling the barriers of her shyness slacken just a little.

"What type?"

"The sensitive type," Clara answered.

"Oh, you'd be surprised how sensitive I am." Cal smiled, stroking Hickory's nose. "Just like my aunt."

"Mrs. Quigley?" Clara screwed up her nose. "That woman seems as sensitive as nails."

Cal thought about this. "She seems that way, but just you wait. She's got the softest heart you'll ever see."

Clara looked through the open stable door out toward the gardens, now veiled in velvety darkness. "It's getting late, Caleb."

"Cal."

"Right, Cal." She smiled at him. It felt nice to speak with someone other than Peggy. To have someone interested in talking about her own past and life. "Well, Cal, I'd better get back to the house, in case Miss Peggy awakes."

"Yes, and it's not right for you to be out in the dark with a handsome young gentleman. Folks might say your mistress is corrupting your sound sense." Cal ran his fingers through his shaggy dark blond hair, studying her with a look that seemed appraising.

Clara lowered her eyes, feeling her cheeks redden. "Good night, Cal."

"Good night, Clara Bell. And good luck with your mistress."

"Thank you." She breathed out, her eyes momentarily locking with his.

"Any time."

"Clara, you're back. I thought you'd left me." Peggy looked up at her maid from her seat at the windowsill, the remnants of recent tears still glistening on her cheeks. What a beautiful mourner Miss Peggy made, curled up in a puddle of cool moonlight, watching the carriages below as they passed by, bearing finely dressed ladies and gentlemen on their way to card parties and galas.

"No, ma'am." Clara entered the room, balancing a tray of ham and cider as she shut the door. "I went to fetch you some supper, miss. Thought you might be getting hungry."

"Clara, you're so good to me."

Clara brushed the comment aside, placing the dinner down on the small end table before her mistress.

"But I don't think I shall eat. Clara." Peggy reached for her maid's hand, her voice suddenly heavy with urgency. "Promise me you shall not leave me tonight." Peggy appeared so forlorn that Clara did not know how to further disappoint Miss Peggy.

"I can stay with you, Miss Peggy, if you like," Clara answered, her shoulders drooping with fatigue. She'd have to find a way to get some sleep in one of these armchairs, or on the floor.

Peggy proffered a tenuous smile. "Thank you, Clara." Peggy cast her eyes once more out the window, toward the street below.

"Oh, look!" Peggy pointed, and Clara's eyes followed to the spot on the street where her mistress's attention had been drawn. A grand carriage with an enclosed body, accompanied by a smartly dressed driver and footman, sped past. "That's . . ." New sobs rendered Peggy's words almost inaudible. "That's . . . Meg . . . CHEW!" Her head collapsed onto the windowsill.

"Come away from the window, Miss Peggy." Clara helped her mistress into bed and then chose the softest chair, filled with downy stuffing, beside the window.

In the pitch dark of night, Clara was jolted awake by an explosion outside the window, followed by a splash of light across the sky.

"Oh!" Peggy had woken too. She glided wraithlike from the bed to the window. "Fireworks!" For a moment, Peggy forgot her misery, distracted by the ecstatic bursts of color and light. But then, she remembered the cause of the fireworks. "They must be drunk on Champagne right now, watching those." But it seemed that there were no tears left for Peggy to shed. She took Clara's hand. "Clara," she spoke, "we should have been there tonight."

Clara stood beside her mistress as they watched the bright display overhead. It was flattering, having so quickly become her lady's confidante and friend. And yet the burden of being such a close ally of Peggy Shippen's did not escape Clara's thoughts.

When it was over, Peggy repeated her lament: "Now they will go back to dancing. We should have been there."

"There, there, Miss Peggy. Back to bed now," Clara answered soothingly, hopeful that the worst of the night was now past. She helped Peggy back under the covers, tucking her in the way Oma had done with her when she had had a nightmare as a young girl.

"Clara?" Peggy looked up from her feathery pillow. "You won't leave me, will you?"

"I will stay right here in this chair, Miss Peggy," Clara said, her tone soft. She knew how much Miss Peggy needed her.

Later, maybe hours later, Clara heard horses halting below, whispered voices rising up from the street. Peggy stirred from her light sleep.

"What is that, Clara?"

"Let me see, my lady." Clara rose, groggy, and approached the windowsill. The carriage was familiar—unmistakable. Hadn't she seen that carriage earlier that same day?

"My lady, I think you had better come look."

"Who is it?" Peggy flew from her bed to the window. "Can it be?" she gasped, her voice airy. "Johnny!" She turned from the window. "I must go to him."

"No, Miss Peggy." Clara held her in place. "You stay here. I will go to the door to see what he wants. If your parents awoke to find him here at this hour, they'd be very unhappy."

"But I *must* see him." Peggy's voice was decided, and Clara felt her own resolve fading against the hope in her mistress's face.

"But, Miss Peggy, your father forbade you from attending, and I can't imagine what he would say if . . ."

"Hush, Clara," Peggy snapped, her tone suddenly chilly. "You forget your place." Peggy was running her hands through her hair, straining to see her reflection in the darkened mirror.

"Yes, miss," Clara sighed, lowering her eyes. "But might I suggest that you not conduct this rendezvous in this house? Your parents would never stand it." Clara could see Mrs. Quigley's disapproval clearly in her mind. "How about this, Miss Peggy: you go down, *quietly,* to the garden. I will meet Major André at the door and show him around back. We cannot wake the house."

"Fine." Peggy pinched her cheeks, drawing a rosy blush to the surface of the skin. "But be quick about it."

Hours ago Clara had been delirious with relief that her mistress had been kept away from this dapper officer, and now she was the lead coordinator of an illicit midnight meeting, sneaking about like a thief in the night. But Clara brushed this unpleasant realization, as well as the image of Oma's disapproving face, from her mind, and she padded her way down the stairs and slipped noiselessly to the front door.

The wooden door groaned as Clara opened it, threatening with every inch of movement to wake the house. She poked her head through the sliver of the opening and saw André, his eyes lined with charcoal, his head adorned in a spectacular turban of scarlet silk. "Major," Clara whispered. "Major André, this is highly unorthodox." She wouldn't let him off too easy. "Judge and Mrs. Shippen are sleeping. The whole house is abed."

"I had to see Miss Shippen, Clara." In the flickering light of the street candles, André's face looked tired, and his breath smelled sweet with wine. Behind him, a few steps below, stood Robert Balmor. Clara straightened her posture automatically, avoiding the secretary's overconfident gaze.

"You'll let me in, won't you, Clara?" André cracked a lopsided grin. Now was her opening—she could ask for some message, some promise of a later visit. He could come back tomorrow, through the front door in the light of day. Yes, she'd ask André to leave a note and then send him away, Clara decided. But then she remembered Peggy waiting in the garden; how would she face her mistress if André didn't appear? Clara dropped her shoulders.

"You must go around back." Clara could not believe her own words. "Miss Shippen is in the garden. She knows you're here."

Clara shut the door and tiptoed her way through the front hall, past the parlor, and let herself out into the garden, where the two gentlemen were just arriving from the alley.

"Johnny."

Clara spotted her mistress in the dark orchard, waiting in the garden like some midnight spirit. Clara blushed to think that all that lay underneath her mistress's white dressing gown was a sleeping shift.

Major André crossed the orchard and embraced Peggy, who collapsed into his arms. He kissed the top of her head, a tender gesture.

"Hello, Clara." Robert Balmor hung back, lingering beside her.

"Hello, Robert." Clara turned to the secretary.

"We missed you tonight. We both missed you." Robert removed his tricornered hat and ran his hands through his dark hair.

"You know we were prevented from coming, I'm sure?"

"Yes, we heard the news this afternoon. Major André was most distraught." Even in the darkness of the garden, Clara felt Robert's gaze fixed on her.

"As was she." Clara turned back to Peggy and saw that she and the major were holding hands now, walking slowly under the arbor, their voices so low that Clara could not discern their words.

"Did he enjoy himself with Meg Chew?" Clara asked.

"Oh, yes. They made a fine pair at the joust. And they danced all night."

Clara nodded. She hoped her mistress would not hear this version of events.

Robert continued. "But he would have preferred to have Peggy with him. He kept telling me so. That's why, as soon as the festivities were over, he was determined to come see her. He escorted Miss Chew home and then we came straight to Fourth Street."

Clara felt her heart swell at André's loyalty, his affection. It would make her mistress so happy.

"I wonder if they will be married," Clara said absentmindedly. But when Robert didn't answer, she regretted the remark. It was too forward.

Robert shifted his weight from one foot to another.

"Miss Bell," Robert said, his voice quiet. "May I have the dance I was hoping for tonight?"

Perhaps she was caught up in the mood of the garden, her mistress's contagious contentment, the wispy splashes of moonlight through the trees. She took Robert's outstretched hand, allowing him to bow to her, and they began to sway.

Glancing over his shoulders, Clara squinted her eyes to look across the garden. In the feeble light, she could just barely see the pair of them, embracing, dancing to imaginary music.

What a fine pair they made. Like two wraiths, separated by circumstances, their love merely an ephemeral, haunting dream.

"What are you thinking about, Clara?"

She focused her eyes back on her own dancing partner, disoriented. "Hmm?"

"You look happy, Clara. I'm happy to be here with you, too." Before she understood what was happening, Robert smiled, and then, unexpectedly, his lips touched her own.

First she felt alarm, as Robert's lips touched hers, his skin soft and gentle. So, this is kissing, Clara thought to herself. How strange to be kissing a man. And then, she decided that it was not all bad. In fact, it was quite nice. She lifted her arms so that her hands grazed his hair, the back of his neck. Perhaps she was behaving improperly—even after she had judged her own lady's indiscretions—but she allowed Robert to continue kissing her, his lips parting so that he could press his tongue against hers. He tasted like tobacco and wine, but she didn't find either flavor bothersome. She leaned her body against his, slowly, growing warm in the cool evening air.

An explosion overhead. More fireworks. But, to her disappointment, Robert pulled his lips away from hers.

"Fireworks!" Clara looked up at the sky. My, she almost sounded like Peggy Shippen, she thought to herself.

"No, those are not fireworks," Robert said, the tension in his voice snapping the softness of the previous moment.

"What's the matter?" Clara turned to him, dazed. She looked across the garden and made out the silhouette of André's and Peggy's bodies, dark against the orange glow of the sky.

"Those are not fireworks," Robert repeated, putting his hat back on his head. "The fireworks ended at the Wharton mansion over an hour ago."

"Balmor!" André crossed the garden, trotting toward them. A sudden burst of light filled the garden with an orange glow, and Clara saw that André's handsome features were tight with concern.

"Balmor!" André shouted again.

"Sir?"

"Rebel fire. We must report to Howe, see what our orders are." André walked at a crisp clip now across the garden. Robert hurried to keep apace.

"Are the rebels in the city, sir?"

"Not yet, from the looks of it." André glanced back in the direction of where the explosions had occurred.

Peggy was at Clara's side now, clutching her hand.

"Darling, I must go." André turned toward them. "Peggy, stay inside. Tell your family to stay inside."

"Johnny, where are you going? I'm scared you'll be hurt." Peggy ran to André and clutched his chest.

"Don't fret, my darling," André scoffed. "It's a ragtag mob of farmers, half of them armed with nothing more than pitchforks. We'll beat them back before the sun rises." André kissed Peggy on the cheek while Robert squeezed Clara's hand once, a silent communication between them. Without another word from André or Robert, they were off.

DAYLIGHT BROUGHT with it the sound of distant cannon fire, but no word from Major André. In fact there was no news from the outside world at all, as the city of Philadelphia remained huddled behind barred doors, unsure of which color they might see on the uniforms once they reemerged. Stores remained closed, houses remained shuttered, and the newspaper did not print that morning.

An eerie calm descended over the Shippen home, as over the rest of the city, while the residents waited. Waited for what, they didn't know. They heard the occasional explosion sounding from some distant farm or woodland copse, but they could only imagine how the scenes of the battlefield were actually unfolding.

Clara scavenged what information she could as she observed the street below Peggy's window. Fourth Street was empty of citizens, but flooded by men in red. British officers and soldiers scurried through the streets, some in marching formation, others in erratic clusters of two or three.

"I suppose I should dress, just in case." Peggy sat at breakfast, utterly bored by this disruption to her social calendar. Her mother, complaining of a headache and having dedicated the day to prayer, was not at the table to hear the comment. Betsy and the judge exchanged a meaningful look.

"Yes, I'll dress." Peggy pushed herself back from the breakfast table, waving Clara forward from where she stood by the buffet. "If André pushes his way through in time for dinner or dancing tonight, I should be prepared."

Judge Shippen sighed, dropping his fork to rest his head in his hands.

"Don't worry, my dear papa." Peggy swooped down beside her father, kissing his cheek. "I'm sure our boys will be back in no time."

"It's not the troops I worry about, Margaret."

In the late morning, while Peggy was putting the final strand of pearls around her high-vaulted *pouf,* Clara heard the familiar sound of carriage wheels outside the Shippens' front door. She went to the window and looked out over the street, where she spotted André and Robert approaching. Trailing behind them was an open cart, laden with goods.

"They're here," Clara announced to Peggy. "André and Robert."

"They are?" Peggy slid her feet into a pair of light blue heels and flew to the window. "Thank heavens I'm dressed. But I knew he would come." She flitted out of the bedroom. "Johnny!" Peggy bounded down the carpeted hallway and descended the stairs two at a time, nearly knocking over a startled Betsy on the way down.

"Clara, send them into the parlor," Peggy ordered her maid.

"What news? Come in, come in." Clara opened the door before they had time to knock, and she ushered André and Robert into the parlor, where Peggy waited. Though Robert was staring at her, Clara kept her gaze fixed on her mistress and Major André, eager to hear the report from the front.

"Johnny." Peggy rose from the chair and ran to him, collapsing into his arms. "Oh, you're all right! You're all right! I was so worried." She began to lay desperate kisses on his neck, but he pulled her off with uncharacteristic indifference. Clara quickly understood why—on the threshold of the room appeared Judge Shippen and his wife, her face appearing even more pinched than usual. Betsy, the Quigleys, and Hannah joined the small assembly, all listening intently for the update.

"Peggy." Major André's voice was formal as he removed his tricornered hat. "Judge Shippen, Mrs. Shippen." He bowed reverentially.

"What news?" Judge Shippen placed a tenuous arm on his wife's shoulders.

"I come to take my leave." André stared at the hat he held in his hands.

"What?" Peggy gasped as those outside the room began to whisper to one another in confused urgency. Clara held Robert's eyes for a brief moment before she lowered them. He, too, would be going.

"Philadelphia is lost," André explained. "The French are threatening to engage our navy off the coast, and the Crown has made the strategic decision to abandon the city."

Peggy winced at the word: *abandon.*

"We have been ordered to evacuate the city immediately." Major André now addressed the judge, avoiding Peggy's eyes.

"But how can this be?" Peggy's face was white, her voice as flimsy as a wisp of cloud.

"General Clinton, our new commander, has ceded the city to the rebels."

"Where shall you go?" the judge asked, his lips in a tight line.

"We will retreat to New York, where we will consolidate our forces without the molestation of rural raiding parties and a hostile local population."

Peggy melted into her hoopskirt, stopping only when her tiny frame landed on the carpeted floor.

"She's fainted." Clara approached her mistress. Betsy and Mrs. Quigley huddled over her, striving to revive Peggy. Robert carried her to the sofa, where he placed her down and felt her forehead.

"Clara, run to the kitchen and fetch the smelling salts," Mrs. Shippen said.

"Yes, madame." Clara obeyed. When she returned to Peggy's side, André had placed his hat back atop his head, ready to depart.

"We cannot linger long, I'm sorry to say." André turned from the judge to his secretary. "Balmor, we must go."

"I'm awake, I'm awake." Peggy opened her eyes, pushing aside the salts Clara brandished and trying to rise from the sofa. "Johnny, you can't really mean it."

Mrs. Quigley prevented Peggy from jumping up.

"Peg, I regret if I have caused you distress." André approached the sofa and took Peggy's hand in his. Clara, aware that Robert was still trying to catch her eyes, turned her attention instead on Judge and Mrs. Shippen, just in time to see Mrs. Shippen scowl.

"This is inappropriate—look at him taking her hand!" Mrs. Shippen hissed into her husband's ear.

Peggy either did not hear or did not heed her mother's scolding. "Johnny, you cannot leave me," Peggy begged. "Remember what you told me—the promises we've made?"

"I must go. I am to escort the general out of the city." Another explosion shook the windows in their frames and the noise seemed to rouse André, fortifying his resolve. Dropping Peggy's hand, he rose from the sofa and adjusted his hat.

"Judge Shippen, Mrs. Shippen." He nodded his head. "Misses Betsy and Margaret Shippen." Another jolt of his chin as he allowed his eyes to rest momentarily on Peggy. With that, he turned on his heels, nodding at the judge before walking stiffly to the door.

"*Wait!*" Peggy shrieked, rising from the sofa and flying across the hall to stop him at the door. Outside, the scurrying troops hustled past, frantic to complete last-minute duties before the evacuation. "Johnny, how can you leave me?" Peggy took the scene in through wide, unblinking eyes.

"I am honor-bound to serve my king, at the expense of my own wishes, Miss Shippen." André's voice was soft now, apologetic. "I do regret the sadness it may cause. But I must do my duty."

"Take me with you!" Peggy pleaded, wrapping her arms around André.

"I knew this would not go well," Robert muttered under his breath. Clara lingered near the front window, ready to provide the smelling salts should her mistress collapse again. For the first time, she looked directly at Robert and addressed him. "So you will go to New York as well, Robert?"

"Where he goes, I go," Robert answered.

"You are not traveling light." Clara pointed to the wagon behind their horses.

"You know our quarters have been at Benjamin Franklin's mansion? Well, André decided to leave the old mad scientist with a little surprise upon arrival back home. He'll walk in to discover his very large portrait missing, as well as his books, his china, and some lamps."

"That's as good as stealing, Robert." Clara looked back at the mountain of confiscated goods.

"I do not give the orders." Robert shrugged his shoulders. "Besides, they are treasonous criminals. Everything they have, they owe to King George."

Clara bristled at this. "Many in Philadelphia agree with those so-called *treasonous criminals.*"

Robert arched his eyebrows, pausing a moment as he stared at her with a new expression. Was it surprise? Contempt? "Don't tell me, Clara, all this time I've been sweet on you, and you've been a rebel sympathizer?" Robert's tone teetered on mocking when he spoke next. "Such a pretty little neck you have. It'd be the loveliest one at the gallows."

He stared at her, but Clara averted her eyes, looking out over the roiling street. "Benjamin Franklin and George Washington simply believe that the people in the colonies have the same God-given rights as any subject of your king."

"Last time I checked, Clara, he was *your* king as well as mine. And divinely anointed at that."

"How has God anointed King George any more than he has anointed the common cobbler? Or you and me?"

"Well, aren't you quite the little daughter of liberty?" Robert stared at her, and Clara let her silence answer him. He opened his mouth to continue but another explosion rocked a nearby street and both Clara and Robert's attention returned to the scene before them.

"Balmor, ready the coach," André barked at his secretary over the din. Robert turned once more toward Clara, tipping his hat as he took his leave. "Miss Bell, no hard feelings. I wish you the best."

"And the same to you, Robert." Clara curtsied, noticing that Robert did not look at her again as he hurried to the coach.

Peggy was clinging to André in the doorway, refusing to let him go. "Johnny, you cannot leave me!" She was trying to kiss him, but André kept thwarting her attempts. "You love me, remember? You told me!"

"I am very sorry, Miss Shippen. More sorry than you know."

"Edward, get hold of your daughter," Mrs. Shippen hissed at her husband, aghast. "How can she carry on like this?" The servants huddled nervously, awaiting orders as they looked out over the street and the more immediate chaos on the doorstep.

"Let them have their goodbye. It will be over soon," the judge answered.

"Will you write? I'll come visit you," Peggy pleaded.

"It will be impossible to cross enemy lines." If André was feeling any emotion, it appeared to be embarrassment as he tried once again to free himself from Peggy's stubborn grip.

As he shook her loose, Peggy's shoulders sunk. "Then you must promise me . . ." She began to sob. "After the war is over, after you win, come back and get me. I'll go anywhere with you—London, Paris, New York. Anywhere!"

André's stoicism was unflappable. "My lady, I fear our victory is not the certainty we once hoped it would be. I am not in a position to make any promise like that."

This left Peggy bereft of hope, and she closed her eyes. When she opened them, she stared up at her lover through a veil of tears. "Then, at least, leave me something to remember you by, my love?"

André looked to the loaded cart behind him. "How about something from the Franklin mansion? A cup and saucer?"

"No." Peggy wept, overwrought with grief. "I don't want something from Benjamin Franklin, I want something from *you*!"

"Such as?"

"How about a lock of your hair?" Peggy ran her hand tenderly through his dark waves.

André reached into his pocket, removing a small silver blade. Delicately, with careful hands, he reached to the bottom of his ponytail and sliced a thin strand of his dark hair, which he presented to Peggy.

"Would you like a lock of my hair as well? To remember me?" Peggy asked, running her fingers through her own curls.

"No, I must go." André shook his head. Noting the disappointment on Peggy's face, André continued: "I'd rather you preserve this perfect little head of golden hair."

"I reckon you're just about as distraught as your mistress is." Caleb sidled up to Clara, standing beside her on the step.

"Pardon me?" Clara turned to him, distracted by the scene before her, as well as the quarrelsome manner in which she'd bid farewell to Robert. "What do you mean?"

"I bet you are sad to see André go. Or, I should say, André's secretary." Caleb did not look at Clara as he spoke, but rather kept his gaze fixed on the street, his jaw clenched.

"You refer to Robert."

"You'd know his name better than I would." Caleb shrugged his shoulders, running his fingers through his hair. "Seems like you're quite upset to see him leave, Clara Bell. And I shouldn't wonder why, given the way you two feel about each other."

"Caleb." Clara shook her head, prepared to correct his error. "You are quite mistaken. In fact, we've just parted ways in an argument."

"I'd argue with him too, if I were you. It's not right for a man to kiss a girl one night, and then leave her the next day." Caleb turned his eyes on her for the first time, and Clara felt her cheeks flush at the accusation they held.

A panic gripped her. "Do Mr. and Mrs. Quigley know as well?"

Caleb spit out a quick, bitter laugh. "And here I was, thinking you were on our side. Sure didn't look that way last night."

"Caleb, please." How could she explain herself?

"Not to worry, Clara, it was only I who had the pleasure of watching your midnight meeting with the major and his secretary." Caleb tilted his head to one side, endeavoring to sound light-hearted as he spoke. "I think you all thought you were being stealthy, having your party outside in the garden. I guess you forgot that I sleep in the stables."

"Caleb, it wasn't how it looked." She put her hand on his arm but removed it quickly, alarmed by the look he threw at her.

"Your secret is safe with me, Clara." Without a smile, Caleb turned and walked toward the kitchen. Clara meant to follow him, but was distracted by the sound of André's carriage as it rolled away from the Shippen doorstep.

"Johnny." Peggy, clutching André's lone raven-colored curl to her chest, watched the carriage go. Peggy brought the memento to her lips, kissing it as her tears splashed on her hands, her lips. Clara gazed at her mistress and could not help but pity her. She cradled the lock of hair so desperately, as if to comfort herself, to assure herself that John André, so quickly gone, had in fact existed.

III.

I haven't caught my breath before there comes another knock on the door.

It's that bothersome aide—the one who always lurked around the house and asked too many questions. I let him in and show him to the parlor, where he's met by General Arnold.

"Greetings, General Arnold!" The aide enters with all the self-importance that often accompanies those delivering news about people more powerful than themselves. "General George Washington, accompanied by the honorable Marquis de Lafayette, Alexander Hamilton, and the rest of his staff, shall be arriving in just a matter of minutes." He smiles, thinking he's just delivered an announcement that will make Arnold happy. He understands so little of what has actually gone on in this household.

Arnold looks to his aide, and I see he's laboring to keep his face from betraying life-threatening panic. Managing some quick, mumbled statement about needing to go to West Point immediately, to "prepare the welcome reception for General Washington," my master taps the aide on the shoulders in a gesture of forced camaraderie.

The aide looks at me, confused, and mutters a half-audible question. "A welcome reception? I thought the entire group was to breakfast here with Mrs. Arnold?"

I look down at the floor, feigning ignorance. It's the cloak I've worn so long now; no one has ever suspected me of being capable of anything more.

Arnold departs the room and lopes into the dining room, from where he cuts into the buttery and flees, like a thief on the run, out the back door. He's been crippled since his campaign in Canada years ago, but on this one occasion I see him run, run like a youth with strong bones and a light heart. He runs to the stable, and just seconds later he is atop his horse, galloping across the plateau of the yard and down the steep incline to the river. As the shrubs conceal the rapid steps of the horse, it looks like my master is in flight, soaring to the river, to the ship called Vulture. *It almost looks like he might make it.*

CHAPTER THREE

"Arnold Will Always Be My Enemy"

June 1778
Philadelphia, PA

FOR DAYS the streets outside roared with song and the ringing of church bells, and the crowds organized a parade to welcome their new military commander, Major General Benedict Arnold, and his ragtag horde of colonial conquerors. But Clara had never heard the Shippen home so quiet. No more invitations came, boasting of Champagne parties hosted by smitten British officers. André no longer sent poetry and drawings for Miss Peggy, and gossip and news no longer arrived after Peggy and Betsy's cocktail parties. These days, when there was news to be had, it traveled in through the servants' quarters.

"That new military governor, Benedict Arnold, has taken up residence in the Penn mansion." Hannah arrived in the kitchen, red-faced from her morning outing to Market Street, as the rest of the servants were having their tea around the kitchen table.

"Well, he didn't waste much time taking the nicest home for himself, did he?" Mrs. Quigley helped Hannah as the cook spread a cold chicken carcass out on a long wooden cutting board, its fractured neck dangling akimbo. Clara slid to a seat farther down the table to have her breakfast.

"It's all they are talking 'bout down in Market Square—how he's closing everything down and routing out the loyalists." Hannah began plucking the feathers from the lifeless bird with expert fingers. "Why, I went over to the spice merchant to pick up some salt, and Mr. Wyatt told me there was none to be had—not even for Judge Shippen himself. Benedict Arnold's seized it all!" Hannah gave a good yank, and a fistful of downy feathers came free from the carcass, raining down over the breakfast table like a dusting of snow.

"So it was for the best that the judge did not side publicly with the British." Mr. Quigley picked a loose feather out from his teacup. "It made his finances very difficult, but at least no one can call him a Tory."

"Well, his daughters didn't help him any, that's for certain, what with Miss Peggy dancing with every British officer who came through town. We might not have evaded the Tory title just yet." Hannah raised her eyebrows in warning.

"Will General Washington be coming anytime soon?" Mrs. Quigley asked. The housekeeper was struggling to collect the white feathers in a sack, which she'd give to Brigitte to refill the mattresses and blankets.

"He's still camped up in New Jersey. Trying to chase the Brits north." Hannah tugged on the dead bird, dislodging another large clump of feathers.

"I'm happy that chicken didn't have to endure this fate while he was alive." Clara eyed the balding carcass with a combination of sympathy and disgust.

"Good morning, all." Caleb stepped into the kitchen from the direction of the stables, a piece of straw hanging out of his mouth. Unlike Clara, Cal had managed to slip away from the Shippen home for a few hours on the day that the city gave its parade for Benedict Arnold. He had come back rosy and smiling, telling the servants at dinner what a merry man Benedict Arnold seemed to be.

Cal now eyed the chicken carcass on the table. "Planning to tar and feather someone this morning, Hannah?"

"You, if you're not careful! Mind not bringing the whole hay-loft in here with you the next time you come in?" Mrs. Quigley pulled the straw from her nephew's mouth and poured both him and Clara full cups of tea.

Clara, who had enjoyed spending more time in the servants' quarters the past few weeks, nevertheless felt ill at ease as she saw Cal enter the kitchen. He had been treating her with a cool cordiality since the night she'd kissed Robert Balmor.

"Will it be another day of moping and drawn shades for Miss Peggy?" Caleb turned his eyes on Clara, scooping a big spoonful of plum jelly onto his bread.

"That girl." Hannah shook her head. "Crying in her bedchamber, looking at that Major André's drawings and his lock of hair. You'd think she'd been widowed."

"André didn't even seem that torn up about leaving her." Mrs. Quigley wrinkled her brow. "Certainly not the way Miss Peggy was."

"Don't imagine he was, from the looks of it. He'll be in New York and onto his next victim by now." Hannah sighed.

"You have to wonder how many Philadelphia belles are left behind, crying in their beds with André gone north." Cal looked at his aunt as he took a sip of tea. "And that Robert Balmor, André's secretary, I imagine he broke a few hearts as well. Or, at least one." Caleb turned his eyes on Clara, and her cheeks flushed a deep crimson.

Caleb had not told his aunt and uncle what he knew, mercifully, but he had seemed determined to torment Clara with his knowledge.

Clara lifted her chin and took a sip of her tea. She cared nothing for Robert Balmor, and in fact had felt relief each time she'd remembered that both he and André were gone. Letting that man kiss her had been foolish and naïve, but it was none of Cal's business.

"Well, regardless of how sad it made Miss Peggy to see André go, I think we can all sleep easier at night knowing that the dashing major is hundreds of miles away from the Shippen home. That boy was trouble." Mrs. Quigley nodded.

"Indeed, Mrs. Quigley, we all feel nothing but relief." Clara looked directly at Caleb and placed her teacup down, a little too firmly. Cal noticed as the cup spilled, and he raised an eyebrow.

"Oh, I look a fright! I'm so pale. And my hair, it's so flat. Clara, you must do me up, like I used to look. I don't want Stansbury thinking my looks have left along with the British."

Peggy had surprised Clara that morning by declaring her intention to dress and pay a visit to the china merchant.

"I could use a little bit of gossip to cheer me up. Of course, there isn't likely to be much gossip now that the city has been abandoned."

Philadelphia was far from abandoned, Clara wanted to say, but she bit her tongue. No, in fact, as she looked out on the cobblestone streets, the city felt more alive now than it ever had while under British occupation. Colonists in support of Washington and the Continental Army had returned in hordes, once again taking up residence and reopening shops to sell soaps, candles, yarn, and tobacco. The residents who walked the streets might not dress as elegantly as the British had, but their faces were animated with greetings, grins, and hearty laughter.

"If I'm going calling, I might as well look my best," Peggy sighed while Clara styled her hair. Her vanity had returned, at least. That, Clara decided, was a sign that her despair was lifting.

"Have that stableboy accompany us," Peggy said, "in case I buy anything. Though of course Papa will tell me there is no money to buy anything new."

Clara reluctantly invited Cal, who agreed to join them on the outing. As they set out into the early summer day, Peggy marched a few feet ahead of them, clutching her parasol tightly as if she planned to use it for protection against the city's residents rather than from the sun. Clara and Caleb walked behind, avoiding eye contact or the free conversation that they had previously shared.

"What a vulgar town! It looks like Boston!" Peggy gasped as they turned onto Market Street. Colonial soldiers marched by in a loose formation. Clara agreed it looked sloppy when compared with the tight regimental movements of the British troops, but the sight still thrilled her.

"You'd think they could at least coordinate their outfits. Now I see why Johnny always referred to them as ragtag." Some of the men barely looked dressed at all—their breeches fraying at the bottoms, their toes peeking out from disintegrating boots, their jackets mended so many times you could no longer tell what the original color had been.

On nearly every corner, merchants had set up impromptu stands selling fruit, fish, and flowers, and small boys ran down the streets, asking for pennies in exchange for the latest news from the military engagements to the south and the north.

"Enlist now and join General Washington in the fight against tyranny! Let's show that blind tyrant what real leadership looks like!" A local militia leader stood on an empty fruit crate, calling out to the crowd of young men that had gathered around him.

Clara glanced at Caleb, his eyes fixated on the militia leader. She longed to share some communication with him, to ask him if he was as excited by the scene as she was. But when he turned toward her, she lost her courage and averted her eyes, turning them back to the figure of her mistress.

"Well?" Miss Peggy had noticed them lagging behind. "Keep up, you two."

They sped up, walking for several moments in silence. Eventually, Cal spoke.

"Sure looks different around here with the redcoats gone." Caleb kicked a pebble a few feet ahead of their steps.

"Aye." Clara nodded. "A change for the better."

Caleb glanced sideways at her but offered no reply.

"I mean it." A loose cluster of militiamen marched past, nodding their heads at Clara and Caleb. Peggy, Clara noticed, did not turn to acknowledge them.

"You don't miss your Robert Balmor, then?" Caleb jerked his chin.

"He's not *my* Robert Balmor, Caleb." Even she was surprised by the edge in her voice, like the blade of a knife.

"Not anymore, since he's left," Cal answered. "I just never saw you as the type to get sweet on a redcoat, Clara Bell."

Clara shook her head, preparing to defend herself from Cal's accusations. Preparing to tell him that she had felt nothing for John André's secretary, and that she now realized how foolish she had been to let Robert kiss her. How she had been swept up by her lady's enthusiasm. But before she could form this answer, she noticed Miss Peggy had halted, and she almost bumped into her where she stood.

The shop in front of them, Halbrooke hat shop, was closed. The door was barred shut, there was no movement inside. The hearth looked cold and gray, like a fire had not been lit in it for days.

Coffin and Anderson, the dress shop where Peggy's Turkish costume had been sewn, was similarly shuttered. As they approached Joseph Stansbury's china shop, they found a similar scene.

Peggy gasped. "Closed. All of them. What is the meaning of this?"

Caleb walked up to the storefront of Stansbury's shop and pressed his face against the glass, peering inside. Clara looked down at her feet and saw a notice.

"Caleb, look." He stepped beside her and Clara read aloud so that both he and Peggy might hear.

> Martial Law has been declared by Philadelphia's Military Governor, the Major General Benedict Arnold. All goods which were illegally brought into the colony of Pennsylvania on English ships from English shops are now the property of the Continental Army.
>
> Military Governor, Major General Benedict Arnold

"What a nightmare." Peggy stared at the words as if they carried news of the scarlet fever. "What have they done to poor Stansbury? And where did all of Coffin's fine dresses go?"

"It makes sense, if you think about it." Cal was still scrutinizing the notice.

"How, pray tell, do you think it makes sense?" Peggy turned, incensed. Clara braced herself—she could have slapped Caleb for provoking Miss Peggy like this.

"All these goods were from the British." Cal stared into Peggy's face, undaunted. "They were selling to us Americans, then taking our money back to enrich the king. Isn't it bad enough he was taking our wealth through illegal taxation? But to continue to fund his government with our own money? Arnold put a stop to it."

Peggy stared at Caleb as she would a piece of rotting fruit on the street. "So you think all those perfectly fine goods should just be taken? You think Arnold has that right?"

Cal shrugged his shoulders. "He is governor now. He's trying to make sure no more of our money ends up in King George's hands."

"They let these street urchins sell rancid meat on every corner, and then close down the artists who sew our silk? Oh, this is *ridiculous*!" Peggy walked on, leaving Cal and Clara behind.

"You know, you really shouldn't provoke her like that." Clara glowered at Cal before turning to catch up to her mistress.

"Why not?" Cal kept a pace beside Clara. "Am I not entitled to an opinion?" He seemed casually amused by the exchange.

"You may have your opinion, just keep it to yourself," Clara snapped. "Now I shall be the one left to cheer up her sour mood."

"I am a free man with my own opinions, and I'll share them when there is a place for them. I suggest you begin to do the same, Clara Bell."

Clara had an opinion on Cal and his prying ways, and she was about to tell him so when a dog bounded up Market Street, cutting a path directly for Peggy. Clara saw the muddy animal approaching and attempted to alert her mistress to look up from the notice, but she was too late. The dog leapt at Peggy's skirt, now barking.

"Away!" Peggy shooed the dog in disgust, kicking at the speckled white mutt.

"Here, boy." Caleb whistled, trying to distract the animal. "He just wants to play, don't he?"

But Peggy's kicking only served to further excite the dog, and he continued to jump at Peggy, clawing his way up her petticoat and dirtying the light blue silk in the process.

"Get down, you beast! Get down!" Peggy tried ineffectively to swat the dog with her parasol, then kicked it with her small leather boots. "Somebody do something!" Peggy shrieked. Passersby chuckled as they walked on.

"Off of the lady, Barley! You no-good mongrel!" A burly, bold-featured man, his brown hair flying in the wind, hollered in their direction from the open window of a carriage. "You mutinous dog. Come now!" The brawny man tipped his head and then let out a guffaw, before speeding off in the carriage, the wheels splashing lumpy mud on both Clara's and Peggy's petticoats.

"My heavens," Peggy gasped in horror, her wide eyes following the carriage down the street. "Who was that wild man?"

Clara looked to Caleb, who was watching the carriage with admiration painted across his features. "That, ladies, is the Hero of Saratoga. The Cripple of Canada." Both Peggy and Clara looked to him, awaiting further explanation. "The man who took all of your new hats and dresses, Miss Peggy. The new commander of Philadelphia. That is Benedict Arnold."

"I REFUSE to go."

Clara looked up from her position in the corner, where she sat stitching a new nightgown for Miss Peggy. It was a balmy evening in early July, but still a fire was lit in the parlor. Her mistress now threw the invitation into this fire, spitting at it once for good measure.

"I flatly refuse. Anything hosted by that . . . *impostor* . . . Benedict Arnold—no, I would never think of attending."

"Please just listen, Peggy," Betsy spoke diplomatically. "It's the first social event since the Americans took over the city, and it would give you a chance to see all of your friends—Meg Chew, Christianne Amile, Becky Redman—they are all going." Betsy was sitting in a wooden chair before the drawing room fire, diligently stitching the pieces for her bridal trousseau, while her sister paced the room. Clara sensed a newfound ease, a certain confidence in Betsy ever since the British had left. It was as if her status in the household had somehow risen and she suddenly found herself on more equal footing with her younger sister.

"Peggy, you would not have to talk to Benedict Arnold at all. There will be other gentlemen there."

"But it's *hosted* by Benedict Arnold," Peggy protested. "It's bad enough this city threw a parade for him when he arrived. But have we really sunk so low as to attend his parties?"

"The party is given in honor of the French ambassador," Betsy answered. "As such it shall be a very genteel crowd."

Peggy pursed her lips in a scowl. "All gentility left this city with the British army."

"And it shall be in the Penn mansion. Even you, the favorite of the British regiment, has never been invited to a party there." Betsy held up the beginning of a shift, checking the length of the arm.

"To think of that creature occupying the Penn mansion. Why, he's not fit to share the same continent as General Howe, let alone displace him from his quarters." Peggy looked into the fire angrily, watching the invitation from Major General Arnold as it smoldered in the flames.

"Well, I shall go," Betsy said, staring down at her needlework.

"Betsy, you cannot," Peggy gasped, incredulous.

"Why can't I?" Betsy looked up. "Neddy is a supporter of the colonials."

Peggy pursed her lips into a tight frown, and Clara was grateful that it was Betsy on the receiving end of that stare and not herself.

"There, I said it," Betsy continued, defiant. "Now that the British are gone, I will say it as if it's not some secret of which I'm ashamed—my fiancé wants to serve for General Washington. And besides, I'd quite like to attend a party. It's been so long."

"Betsy, setting aside the fact that you've just told me you plan to marry a traitor"—Peggy shook her head—"for us to go to Arnold's ball is to lend credibility to the event. Of course they want the Shippen girls there. That's why it's so important we snub them. Our absence will send a message that we do not consider him a friend, don't you see?"

"I see, yet I don't understand the point in deliberately affronting the new military governor of Philadelphia."

"Why are you suddenly taking such an interest in your social diary, Bets?"

"Benedict Arnold is likely to be here for a long time, and we need not make an enemy of him," Betsy reasoned.

"Bendict Arnold will always be my enemy," Peggy retorted, turning back to the fire. "Driving Johnny and the British out, allowing all the riffraff back in, shutting down the shops. I hate the man, and I always will!"

In the end, Stansbury succeeded in convincing Peggy to attend Arnold's ball by appealing to her vanity: if she removed herself from society at the height of the season, wouldn't she lose her status as Philadelphia's favorite belle? Might she be ceding her title too willingly to Meg Chew, or Christianne Amile, or Becky Redman?

Peggy agreed to attend, though that didn't stop her from hurling insults at the evening's host. "I see no reason why that old cripple should host a dance when he himself cannot walk without a cane."

The evening of the event arrived, a warm night in early July when the days were long. Clara opened the bedroom windows, allowing the aromas of the garden and the chirps of birdsong to float in while Peggy dressed.

"If I'm going to go, I might as well go looking my best." Peggy stood with Clara before the mirror, eyeing her figure in nothing but her shift and her corset. "My goodness, I've turned to skin and bones since the British left. Look at me." Peggy turned a slow circle before the mirror, tracing her hands from her waist to her hips.

"You haven't been eating enough, my lady." Clara held the hair curler over the hearth to heat it.

"I'm sick of the food we have. It's always the same: fowl or salt fish, potatoes without butter, vegetables. And there's never enough of it." Peggy turned to her third favorite line of complaint: after the topics of her hatred for Benedict Arnold and her aging wardrobe, she most often railed against the meals that Hannah prepared for the family.

"I can't even have guests over. We don't have enough food to give them," Peggy said sourly.

"We will have better food, and more of it, once the war is over and your father starts his trading business back up." Clara gave the answer she most often heard in the servants' quarters.

Peggy frowned at this. "And in the meantime, I suppose I shall keep wasting away."

"Now then, enough gloom for such a pretty evening. What would you like to wear to the party?" Clara posed the question with what she hoped would be contagious enthusiasm.

"I have an idea," Peggy said, a devious smile tugging at the corners of her mouth. "Why don't I wear the purple gown? It *is* the color of royalty, after all, and these colonials claim they don't want a royal."

"All right." Clara agreed, crossing the room to the wardrobe. "The plum gown in velvet?"

"No! Lord, Clara, velvet? Do you mean to roast me alive? It's July! I mean the taffeta, in lavender."

"As you wish."

"It's a shame there will be no men of import at the party." Miss Peggy stared at herself in the mirror, sighing. For the first time since André's departure, she'd taken an interest in fixing up her appearance, and she was resplendent in lavender taffeta with lemon-yellow piping, the stomacher of her gown cinched to rest snugly on her tiny waist. Her hair, its golden color enhanced by the summer sun, was piled high atop her head in her favorite style, and she wore amethyst jewels—a choker, a bracelet, and a pair of chandelier earrings.

"I suppose since we're all so equal now, you might as well come with me tonight, Clara. After all, Mr. John Adams would say a maid is of the same status as her lady anyhow, nay?" Peggy fiddled with an earring, staring at Clara through the mirror. "Come with me tonight. I don't much fancy the idea of chatting with Meg Chew, and Betsy is no fun. And that way if I wish to leave early, I can blame it on you falling ill."

The invitation, however coarsely it was delivered, made Clara smile; her lady wished to speak with *her* more than anyone else at the party. And how exciting to attend a fête at the home once occupied by the Penn family, and now presided over by the commander of the army in Philadelphia. If only Oma could see her tonight, attending such an event with the Shippen girls.

Mrs. Quigley had helped Clara select a simple, clean dress of pale yellow cotton, which fit her well and complemented her own blond hair. Mrs. Quigley had loaned her a necklace of small pearls, and Miss Peggy, in a moment of rare magnanimity, had even suggested that Clara borrow her hair curler. Though she was dressed in fabrics and accessories of much less value than Miss Peggy or Miss Betsy, Clara felt pretty as she prepared to depart for the mansion.

"You look nice." Cal hopped down from the Shippen carriage, stuffing his hands into his trouser pockets. Clara waited out front in the warm evening. A carriage rolled past, its footman nodding his greeting, but otherwise the street was quiet.

"Thank you." Clara turned from Cal back up toward the front door, hoping Peggy and Betsy would hurry up and come out. Standing here alone with Cal made her uneasy.

Cal had a piece of straw in his mouth. "Clara, I've been meaning to apologize." He paused, shrugging his shoulders. "For my remarks about Robert. It was just that . . ."

"Finally!" The front door opened, and Betsy stood there. "Peggy, I thought you were going to keep me waiting all night."

Peggy emerged behind her sister. "What are you in such a hurry for? It's not as though the party shall be any fun."

Betsy climbed quickly down the stairs, her skirt bunched up in her hands. Cal looked once more at Clara, his eyes full of the words he had hoped to say.

"We shall have to drive quickly, Cal." Betsy extended her hand, and Caleb opened the coach door, helping her into the carriage.

The hour was close to eight o'clock, and yet the sun had not begun to set on what was one of the longest, warmest days of the year. As Caleb spurred the carriage onward, north up Market Street toward Sixth, Clara felt the breeze on her cheeks and pushed aside the troublesome, unresolved quarrel with him. It was a lovely evening and she allowed her mood to lift, even somehow managing to drown out the bothersome arguing of Peggy and Betsy opposite her.

"I suppose you'll find Neddy and vanish for the rest of the evening to discuss boring things." Peggy looped her pinky-finger through a curl of hair, looking away from her sister as she insulted her.

"There is nothing boring about Neddy's military service, Peggy," Betsy snapped. "His captain has commended his diligence and attentiveness so far."

Peggy sighed. "I suppose that's all everyone will be speaking about at the party, colonials this, and colonials that. I'm bored of it already. Thank goodness I'll have you with me, Clara. We can leave early." Clara nodded obediently, hoping she'd be able to stay long enough to catch a glimpse of General Arnold.

The carriage slowed to a halt before the Penn mansion, an old brick home awash in the golden glow of predusk sunlight. Three steps from the street led them to a white door beneath a crisp white pediment, which stood out against the redbrick façade. The music and chatter filling the front hall spilled out through open windows onto the street. "This is nice," Peggy admitted begrudgingly.

"See, you're glad I insisted you come," Betsy gloated. She herself looked very pretty in a simple gown of light green silk with pink ribbons, and she had confided to Clara that it was Neddy's favorite dress.

"I didn't say that," Peggy retorted, stepping out of the carriage and taking Caleb's outstretched hand.

When it was her turn to be helped down by Cal, Clara extended her hand.

Was it her imagination, or did he give her hand a gentle squeeze? "Have fun in there," he whispered. She could never tell if he was teasing her or being earnest.

The ladies made their way up the front steps and were welcomed into a spacious hall, filled with wigged footmen carrying trays of Champagne and a military band playing upbeat music on the fife and drums.

"Marching music," Peggy grumbled, accepting an outstretched glass of Champagne.

"I'm going to go find Neddy." Betsy took a glass for herself and left her sister's side without another look.

"Peggy Shippen, is it you?" A brunette beauty in a cream-colored gown glided toward them. "Have you finally deemed us worthy to grace us with your presence once more?"

"Oh, hello, Meg." Peggy smiled halfheartedly, exchanging kisses on the cheek with a young woman Clara immediately knew to be Meg Chew.

"I have not seen you in ages, Peggy. I hope you are well?" Meg studied Peggy's appearance from the top of her hair down to the hem of her gown.

"Quite." Peggy took a gulp of Champagne. "And you, Meg?"

"Oh, I'm just splendid." Meg Chew tossed her head, sending her flower-trimmed curls bouncing. "It feels good to have an occasion to put on a gown once more, does it not?"

"Indeed," Peggy agreed, looking as glum as a weed next to her rival's splendor. She took another sip and drained her glass.

"But when was the last time I saw you, Peggy?"

Peggy shrugged her shoulders, still looking around at her fellow partygoers. Clara guessed that she was seeking some gentleman to deliver her from this exchange. Finding none, Peggy turned to her maid, proffering her empty flute. "Please fetch me more Champagne, Clara." Clara curtsied and took the glass, seeking out a wigged footman.

"Oh, I recall it now, the last time I saw you, Peggy, was just before the Meshianza Masque."

"Excuse me, some more please." Clara found a nearby footman. Returning to the ladies' conversation, she saw that Meg Chew was still chatting gaily.

"You know, I must tell you, I felt downright awful for attending the Meshianza with Major André in your place." Meg placed her long fingers on Peggy's hand. "Peggy, it didn't feel right. We just had *so* much fun playing dress-up together, dancing all night, pretending to be Turkish barbarians." Meg tossed her head back in mock embarrassment. "We were like a couple of wild heathens!"

"Oh, I know." Peggy pulled her fan from her purse and waved it a bit too quickly. When she spoke again, her tone was one of forced gaiety. "He was so sad as well. And I just worried that my dress would be too tight on you, given that I'm so much more petite than you are, Meg."

Clara was standing there holding out the glass of Champagne, watching Peggy's face twist into a wicked grin. "But don't feel too sorry for me, Meg. You see, Johnny rushed to escort you home safely and then he came over to see me." Leaning close, Peggy whispered, "We had quite the evening, as well."

Peggy was exaggerating, Clara knew. She was neglecting to tell Meg that Major André had left in a hurry once the battle had begun, and that she hadn't heard from him since his departure. But she must have been satisfied by the deflated look on Meg Chew's face.

"Oh, good," Meg said, her lips curling into a forced smile. "And have you heard from Major André since he arrived in New York?"

Peggy shook her head. "No, he told me he could not write across enemy lines."

"I see," Meg replied. "Well, if I hear from him, I'll be sure to fill you in on his news. I know you must be very anxious to hear of his well-being just as I am. We were all such dear friends, weren't we?" Clara marveled at how these women could trade such cutting barbs, all the while maintaining the picture of smiling amity.

"Thank you, Meg. You are too kind," Peggy said through clenched teeth. "Oh, Clara, you're back." Peggy noticed her maid beside her and reached for the glass of Champagne. After several gulps, Peggy looked once more at Meg. "Excuse me, I think I drank that too quickly. I must go sit."

"Oh dear, yes, go rest. And please do take care of yourself. I hate seeing you so . . . well, so much less vibrant than you used to look." Meg Chew cocked her head, a sympathetic pout puffing out her lower lip.

"Your concern for me is so touching, Meg." The ladies curtsied and Peggy turned on her heels, pulling Clara down a hallway. Once they reached the safety of a private library away from the crowds, Peggy slammed the door.

"The nerve!" Peggy trembled, jerking her head of curls in tight, tense movements. "That imbecilic cow! She thinks Johnny would write *her* before he'd write me? Why, it was all I could take not to claw that stupid smile right off her face!" Peggy stomped her feet as she approached the mantelpiece. Her hands trembled, and Clara was afraid she might spill her glass of Champagne all over the carpet—or worse, hurl it across the room.

"Come now, Miss Peggy, you mustn't let Miss Chew upset you so." Clara reached forward and removed the glass from Peggy's hands, placing it on the mantel. "You know that you were the favorite of Major André."

"Oh, forget it, Clara. What does it even matter, really?" Peggy collapsed onto the sofa and kicked her feet up, clutching her abdomen where it was held in by the unforgiving corset. "I'm not a fool. I know Johnny is gone."

"Oh, miss." Clara knelt down beside her mistress. Through the door of the library she heard loud clapping, a thunderous cheer, coming from the front hall. Someone had made a roaring entrance into the party. "It may seem that way, but the party out there seems quite gay. Why not at least try to enjoy yourself for a little while?"

When Peggy had collected herself and reentered the hall, the large space teemed with women in bell-shaped ball gowns and colonial gentlemen exchanging news about George Washington and the Continental Congress. The women appeared to Clara as familiar faces—the same Tory belles who had mingled so happily with the British officers at Lord Rawdon's soiree. But the landscape of male faces was entirely new. These men did not wear perfectly powdered wigs, and their jackets were not the bright red of the Crown's men. These men were scruffier—their suits less tailored, their pants frayed, their faces whiskered. Peggy would not have agreed, but Clara found the informal mood preferable to that of the stilted card party at Lord Rawdon's.

At the center of the hall, surrounded by a dozen or so admirers, stood two new faces—late entries to the party. One of them wore a beige silk suit and a fine wig of bright orange curls. His face was made-up like a woman's, blanched with white powder and bright rouge on his cheekbones. Standing beside him was a broad-chested American officer who had a small crowd in uproarious laughter over something he'd said. Clara studied this second man—his animated gestures, his large, prominent facial features, his unruly tufts of graying brown hair that were barely contained by a ribbon tied at the nape of his neck. While his upper body appeared athletic and robust, he stood in a slightly stooped posture, leaning on a jeweled cane. That man, Clara knew, was the host, the same man who had splashed them with his carriage.

"Benedict Arnold." Peggy was watching him as well.

"Yes, ma'am," Clara said, nodding. She scanned the room—there was only one couple in the hall that seemed as unhappy as her mistress. The couple, abstaining from all Champagne or hors d'oeuvres, stood in the corner, muttering only to themselves. The man, with a long, oval face and pale blue eyes, appeared to be about the same age as his host. The lady, a few years older than the Shippen girls and dressed in plain homespun, looked as though she'd just bit into a lemon wedge.

"Miss Peggy, who are they?" Clara remembered Mrs. Quigley's instructions that it was rude to point, and instead gestured with a subtle nod of her chin. "That couple in the corner? They seem even more bored than you."

Peggy turned her eyes in the direction of Clara's glance. "Good gracious, *they* are back? Well, now we know for certain that there will be no fun in Philadelphia all season."

"But who are they?" Clara studied the man—tall, thin, serious. He, like the woman who accompanied him, wore the homespun garb that was customary among the patriots.

"The Reeds. Joseph and Blanche Reed. Blanche Reed once fancied herself to be in the same circle as Betsy, Meg, Christianne, Becky, and me. Can you imagine? Just look at how she dresses."

"And her husband?"

Now Peggy lowered her voice. "Oh, yes. Joseph Reed is fanatical. One of the first to advocate separation from the Crown. Apparently he's too radical even for that tobacco farmer, George Washington." Peggy spoke the name with disdain. "Joseph Reed of course fled when the British sacked the city, but I guess he's come back now, like some buzzard hoping to pick the last morsels of life from the carcass of our precious Philadelphia."

"I see," Clara said. Sensing Peggy's worsened mood, Clara regretted her question.

"Hello, Peggy." They both turned to see a young woman of Peggy's age approaching. She had a pretty smile, though her shapeless frame was less alluring than Peggy's or Meg Chew's.

"Oh, hello, Christianne." Peggy turned to the newcomer, a genuine smile lighting her face. Unlike Meg Chew or the Reeds, this was a guest whom Peggy seemed relieved to see. They kissed each other's cheeks.

"Lovely party, isn't it?" Christianne stared at Peggy, admiring her gown.

"I suppose so," Peggy answered in a clipped tone.

"I'm happy to see you." Christianne studied every inch of Peggy's appearance—from her dress to her amethyst jewels to her curled hair. "I think you look lovely; I'm not sure why Meg Chew had said that you had given up on society."

Peggy frowned. "So she is spreading rumors about me?"

Christianne threw a guilty look in Meg Chew's direction before answering Peggy. "She said that you flatly refused to socialize now that André was gone."

"She *wishes* I had given up." Peggy snapped. "I simply have no appetite for boring parties, not when I'm used to the fun we had with the officers, that's all."

"Did you see that the Reeds are back?"

"Yes," Peggy said. "That's how you know that the fun is gone."

"Well, I think that tonight is just lovely." Christianne looked around the room, her eyes roving in the direction of General Arnold.

"Perhaps." Peggy shrugged. "I can't find Joseph Stansbury. Where is he?"

"Oh, you haven't heard?"

Peggy shook her head.

"He's gone to New York on urgent business."

"What sort of business?"

"I'm not sure of what type. All I know is"—Christianne paused, as if to make sure she had Peggy's full attention when she delivered the last part of her sentence—"is that Major General Arnold told me that he'd sent Stansbury to New York on business." A self-satisfied pause. "Have you met Major General Arnold and the ambassador yet?"

"No." Peggy was fanning herself, already bored with the conversation.

"Oh! Major General Arnold is such a nice man. Over there." Christianne nodded toward the two men. "That's the French ambassador, the finely dressed one with the orange hair. And beside him"—Christianne's voice was pregnant with admiration now—"that's Benedict Arnold. The American war hero."

"Seems like a vulgar type, no?" Peggy looked at the American officer like she'd look at a plate of day-old food.

"Oh, not at all. I've just met him," Christianne answered, her cheeks reddening to match her giddy tone. "He's lovely. So very nice. And humble. To think, he single-handedly turned the tide of the entire war with his bravery at Saratoga."

"I'd like to ask him when he will open Philadelphia's shops again so we can buy fabric," Peggy grumbled.

"That's you, Peggy Shippen, always thinking about your next dress." Christianne giggled. "If you'd like, I could ask him," Christianne offered. "He *is* the one in control of such matters now, after all."

Peggy thought about this but did not respond to her friend's offer.

"Well, I am going to go back to him. He's telling the story of his winter siege in Canada. The first time he was shot in the legs. But of course, he was shot again in Saratoga. Can you believe the bravery?" Christianne kissed Peggy once on the cheek and scurried off, weaving her way through the crowd surrounding Benedict Arnold.

"Ridiculous how they're fawning all over him like he's King George the Third," Peggy mused, glowering at the general and his surrounding admirers.

"Did you hear what he did when they tried to amputate his wounded leg?"

"Pointed his gun at the surgeon and told 'em he'd rather die than be without his leg!" Two guests shoved their way past Clara and Peggy in an attempt to get closer to Arnold.

"Perhaps we should try to meet him?" Clara prodded tentatively.

"Oh, what for?" Peggy threw another petulant glance toward Arnold. He stood in conversation with Christianne Amile, who had managed to jostle her way back to his side. "Look at Christianne—never managed to get any attention from the British gentlemen, now in a swoon over that American. That just goes to show how inferior their tastes are. I'm surprised they don't all think Blanche Reed is a beauty."

Peggy stood alone, with no suitors and no company but Clara, drinking several more glasses of Champagne in quick succession. Clara knew Peggy clung to her haughtiness as the last line of defense against utter despair. Finally, eager to clear the sour and unattractive smirk from her lady's face, Clara proposed a new tack.

"Well then, let's at least pay our respects to the French ambassador," Clara suggested.

"Oh fine, *him* I will talk to," Peggy agreed, draining the remnants of a final glass. "He has at least spent some time in a royal court." Clara did not respond with the thought that then crossed her mind: that Miss Peggy had not spent any more time in a royal court than the rest of the colonials at the party.

"Maybe we can ask him why his king would be so foolish as to side with the rebels." Peggy giggled, her tongue made reckless by Champagne and bitterness. "Fine," she sighed, her head tilting to one side. "Let us go pay our respects." She took Clara's hand and began weaving her way through the thick crowd.

There was much shoving and elbowing, as people waiting in a line did not appreciate Peggy cutting in front of them.

"Watch out, Miss Shippen."

"Excuse me, Miss Shippen."

Irritated guests felt less need to pay homage to this woman now, her status so visibly diminished since the departure of her British admirers.

"This is ridiculous," Peggy snapped. "I don't wait in line to meet people."

"Behave, Peg." Betsy had appeared beside them in the crowd. She looked away from her sister toward the center of the crowd. "Major André is not the *l'homme d'honneur* in Philadelphia anymore. Benedict Arnold is. From the looks of it, Christianne Amile is his favorite. So the gentlemen will be lining up to dance with *her* now." Betsy watched her sister, the hint of a gloating smile spreading across her features.

"Oh, we'll see about that," Peggy answered, fixing her gaze on Arnold as the fog of Champagne seemed to lift from her eyes. Clara noticed a look of determination cross her mistress's face, which she hadn't seen in weeks. She was not certain to what purpose Peggy had set her mind, but, whatever it was, she knew Peggy would have it.

As THE evening grew dark and the hall dimmed into the amber glow of candlelight, the crowds thinned. Guests—glutted on Champagne and rich desserts—sought comfort on the plush couches or departed for more private conversations in a dark study or on a shady garden path. Now only the host remained in the front hall, along with a small cluster of admirers. Around Benedict Arnold stood an aide-de-camp in the Continental uniform, the French ambassador, and Christianne Amile, who still looked on with the same smitten expression.

"You see the way Christianne looks on like a hopeless puppy? The French ambassador must be so underwhelmed by our society here in the colonies. Perhaps I should give him a little excitement." Peggy had at last inched herself close to their host, and she now fidgeted with her hair.

"Hold this, Clara." Peggy stuffed her fan and her empty glass into her maid's hand and then glided the remaining distance across the room so that she stood before the major general.

"Ah." Benedict Arnold turned from Christianne when he saw Peggy approach, smiling politely as he had with all his guests. "And who do we have here?"

"Major General Arnold, it is an honor to meet you, sir." Peggy extended her tiny hand toward her host for a kiss, as she curtsied low. "I'm Margaret Shippen, but you may call me Peggy."

"I know who you are, Miss Shippen." General Arnold took Peggy's outstretched hand and held it to his lips, staring down at her in her curtsy. "My whole regiment knows who you are." Christianne looked on as well, the smile slipping from her features.

Peggy locked her eyes on Arnold, flashing her coquettish grin. "Am I that famous, General?" Peggy rose slowly from her curtsy, cocking her head to the side. It was like observing a flower blooming before her very eyes—Clara was as awestruck as the rest of the captive crowd as Peggy surged back to life under the heady glow of male flattery.

"Infamous, I daresay." Arnold raised his eyebrows suggestively.

"Oh," Peggy gasped, bringing her hand to her cheek in a gesture of exaggerated modesty. "Infamy is not a good thing, I fear."

"They say that you had an army of British men at your feet." Arnold eyed Peggy up and down, as if to size up the woman behind the tales he'd been told.

"And they say that you had an army of British men on *their* feet, running in the opposite direction of Saratoga," Peggy rejoined.

Arnold and his aide erupted in delighted laughter. While Peggy's figure seemed to blossom, growing more irresistible under the attention, Clara noticed Christianne Amile's posture experiencing the opposite effect—the poor girl appeared to be sagging beside the distracted Arnold like a wilting flower.

"Her wit is as quick as they say it is," Arnold said to the ambassador and the other gentleman beside him, a dapper, dark-eyed attendant with white powder in his hair. "Miss Shippen, allow me to introduce you to my companion: His Excellency, the French ambassador, le Comte Conrad Alexandre Gérard."

"Ah, *l'homme d'honneur,* the guest of honor." Peggy curtsied, bowing her head as she offered her hand to the ambassador for a kiss. "*Votre Excellence,* Your Excellency." She was delighted, Clara could see, to be playing the coquette once again.

"*Enchanté.*" The count flashed a toothy smile at Peggy. "Zee *honneur* is all mine. And I see zat you speak French, mademoiselle."

"*Mais bien sûr.* But of course, Excellency. All the young ladies who hope to think of themselves as accomplished must speak French. We may not be as impressive as the ladies of your court in Versailles, but I do hope that we don't disappoint you entirely."

"But you do not disappoint in the slightest, mademoiselle."

"Is Your Excellency enjoying himself tonight?" Peggy focused on the ambassador as if his response alone was all that interested her.

"Mademoiselle Shippen, I must admit I have been somewhat homesick for my mother country. But when I gaze on you, your beauty, well, I could be back at Versailles."

"The ambassador is much too kind." Peggy fixed her gaze on Arnold, flashing a beguiling smile. "We all know that the French court is the height of gentility. Nothing like our rough little assembly of colonial patriots. Nevertheless, I am happy to provide some small succor to an ally of our cause."

Our cause? Clara was stunned at hearing her mistress bandy such language. And poor Christianne, standing beside Arnold, was completely forgotten.

A pair of guests now approached to pay their respects one final time before taking their leave. Arnold bid them a quick farewell and then turned back, repositioning himself so that he stood closer to Peggy than the ambassador. "Now, Ambassador, with beauty such as this to protect, do you not agree that you must aid us in our fight, *monsieur*?" Benedict Arnold had locked his eyes on Peggy and now seemed unwilling to remove them. At this close distance, the vast difference in their age was glaring; to Clara it seemed that Arnold was twice Peggy's age.

"Major General, I am overcome by your kindness." Peggy

dropped her eyes to the floor demurely, leaning forward so that Arnold might steal a furtive look down the front of her gown.

"Miss Shippen, will you allow me to make one more introduction?" Arnold moved closer to her, so that the ambassador and Christianne Amile were now entirely removed from the conversation. Sensing their exclusion, the two of them splintered off into their own, less-than-easy dialogue.

"Please, sir," Peggy said in her breathless manner, a performance Clara had only seen used on Major André.

"Miss Shippen, please meet my aide-de-camp, Major David Franks."

"A pleasure, Major Franks." Peggy extended her hand to the man beside Arnold.

"The pleasure is entirely mine, Miss Shippen," Major Franks stammered, clearly the latest in the line of men to fall enchanted before her that evening.

"I hope you're taking good care of our national hero, Major Franks?" Peggy cocked her head. "He's a special favorite of General Washington's. We Philadelphians would not want anything to happen to him while he was here."

"I . . . uh . . . well, I try, Miss . . . Miss . . ." Major Franks groped for her name.

"Shippen." Peggy obliged him, and Arnold erupted in jocular laughter.

"Miss Shippen, you must go easy on Major Franks," General Arnold interjected. "He's a young man and therefore, I fear, ripe for heartbreak. I am older, more seasoned in the beguiling ways of the fairer sex. I am less at risk against your charms myself."

"Well I've always loved a challenge." Peggy flashed a dazzling smile as she inched closer to Arnold, lowering her voice so that it seemed as if she spoke only to him.

"Ah, the little lady says she is up for a challenge." General Arnold looked down at Peggy as if he would gobble her up.

"I *am* up for the challenge," Peggy replied with a lopsided grin, and then, leaning in so that just Arnold could hear her, she breathed the words in his ear. "The question is, General Arnold, are *you* up?"

THE MOOD in the carriage on the way home was tense, and Betsy seemed to flinch each time the horses dragged them over a deep rut in the cobblestones.

Finally, Betsy looked across the carriage at her sister and broke the silence, demanding to know why she had waged such a full offensive of charm and attention on a man whom she had earlier declared her sworn enemy. Clara, utterly confounded by her mistress's behavior, also could not understand what she'd just witnessed.

"I can't figure out why you care who I flirt with, Bets, unless you're worried I'm coming after Neddy." Peggy spoke calmly, which further inflamed her sister's irritation.

"You'd never," Betsy gasped. "And besides, Neddy would never throw me over. Especially not for you."

"Suit yourself," Peggy said.

"He would not! You're not his type. Neddy told me so himself."

"I don't care if I'm Neddy Burd's type." Peggy tittered, glancing out the carriage window.

"It was shameless, Peg, the way you fawned all over General Arnold like that," Betsy continued. Through the coach opening, Clara saw Caleb laughing to himself—he was far enough removed that he found the Shippen girls endlessly entertaining.

"And that poor Christianne Amile . . . Such a nice girl, and completely smitten by Arnold, and you waltz right in and elbow her into the corner," Betsy continued. "I thought she was your friend."

All Peggy offered by way of an answer was a giggle.

"And a man that old! He's thirty-seven, Peg. You're only eighteen. Father would never let him court you."

"Does Father have a say in what I do?" Peggy asked, unfazed.

"But you would not want him to court you, would you?" Clara piped up, seeking clarification.

"Why ever not?" Peggy stared back at her maid, defiant.

"No, she'd never," Betsy answered. "You would not, right, Margaret Shippen?"

Peggy looked derisively at her sister. "Are you *trying* to sound like Mother?"

"Peggy, I mean it. You are not actually interested in Benedict Arnold, are you?"

"Oh, you girls are such simpletons." Peggy leaned her head back against the carriage and sighed. "Bets, I expect it from the farm girl"—she pointed at Clara—"but you?"

"Sometimes I really do not understand you, Margaret Shippen." Betsy looked at her sister disapprovingly.

"It's simple enough to understand, even for a pair as naïve as you two," Peggy spoke clearly, calmly. "If you can't break the rules, you might as well seduce the man who makes them."

IV.

My lady is wavering between hysteria and spells of eerie quiet. The hysteria I can manage; I'm familiar with her tantrums. At least when she's in the throes of a fit, she's screaming exactly what is on her mind. It's the cool, calculating calm that has always unnerved me more. When she's like that, no one—not even me—is capable of understanding what is happening behind those icy blue eyes.

Mistress disappears, grabbing a goose-down pillow and holding it over her face. I hear her muffled screams, which she releases into the feathers, and I'm glad for their quieting influence.

"My lady, they are approaching." I watch out the window as they ride up in a storm of churning dust, leather boots, and horse hooves. The dog in the kitchen barks and pushes his way out our front door, sending a few of the approaching horses into skittish whinnies.

His head stands out from all the rest, even with their identical tricornered hats and matching dark blue officer's coats. General Washington always stands out, on account of his unusual height. His ease atop the horse is surprising.

"What a lovely place!" He roars it good-naturedly to his riding companion, the Marquis de Lafayette. "Arnold has arranged for quite the plush perch for himself and Mrs. Arnold." Washington and his young friend laugh, his laugh a booming, contagious sound that originates from somewhere deep within his barrel of a chest.

The military party approaches the home as a unit, a herd, their camaraderie evident in the way they banter and jostle with one another, the way they quip like old friends. I suppose that is inevitable after the trials they've endured together: victory in battle, defeat in battle, the bone-numbing cold of their winter together at Valley Forge. They've been to hell and back, this group, and now all they expect is a nice warm breakfast with a fellow patriot and the charming wife of whom he's so often boasted.

"Here we are, men." Washington steps down from his horse, his height alarming even after the stories I've heard about his uncommon stature. He removes his tricornered hat and uses it to point across the river. When he speaks, his men listen with rapt attention. "There stands West Point. The key to the continent. Boys, our future could be made or broken on those granite cliffs."

I wonder, as I study his large features—his placid eyes, his wide, honest brow—does Washington know already? Or is there still time?

CHAPTER FOUR

"The Most Beautiful Little Patriot in All Thirteen Colonies"

July 1778
Philadelphia, PA

"CLARA, SIT."

"Yes, Miss Peggy."

"You seem to enjoy sewing."

Clara nodded, lowering herself into the chair opposite her mistress.

"You are always fixing my gowns, since they are as old as Abraham and Sarah."

Clara lowered her eyes, smiling under her mistress's flattery. "I try, miss."

"And you stitch all of my shifts and undergarments."

Clara waited to see where her mistress was directing the conversation.

"How would you like to help me with something very important?"

"I'd like nothing more than to be helpful."

"Good, then you must teach me everything you know about stitching. And you must do so in the next quarter of an hour."

It was the morning after the party given by Benedict Arnold for the French ambassador. Clara noticed, with surprise, that her mistress had risen early, attended breakfast with her family, and even spoken kindly to them at the table. After the morning meal, she had requested that Clara bring her a cup of tea, a fresh kerchief, and her stitching frame so that she could do some needlework in the parlor. It was the last thing Clara had expected to hear from her mistress, and for a brief moment she had entertained the foolish thought that her mistress might actually have been interested in a morning of simple, industrious activity.

"I will try, my lady." Clara now set down the tray of tea on the table and joined her mistress in the parlor. "I see you have your stitching frame set up. That's the first step."

"Yes, but why must I use this contraption?"

"To keep the linen taut, my lady."

"Very well. I want to sew in little golden stars, and then I want to stitch a motto on this kerchief." Peggy looked at the blank kerchief. "And I'll finish with my initials, of course."

"All right then. We shall start with the stars. Which color?" Clara held up two spools, one of a dark gold and one of a cheery yellow.

"Hmm, which one looks more like the color of the stars on the rebel flag?" Peggy eyed her options, brow furrowed.

"I suggest we select this one." Clara picked the gold spool, intrigued to find out more about their morning's task.

"Fine." Peggy nodded her agreement. "You thread the needle, Clara. I don't want to prick my fingers."

Clara prepared the needle and handed it to Peggy, a long tail of golden thread dangling behind it. "Now, would you like your embroidery in the corner of your kerchief? Or right in the middle? You must choose your spot."

"Right in the middle," Peggy answered.

"Then right about here is where you should make your first stitch." Clara pointed to the center of the kerchief, stretched out over the circular stitching frame.

"Oh, I feel so clumsy, and my hands will shake and ruin it. Can you do it for me?" Peggy handed the threaded needle to her maid, smiling imploringly.

"All right then. I'll do it this time, and you watch so that perhaps you'll be up for it next time."

Clara sewed quickly with expert hands as her mistress hovered, looking on with half interest. Peggy instructed Clara to stitch a miniature constellation of gold stars, just like Betsy Ross had done, offering criticism whenever she didn't approve of a star's size or position.

"Now, below the stars, I want you to stitch a motto," Peggy directed.

"What's that, my lady?"

"I want you to write: 'Don't Tread On Me.'"

Clara looked into Peggy's face. "Miss, you want me to stitch in the patriots' motto? The one Mr. Benjamin Franklin came up with?"

"That's right." Peggy stared back at her maid, defiant. "That's what I said. Do it."

"Well . . . all right. If that's what you say."

"It is what I say," Peggy answered. "And do it quickly, as I'll need it today."

So her lady had gone from Tory to patriot in one day; she must have enjoyed herself at the party last night after all.

HANNAH HAD not yet started to cook the midday dinner, and Brigitte had barely emptied the chamber pots, before Major General Benedict Arnold knocked on the front door of the Shippen home, asking if he might call on Miss Peggy Shippen.

"I knew he'd be here before luncheon." Peggy watched through her bedroom window as his formal carriage rolled to a halt, flanked by a military escort of soldiers atop strong horses. When the coach door opened he limped out, supported by his silver-tipped cane.

Clara knew from her mistress's satisfied expression that the day was going according to some precise plan she had laid out, as if they were all mere marionette puppets, playing in a show that they themselves did not know existed.

"Well?" Peggy turned to her maid. "What are you waiting for? He's limping his way up the front steps—hadn't you better go answer the door?"

"MAJOR GENERAL Benedict Arnold to see you, sir." Clara found the words surprising, even as she uttered them.

"Please show him in." Judge Shippen received the burly American officer in the parlor, his shock at the visit plain on his face. "Major General Benedict Arnold, I am certain that we do not deserve the honor of a visit from our new governor so soon after your arrival to our city. This is too kind of you."

"Hullo and good day, Judge." Benedict Arnold limped his hulking frame into the parlor. Clara recognized the same swarthy dog from the day Arnold's coach had sped past Peggy.

Judge Shippen fidgeted with the sleeves of his threadbare coat as he directed his guest. "Welcome, General Arnold, please sit."

"Much obliged, Judge Shippen." Arnold doffed his tricornered cap and took the seat offered him. His frame appeared too hefty for the finely carved wood beneath it.

"Thank you for receiving me, Judge." Benedict Arnold's voice was a strong baritone, reverberating off the upholstered walls of the Shippen parlor.

"But of course, General Arnold. And I must offer my sincere regrets on behalf of my wife; Mrs. Shippen suffers from chronic headaches. Perhaps if we had had more notice of your visit, she might have—"

"Down, Barley, sit!" Arnold bellowed at his dog, the mutt's tail wagging precariously close to a porcelain vase. "What was that you said, Judge? Oh, no worries about the missus." Arnold propped his jeweled cane against the chair's armrest and stretched his wounded left leg out before him. "Feels good to take a load off, eh, Judge?"

"Indeed, General," Judge Shippen answered, his lips pressed tightly together.

"Mind if I smoke in here?" Arnold removed a pipe from the pocket of his military jacket.

"As you wish, please." Judge Shippen nodded. "And perhaps something to eat?"

"I'll never turn down food, Judge, as you can probably tell from my frame." Arnold patted his belly with one thick hand as he lit his pipe with the other.

"Clara?" Judge Shippen summoned the maid into the room. Clara noted the twitch in the judge's jaw as he told her to bring them a plate of apples, cheese, and nuts.

"Right away, sir." Clara curtsied and left the judge coughing in a cloud of Arnold's smoke. Not only did the judge disapprove of tobacco smoke in his home, he wasn't particularly fond of receiving visitors, especially those visitors whose political alignments were as clear as the ones held by the city's new military commander. Nor did he seem enthusiastic about exhausting his limited food stores on superfluous midday visits.

Nevertheless, Judge Shippen was well-bred enough to know that the occasion warranted a courteous display. When she reentered the parlor with a tray of food, Clara found the judge conversing with his guest. "How are you finding our city, General Arnold?"

"Oh, delightful, just delightful." Arnold disregarded the formality of his host, leaning forward like the two men were old friends.

"The food, Judge."

"Thank you, Clara. Place it here." Clara deposited the plate of food between them. Before she had stepped back from the table, Arnold had reached for an apple piece and bit into it with gusto. "I must tell you, Judge, the city has not disappointed. I had never seen so many pretty faces as I did at the party at my home last night."

Judge Shippen's cheeks blanched, but he managed a pinched smile. He looked at the food, but did not touch it.

"Nice to be in the society of gentlemen again, Judge." Arnold exhaled a pungent fog of pipe smoke. Clara liked the familiar scent; it reminded her of Oma, who had sometimes spent the warm evenings on the farm indulging in her one vice. "Philadelphia seems like a genteel town—so different from the savage wilderness of Ticonderoga and Saratoga. Speaking of Philadelphia's charms, Judge, is Miss Peggy Shippen at home this morning?"

"My daughter, well, in fact . . ." The judge stammered, grasping for some suitable reply, but was interrupted.

"Can it be true?" All eyes in the room turned to the doorway, where Miss Peggy stood, a vision in bright blue silk, ruby jewelry in her hair and on her limbs. Now Clara understood her lady's particular interest in her wardrobe earlier that morning—she wore the colors of Betsy Ross's flag.

"Can it be true that Major General Benedict Arnold is paying me a visit in his first week here?" Peggy crossed the room, her face the image of flattered humility. Arnold wrestled with his wounded leg as he struggled to his feet, leaning on his jeweled cane as he bowed. Peggy extended her hand to him for a kiss.

"Miss Shippen, thank you for taking my visit." Arnold looked at her, his large features lit up with boyish excitement.

"It is I who must offer thanks, General Arnold." The scent of Peggy's rosewater perfume wafted as far as the threshold of the parlor, where Clara stood, awaiting further orders from the judge or her mistress. "I shall be able to tell my grandchildren some day that I once received the hero of the colonies in my own parlor." An intangible attraction bounced between the two of them, Clara noticed. Some subtle shift that made all the men—Arnold, his uniformed attendants in the corner, even her own father—sit up a little more straight, a little more alert. Even Clara found it hard to peel her eyes from her mistress's dazzling entrance.

"Ahem." Judge Shippen shifted in his chair, looking from his daughter to the large man, twice her age, who had come to court her in his home.

"General Arnold, may I sit beside you?" Peggy tiptoed to his side, nearly stepping on the dog before she noticed him curled up at his master's feet. "Oh, ho! And who is this adorable little creature?" Peggy leaned over, clucking sweetly at the dog.

Peggy hated dogs, and this one especially. That much Clara knew.

"This here is Barley." Arnold stroked the dog behind the ears, offering him a generous piece of cheese. The judge cringed as he watched.

"I think I saw him in the street once, shortly after you came in." Peggy smiled, as if the memory were a sweet one. "He wouldn't leave me alone."

"Can't blame him!" Arnold retorted, guffawing at his own joke.

"What a charming little name, Barley." Peggy petted the dog once, her hand recoiling the moment Barley attempted to lick her.

"Aye, he's named after the essential ingredient for his favorite drink—ale."

"How clever." Peggy tossed her curls back so that her ruby earrings danced alongside her laughing features.

"Stuck by me loyally in Canada during the siege of Quebec, more loyally than some of my own men, mind you. Plus we love ale, don't we, Barley?" Turning back to Peggy, Arnold stretched his hand out and one of his aides placed a chair for her on the other side of Barley.

"The siege of Quebec is now a famous tale. I hope you don't mind my saying so." Peggy fluttered her eyelashes toward the floor. "There is nothing I'd love more than for you to regale us with some of the tales of your heroism." Peggy stared only at the officer, as if oblivious of her father, and everyone else in the room. "Perhaps you can tell us how you came to be General Washington's most favored compatriot?"

"Oh, ho ho! Is that what they say about me? Miss Shippen, you are too kind. The general, Mr. Washington, is a good man. Too fair to have a favorite. I can oblige with my tales though, if you'd like. Which battle would you like to hear about, Miss Shippen?"

"Oh, there are so many from which to choose. Where to begin?" Peggy furrowed her brow as if she were genuinely confounded. "We've been hearing of your bravery at Canada, and then also at Fort Ticonderoga, and of course at Saratoga. I can't pick which one I'd like to hear first."

The general laughed, an unchecked, booming laugh that roared like cannon fire. "How about I regale you with a little bit from each one?"

"Oh, but that would take ages." Judge Shippen rearranged himself in his chair. "How about you pick one, the most riveting story. We would hate to waste too much of your time, General Arnold."

"I've got time, Judge. How about over a jug of ale, shall we say?" Arnold looked to his host. "If I may be so bold as to beg some ale from you? We soldiers don't like telling tales without it." Arnold smiled, an expression of mischievous merriment, and Clara decided that perhaps Benedict Arnold was not entirely unattractive.

"My apologies, Major General, we do not keep ale in the house," the judge replied.

"Not a problem." Arnold whistled, prompting a young, wigged attendant to appear at the parlor doorway. "Franks, you remember Miss Shippen?"

"How do you do, Miss Shippen?" The aide bowed, looking bashfully at Peggy.

"Why, hello, Mr. Franks." Peggy waved to him. "Wonderful to see you again."

"Franks, be a good lad and fetch a jug of ale from the carriage and bring it in here, would you?" Arnold turned back to his host. "I always travel prepared. Another thing that life in the military has taught me." Arnold winked, and if he noticed the judge's anxious expression, he chose to ignore it.

"Miss Shippen, can I tempt you to join me?" Arnold turned to Peggy.

Peggy cast a sideways glance toward her father before turning her attention back on Arnold. "You may tempt me all you like." Her light eyes sparkled. "I'd love to join you in a drink, sir, to toast your brave exploits." Without looking at her maid, Peggy ordered: "Clara, fetch two mugs."

"Just one drink, Peggy, my dear," the judge interjected.

By the time Arnold was done telling about the Battle of Saratoga, the two of them had nearly finished the jug, and Arnold was reclining with a full belly, holding his mug for his dog to lap up the final drops with his tongue.

"You see," Arnold sat back, his left leg outstretched, his voice loud and commanding, "the musket fire from that damned lobsterback soldier in Saratoga had gone right into the old wound in my left leg. The leg which had already been shot in—"

"In Quebec, certainly. The winter's siege of 1776, of course." Peggy completed his sentence, leaning forward past the edge of her seat.

"That's absolutely right." Arnold smiled approvingly at his devoted listener.

"Such pain you must have endured. Please, go on, General."

Arnold lifted his empty mug, examining its emptiness, before continuing. "So now, in Saratoga, this musket bullet lodges right beneath my left knee. They insisted that my life was in peril if they did not amputate."

"Oh my," Peggy gasped, pulling her newly stitched handkerchief to wipe a tear from her cheek.

"Am I upsetting you?" Arnold paused. "I can stop."

"Yes, perhaps she has heard enough," the judge spoke, participating for the first time in what felt to Clara like hours. "It might be prudent to continue this another time."

"Please do not stop!" Peggy leaned forward, her eyes fixed on Arnold. "I must hear the end."

"Such a brave little lady." Arnold nodded his head. "All right, so, while the surgeon removed his tools to saw my left leg off, I ordered my men to fix their muskets on him. I told him, 'Doctor, stop it right there! If I lose my leg, you lose your life.'"

Peggy put a trembling hand to her heart.

"They said I'd never walk again, but"—Arnold paused for full effect—"you see me here today."

"And how happy it makes me to see you here. It's a wonder." Peggy nodded.

"And so, at the end of the day, after our victory at Saratoga we had split up Burgoyne's British army to the north from Howe's British army to the south. And we finally secured the allegiance of the French. And I kept my leg. Not too bad for a day's work, if I do say so myself." Arnold winked, tipping his empty mug to his lips to see whether he might sponge one last drop.

Judge Shippen nodded, satisfied that the tale was complete, and mumbled something about checking on his wife. When Arnold did not take his host's cue, the judge abandoned his hopes of showing the general out, and instead excused himself from the room. Peggy now sat alone with her suitor.

Using her new handkerchief to dab the corners of her eyes, she said, "You must have endured such hardship, General Arnold."

"Miss Shippen, please do not cry."

"Fear not, General, they are merely tears of admiration." Peggy made an elaborate display of fanning out her handkerchief, and Arnold noticed its pattern.

"What a nice handkerchief."

"Oh, this old thing?" Peggy handed it to him and Arnold looked it over, studying Clara's handiwork—the small cluster of stars and the patriotic slogan underneath. "'Don't tread on me,'" Arnold read aloud, a smile spreading across his face. "Well, you are quite the patriot, Miss Shippen."

"I suppose I am." Peggy nodded, lowering her eyes. "I carry it with me, always. I stitched it to resemble Betsy Ross's flag. And you see?" Peggy stood up and did a theatrical twirl, allowing her bright blue dress to flare out to half the size of the parlor. "I wore my blue dress with my red jewels in the hopes that I would remind you of our new flag." Peggy smiled, and Benedict Arnold erupted in laughter.

"Bravo!" Arnold's laughter rumbled up from his broad chest and belly. "I daresay, the most beautiful little patriot in all thirteen colonies."

"If it would please you, I'd ask that you keep my handkerchief." Peggy placed a pale, smooth palm on top of his thick, rough hand, folding it over the white linen. "As a memento, so that perhaps you'll always remember me, and this visit we had together. I know I will cherish the memory always."

"I cannot take this from you."

"Why ever not? I'll stitch another. I'm always stitching; I can't stand for my hands to be idle," Peggy said.

"Well, then, I will keep the handkerchief, of course. But please know that even without it, I would never forget the sweet memories of this visit. Not even if I lived for a thousand years."

Peggy averted her eyes to the wooden floor, blinking with chaste humility as she spoke. "Oh, sir, you are too kind. I don't know what I did that I should be so honored with both your visit *and* your kind words."

"You have made me feel so welcome in Philadelphia. And I am so encouraged by your show of patriotism. It gives me hope in the cause." Arnold sat back, massaging his left knee.

"Are you enjoying Philadelphia, sir?" Peggy finished off the last of the ale by pouring it in his mug.

"Very much." Arnold took a sip.

"And the Penn mansion?"

"Oh, it's very comfortable. Though awfully big for just me."

Peggy nodded. "I'd never had the pleasure of setting foot inside before last night's party. That awful British general who occupied it before you, what was his name? Howell?"

"Howe." Arnold corrected her.

"Oh, yes, Howe. Now I remember." Peggy shrugged her shoulders. "Not that memorable, I suppose." The two of them shared a laugh. "Well, he was in there before you, and he never invited us poor Philadelphians into his home."

"He didn't understand the people. Wasn't one of 'em, the way I am."

"How I admire your humility." Peggy smiled. "Speaking of the people," she continued, "it's been quite hard for all of us, not having any stores opened in Philadelphia."

"Oh, I plan to reopen them." Arnold waved his hand nonchalantly as he smacked the cork stopper back into the neck of the empty ale jug. "We just had to close them for a bit while we did inventory. All those goods were shipped from England, you see. We didn't want to be sending any more profits back for the Crown's enrichment. Not when they're trying to kill us all."

"Well, where did everything go?" Peggy asked. "All those beautiful petticoats, and clocks, and china, and mahogany furniture. I hope you didn't destroy it all."

"No, my lady! We would never destroy such valuable items. We have them all safe and sound." And then Arnold was struck by an idea, an idea he thought had originated in his own mind, even though Clara knew otherwise.

Arnold smiled as he asked, "Miss Shippen, would you like to see the goods?"

"IT'S NOT right. Something about it does not seem right." Clara stepped into the quiet kitchen, muttering to herself as she searched out a late lunch. "Oh!" She started when she saw Caleb, hands stained bloodred beside the stove. "Caleb, what in heavens' name are you doing?"

"Hello, Clara Bell. I didn't mean to give you a fright." He chuckled to himself, holding up his hands. "What does it look like I'm doing? Stewing cherries for Hannah, for the preserves. You'll thank me when we have jam this winter."

"I see." Clara nodded, walking farther into the kitchen and removing a piece of brown wax paper from atop a half-eaten pigeon pie.

"That is one of Hannah's tastiest dishes. You should have a slice." Caleb watched her as he worked. "Where were you during luncheon?"

Clara wanted to tell someone, but she hesitated, pondering how much to divulge about how she'd spent the past hour. "Well, why should I tell you? You who seems to know everything, anyway."

"I suppose I deserve that." Cal wiped his hands and placed down the rag, approaching Clara. "I've been trying to apologize to you for days, Clara Bell."

She fixed her gaze on the far side of the room, avoiding his eyes.

"But you've been avoiding me."

Now she looked up at him, his hazel eyes close to hers. She sighed, feeling her anger with him lessen. "I'm *not* sweet on Robert Balmor."

"I know you're not." His tone was soft now, his eyes earnest.

"And I'm sorry I gave you a hard time about it. It was just that I was . . ." His voice trailed off. "Well, never mind it now. It's in the past." His hand went to her arm and rested there, a gentle pressure. "Now will you tell me what's got you so upset?"

She nodded. She did wish to tell someone. "Cal, I've been helping Miss Peggy sort her pile of gifts." She served herself a slice of the pie and sat down at the table.

"And these gifts wouldn't happen to be from a certain General Benedict Arnold?" Caleb leaned on the table beside her. "I saw her ride off with Mr. Big Britches himself this morning, shortly after she received a visit from him."

Clara nodded, telling Cal all that Miss Peggy had told her about this morning's errand to Benedict Arnold's home.

"Well, are you certain that Miss Peggy saw it correctly?" Caleb had turned back to the fruit preserves, his face serious as he questioned her.

"How could she see anything other than what was there?" Clara asked, serving herself a second piece of the pie. "She described row after row of confiscated merchandise."

Caleb thought about this. "The goods must have been taken from Philadelphia's stores when Arnold and his men declared martial law and closed them."

"I'm telling you, she described tables, chairs, dishes, chandeliers, foodstuff. And the dresses, you would not believe the dresses she returned home with. I thought Miss Peggy's eyes were going to pop clear out of her head."

"Where is Arnold keeping all of these goods?" Caleb asked.

"The alley behind the Penn mansion," Clara said, her mouth full of food.

Caleb nodded.

"The way Miss Peggy spoke of it, it seems all of the goods are sprawled out back there. Wagons and wagons full of clothing, shoes, household wares. All of Philadelphia's wealth, right there behind his home."

"What could he be planning to do with all them goods?" Caleb asked.

"Give them all as gifts to Miss Peggy, from the sound of it." Clara poured herself a mug of cider. "A drink?"

Caleb nodded, wiping his hands on the soiled rag. "But he can't simply be planning to give them all as gifts. Not with that many goods." Caleb sat opposite Clara, thinking for several moments before answering. "Arnold must be planning to sell them."

This triggered a thought. Clara frowned, sliding a full mug toward Cal. "You know the British china merchant? That Joseph Stansbury?"

Caleb nodded. "Miss Peggy's friend."

"The other night at the party, when Miss Peggy met General Arnold, I overheard Christianne Amile telling Miss Peggy something interesting." Clara considered what she was about to say before continuing. "Miss Peggy asked why Stansbury was absent. Christianne answered that Stansbury was in New York. She said that General Arnold had that china merchant conducting business for him up there."

Caleb narrowed his eyes as he looked at Clara. "But New York is enemy territory. Arnold would have to write a pass to allow Stansbury to cross enemy lines into New York."

"Would the military commander of Philadelphia have that power?" Clara asked.

Caleb sighed, nodding. "Arnold is selling the confiscated goods in New York. And he's using the merchant to do it for him." He thought about this, his brow knit together. "I can't believe Arnold would do it."

They sat across from each other in thoughtful silence, Clara sipping her drink. Caleb spoke first. "He *is* always complaining about how the Continental Congress owes him thousands. Why, Arnold has railed against the Congress for years, griping about their debt to him. Guess they never reimbursed him after he fed and quartered his men in Quebec for the entire winter of 'seventy-six. And after he lost a leg for them."

"Yes, but to take your money back in such a dishonest way?" Clara frowned.

"Lots of 'em dabble in the black market, I suppose. You saw the cartload full of goods André left town with."

Clara's eyes widened. "But I never exactly thought of Major André as a pillar of virtue."

"But he's not the only one who does it." Caleb rubbed his chin with his fingers.

Clara sighed, her mood hardly lifted by this conversation.

"He'll get found out. Sooner or later." Caleb gripped his mug of ale.

"I don't think so." Clara shook her head. "Who would dare stop Arnold? He's beloved by the whole city, the whole thirteen colonies."

"I'll tell you who—that Joseph Reed," Caleb answered. Clara's mind went back to the evening of the party at the Penn mansion, and the plainly dressed couple standing alone in the corner, scowling at their host. Miss Peggy had spoken of Joseph and Blanche Reed with such disdain.

Clara's mind was trying to make sense of this. "But how is Joseph Reed in a position to stop Benedict Arnold from selling Philadelphia's confiscated goods?"

"Clara, don't you read the papers?" Cal was grinning at her. "Joseph Reed has been named governor of Pennsylvania."

"But I thought Arnold was already governor?" Clara wondered aloud.

"Arnold is military governor of Philadelphia. He runs the army here. But Joseph Reed is the governor of Pennsylvania's Executive Council."

"So, aren't they on the same side, then?" Clara asked.

"Oh, sweet Clara Bell." Cal eyed her in a quizzical way, as if trying to prevent some deeper emotion from spilling through his playful, hazel eyes. Clara shifted in her seat.

"What, Caleb? Why are you looking at me like that?" She broke his eye contact, trying to dispel the awkwardness she felt at the intensity of his stare. "Anyhow, aren't Arnold and Reed on the same side?"

He blinked, and he was calm, lighthearted Cal once more. "That's what you would think. But when you're in a position of power, your friends can become more dangerous than your enemies."

"Meaning?" Clara asked.

"Meaning Joseph Reed and Benedict Arnold are bitter rivals."

Peggy would be so thrilled to hear it.

"CLARA, CAN you believe how much he sent me back with?" Peggy was a woman possessed, her spirits soaring higher than Clara had seen in months. "Come in!" She pranced around the bedroom, sorting and re-sorting the piles of new gowns, hoopskirts, jewelry, ribbons, and shoes. All the goods Arnold had stacked into the carriage and sent back to the Shippen household from his back-alley cache.

"I thought we had put them all away." Clara eyed the mess

sprawled across her lady's bedchamber, shoulders sagging at her work being undone.

"Oh, but I wanted to see them again," Peggy sighed, enfolding herself in a shawl of feather-light cherry silk. "Betsy is going to be so jealous. Why, not even John André could have provided me with such fine clothing."

"You have so much, perhaps you might share some of it with Miss Betsy." Clara scooped up a pair of satin shoes from the crowded rug.

"Perhaps." Peggy considered the suggestion. "If I find something I don't like. You're so kind, Clara."

Clara didn't respond as she deposited the shoes back in Peggy's armoire.

"Arnold must be the richest man in Philadelphia." Peggy spoke in a singsong manner, fiddling with the shawl before the mirror. "Will there even be enough parties to wear all these gowns to?"

Clara removed an emerald gown from the bed and hung it in the wardrobe.

"I'll just have to tell Arnold to host lots of balls at the Penn mansion." Picking up a lightweight salmon skirt, Peggy went twirling in a circle until she fell to the ground, melting into a pile of clothing. "Can't you just imagine it, Clara? Little old me—presiding over galas in the Penn mansion! Lady of the house . . ." Peggy's mind raced forward into her fantasy, and she fell so deeply into the imaginary scene that she forgot the words necessary to narrate it.

The gifts kept coming all throughout the summer. Each time Benedict Arnold came calling, accompanied by his dog Barley, he'd appear with a treat. Sometimes it was a bottle of Champagne, sometimes it was a new hat in the latest style being modeled in Europe. Sometimes it was an invitation to a dinner party or card game at his home. He never showed up empty-handed, and Peggy never failed to greet him with her most effusive praise, her most appreciative smile.

Peggy no longer complained to her father that she was hungry or tired of the food that Hannah cooked. She ate with Arnold at least once a day, taking either luncheon or dinner with him, if not both.

"Clara, you won't believe how much I ate today." Peggy had just returned one stifling afternoon in late summer, demanding that her maid unfasten her corset. "I'm going to burst. We started with baked sole and beef fillets with morels and truffles, followed by goose and peas and roasted duck. Next we had gooseberry tart, sweetbreads, plum pudding, fruit and nuts. And Champagne—a Champagne refill with every course!" Peggy let out a long belch. "Arnold told his footmen to make sure that my glass was never empty."

"That sounds lovely, miss." Clara pulled on the stays to loosen them, thinking hungrily of the feast her mistress described. How Clara would have loved to savor a bite of beef fillet. Still, she and the entire Shippen household had no reason to complain of hunger. Even though most of their luncheons were made up of salt fish these days, it was better than their countrymen who lived outside the city—starving and struggling to stay fed on what they could forage or hunt. Some of them, Cal said, would have considered squirrel meat a feast.

"I must watch myself or I might get fat under Arnold's constant indulgences." Peggy stepped out of her corset and looked approvingly at her now revealed figure in the mirror opposite her. It was true that she had regained the soft curves that she had lost after André's departure; her waist still thinned to a narrow middle, but beneath it and above it, her hips and bust had bloomed outward into a full, feminine silhouette.

"Though Arnold tells me that I'm perfect just as I am." Peggy flopped onto her featherbed, and before Clara had finished removing her shoes, she was snoring in a heavy, feast-induced stupor.

In addition to filling Peggy's stomach with endless meals and bubbling Champagne, Benedict Arnold stopped by the Shippen home regularly that summer, paying his respects to Judge and Mrs. Shippen and inviting Peggy on a steady parade of outings. Whereas André had wooed her with the chivalry of a man visiting a brothel—luring Peggy away from soirees for clandestine midnight meetings—Arnold wooed Peggy in the broad daylight of his good and honest intentions. Clara noticed, with relief, that her mistress responded in kind. Peggy now behaved like a genteel belle of unimpeachable virtue. Arnold seemed to take pleasure in spoiling Peggy, and she showed her delight generously and gratefully. He took her to the theater, and for picnics along the Schuylkill River, and gave dinner parties with her as his hostess whenever an honorary came to town. On such occasions, Peggy would fill the home with her beautiful companions—inviting her sister, and Meg Chew, and Christianne Amile, and Becky Redman. In the past, Peggy would not have allowed her rivals to get so close to the man she had set her sights on. But Clara knew—as she watched Peggy adjust Arnold's cravat, feed him tasty morsels of gooseberry tart, sit on his knee and light his pipe for him—that this time around, Peggy Shippen felt absolutely no threat. She held Benedict Arnold's generous heart in her fair, soft little hand and she, and everyone around her, knew it.

It was a Saturday afternoon in late August. Arnold was driving Peggy and Clara back to the Shippen home in his spacious carriage.

He'd taken his lady and her parents to a matinee comedy, the subject of which was a very blind King George III requiring all sorts of assistance to help him read the Declaration of Independence. Halfway through the performance, Mrs. Shippen had complained that her headache had grown too severe as to allow her to enjoy the performance, and her husband had asked Caleb to escort them home. This left Peggy and her maid to be delivered home in Arnold's carriage, a responsibility Arnold had happily accepted.

Though she and Cal had watched the show from the rear of the theater, like the other servants, Clara had enjoyed herself that afternoon. She had never been to a play before, and she found it amusing how the men jostled about in costumes and masks on stage. Arnold and Peggy, however, had left the theater in foul spirits. "The signing of the Declaration of Independence—it's the moment of this fight for liberty that people will always remember." Arnold sat beside Peggy in the carriage, his brow stitched in a tight knot. "Jefferson and Adams always get all the credit. You know why I wasn't present when they signed the Declaration of Independence?" Arnold looked up to Peggy.

"Why, my love?" Peggy asked, her voice gentle.

"I was defending Fort Ticonderoga. And Lake Champlain. Someone had to be there, or else Burgoyne and his entire army would have streamed down from Canada and ended our war for liberty before it had even started. There would have been no Declaration of Independence if not for me!"

"Yours was a far nobler pursuit, my dear Benny." Peggy comforted Arnold with a light pat of her hand. "With what you've suffered for the cause, you are entitled to a large share in the glory."

But Arnold did not appear consoled. "Did I not deserve to be there? To have my name memorialized on that document?" Arnold's features screwed up in a frustration that he'd never before shown in Peggy's presence. "Instead, I'm here in Philadelphia three years too late. And putting up with that snake, Reed, besmirching my name at every dinner party he attends."

"Well, of course you deserved to be there for the signing," Peggy answered, cowed by Arnold's nasty mood. "But no one shall ever remember their names—all crowded on that piece of paper like lines of a child's scribble. But yours, Benedict Arnold, yours is a name which shall be remembered by history. You mark my words, dearest."

Arnold thought about this in silence, wincing and clutching his leg protectively as the carriage jostled over the cobblestones of Fourth Street. Finally, he looked up and answered. "You are right, my sweet Peg." He nodded, his melancholy evaporating under her attention. "You are my angel, always here to point out the good." He placed a soft kiss on her cheek, which she received with an adoring smile.

"Ugh," Peggy gasped.

"What?" Arnold looked at her, his face growing concerned.

"Look who it is," Peggy answered, her voice now with an edge to it. They pulled up alongside a carriage, plainer and smaller than Arnold's, and Clara detected the familiar, oval face.

"Joseph Reed." Arnold lowered his voice to a menacing snarl.

"Everything about that man is dull. Even his carriage." Peggy watched the man, her expression as taut as if she'd just drunk from a bitter draft. Reed, for his part, had not yet noticed Arnold's carriage beside his.

"Well, of course. Because he's so frugal and honorable, right?" Arnold's tone dripped with contempt. "Above reproach, that Joseph Reed. All he cares about is his country. Joseph Reed is a man without vice, didn't you know, Peg?"

"I can't stand to look at him. That long, pale *moonface*!" And then, Clara noticed, a sly smirk began to spread across the features of her mistress's face.

"Benny, I think I have an idea. A way to show Mr. *Moonface* just how highly we think of him."

Arnold looked from Reed to Peggy. "What's that?"

Peggy cocked her head, leaning close and whispering something into her suitor's ear.

"Ah! Ha ha ha! Peggy, you're terrible." Arnold's thunderous laughter shook the carriage.

To the groom, Peggy called out: "Keep apace with Reed's carriage." Turning back to Arnold now, Peggy snickered. "Do it, Benny, hurry!"

And to Clara's utter mortification, she watched in frozen horror as the commander of the Philadelphia army pulled himself to a stand in his carriage, bent over, and pulled his breeches down. When Reed did suddenly notice the carriage lingering beside his, with the military commander of Philadelphia fully exposed before him, the look of horror only prompted Peggy into further hysterics.

SUMMER STRETCHED on in Philadelphia, the sun's rays warming the Schuylkill River and promising a good harvest of the farmland around the city, and a tenuous period of truce reigned in the Shippen home. Mrs Shippen and Betsy were so busy planning Betsy's December wedding that they paid little attention to Peggy's routine, nor did they notice when she stayed out later than perhaps was prudent. Judge Shippen, though not pleased with his young daughter's budding relationship with the city's much-older commander, at least seemed resigned to the courtship. His daughter had finally stopped complaining about the scarcity of food and wine on their table and the absence of new silk in her wardrobe.

As the days shortened and crisp, clear air settled in around them, carrying with it the first hints of the coming autumn, Clara found herself starting to feel at home for the first time since she'd arrived at the Shippen home. Peggy was happy, and thus treated Clara kindly. Betsy was equally happy, visiting with Neddy Burd and planning for a life after the wedding. Mr. and Mrs. Quigley seemed satisfied with the work Clara was doing—guiding her with a gentle firmness and giving her plenty of opportunity to help in the home. Hannah, it seemed, had come to appreciate Clara's constant company in the kitchen, and had taken to saving her extra-large pieces of pie for dessert. "We need to fatten you up, girl. Didn't they feed you on that farm?"

Her only complaint that autumn was the absence of Cal. The cooler weather brought with it plenty of new work for him, often drawing him out of doors and away from the Shippen home for days at a time. She'd watch him return to the kitchen late at night, sleeves rolled up and glistening with sweat after long days outside. He had a winter's worth of firewood to collect from the nearby woods, a smokehouse and root cellar to stock, and the raking to complete, not to mention his regular work as a horse groom and footman. When those chores were done, he'd turn next to the apple harvest.

Clara begged Caleb to let her help with this last job. "I worked outdoors at the farm. And besides, Peggy barely needs me now that she spends entire afternoons with Arnold," she'd coaxed as Caleb had wiped his brow, nearly collapsing at the servants' dinner table at the end of a particularly long day. He'd finally acquiesced, enlisting her help in picking the apples that grew in the Shippens' small orchard. They made an efficient team, working side by side with stretches of laughter and stretches of amicable silence. He'd prop the ladder and climb high into the trees, tossing down apples. She'd catch them, deposit them into brimming barrels, and deliver the haul to Hannah for fresh applesauce, apple butter, apple bread, and apple tarts. Clara loved the afternoons in the golden sun of late autumn. When they'd take breaks, Caleb would sit on a low branch and strum his guitar while she, propped up against the trunk of the tree, would eat apples until she grew full and sleepy. The evenings in the kitchen were just as pleasant, as she'd sit at the table playing cards with the rest of the servants and take greedy inhalations of the air, heavy with the aroma of the cooking fruit.

Caleb was different from the Quigleys, or Hannah and Brigitte. He was a friend, perhaps the first close friend she'd ever had. And certainly the first boy she'd ever been close to. She noticed herself looking forward to meeting Caleb in the kitchen at mealtimes, or in the evenings at the end of their days. He'd always ask her how her day with Miss Peggy had gone, and he'd listen intently as she'd describe the list of activities they'd completed. He would fill her in on the progress he'd made in the smoking of the meat or winterizing the barns.

Sometimes, at the end of a long evening of good-natured chatter beside the hearth, Clara would leave Caleb to retire to her bedroom and she'd find, to her surprise, that his presence lingered with her even after they'd parted ways. She often spent nights, after her prayers were completed, lying in bed and replaying the conversations she'd had with Cal. Wondering about Cal. Did he think of her as often as she thought of him? But always, these daydreams about Cal were accompanied by Oma's stern warnings: boys only brought trouble. For Clara, the most important thing to do was to work hard and keep her employers happy. She reminded herself of this each morning as she rose from bed, scolding herself for the fact that he was often the first person she thought of.

And her hard work seemed to be noticed by all whom she served. Even General Arnold had come to enjoy Clara's presence in his life, it seemed. When he'd send Major Franks over in a carriage laden with gifts for Peggy, he'd always include something extra for Clara: a small jewel, a vial of cordial, or a silk sash. To Clara's surprise, Peggy wasn't jealous of the gifts her beau bestowed on her maid—it actually brought a smile to her face.

"He's a smart man, my Benny. He knows the strategy of a siege: you must win the support of the locals. The way to victory in conquering a maiden's heart is by winning over her maid."

THE COOLER weather brought with it news from Europe that seemed to cheer everyone in the colonies, including General Washington himself.

"Spain has joined France in supporting our war for freedom!" Caleb rushed, breathless, into the kitchen, waving a discarded newspaper. All the servants paused their morning chores. Even Brigitte looked up from her sweeping to listen.

"'The declaration of Spain in favor of France has given universal joy,'" George Washington was quoted as saying in the *Pennsylvania Packet*. "'The poor Tory droops like a withering flower under a declining sun.'"

And yet, there was one Tory who did not appear to be withering, but rather seemed to be blooming before Clara's eyes.

"A splendid day for a picnic." Peggy looked out her bedroom window as Arnold's carriage halted on the cobblestone street below. The door opened and Barley the dog hopped out, followed by Arnold's hulking frame, tenuously supported by his jeweled cane.

"His leg continues to worsen," Peggy observed, her shoulders dropping. "He can barely walk."

For their picnic, they chose a meadow of sun-warmed grass beneath a willow on the bank of the Schuykill, a half hour's ride out of the city. Clara stepped out of the carriage, carrying the picnic hamper, and admired the spot. Their view along the river looked directly across at Mount Pleasant, one of Pennsylvania's largest mansions.

The mansion had been constructed in the fashionable Georgian style and was made up of white and red brick. Rows of clean windows pierced its façade, including a grand picture window in the middle over the front door. Atop the house was a rooftop balcony, and Clara imagined sitting up there on a pleasant night, looking down on the shimmering surface of the Schuylkill. The leaves on the surrounding trees had just begun to change color, and the tapestry of rich amber, bright yellow, and deep burgundy surrounded the mansion. Somewhere in the distance, a fire warmed a farmer's cottage, filling the meadow with the welcoming scent of the cozy hearth.

Arnold had prepared a hamper full of apples, goat's milk cheese, bread, marmalade, wine, and grapes for the occasion. Clara had slipped into invisibility, as she always did when Arnold and Peggy became consumed with each other. As she spread the blanket out on the grass, her thoughts turned to Cal, and how nice it would be for them to take such a picnic as this one. It wasn't until she noticed Barley nosing his way into the food hamper that Clara came back to herself.

"How about some wine, Clara?" Peggy sat on the blanket, adjusting her straw hat to shield her eyes from the sun.

"To your health, madame. You look fairer today than you've ever looked before." Arnold kissed Peggy's cheek, clinking her wineglass against his own. Her coral gown was the perfect complement to the shades tinting the leaves on the trees, and her cheeks had a rosy hue from the gentle breeze.

"Benny, you say that every day." Peggy took a sip of her wine.

"Because it's true, Peg—every day that I see you, you are prettier than the day before."

Peggy smiled, feeding herself a slice of apple. "You seem nervous today." She looked at him, watching him drain a full glass of wine. He gestured toward Clara for a refill.

"Please don't drink too much wine, Benny."

"Why not?" Arnold asked, his face wounded.

"Because you'll fall asleep in the middle of our picnic," Peggy answered, handing the wine bottle to Clara. "Put that back in the hamper."

"Can't I take a nap beside you?" Arnold asked, frowning as the maid tucked the wine out of sight.

"No, that's not fun for me," Peggy answered, her tone flat. Arnold put his glass down, picking at a piece of bread. They ate in silence for several minutes before Arnold spoke again.

"I suppose I'm nervous because . . . well, because there's something I'd like to discuss with you." Arnold looked at the river, at the dog, everywhere but at Peggy. Clara took several steps away from their picnic blanket, a swell of discomfort rising within her as she sensed the serious nature of the conversation.

"Miss Shippen, I think it's apparent that I feel a great . . . affection . . . for you. A feeling which, I confess, sometimes I allow myself to indulge in. In my daydreams, sometimes I allow myself to wonder—could a woman of your beauty, your spirit, your kindness, ever feel this way in return for me?"

Peggy looked him squarely in the face, blinking as she answered, matter-of-factly. "Yes."

Arnold was stunned and lost the words with which he had intended to continue. "I . . . I . . . I beg your pardon?"

"Benedict Arnold, I could be in love with you, yes." Peggy swatted a fly, her curls bouncing under her bonnet as she ducked her head. "Of course I could be in love with you. But I'm not. At least, not yet."

His face did not clearly spell his emotions—was he hopeful? Discouraged? Clara could not tell, most likely because he himself did not know what to make of Peggy's stony declaration. "These things take time, I realize that. It only makes me appreciate you more, Peg, that you are allowing your feelings to progress in a modest and natural way. It speaks of a genuine attachment, not some passing fancy."

"Well, it's not just that I want to take things slowly," Peggy answered, her tone dry. She was usually all affection and playfulness with Arnold; right now, Clara noted, she seemed crisper than the autumn air. "There's something else."

"What is it, my love?" He leaned toward her, his face heavy with yearning. "Please just tell me what it is, and I will do it. If you require me to run to the moon to prove my love, it is not a task too large."

Peggy arched her eyebrows. "You will not be *running* anywhere, Benny, we both know that."

Arnold stiffened his posture. "There is nothing I wouldn't do to prove my devotion. And win yours in return."

Peggy looked dreamily out over the river. Her reticence only seemed to further agitate her suitor.

"Well? What is it? In what way am I deficient?" Arnold asked. The skin where his whiskers sprouted from his cheeks flushed a deep red. "I am sure that, whatever it is, a remedy exists."

Peggy glanced back to meet Arnold's eye. "I so love to dance. I can't imagine myself marrying someone who couldn't dance with me."

Clara felt that the slightest breeze could have knocked her flat on her back. Arnold had just finished professing his ardent devotion to Peggy, and she had answered him by telling him that she loved to *dance*?

Clara wished that Cal had been there to witness the scene, for she felt certain that he would never believe her. Here was a man who had spent the past six months courting her mistress—feeding her, spoiling her with gifts, giving her whatever she desired—and Peggy was sitting opposite him, finding fault with the fact that he had been crippled while serving his country?

Clara was tempted to stare, open-mouthed, just as Arnold was doing, but she concealed her amazement, pretending instead to be distracted with throwing a stick for Barley.

"Benny, it's one thing that you're so much older than me; that fact we cannot change. But to think that you might not be able to keep up with me, not for a lack of energy, but because of your *condition*." Peggy jerked her chin down toward Arnold's left leg, which was extended on the blanket. "I suppose I have always maintained hope, ever since I met you, that perhaps you could grow stronger, and heal. Reteach yourself to walk, my love, and then I would reconsider your offer."

For once, Benedict Arnold seemed to see Peggy Shippen's behavior for what it was, and not through the glossy sheen of love and admiration by which he'd been dazzled. The look on his face shifted, Clara saw. The hopeful and besotted suitor now appeared as a tired old man, stunned and offended.

"I think the picnic is over," Arnold answered. And from the silent tension that hung in the carriage throughout the ride back to the Shippen home, Clara deduced that her mistress had finally found the boundary of male indulgence.

V.

I hear General Washington and his party arrive at the front.

"Anyone else fancy a bite to eat?" When Washington speaks to his officers and attendants, it is all casual camaraderie. Yet it is visible in their expressions, their movements, their attentiveness—they revere him as a god among men. As he crosses from the horse post to the house, his party moves with him like a school of fish guided in perfect unison.

George Washington is as the newspapers say he is: "always the tallest man in his company." He removes his tricornered hat, yet still he must bend as he passes through the doorway so as to avoid grazing the crown of his head.

"Mrs. Arnold will be right down," I say, with a quick curtsy. To my shock, he stares me broadly in the face as he replies: "Thank you, young lady." He has a deep voice and an open, friendly manner about him that soften the impact made by his imposing figure and his formal military regalia. He is dressed in a uniform coat of a deep navy blue with gold buttons and cuffs. Epaulets of gold satin and fringe rest atop his broad shoulders, enhancing their already wide appearance. Under the military jacket is a snugly tailored vest of white and breeches of nankeen. A light blue sash crosses from his right shoulder to the left side of his waist, and a neckerchief conceals his thick neck. Leather riding boots with spurs climb over thick calves until they reach his knees. He seems to take up half of the space in the drawing room as he looks around approvingly.

We all hear the footsteps at the same time and turn to see my lady descending the stairs.

"General Washington!" Her voice is sweetened with the tones of pure delight, as if seeing him is the high point of her year. My lady's attire is unusually casual, but he does not know this—he probably credits the abnormally warm September weather. She wears a cool dress of white linen with lace detailing at the sleeves and collar. A sash of light blue, stitched with pink and yellow flowers, ties snugly around her waist, showcasing her famous figure. Her blond hair is not piled high on her head, but in a loose chignon bun that rests on the nape of her neck. She looks early-morning fresh, unblemished, excruciatingly beautiful. You'd never know that inside she teems with anxiety and anger.

"It is the legendary Mrs. Arnold." Washington and his men bow deeply upon her entrance. She extends her hand for a kiss from the general.

"I must confess, my lady, my men were worried about being late this morning only because they didn't want to keep the charming Mrs. Arnold waiting."

She laughs, and for the first time I see that her gestures are labored, forced. But Washington suspects nothing; for even now, Mrs. Arnold still shines brighter than most women.

"I think they are all half in love with you." Washington offers the compliment with a gallant smile.

"Oh, I'm sure it's not true." She clutches her side, takes a moment to collect herself, and then walks toward the dining room. They follow her.

When she speaks again, her voice is cool, calm. "General Washington, Excellency, I must make apologies for my husband. Major General Arnold is not here this morning because he is preparing a grand reception for you over at West Point."

"Is that right? It's very kind, but surely not necessary. His presence at breakfast would have been all the reception I needed."

"Yes, well." She tries to smile, but her frailty is obvious. At this point, General Washington takes note.

"My lady, are you well?"

"Oh." She manages a smile. "With the little one consuming all of my energy . . . I'm afraid I'm left with very little with which to entertain. It's nothing—simply what ails all new mothers. I'm quite all right, thank you." She ushers them toward the dining room table, which is spread with two loaves of bread, slices of ham, bowls of fresh cream, sliced peaches, a pot of tea, and a pitcher of ale.

They sit at the table, with Washington at one end and my lady at the other. Their chatter is boisterous and merry, with all of them vying for their hostess's attention. Washington likes to laugh loudly and often, and his aide Alexander Hamilton appears well-practiced in soliciting his general's merriment.

As I'm refreshing the men's ale mugs, a messenger comes in. He wears the same ragged uniform as the man who delivered the fateful message to Arnold hours earlier, as well as the same harried, exhausted expression. My hands begin to tremble, rattling the pitcher of ale.

"Yes, come in," my mistress says, her voice smooth like syrup, her face betraying not the slightest concern. "Marquis de Lafayette, more peaches?" She doesn't look in the direction of the messenger as he hastily hands General Washington the letter. I pour the ale, trying to steady my hands.

"Where do you come from?" the general asks the messenger.

"North Castle, sir," the messenger says. "On an urgent errand from Colonel Jameson, Your Excellency."

"What is Jameson up to that can't wait until I've finished tasting Mrs. Arnold's delectable peaches?" Washington quips good-naturedly, but he opens the envelope.

It's the general's quick gasp that pulls all our eyes to him. The letter quavers like a wind-blown leaf in his hands, and over the letter appears his face, now drained of all color.

"He has betrayed us. Benedict Arnold has betrayed us." Washington says it with quiet incredulity. "If not him, then in whom can we trust?" My eyes, like all those in the room, stare into the beautiful face of my mistress.

I see, as the men do, the panic, the bewilderment and despair of a woman who has just found out that her husband is a traitor. I see all that, but I also see something they do not; I see that the pain she shows is nothing more than a mask. A painfully beautiful mask.

CHAPTER FIVE

"Stuck in the Mud"

November 1778
Philadelphia, PA

I'VE RUINED *everything*!" Peggy was inconsolable. "I took an incredible risk, saying what I said. I knew it was hazardous . . . that he might take it the wrong way. But I thought his affection for me was strong enough that it would sustain such a blow. Oh, it was so foolish."

Peggy cried to Stansbury in the window seat of her home's front hall, keeping her voice low so that her mother and sister, sitting in the parlor across from them, would not hear. The view onto the busy street only seemed to deepen Peggy's melancholy, for none of the carriages that passed belonged to Arnold.

"It's so unlike you, Peg, to make such a misstep." Stansbury mirrored her quiet tones as he looked through the window at the cold drizzle. "And you were so close to attaining your prize."

Peggy nodded.

"Why did you offend him like that?" Stansbury asked, taking a cup of tea from Clara. "Bring me some sugar," he ordered the maid, without glancing in Clara's direction.

"Because it's the *truth*! I do want him to heal, to reteach himself how to walk. I don't want to marry a cripple." Peggy wiped her wet nose on the back of her palm.

Since the afternoon of their picnic, Arnold had not visited the Shippen home. He had sent no gifts, no letters, no invitations. At first, Peggy comforted herself with the idea that Arnold's pride had been wounded, but his affections remained as they had been. Days passed, threading together to form weeks. Finally, when the weeks had stretched to a full month's time, and Arnold's carriage still had not appeared through the window of her bedroom, Peggy began to lose hope. It was now just under two months until her sister's wedding, and Peggy was predicting—for the first time in her life—that she herself would end up unwed, an old maid.

That gray afternoon, a bundled and blanketed Judge Shippen sat in his armchair in the parlor, reading a thick book in determined silence. Beside him sat his wife. Mrs. Shippen and Betsy spent most of their free time stitching, working feverishly on the linens for Betsy's trousseau that had to be ready for her Christmas wedding. On this chilly day, the only other visitor to appear at the Shippen door was Christianne Amile, who had come over to help Betsy sew. Having received a perfunctory greeting from a still-sulking Peggy, Christianne entered the parlor and took a seat beside Betsy in front of the fire. The afternoon was damp, and the two girls asked Clara to bring them warm cider to keep their fingers nimble as they sewed. The more Betsy and Christianne drank, the bolder they became, exchanging horror stories they'd heard from other women about their wedding nights.

"My mother tells me that she hid under the bed on her wedding night," Christianne whispered to Betsy, her tongue loosened by several mugs of mulled cider.

"I cannot blame her, after what I've heard about wedding nights," Betsy replied, giggling.

"Elizabeth Shippen, mind your manners and remember that you are a lady." Mrs. Shippen threw a barbed look at her daughter from where she sat, stitching in an armchair.

"Yes, Mother," Betsy assented, momentarily halting her giggles.

"Clara?" Peggy called from her perch in the front hall. Peggy, uninterested in sewing, had sought privacy across the hall with Joseph Stansbury, and she sat there now as the china merchant tried to console her.

"Yes, Miss Peggy?" Clara paused before them.

"Have any letters come for me today?"

"I'm sorry, no, Miss Peggy."

Peggy's shoulders dropped.

"More cider, please, Clara!" Betsy called from the other room.

"And where's my sugar?" Stansbury asked, gesturing toward his waiting teacup, as if sugar were easy to come by these days.

"Oh, Stan, we don't have any sugar. Not since Arnold stopped—" but Peggy didn't finish her thought before she pressed her forehead against the cold glass of the window, crying once more.

"Don't." Stansbury put a hand on Peggy's shoulder. "More cream, then." He looked at Clara.

"Right away." Clara curtsied and excused herself.

"I think Miss Peggy actually possesses genuine feelings for Benedict Arnold," Clara said, stepping into the kitchen to refill the family's mugs of cider. It was warm in there, and Cal was nibbling on a piece of Hannah's fresh-baked pumpkin bread. Clara longed to take a seat beside him rather than return to the front of the house with its damp drafts and glum faces.

"Is it possible, Clara Bell? Can she feel real emotions?" Caleb teased her, placing his fork down and refilling the cups Clara handed him.

"Caleb, I really believe she does." Clara nodded. "And I need more cream too, for the merchant. And a bite of that pumpkin bread."

"Of course you do." Caleb handed her a sliver of bread, flashing a half grin that he sometimes fixed on her when they were alone.

"The two of you plan to eat all that pumpkin bread before the family's had any?" Hannah hollered at them from the corner where she stood, spreading the pumpkin seeds on a rack for roasting.

"I mean it, though." Clara finished her thought, her mouth full. "I believe Miss Peggy has fallen for Arnold."

"Sweet, innocent Clara Bell sees only the best in others." She didn't know why, but the way Cal looked at her as he said it made her blush. Taking the cider and the cream saucer, she went back out into the front of the house.

Clara found Miss Peggy where she had left her, Stansbury holding her hand in his own as she stared forlornly out the window. "Can you write to him, Peg?" He was the only person who had not yet tired of Peggy's perpetual gloom.

"I suppose," Peggy answered, blowing her nose in one of the dozen "Don't Tread On Me" handkerchiefs she'd had Clara stitch for her. "But is that unbecoming? Won't that make me appear desperate?"

Clara delivered the cream to Stansbury and entered the parlor with the cider mugs. In spite of her faith in the genuine nature of Miss Peggy's affection for Arnold, Clara nevertheless felt that her mistress deserved the punishment she was enduring. Hadn't she always complained to Caleb about how Peggy Shippen had reduced Benedict Arnold, a war hero, to a groveling fool at her feet? And hadn't Peggy met Arnold's declaration of love with a cold, flat statement that she could not love a cripple? It wasn't kind. And Arnold had a right to be stung by her harsh rejection of him. But Clara did hope he'd return—both for the happiness of Peggy and the harmony of the Shippen household.

"Perhaps a bit of gossip might lift your spirits," Stansbury spoke in his clipped British accent. "You'll never believe who I crossed paths with last time I was on business in New York."

"Who?" Peggy asked, eyeing her companion through her tears.

"A certain major. A certain dark and handsome Brit by the name of John André."

"Oh," Peggy gasped, momentarily pausing her sobs. The window beside her rattled as a gust of cold rain slapped the glass.

"He asks after you, Peg." Stansbury leaned close. "Every time I see him, he asks about you."

"He—he does?" Peggy's face appeared soft in the gray light—a fleeting moment of vulnerability.

"He's asked me if you would read his letter, if he wrote."

But Peggy shook her head, her face now serious. "Stansbury, that is the past. A girlish fancy. I've set my sights on Arnold now. He's the one I want." The china merchant did not argue. "Besides," Peggy continued, "everyone knows that the colonials are going to win the war. I'm not going to marry a Brit." With that, Peggy leaned her head back and closed her eyes, a posture of defeat. The merchant was finally quiet, sipping his tea in silence beside her.

Clara looked past her mistress and out the window at the street below. The cobblestones were slippery in the cold rain, and passersby scurried along, their cloaks and capes pulled over their heads in futile attempts to remain dry. Carriages rolled by, pulled by horses with heads slumping against the onslaught of rain. And then one carriage stopped. Clara recognized the coach immediately, even though it hadn't appeared outside their home in a month.

"Miss Peggy?" Clara spoke, still staring out at the street.

Peggy blew her nose and turned toward the maid. "Oh, what now, Clara?"

"Major Arnold has come calling." Clara kept her gaze fixed out the window. The announcement triggered a flurry of activity. Peggy sat up, her back stiff as she turned toward the window. She saw what Clara saw.

"It's Benny!" Peggy shrieked, a smile illuminating her face. "Oh! How do I look? I must look a fright, with all this crying. Oh, Clara, how is my hair?"

"You look wonderful, Miss Peggy. Now, why don't you go take a seat in the drawing room and I'll show him right in." Clara practically pushed her mistress away as she turned back toward the window. The carriage door opened and out hopped Barley the dog. There was a moment's pause before Benedict Arnold emerged—his legs first, then the rest of his body—alighting from the carriage with uncharacteristic nimbleness. Yes, something was different. He had no cane. Clara could hardly believe her eyes as Arnold lowered his hat to shield his face from the rain and began to march across the street.

"Ready, Barley? Here we are." Arnold climbed the Shippens' stairs with a youthful vigor that Clara had never before seen in him. Before he could knock, Clara had opened the door.

"Major General Arnold!" Clara curtsied, not attempting to conceal her surprise or delight. "Please, come in."

"Clara, good to see you." Arnold's merry voice roared throughout the hall, his mood as light as his footsteps. "Where is that pretty mistress of yours?" Clara had no doubt that Peggy could hear Arnold from the drawing room—his voice echoed off the walls.

"Benny?" Peggy appeared in the hall. "Is it really you?"

"It's me, Miss Peggy Shippen." Arnold spread his arms wide,

taking a theatrical bow before her. "Standing before you, like you requested." He crossed the room without the aid of a cane, walking on both legs as if he'd never suffered a battle wound.

"Oh, Benny, look at you!" Peggy flew to him. Once together, they embraced, showing no modesty as he kissed her, right there before her father, mother, and sister and the parlor full of servants.

Stansbury looked on, a smile on his face as he turned to Clara. "Well, Cupid has given our general a more mortal wound than all the host of Britons!"

Clara watched the two lovers as they kissed, oblivious of their surroundings. But Clara couldn't help but wonder: Was it Cupid who had determined this string of events, or had her mistress somehow arranged the entire thing?

Peggy was rapturously happy to be reconciled with Arnold, so Clara braced herself for fresh fighting when she heard the news on Christmas Eve: Judge Shippen had turned down Arnold's request for his daughter's hand.

"Is it true?" Clara was in the pantry that evening with Mrs. Quigley, skimming the tops of the milk jugs to separate the cream. "Did the judge really tell Arnold he would not give permission for the major to marry Peggy?"

"That's *Miss* Peggy to you, Clara, and don't you be forgetting your place." Mrs. Quigley looked at Clara sternly.

"I'm sorry, ma'am, *Miss* Peggy. Did the judge really tell General Arnold he could not marry Miss Peggy?" Clara scooped a dollop out of the next pitcher and added it to the bowl. Hannah would use the cream for Christmas dessert.

"Well, I don't like to gossip." Mrs. Quigley sighed, stopping up the skimmed milk jugs. "But that's what I heard His Excellency telling the missus when I was in there this morning."

"We must ready ourselves for a storm." Clara exhaled slowly. "Miss Peggy will be a fury."

But Peggy wasn't in a rage, Clara noted with shock, as she entered her bedroom the next day. "Clara, hello," Peggy called out to her maid from her spot under the bed cover.

"Merry Christmas, Miss Peggy." Clara entered with trepidation, passing before her lady's bed to deposit an armful of firewood on the hearth.

"Are those Hannah's stewed apples I smell coming up from the kitchen?" Miss Peggy inhaled a long, languid breath, kicking aside the coverlet. "They smell absolutely divine." Clara looked at Miss Peggy. Her mistress didn't appear distressed at all. In fact, she appeared downright cheery this morning.

"Clara." Peggy rose from her plush mattress and approached her maid. "I have something for you." She tiptoed back to her bed and bent over, reaching under the bedframe to retrieve a large package wrapped in discarded newspapers with red ribbon. "Merry Christmas." Peggy handed the package to Clara with an eager smile.

"For me?" Clara had never had a Christmas present before—at least not one wrapped with red ribbon. In past years Oma had made her a special breakfast on Christmas morning, and one year she had found a way to give Clara a basket of oranges—but a real, proper present?

"Miss Peggy . . . I can't accept such a—"

"Don't just stand there, open it." Peggy giggled. Clara obeyed, peeling off the paper and carefully removing the red ribbon.

"May I keep the ribbon?" Clara asked, embarrassed by how silly her request must sound to Miss Peggy.

"I suppose, if you'd like. Go on, open it." When Clara pulled aside the paper, she could not help but gasp.

Miss Peggy had given her a velvet gown of deep, nighttime blue. Around the collar and wrists were embroidered lace details that looked like fresh-fallen snow. The skirt was full, like one of the proper gowns worn by Peggy and Betsy Shippen to their balls. Clara held her present before her, afraid her dirty hands might sully the pristine velvet. This gown would likely have cost an entire year's worth of her wages. For several moments, she did not speak.

"What's the matter, cat got your tongue?" Peggy looked at Clara, giggling. "What do you think?"

"Miss Peggy." Clara turned from the gown to her mistress. "This is too generous. I've never dreamed of owning a gown like this. I . . . I don't know what to say."

"Merry Christmas, Clara." Peggy leaned forward and kissed her maid's cheek.

"Miss Peggy, I . . . I can't keep this."

"Don't be silly. Of course you can, and you'll wear it to Betsy's wedding next week. You'll need something nice to wear."

"Goodness." Clara brought the lush velvet to her cheek and reveled in the feel of the plush, downy fabric against her skin.

"Do you like it?" Peggy smiled.

"Oh, Miss Peggy, I love it."

"Good!" Peggy took Clara's hand in her own. "I'm so glad. You are so good to me, and I wanted you to know how I cherish you so, Clara."

"Miss Peggy, thank you." Clara lowered her eyes, and then she remembered: "I have something for you too. Let me go and fetch it." Clara flew down the stairs to her bedroom and returned, several minutes later, carrying the gift she'd made for her mistress.

"A crown," Peggy gasped in delight when she saw the head wreath Clara had fashioned. It was what she and Oma had always made at Christmastime; she'd collected several bows of pine needles and threaded cranberries, baby's breath flowers, and pine cones into a woven wreath. It was nothing fancy, but it was fragrant with the aroma of winter pine and looked beautiful on top of Peggy's blond curls. "Look at me, I look like quite the Christmas spirit!" Peggy clapped in delight as she eyed herself in the mirror. "Oh, I love it, Clara."

"I'm afraid it's nothing compared to my new gown." Clara looked once more at her dress.

"But you made it with your own hands, and that makes it special," Peggy answered.

"Still, I fear I will never be able to thank you sufficiently for my new dress."

"You don't have to thank me. Benny offered it to me first, but you know what I said? I said, this dress will look delightful on Clara."

Had happiness truly changed her mistress? Clara felt guilt as she recalled the nasty thoughts she had allowed herself to hold against Miss Peggy. And then she remembered, with a sense of dread, that the judge had prevented Arnold's suit for marriage. Perhaps all of Peggy's joy would be dashed after all. But did Peggy not know yet?

"So, how is the general doing?" Clara proceeded cautiously forward.

"Oh, he's splendid." Peggy turned back to the mirror and adjusted her head wreath.

"Any . . . any news with him?" Clara asked warily.

"Well, I turned him down again," Peggy said nonchalantly, as if she were commenting on the weather. "Well, not me exactly. But Papa did."

"You—you know about that?" Clara's mouth fell open in shock. "So it's true? Your father said no to General Arnold when he asked for your hand in marriage?"

"He did," Peggy answered, swiveling her head so that she might see her new wreath from various angles.

"And you . . . you aren't upset about that?" She certainly did not appear to be.

"Ha!" Peggy tittered. "Papa only told Arnold no because I told him to, Clara."

Clara attempted to understand her mistress's logic, but found this latest development baffling. "Miss Peggy, such a move hardly seems wise. I thought you had hoped to marry the general?"

"Clara, if I sought your opinion, I'd ask for it." Peggy turned and stared her maid straight in the eyes with what felt like a warning. "I know what I'm doing."

"I'm sorry, Miss Peggy, it's just that I don't understand. When you were apart for a month, you were crying every day, talking about how much you loved him and how you could not believe you might have lost him."

"Yes, and look what happened. I reject him once, he teaches himself to walk." A look of smug satisfaction crossed Peggy's face. "I reject him again, what do you think he'll do for me this time?"

Christmas dinner at the Shippen home lifted Clara's spirits. The servants' quarters were abuzz with the news that General Washington had swept through Philadelphia two days prior, on a top-secret errand to meet with the Congress and discuss the coming spring military campaign. Caleb insisted that he'd seen the general riding in his carriage up Market Street.

"You did not see him any more than you saw King George himself." Hannah scoffed, slapping Caleb's hand aside as he tried to pick a piece of the crispy ham from the platter where it sizzled, waiting to be served to the Shippen family.

"Did too, honest," Caleb insisted.

"Where was he going?" Clara asked, chuckling as she watched Caleb try once more to pilfer a piece of the crispy meat.

"To Joseph Reed's home. He was calling on the governor and his wife."

"Ha! Well, don't tell Miss Peggy that the Reeds had a visit from Washington and she didn't," Clara warned him.

"It is strange that he didn't visit Benedict Arnold, seeing how he is the military commander and all," Caleb agreed, removing his hand just in time to avoid Hannah's swift slap. "I wonder if it bothered Arnold."

Clara, knowing how touchy her mistress's beau could get, was certain that it had.

"What did he look like?" Mr. Quigley quizzed Caleb, clearly intrigued and yet trying not to forfeit his customary formality.

"He was with Martha," Caleb answered.

"That's Mrs. Washington to you," Mrs. Quigley said, hoisting a platter of squash and potatoes from the table before exiting the kitchen.

"Yes, Auntie, I do apologize," Caleb called after the woman's departing figure. He turned back to Clara. "He was with Mrs. Washington."

"And what was she like?" Clara asked, her head tilting to one side. "Pretty?"

Cal shrugged his shoulders. "Not as pretty as Miss Peggy, that's for certain." For a reason she did not fully understand, Clara felt jealous to hear him speak this way of another woman's beauty, even though she herself knew her mistress was attractive. Cal continued: "Mrs. Washington is a little lady. Plump."

"What did she wear?" Hannah joined in.

"Do you think I noticed what she was wearing?" Caleb smirked.

"Yes, I do," Clara answered.

"Fine, but only because she was with the general." Caleb crossed his arms.

"Of course." Clara laughed.

"She was dressed plainly in a maroon gown and linen head cap. But he—well, there was nothing plain about him." Now Caleb's voice was thick with admiration as he recalled the scene. "The general was dressed like we always see him in the papers—the blue military uniform with the gold epaulets. He must have taken up half the carriage. He waved to the crowds in the streets. He saw me, I swear it."

"You know he fought off the entire French Army back at Fort Necessity in the French War?" Hannah said aloud to the kitchen, adjusting the stewed apple where it rested in the roasted pig's mouth.

"When he crossed the Delaware on Christmas Eve two years back, the river was frozen, but it melted when he put his boat into the water," Caleb answered her with another volley of Washington lore.

"All right, all right. That's enough of that." Mrs. Quigley reentered the kitchen, her stern expression warning them that even though it was Christmas, they were not off duty just yet. "The Shippens are ready for their Christmas dinner."

THE FAMILY took their main meal at midday and then retired for naps, so the servants could dine together in the late afternoon. Peggy was snoring in her bed in time for Clara to join the other servants at the kitchen table. The feast that Hannah prepared was unlike any Clara had ever eaten; no salt fish was served at this meal. Hannah had loaded plates with fresh bread, butter, gooseberry jam, fish stew, smoked herring, meat pies, roasted potatoes seasoned with mushrooms and rosemary, and the leftovers of the ham and goose, which the family had already enjoyed at dinner. Mr. Quigley even allowed the servants to break from the usual cider and open bottles of wine for the occasion.

"Hannah, you've outdone yourself once more." Mr. Quigley called the servants to the kitchen table, where they congregated around the spread. The old cook was beaming, her rosy cheeks matching the color of her fiery hair.

Clara had woven Christmas wreaths for each of the women in the kitchen, so she, Hannah, Mrs. Quigley, and even Brigitte came to the table looking like a "band of woodland fairies," as Caleb said. For the men, she'd crafted pine bough neckties, which Caleb and Mr. Quigley wore good-naturedly, even though they complained that the pine boughs would drop into their stew.

"Help me put this on," Caleb asked her as the other servants took their seats. She obliged, reaching for his collar to tuck the necktie around his neck. With him this close to her, Clara breathed in his scent. The pine mingled with the familiar fragrance of Caleb's clothing, a mixture of wood-fire smoke and the stables. She looked up into his eyes, just inches from hers, and she felt her entire body growing warm.

"Merry Christmas, Clara Bell." He smiled at her.

"Merry Christmas, Cal," she answered, trying not to sound timid.

"Did you make a Christmas wish?"

"Oh, just that we win this war soon," Clara answered.

"Mine was of a more personal nature," Caleb said. When she didn't prompt him, he continued. "It's about someone . . . someone else besides me."

Petrified of crossing some line she did not yet understand, Clara finished tying Caleb's tie and turned for the stove. Her hands shaky, she busied herself with helping Hannah deliver the final dishes to the table.

Mrs. Quigley had shown a moment of rare recklessness and allowed them to festoon the kitchen with fresh white candles, so that the room was filled with a twinkling, amber glow as they sat down to dine.

Mr. Quigley led the servants in a prayer of thanksgiving for the feast, and he added a wish that the war might end with all in the Shippen household safely delivered, before he raised his glass in a toast.

"My friends." The old man, usually so stern and formal, looked around the table now with a paternal softness. "What a blessing it is to sup on such a spread while many around us are forced to go without. Please join me in a toast to our cook." Mr. Quigley turned his gaze to the opposite end of the table, where Hannah sat, lips pursed in a bashful smile. "To Hannah, the endlessly resourceful master of the kitchen."

"Aye, aye!" The kitchen erupted in unanimous chorus.

"Thank you, sir." Hannah blinked, looking bashfully to her sister.

"And of course, to General George Washington!" Mr. Quigley continued.

"To freedom!" Mrs. Quigley added, her cheeks flushed with the drink and merriment.

"To America!" Caleb answered his aunt, his eyes fixed intently on Clara, "and the pursuit of happiness!" When he winked at Clara, she felt her stomach flutter with a mixture of fear and excitement.

As DINNER ended, Hannah, who was feeling merry after several glasses of wine and much praise over her Christmas cooking, went outside and clipped a sprig of mistletoe, which she hung over the pantry doorway. This prompted teasing from Caleb and Hannah, who insisted that Mr. and Mrs. Quigley exchange a kiss. The couple refused, instead offering refills of drink to their companions around the table. The wine was finished even before the plates had been licked and scraped clean.

"All right now, I declare that Brigitte ought to get a day off from her duty of scrubbing dishes," Mrs. Quigley announced, rising to carry the emptied plates to the washbasin.

"I agree," piped up Hannah. So all the servants, jolly from the abundance of savory food and the wine bottles they'd drained, decided to split up the task, working together to scrub the dishes and platters while Caleb strummed out Christmas carols on his guitar.

LATER THAT night, Clara stood in the kitchen alone. She had offered to finish polishing the last of the silver so that the yawning Hannah and Mrs. Quigley might retire to their beds. They had accepted her offer, and the rest of the servants had bid Clara a good night.

Clara now stood with the final silver cup in her hand, humming Christmas carols as she polished.

"You know what that means, Clara Bell?"

Clara looked up, startled. She hadn't heard Caleb reenter the kitchen.

"That." Caleb walked slowly toward her, pointing up at the mistletoe that Hannah had strung overhead.

"Yes, of course." Clara looked from the plant back to the cup in her hand. Cal now stood just inches from her; she felt her heartbeat quicken at the thrilling yet terrifying proximity of his body to her own.

"Have you ever been kissed under the mistletoe?" He tried to sound light, yet he didn't smile.

"No." Her hands were trembling, even as she regretted how innocent she must appear. Never been kissed under the mistletoe. Never been kissed at all, in fact, except for that one kiss Robert Balmor had planted on her lips before she'd even known it was coming. She spoke again, mostly to fill the silence between them. "Oma called it a pagan tradition—we never hung it at the farm."

Cal laughed, standing so close to her now that she smelled the pine bough draped around his collar. She looked up into his face, the yearning so evident in the light hazel of his eyes. "Sweet, innocent Clara Bell."

"Cal, I . . ." Her breath was uneven.

"Yes, Clara?" His face, his earnest face, betrayed hope.

Did she want him to kiss her? Part of her did, yes, of course. Part of her thought often about kissing Cal, longed for that kiss. But a larger part of her was terrified at the idea. Hadn't Oma always warned her against foolish notions and fickle men? Lust was dangerous. And love was a luxury for people with the last names of Shippen, Arnold, Burd, or Chew—not for the two of them. Two penniless orphans, they were. How could she, Clara Bell, consider loving someone when she was not even the master of her own fate?

"Never mind." She lowered her eyes, snapping the moment between them as she resumed scrubbing the cup in her hands. And then, her tone matter-of-fact, she added, "I better be finishing up this silver and getting to bed, or else I'll never be able to rise tomorrow morning."

Betsy Shippen's wedding day dawned clear and cold. Clara still felt full from the Christmas feast and she did not know how she would sit down to another meal of its size.

As the wedding ceremony and the wedding feast were to be held in the Shippen home, the servants and the Shippen ladies scurried about all morning, scrubbing the floors, dusting the mantels, lighting the fires, and polishing the silver before rushing off to dress. Clara tried to convince Peggy to dress plainly on the wedding day, so as not to outshine the bride, who wore a simple dress of cream-colored silk with lace detailing around the neck. Still, Peggy looked resplendent in a gown of pine-green velvet embellished with gold. When Peggy entered the crowded Shippen drawing room with a beaming Arnold, Clara noticed how her mistress drew the attention to herself.

"Miss Peggy looks quite nice." Caleb appeared beside Clara. He had cleaned up for the occasion, combing his light brown hair back with water so that his face looked fresh and clean. He wore his only suit, a black three-piece with a jacket, vest, and knee-breeches, which Mrs. Quigley had sewn for him. At his collar he wore a cravat that Clara had never seen before.

"She does, doesn't she?" Clara gazed at her mistress, who stood on the opposite side of the drawing room whispering something into Arnold's ear. "I just hope she doesn't take the interest away from the bride."

"No, she won't," Caleb answered quietly. "But *you* might, Clara Bell."

Clara turned to him, unsure of how best to answer. She'd worn the blue velvet Peggy had given her, and Mrs. Quigley had curled her hair. It was true that she had felt pretty as she'd allow herself to gaze, vainly, into the mirror. But the way Cal looked at her now, the way he had looked at her since Christmas night, confounded her. Like he was trying to read her thoughts.

She mumbled, "Thank you," before Judge Shippen asked the room to quiet. Caleb stood by her throughout the wedding ceremony. And when he secured the seat beside her at the servants' dinner, Clara did notice how her heart leapt with something that felt like joy.

NEDDY BURD had arranged for a military escort as he drove his new bride away in the carriage, so all the wedding guests gathered on the streets to wave them off.

Clara lingered in the cold. She stood there long after the carriage had clipped away and the guests had either departed or returned into the warmth of the Shippen home. She sat on the stoop of the house, her cloak pulled tightly around her neck, imagining the ways in which her daily life might change now that Betsy would be out of the house. Mrs. Shippen would have more time on her hands, that was for certain. Would she turn a more exacting eye on the household management, specifically her servants? Or perhaps she would refocus her attention to her youngest daughter and the task of getting Peggy married. Or would the two of them, mother and daughter, maintain their frosty standoff, allowing the household to go on in a tenuous harmony? And wouldn't Arnold be eager to have a wedding of his own now that he'd attended Betsy's alongside Peggy? But mostly she was thinking about Cal. She was trying to understand her thorny, confused emotions. It was true that when she wasn't with Cal, she thought about him. She longed to be in his company. And yet, when he appeared, her heart would lurch, her nerves would tighten. The sight of his face, his shaggy dark blond hair; even now on the dark front step, the thought filled Clara with waves of joy and fear. Why was it so hard for her to accept, fully, the fact that she was falling in love with him? Clara ruminated on this, alone, for a long while. Or she had thought she was alone, when she heard a familiar, gravelly voice.

"I had to leave the Penn mansion."

A pause, and then a second voice asked, "Why?"

Clara knew who's was the second voice, even in the pitch-dark evening. Peggy and Arnold must have wandered farther up the street to find a private place to talk. In the shadowed lane, Clara could now make out the outlines of their two figures, clutching hands, just a few feet from her. Arnold leaned heavily on his cane.

"Reed was making trouble for me, asking why a public servant in the military needed to be quartered in the grandest mansion in Philadelphia."

Peggy was silent. If Clara was close enough to hear the grinding of teeth, she was certain she would have.

"The news is not grievous though." Arnold continued, "Do not fret, Peggy."

"How could I not? You've been forced out of your home. I *hate* that Joseph Reed!" Peggy spat.

"Peggy, please." Arnold sounded alarmed. "You must not speak like that. Anyone could hear. Reed himself could hear."

"Let him hear it. I hope he does."

"I cannot bear to see you this upset. You must calm down."

"I . . . I . . ." Peggy reined in her temper. "I'm sorry. It's just that, I hate to see you suffer at the hands of that vile man."

They stood in silence. When Arnold spoke next, his voice sounded upbeat. Even proud. "I tell you it's not bad, because I've replaced that place with something even better."

"What do you mean?" Peggy asked.

"Land. Lots and lots of land," Arnold answered.

"Is it true, Benny?"

"It's in gratitude for my service."

"Where is it?"

"New York," he answered.

A pause. A long silence. Clara told herself that she ought to go inside, yet she was interested to hear her mistress's reaction to this news. After all, it would no doubt affect Clara's life as well.

"New York is so far away, Benny. Philadelphia is my home."

"Yes, but just wait until you hear what the offer entails, my sweet Peggy. A hundred and thirty thousand acres of land. It's been seized from the royalist Johnson family's estate on the Mohawk River. Peggy, I've seen that land, I've fought up there. That was where I beat St. Leger. It's the most beautiful spot. We could raise up a beautiful mansion, and fill it with happy children and servants."

"Oh, Benny, it is lovely to think about, but—"

"But wait, my dear girl. There's more."

"Oh yes?" Peggy's voice still contained hope.

"In addition to the land tracts in New York, I've . . . I've made a purchase closer to home."

"What sort of purchase?" Peggy was growing more intrigued, Clara could tell by the tone of her voice.

"Have you ever heard of Mount Pleasant?" Arnold asked.

"Mount Pleasant? The mansion on the Schuylkill?" Peggy knew Mount Pleasant.

So did Clara. Clara recalled their picnics on the Schuylkill. Many of them had taken place on the patch of grass right across from Mount Pleasant. Peggy had always marveled at the mansion, with its many windows, its sloping hills and rooftop balcony. Clara had always assumed that there was just as much chance that her mistress would live at Mount Pleasant as there was she'd live in King George's palace.

"That's it," Arnold answered. "The place John Adams himself called the 'most elegant seat in Pennsylvania.'"

"You didn't buy it." Peggy's voice quivered. "You couldn't possibly have bought Mount Pleasant."

"I did," Arnold replied.

"Oh, Benny!" Peggy pulled Arnold toward her in a kiss, so that their outlines joined against the backdrop of the sparsely lit street.

Clara could not watch what should be a private moment. She felt, as she had for much of her service at the Shippen home, as if she were witnessing scenes in which she had no part. She rose from her seat on the steps, turning back indoors. And then, in the quiet night, Clara heard the words that her mistress had so long withheld: "Benedict Arnold, I love you."

"GRAB YOUR pots and pans and let's go!" Mrs. Quigley threw on her wool cloak and yelled into the full kitchen for the rest of the servants to do the same. "You think the New Year will wait until we're all ready for it?"

"What do I grab?" Clara asked, spinning around, looking for someone to guide her in the New Year's Eve mayhem of the Shippen kitchen. She saw Cal slip out the door for the yard, and she feared she might fall too far behind to find him again.

"Find a pot and a pan, or else a pot and a pewter spoon. Anything that'll make a devilish noise when you bang 'em together!" Hannah's thick frame was even wider under scarves, a cap, and a heavy wool coat as she hurried for the door.

Clara reached into the cupboard and grabbed two pewter mugs, hoping that they would serve her purpose. She retrieved her cloak and woolen hand muff from the hook and slid her cap snugly onto her head, and then she was out the door, hurrying to catch up with Cal.

Ten minutes remained until midnight, and the entire city of Philadelphia seemed to be out in the streets, all marching through the cold, snow-speckled night toward the square outside of Independence Hall.

"There she is. Hello, Clara Bell." Caleb was walking between the Quigleys, a noticeable bounce in his step. Just ahead walked Judge Shippen and his wife, whose hands were pressed to her ears in an effort to muffle the din in the street. Accompanying the judge and his wife were Betsy and Neddy Burd, who had joined the family for the evening. Peggy had dined with Arnold, and Clara had not yet seen her that evening.

"What is all of this?" Clara asked, looking around at the crowd in the street that seemed to be multiplying by the second. She was determined to stay close to Cal and not to get separated in the throngs. Enough of her shyness, enough of her breathless panic. She cared for Cal, and he seemed to care for her, too. Tonight was the night that she might finally let him kiss her. The thought brought a happy flush to her cheeks, and she smiled in his direction before burrowing more deeply into her scarf.

"Oh, just a fun little New Year's tradition, dearie. Didn't you and your grandmother ever do it?" Mr. Quigley held a lantern to light their path. He wore his formal suit even in the frigid midnight temperatures.

"Nothing like this, sir," Clara answered.

"Let me guess, Clara Bell." Cal teased. "Always asleep by midnight?"

She threw Cal a sideways glance and noticed his smile, his energetic gait—what had him feeling so merry?

"Well, here in Philadelphia, the town gathers in the square, and when the church bells strike midnight, we all offer up a yell and bang the pots and pans like it's the end of the world." Mrs. Quigley chuckled. "It's to ward off the bad spirits, usher in good luck for the New Year."

"Oh, I see." Clara laughed, hustling to stay apace with Caleb as they marched through the crowded street.

"Caleb, my dear, you be sure to make a special wish at midnight. You are the one who needs the luck this coming year. More so than any of us," the housekeeper said, before she was jostled by a young man running past her. Clara could not help but detect the look of concern that had crossed Mrs. Quigley's face as she had spoken to her nephew. And the mischievous glimmer in Cal's eye.

"What does your aunt mean?" Clara asked. She saw that the Quigleys and Hannah had been separated from them by the growing crowd.

"I've got news, Clara Bell."

Clara pulled her scarf higher around her ears, turning to face him. "What is it, Cal?"

He stopped short and she paused to face him. The crowds rushed past them toward the square, as Clara and Cal faced each other, an island in the stream of bodies. His eyes were alight, his gaze intense. Her stomach did a turn as she realized just how terribly she longed to kiss him. And then, for some reason she could not explain, she understood that that would no longer happen.

"I'm leaving," Cal said.

A short punch of air left her mouth, filling up the frigid night with a misty little cloud. She could not answer as she stared at him. After what felt like an eternity, Cal continued. "Seeing General Washington right before Christmas made me think; he was rushing off to meet his men and continue the fighting. And just last week, he issued an urgent call for more volunteers. This country needs men to fight if we are to have any chance at winning our freedom." Cal paused. "How can I stay back? Hanging around the Shippen home, serving no purpose . . ." Cal allowed the words to drift off but he did not finish his thought.

"Of course you serve a purpose, Cal." Clara tried to keep her voice steady, even as she heard it catch on the words.

"But here is my chance, Clara, to serve something so much larger than myself. Or than any of us. How can I not answer the call?"

Her shoulders dropped as she saw the resolve on his face. The determination.

"The cause is liberty, Clara. Think about it, I have the chance to serve General Washington!" Cal's voice teemed with excitement, with passion. And though Clara's heart felt as if it had been trodden over by every reveler in the packed square, she forced a smile. She could not rob him of any of his happiness in this moment. "Of course you must go, Cal."

And then, the square erupted in noise, and Clara instinctively brought her fingers to her ears.

The clock struck midnight, and the square around them roared with a din the likes of which Clara had never heard. All around her, servants and gentlemen alike were cheering and hugging, banging pots and pans in between kisses and well wishes.

"Happy 1779!

"Long live the colonies!

"To liberty!

"God Bless George Washington!

"And Benjamin Franklin!

"To France!"

The square was full of midnight revelers, and swelling in size every minute. Many in the crowd held candles or lanterns aloft, and the faint light from the wicks illuminated the flakes of snow as they fell, cloaking the city in an ethereal glow. Somehow, in the mayhem of hugs and cheers and song, Clara had lost Cal. She pushed back against the jostling crowd, looking for him.

"Cal?" She called out to him, but her voice was a feeble cry against the torrent of noise. Wine bottles and mugs of ale were being passed around as the crowd broke out into sporadic verses of "The Liberty Song."

Some even yelled prayers in honor of their local military commander, whom Clara knew to be in the crowd, somewhere, with Peggy.

As she listened to the bells, and watched the laughter and hugs of strangers, Clara felt oppressed by sadness. Cal was leaving. This new year would be a year with him gone. Removed entirely from her life. And it would be the first year of her life that she would live entirely without Oma's presence. She had no idea what the future with Miss Peggy held for her, and she could not help but feel desperate when she thought about how little control she had over the events unfolding around her. These thoughts hung heavy on her and suddenly, amid the crowds and cheer of the square, Clara felt lonelier than she ever had in her life.

"Happy New Year, girl." Mrs. Quigley appeared, taking ahold of Clara to give her a quick kiss on the cheek.

"Happy New Year to you as well, Mrs. Quigley."

"Clara, what is this? Don't cry, my girl." Mrs. Quigley pulled her in for another hug. "There, there. You've got much to give thanks for, Clara, my dear. None of this sadness." As the old woman pulled away, she whispered, "Your grandmother would be proud if she could see you tonight."

"I don't know about that." Clara sniffled. "But I do hope she is looking down on me," Clara answered, managing a feeble smile as she choked back further tears.

"Aye, that she is, my dear."

"Happy New Year, Clara Bell." Mr. Quigley joined them, giving Clara a quick kiss on the cheek.

"Same to you, Mr. Quigley."

"We are glad to have you with us," Mr. Quigley replied, allowing the hint of a smile to curl his lips.

"And I am grateful in return, sir."

"Let us offer a prayer for our general, and his men down in Middlebrook, New Jersey. May they survive the winter, and live to win the war in the New Year."

Clara looked through the crowds, frantic to find Caleb, but all she saw around her were the faces of happy strangers. Meanwhile, the church bells kept ringing, chiming out a merry chorus while the crowd sang out in unison the refrain of "The Liberty Song."

In Freedom we're born and in Freedom we'll live.
Our purses are ready. Steady, friends, steady;
Not as slaves, but as Freemen our money we'll give.

And then, through the masses, there emerged a familiar face. Then a second familiar face.

"Clara." Peggy was weaving her way through the mob, pulling a limping Arnold and his silver-topped cane behind her. "Clara, there you are!" Peggy wore a hooded cape of scarlet, the wisps of blond hair peeking out from under the cape and ringing her face like a snow-laced crown.

"Miss Peggy, General Arnold, Happy New Year." Clara offered a smile as her mistress and Arnold approached. But Peggy didn't want a smile, she wanted a hug, and she pulled Clara to her.

"Oh Clara, I am so happy." Peggy's laughter glittered like the snowflakes, mingling in the air with the chiming of the church bells. "Oh, Clara, isn't it wonderful? Benedict and I are getting married!"

Though Clara had dressed Peggy Shippen every day for a year, wedding tradition dictated that the bride's mother and sister dress her on her wedding day. Betsy had returned home for her sister's wedding. That morning, Clara made herself useful in the bedchamber, serving them breakfast on trays and running errands when they needed the curling iron reheated or fresh vials of rose-water poured.

Peggy had woken early that morning. It was early April and the days were not yet long, so it was dark when Peggy called her mother and sister to her bedroom. Clara answered their summons and brought up trays of tea and toast while the ladies shook off their grogginess.

"Clara, is it ready?" Peggy was the only one who had risen fresh-faced and brimming with energy. "Show me the gown."

"Yes, Miss Peggy." Clara ran to her own room and fetched the white lace gown she had been tasked with preparing for the day.

"It looks just as it did when I wore it," Mrs. Shippen noted, running her hands along the bottom of the skirt to fluff it. "What a blessing that you are my exact size."

"I suppose," Peggy said, tight-jawed. She had wanted a new gown, but her father had told her he could afford either a new dress or wine for the wedding feast. Peggy, reluctantly agreeing that her mother's old gown had been flattering to her figure, had opted for the wine.

"I would have happily worn it, Mother," Betsy interjected as she unfastened the long line of buttons down the back of her sister's gown.

"Elizabeth, we tried to squeeze you into it and it did not fit," Mrs. Shippen replied with a sigh. "I wasn't going to have you tear it in two at your wedding supper." Betsy frowned and handed the gown to her mother, who finished unfastening the remaining buttons.

"You could have had it, Bets," Peggy said. "I longed for a new gown."

"Now is not the time for extravagance, Margaret," Mrs. Shippen answered.

"It's not so terribly plain, I suppose, thanks to the lace trim Clara added around the sleeves and collar." Peggy looked to her maid, smiling. "Once I add the pearls that Benny gave me, I shall look quite nice, I hope."

Mrs Shippen ignored the remark and began tying her daughter's stays. "You aren't going into your marriage with many linens, Margaret."

"Yes, Peg, your trousseau is lacking," Betsy agreed. "I sewed for months before marrying Neddy."

"Why would I stitch away for months to sew all my household

linens? Benny will just buy us the tablecloths and sheets we need," Peggy said. Clara saw her mother and sister exchange anxious glances. "Mark my words, ladies, today will be the last day of my life that I will have to do without."

Mrs. Shippen creased her forehead as she looked at her younger daughter. "I fear I didn't teach you enough of Mr. Benjamin Franklin's messages on the value of frugality."

"Oh, Mother," Peggy sighed. "Mr. Franklin again? I'm sick of *Poor Richard's Almanack* and those tiresome sayings."

"Men are always very generous during the courtship, but they appreciate a wife who can manage a household on a budget." Mrs. Shippen ignored her daughter's protests.

"I run my house on our budget each month, Mother," Betsy said.

Clara, who was holding the gown ready for when the corset was laced, saw that Peggy clenched her teeth but held her tongue.

"You'll have to watch yourself, Peg, especially with all the money he must be spending on fixing up Mount Pleasant," Betsy mumbled. "That must cost a fortune."

"Quite true. Margaret"—Mrs. Shippen's brow knit as she looked at her younger daughter—"I wonder how, on an army salary, he afforded that mansion."

Peggy shrugged. "Nothing wrong with an army man doing a bit of business on the side. He's a savvy businessman."

"What sort of business?" Mrs. Shippen reached to Clara for the gown. Clara wondered, had Mrs. Shippen really not heard the rumors around town about Major General Arnold's black market trades? She herself, a maid, had heard hints of the accusation at the spice trader, the butcher, the tea merchant.

Peggy was eager to change topics. "How should I know, Mother? Arnold does not like me to trouble myself with concerns over money," Peggy answered. "As long as it's there, I don't care how he comes by it."

Mrs. Shippen and Betsy exchanged a troubled look before helping Peggy into the gown. Peggy waved her maid forward. "Clara?"

"Yes, my lady."

"Are my flowers ready?"

"Yes, ma'am." Peggy had asked Clara to weave a crown of white flowers, a springtime version of the headdress she had so loved at Christmas, garnished with snowdrops, Dutch crocuses, and hints of pink cherry blossom. Clara had also fashioned a bouquet for the bride to carry with her during the wedding ceremony.

"Clara, you are truly skilled." Peggy placed the wreath atop her head and tucked her blond hair, pulled back in curls, under the flowers. "Well?" Peggy turned around, spinning in a circle for her mother, sister, and Clara. "What do you think?"

Since Mrs. Shippen and Betsy seemed intent on reserving any praise, Clara weighed in. "General Arnold will feel like the luckiest man in Philadelphia when he sees you."

Peggy beamed, crossing the room and taking Clara's hand in hers. Leaning forward, she kissed Clara on the cheek, and the sweet smell of her fragrant crown filled Clara's nose. "Oh Clara, thank you for making my wedding day special."

The courtship had been lavish—the responsibility of the besotted Benedict Arnold—but the wedding was a simple ceremony and feast hosted by the Shippens.

As Clara had predicted, the groom was bashful to the point of speechlessness for most of the day, doing nothing but look on fawningly at his bride as she chatted with her guests. Arnold looked very dignified, Clara decided, in his full military jacket and jeweled cane. He beamed with pride whenever his young wife was present, and it gave him a kind, handsome appearance.

There were few guests for the evening feast—just the Shippen family, with Uncle William Shippen, who had traveled to town for the wedding, and a small number of guests. Peggy had invited Joseph Stansbury, Meg Chew, Becky Redman, and a very shy Christianne Amile. Since Benedict Arnold had no surviving parents and the rest of his family was up north in Connecticut, he had just Major Franks attending on his side. He'd arranged to have a military band of fifes and drums to serenade his bride, and Peggy clapped and delighted in the music as she ate.

Hannah cooked, assisted by Mrs. Quigley and Brigitte, while Mr. Quigley and Clara loaded the candlelit table with platters of food and bubbling Champagne. The food was simple but savory: mutton with mint jelly, roasted vegetables, ham, potatoes, and bread with black currant preserves. For dessert there was a fruit and nut cake accompanied by cherry cobbler and gooseberry tart.

Benedict Arnold spoke before the dessert, toasting his bride and telling her family that he'd loved her since the moment he first met her at the Penn mansion. While Arnold extolled his bride's beauty and virtue, Peggy blushed, and her laughter was as bubbly and intoxicating as the Champagne.

After the family had finished eating, Arnold loaded his bride into a carriage and drove her off, accompanied by the full military escort, to an inn for their honeymoon night.

"Goodbye, Clara!" Peggy kissed her maid before she took Major Franks's outstretched hand and hopped into the carriage. "Clara, I love him so much," she sighed. "How did I get so lucky?" As Clara listened to these words, the image of Cal's face burst across her mind. How terribly she missed him since he'd enlisted. But when she began to cry, Miss Peggy assumed they were tears of joy on her own behalf.

IT WASN'T until the guests had left and the servants had retreated to the kitchen to enjoy their own supper that Clara had a moment to think. And when she did, her thoughts inevitably turned to Cal. He'd left shortly after New Year's Day. It had been a quick goodbye in a crowded kitchen. There was so much Clara would have loved to tell him, but with the eyes of everyone on her, she'd merely urged him to take care of himself and stay safe.

The past few months had been a blur of stitching Miss Peggy's bridal gown, packing up her lady's bedroom, arranging a feast and a party. But now, with Miss Peggy happily married, and Clara taking a moment to pause, her mind was flooded. She felt Cal's absence like an ache in her bones.

"Hello, Clara? Where has your mind wandered off to?"

Clara blinked, seeing once more the crowded kitchen before her, the table set for supper. "Oh, I apologize, Mr. Quigley."

"Daydreaming again?" Mrs. Quigley, still dressed in her wedding attire, served Clara a slice of cold mutton.

"I suppose I was," Clara said, accepting the full plate from the old woman. "Thank you, ma'am."

"I was saying—a toast to your mistress, now happily married." Mr. Quigley raised his glass toward Clara from where he sat at the head of the table.

"Indeed." Clara nodded, lifting her glass. "And to the groom."

"I'll drink to that. Poor Benedict Arnold is finally victorious in his latest siege." Hannah chuckled.

"She's done all right for herself as well," Mrs. Quigley said, taking her seat beside her husband.

"Indeed." Clara nodded.

"Your life will really change now, don't you think?" Mr. Quigley said, as all the servants began to eat. "Moving out of this home, going with Miss Peggy to set up her own household. I'm still shocked that she managed to convince the judge that she should take you with her."

"We all know that she can be very persuasive," Hannah said.

"Poor Miss Betsy didn't get to bring you to help set up her home," Mrs. Quigley said.

Clara nodded. "But Miss Betsy seems happy enough. Mr. Burd is very good to her."

The other servants agreed.

"And I suppose it's good for you that you get to go with the Arnolds. You might be managing the house someday." Mrs. Quigley smiled, a look of encouragement.

"Perhaps, ma'am." Clara nodded. Was that what she longed for—running another's household? The idea contained some enticement, to be sure; managing the household of a lady such as Mrs. Margaret Arnold was certainly a respectable station for an orphan who had started out on a remote farm.

"How long do you suppose it will be before the Arnolds take up residence at Mount Pleasant?" Mr. Quigley paused his eating to take a sip of cider.

Clara thought carefully before saying, "I wonder at that, myself, sir. General Arnold keeps telling Miss Peggy it's not ready for them."

Clara had heard the gossip in town—how General Arnold had taken out a seventy-thousand-dollar mortgage to buy the large home as a wedding gift for his bride, but now could not afford to furnish it.

"Well, they are fortunate to have the judge offering his cottage out back," Mrs. Quigley interjected. "It's no Mount Pleasant, but it'll do for now. I'm sure they can stay there as long as they like."

"Or as long as they need," Hannah said. Clara saw the look that passed between the butler and his wife, and she suspected that she was not the only person at the table to have heard the rumors of General Arnold's financial woes.

THE TABLE had barely been cleared from their small wedding feast before the trouble began for Arnold and Peggy.

It was a warm afternoon in late April. Peggy was taking her tea in the small parlor of the Shippens' cottage, exchanging post-wedding gossip with Joseph Stansbury. Arnold walked in on the chatting duo, leaning heavily on his cane. Clara opened the door for her new master and watched him limp in, noting that his silver-topped cane, once so lustrous, needed a polish and shine.

"Oh, hello, my darling." Peggy rose from her chair and gave Arnold a quick kiss on his cheek. "Stansbury and I are just having some tea and catching up on the latest news."

"Your wife is catching me up on her life since becoming a married woman, General," Stansbury added.

"Ah, well, let's hope she's not telling you too much, at least not about the wedding night!" Arnold rejoined good-naturedly.

"Of course not, my love." Peggy played the role of blushing bride. "Would you care to join us, Benny?"

"I'm afraid I cannot. Peggy my love—" Arnold paused. "Mr. Stansbury." Arnold nodded to the china merchant. "My dear wife, might I be so rude as to demand a minute of your time?"

"Yes, of course. Sit. What is it?" Peggy cocked her head, sitting back down in her chair. Arnold shifted his weight, looking at Stansbury.

"Oh!" Peggy understood. "Stansbury, do you mind giving me a minute alone with my husband?"

"Course not." The merchant rose, kissing Peggy's hand. "It's his right, I suppose."

"You're a dear, Stansbury." Peggy smiled back at the merchant. "It won't be long. We still haven't even gotten to what everyone wore to the wedding."

"Oh my, did you notice how plain Meg Chew looked?" Stansbury put his long, spindly fingers to his mouth in mock horror and Peggy erupted in laughter.

"Shoo, shoo." Peggy waved her friend away. Once Stansbury had gone, Peggy looked back to her husband. "Benny, what is it? You have me very nervous."

Arnold fidgeted opposite her, lowering himself in the chair just vacated by the china merchant.

"It's about Mount Pleasant, Peg." He looked at her as if to gauge her reaction.

"Yes, what about it? When can we move? Before it gets too hot—well before July or August, I should hope. This tiny cottage will not do well in the heat."

"I fear . . ." Arnold paused, changing tracks. "I so much regret that I have to tell you—we shall not be able to move in before the summer. Probably not before winter either."

Arnold told his wife the news Clara had known for weeks. How he had had to take out an exorbitant mortgage to buy the home, and how his military salary did not allow him the monthly funds required for fixing up the home or buying the furniture necessary to move in. He needed time, a year or so, to try to set some funds aside. He begged and pleaded with his wife to understand,

and to make the best of their current situation in the Shippen cottage. They had a roof over their heads, after all, did they not?

Peggy listened quietly, the look on her face growing grimmer as her husband discussed the bitter vitriol his rival, Joseph Reed, was spewing thoughout town. Now that Reed was so publicly questioning Arnold's finances and expenditures, hadn't they better err on the side of discretion and avoid a very public move to Mount Pleasant? And perhaps, would Peggy be willing to put a temporary halt to the credit spending she was becoming known for throughout town?

When Arnold had finished speaking, he seemed to collapse farther into his chair, as if the mere confession of this sobering economic report had cost him all his energy reserves. The room was quiet, filled now by just the sound of the crackling fire.

Peggy stared into the hearth at the decomposing logs. "Well, this is something, Benedict Arnold."

"Please, my pet, what do you think?" Arnold eyed his wife, rubbing his hands together in a nervous gesture.

Finally, Peggy answered him. "What do I think?" Peg met his gaze, her cheeks red. "What do I think? I think it's a shame that my husband is siding with the gossips throughout town over his own wife."

"Peggy." Arnold looked at her, his face draining of color. "Surely you know that that is not my meaning. I simply think that it might be wise if we economize a bit in the next few months. Perhaps you might not purchase quite as many new items at Coffin and Anderson? You can manage that, right, my dove?"

"You want me to live like a pauper?" Peggy leaned forward to sip tea from her full cup just as Arnold reached forward to take her hand, so that the hot drink spilled down the front of Peggy's new gown.

"Look what you've done!" Peggy yelped, reaching for a napkin.

Clara ran to the kitchen and reappeared with several rags, and she began to dab the front of the gown.

"I do apologize." Arnold looked on, his expression helpless.

"Reckless!" Peggy stood up, dabbing the brown stain. "And it's not as though I can replace this ruined gown, since you tell me I shall have nothing new."

"Please, Peggy, I pray you'd not upset yourself." Arnold stared at his wife with a look of growing consternation.

"Don't you scold me, Benedict Arnold! Not when you've deliberately lied to me—lured me out of the comfort of my father's home into this . . . this . . . *shack*! All under the false pretenses that we'd be moving into Mount Pleasant. And now you say we can't afford to live there, and I should be denied all the nice things you had promised me." Peggy's hand flew to her heart as she collapsed backward against the chair. "Oh, what a life I've chosen for myself!" When Peggy cupped her face in her hands and began to sob, Clara was sure that Arnold felt more wounded than he had ever felt on the Saratoga battlefield.

"Just . . ." Peggy struggled to speak through the cries that heaved her chest. "Look . . . at . . . this . . . *HOVEL*!"

The hovel Peggy lamented was in fact a cottage behind the Shippen home, in which the Arnolds had been living since their wedding. Clara didn't see why Peggy minded it so much—the house was small but comfortable, with large windows that opened out into the orchard and afforded plenty of light on sunny days. Arnold seemed perfectly content there, or anywhere, as long as he was near his wife. The only person who really had a right to be put out was Clara. She had given up her private bedroom in the larger Shippen home for a little straw pad on the floor of the Arnolds' new kitchen, which she shared with Barley now that Miss Peggy had banned the dog from Arnold's bedchamber. Though it was humbler, Clara didn't mind her new spot—at least its proximity to the fire guaranteed that it would be warm and bright even once the weather turned cold. And since her mistress would have never dreamed of setting foot in the kitchen, it was as private as a room could be.

Peggy had insisted that now that they were married, they would no longer take their meals with her parents. But, since the Arnolds could not afford a cook of their own, they still depended on Hannah for their meals. This meant that Clara had the task of hauling food from the Shippens' kitchen to the Arnold's kitchen, and then bringing the dishes back at the end of each meal. It was a lot of work, and ordinarily she would have asked Caleb for help with it. But with him gone to the army, her time spent lugging food back to the cottage was just yet another moment throughout the day in which she missed him.

"It's just that the Continental Congress still owes me thousands from the campaigns of 'seventy-five." Arnold tried to quell his wife's temper. "I paid all my men out of my own fortune up in Canada and at Ticonderoga. I'll get reimbursed soon."

"Do *not* try to comfort me with more empty promises," Peggy hissed at her husband, who now wore a look of alarm as he watched his wife rail. "I don't want any more false promises, Benedict Arnold!" Peggy closed her eyes, while her husband looked to the maid, helpless.

"I don't understand why we can't just go back to the Penn mansion." Peggy spoke after a long pause, her face wet with tears.

"I have told you a thousand times, my angel." Arnold winced as he bent to kneel beside his wife's chair, clutching his left leg in pain. "Reed was telling the Congress, and the newspapers, that I was living there illegally. He found out that I wasn't paying any rent."

"Then just pay the rent to get Reed to shut his mouth, Benedict." Peggy, having exhausted Clara's supply of rags, handed the soiled cloths back to her maid and sat back in her armchair.

"Peg, I can't afford to rent the Penn mansion while I'm also sinking my life's savings into Mount Pleasant. For the time being, this cottage will just have to do."

"I'm miserable here," Peggy moaned. "And I despise that Joseph Reed for ruining our happiness."

"My dear, please." Arnold leaned toward his wife to comfort her, but to no avail. "You must calm down; you will make yourself sick." He took her hand in his, but she swatted him away like a bothersome fly.

"My darling, I promise, I will do whatever I can to increase my income so that we can move into Mount Pleasant. You have my word."

"Your word means nothing," Peggy snapped at him. The look on Arnold's face showed such acute pain that even Clara felt his wound, and she excused herself, mumbling something about taking the dirty rags back to the kitchen. Neither Arnold nor Peggy replied as Clara turned to leave.

"My darling Peg, I love you. I will do whatever it takes to make you happy," Arnold said, pleading with her. "Will you believe me, please?"

But Peggy did not reply. She simply buried her face in her hands, so that all that was visible as she sobbed were her curls, bobbing up and down with each gasp.

"Lovely day, isn't it, my dove?" Arnold and Peggy sat opposite Clara in the carriage on the way back to the Shippen home after church. Arnold looked out the window, waving to the small children who ran alongside the carriage, hoping to get a glimpse of the local war hero.

"Mmmm," Peggy agreed absently, burying her nose in the society section of the *Pennsylvania Packet.* "I suppose it is."

It was a lovely day, Clara agreed in silence. Late April, and all of Philadelphia was in bloom. The recent rains had left the ground soft and fertile, with new buds poking their way out from the earth each morning. The days were growing longer and warmer, while all around them the trees hung heavy with cherry blossoms. The horses kicked up splotches of lumpy mud with each step, and the small children who shouted alongside the carriage were splattered in brown, laughing at the mess their mothers—or maids—would have to wash.

"Look at that mud." Arnold watched the scene outside the carriage, erupting in his loud, jolly laughter. He looked to his wife but she ignored him.

"It's a wonder we can drive through it," Clara piped up, so that Arnold would know he was not being completely ignored. Arnold's eyes crossed the carriage to Clara, smiling at her in appreciation.

"Anything interesting in the paper today, my doll?" Arnold tried again to get his wife's attention.

"Here, just take it and read it for yourself." Peggy sighed, exasperated, as she tossed it in her husband's lap.

"Dearest, I didn't mean that you should give it over," Arnold answered.

"No, just read it! I'm done," Peggy snapped, looking out the other side of the window. Then, quietly, she mumbled to herself, "I can't read when you're jabbering away alongside me, anyway."

Stung, Arnold looked from his wife to the paper and unfolded it so that he might scan the front page. "Let's see what filth they've dug up today," Arnold said good-naturedly, perusing the articles. He had not been reading long when his face went ashen.

"My good God." Arnold's mouth fell open.

Clara saw his expression, and then looked down to see the headline. Right there, on the front page, was printed a long article, accompanied by a drawing. Clara knew immediately, from the cane and the broad, stocky body, whom the drawing was meant to portray.

"What is it?" Peggy looked to her husband, acknowledging him for the first time. "Read it aloud, whatever it is."

"It's that devil Reed." Arnold's voice was a quiet tempest.

"Read it aloud," Peggy ordered him.

"Reed has convinced the Pennsylvania Council to make formal charges against me. Eight formal charges."

"What?" Peggy leaned over to read the paper alongside her husband.

"Reed and his henchmen have come up with a whole laundry list of charges against me." He listed them off quickly. "Obtaining illegal personal gain from two British ships, using public wagons to transport personal items, closing the stores in Philadelphia, enlisting my military men to do my own personal tasks, issuing passes for folks to cross enemy lines into New York."

"After all that you've done for this country, Reed is allowed to make such outrageous charges against you?" Peggy spoke, her voice eerily quiet. "It cannot be borne."

"It would be the end of my career if Washington believed these charges," Arnold spoke in barely a whisper. "I'd be finished."

"Ludicrous," Peggy said, her tone defiant. "You're a hero, Benedict Arnold."

"Not according to Reed. According to Reed, I'm a crook and a thief."

"You sacrificed your leg. And thousands of your own dollars on feeding and quartering your men during the Canada and Ticonderoga campaigns—which they have never reimbursed you for."

"What will become of me now?" Arnold's voice quavered.

"What else do they say?" Peggy asked.

"They accuse me of acting disrespectfully to the civilian leaders of Philadelphia."

Clara's mind flew back to the afternoon in Arnold's carriage, and the ghastly display when her mistress had urged Arnold to pull down his breeches to insult Reed.

"Can they blame you?" Peggy chortled. "Anyone would act disrespectfully to that moonface, Reed. And what's the final charge?" Peggy demanded.

"Favoring British loyalists in my personal life." Arnold looked squarely into his wife's face. "They say I have chosen to consort with 'those with well-known loyalist tendencies.'"

This, at last, silenced Peggy's indignation. "I . . . I don't know *who* they could possibly be talking about," Peggy answered, shaking her head.

The carriage came to a halt, jerking them all forward. Clara braced herself so that she did not fly forward onto Arnold.

"Good gracious," Peggy shrieked as her hat fell loose off her head. "Is Franks drunk on rum?"

"What now, Franks?" Arnold hollered out the window to his aide. Neither the horses nor the carriage moved.

"Blasted wheels!" Franks hopped down from his perch and approached the horses.

"What's the problem?" Arnold scowled at his aide.

"Stuck in the mud, sir." Franks poked his head up to the carriage window. "We'll need at least two able-bodied men to push us out of this mess."

"Able-bodied men." Arnold gritted his teeth and spoke in a low growl, his nostrils trembling in silent rage. "I *would* get out and help, but I am no longer able-bodied, not since I sacrificed my leg in the service of my ungrateful country."

VI.

"She's possessed of a fury!" Hamilton scoops up my lady's fainted, inanimate body. The Marquis de Lafayette is mumbling, the shock forcing him to slip back into his native French, while George Washington sits in stony silence, head cradled in his large hands as he stares at the words he's just read.

Peggy is carried up the stairs by Hamilton, and it's not until she's placed down on the featherbed that she revives. She sees us standing over her and resumes her hysterics, shouting about Benedict's betrayal.

"You'll kill my child, I know it!" She wails, her eyes roving around the bedroom but not fixing on any one point. "You shall punish the son for the sins of the father!"

Hamilton tries to soothe her, tries to pull her back to herself, but every time he approaches her, my lady reaches up as if she would claw at his face.

"I won't let you kill my son!" She screams, her features contorted with rage.

"Please, Mrs. Arnold, you are making yourself ill." Hamilton turns to me with a look of deep concern, but I am just as helpess as he is.

I've seen scenes like this many times before, but what unnerves me this time is that I suspect her hysteria might be genuine.

When Peggy speaks again, she's mumbling and pointing at the ceiling.

"Look." She points upward at some unseen menace. "Look! My husband is gone. He's gone there." Her fingers direct our eyes aloft, but when I follow her pointing, all I see is the ceiling overhead.

CHAPTER SIX

"There Is Another Way"

December 1779
Philadelphia, PA

Arnold looked glumly out the window, avoiding his wife's eyes. "There's Major Franks with the carriage. Goodness, I hope he's packed enough ale."

"I hate to think of you making the journey all the way to New Jersey by yourself, and with your leg bothering you as it has been recently." Peggy wrapped a heavy wool cloak over her husband's thick shoulders, her arms lingering around him in a loose embrace. "Oh, Benny, to think of you standing trial before that tobacco planter Washington. How dare they presume to judge you, after all that you've done in this war?"

"There, there, my darling." Arnold leaned toward his wife and stroked her cheek with his rough hand. "You are not to worry about me. My record speaks for itself, and Washington will see to it that I'm cleared."

"But a court-martial sounds so terrifying."

"I've faced worse." Arnold shrugged, the bluster in his voice perhaps more for his wife's sake than his own.

"I hate to think of you having to defend your honor against Joseph Reed."

"A panel of military men will surely not side with Reed over *me*. No, the men will not betray me. They love me."

"At least *they* do, Benny." Peggy sighed.

"And you do." Arnold took his wife's chin in his hand. "May I rest assured of that?"

"Of course, Benny." Peggy jerked her chin free, all seriousness. "But do see about the money they owe you."

"Excuse me, General and Mrs. Arnold." Clara edged forward, carrying the hamper her master had asked her to prepare. "The provisions we've prepared for your journey, General Arnold. Some cold ham and chicken, and some apples with bread and cheese."

"Thank you, Clara." Arnold nodded at the maid. "Run that out to Franks and have him set it in the carriage. He'll have to make room amid all the jugs of ale he's loaded up, I'm sure," Arnold quipped, forcing out a laugh.

When Clara had delivered the hamper and scurried back through the front door, Arnold turned toward the maid. "Clara," he said, as she kicked the snow loose from the bottom of her boots. "You be sure to take good care of Mrs. Arnold while I'm away, you hear?"

"Aye, sir." Clara nodded, lowering her eyes.

"It's no small solace to me, knowing that you are here with her."

"Clara always takes good care of me." Peggy stepped in front of her maid and took her husband's chin in her forefinger and thumb. "I just wish I could take care of *you*. I would make the journey to New Jersey with you."

"Not in this cold, and not in this condition." Arnold placed his hand lovingly over Peggy's swelling belly. "I can't wait to meet our little one."

"He's strong." Peggy smiled. "I feel him moving every day."

"You think it's a 'he'?" Arnold arched his eyebrows, his hand resting on her belly.

"I do. I think you'll have a son," Peggy said, putting her hand on top of his. They stood silently a moment, and the scene almost looked like a moment of tender familial intimacy.

Peggy broke the silence. "You shall have a son soon. All the more reason why you must insist that Congress settles your debt and reimburses you for the small fortune they owe us."

Arnold exhaled a long, slow breath, and Clara noticed just how tired he looked, and he was not even on the grueling road yet.

"It's getting late. It's best I depart. The sooner I'm off, the sooner I may put all of these filthy accusations behind me and get back to the service of my country." Arnold rested heavily on his cane.

"They don't deserve you, Benedict Arnold." Peggy sighed as she looked into her husband's face. "Not after they've treated you like this." They held each other for a long time, and when they separated, Peggy had tears in her eyes. Barley the dog looked equally forlorn, especially when his master ordered him to stay in the parlor and not follow him to the door.

"My darling wife, I can't leave you when you're upset like this." Arnold hovered at the doorway, his brow creased in worry.

"No, no. You must go. Go now so you'll be back in time for Christmas. It will be cause to celebrate indeed if you come back with your name cleared and your purse full with the money they owe you."

Arnold looked down at his wife, his posture stooping. "Even just to have my name cleared would be a victory, isn't that right, Peg?"

Peggy thought about this. "We need the money, Benny." Peggy

clung to his cloak, pulling his hand onto her belly. "So we can finally move. Do it for our son."

"I understand. I'll do what I can." With his head low, Benedict Arnold walked through the door, out into the blustery winter wind and the waiting court-martial.

THAT AFTERNOON, Clara showed Joseph Stansbury into the small parlor, where Peggy sat disconsolately before the fire.

"Is that Peggy Shippen buried under that pile of quilts?" Stansbury marched into the room, his heeled shoes clicking on the wooden floor, causing the loose boards to groan.

"Stansbury." Peggy's face brightened as she said his name. "Just what the doctor ordered to lift my spirits. Oh, don't you look fine! Of course, you always look fine. I don't think I've ever seen you wear the same suit twice."

"Business is good, madame." Stansbury doffed his plumed cap and sat down opposite Peggy. He eyed her appearance, taking in her plain calico dress barely visible under a mound of tattered quilts Mrs. Shippen had given them. The British merchant withheld his ordinary compliments to Peggy's appearance, Clara noticed.

"You called me Peggy Shippen just now. It's Peggy *Arnold,* don't forget."

"Oh! Apologies, old habits persist, Madame Arnold." The merchant winked.

"You know my Benny left this afternoon for his trial in New Jersey?" Peggy held her hands before the fire to warm them.

"Good gracious, what a charade." Stansbury smoothed a loose wisp of his powdered hair, tucking it neatly back into place.

"Shall I have Clara bring us tea?" Peggy offered.

"Tea? Are you the same Peggy Shippen—sorry, Peggy *Arnold*—I used to know? Let us have wine." Stansbury chuckled, and snapped his fingers for the maid.

"Wonderful idea," Peggy agreed, calling for her maid. "Clara, bring us some wine."

"Yes, ma'am." Clara curtsied.

"Oh Stan, if I had known you were coming I would have cleaned myself up. I look a fright." Peggy brushed her hair off her face. "I just never have any reason to dress, or put on rouge, or style my hair. No one invites me anywhere, at least not while these charges are pending. I heard Meg Chew hosted a soiree last weekend?"

Stansbury nodded, averting his eyes.

"She failed to invite me," Peggy said, her tone sour. "Not that it matters. I'd be mortified to step foot out of doors in my condition anyway . . ." Peggy lifted the quilt to show her growing belly.

"Nonsense, Peggy, you have the glow of an expectant mother."

"None of my old dresses fit me. I have to squeeze myself into this shapeless calico."

"Well I think you look as radiant as you ever did at a ball."

Peggy's voice grew wistful. "Remember the balls? Oh, we went to some fun ones, didn't we?" She leaned in and took her friend's hand as Clara served them each a glass of wine.

"To you, my lady." Stansbury held his glass high.

"To fun!" Peggy's eyes twinkled.

"The two are one and the same." Stansbury winked.

"I'm not so fun anymore, I'm afraid." Peggy shook her head. "No one ever visits. Most days it's just Benny and me in here. And Clara. And Lord knows, if Papa didn't pay Clara's wages, I wouldn't even be able to afford her." Peggy took a sip of wine and smacked her lips, savoring the taste.

"It must be very trying for you, Peggy." Stansbury shook his head. "A girl like you is meant to be dressed in silk, not calico."

"Silk? Ha! I haven't been allowed to buy anything on credit in six months."

"I don't know how you tolerate it, Peg."

"Benny tries to stay optimistic. But with Reed besmirching his name to the papers every day—calling him a cheat, and a thief—my husband gets overcome."

"I don't blame him," Stansbury replied, looking around the sparsely decorated interior of the small cottage. "It's drafty in here, isn't it?"

"I'm always freezing in here." Peggy made a face. "I don't know how I shall survive the winter. Will I die of the cold or the boredom first?"

"You and your husband should be in the Penn mansion." Stansbury sipped his wine. "Hosting dinners and dances every night."

"Or Mount Pleasant." Peggy sighed. "But how could we? Not when Congress still owes my husband the thousands that he paid out of his own pocket back in 'seventy-five."

"Such ill treatment from his so-called friends. No wonder he is overcome at times." Stansbury tented his long, thin fingers before his face in thoughtful silence. "You weren't made to live in a drafty cottage, Peggy Shippen. Too bad our country doesn't have royalty—then you could just go to Court to pass the winter."

"Wouldn't that be nice?" Peggy's eyes glimmered at the mere thought of it.

"We used to live like royalty, didn't we, Peg? Card games at Lord Rawdon's, dinners and dances every night."

"Oh, I think of those days very often, Stansbury. How I used to flit about on the arms of the British officers, sipping Champagne and eating oysters. Dancing until the sun came up." Peggy stared into the fire, a feeble smile on her face. "And now look at me . . . I'm poor . . . and fat."

"You are not fat." Stansbury tittered. "You are expecting a child."

"Remember what my waist was like? Now I would break a corset if I even tried to squeeze into one." Peggy curled her lips into a pitiful pout. "You know what I do sometimes? When I'm so terribly bored and it's been day after day of looking out the window at the cold? You know how I keep myself entertained, Stan?"

Stansbury finished his wine and summoned Clara. The maid refilled his cup. "How? Do tell."

"I console myself with the fact that, somewhere in the world, there is still fun like the fun we used to have . . . I imagine what your trips to New York City must be like. I close my eyes and imagine myself there with you, dancing and flirting. Listening to the violins. Do you attend parties with the British officers?"

"I do. They are crawling all over New York, still as dapper as ever. It's just like it used to be in Philadelphia. Remember that winter we had? When André and the men were here?"

"I could never forget it," Peggy answered, her voice dripping with nostalgia. "New York must be so beautiful in the snow with all of those redcoats at Christmastime. I'd give up an entire year of this life just to have one night there."

"It's too bad I can't smuggle you with me on my next business trip up there." Stansbury smirked. "You are far too recognizable to make it across the enemy lines."

"Not anymore." Peggy heaved a sigh. "I bet André would not even know me in this state. But please, Stansbury, do tell me what it's like up there. Let me pretend I'm there, even just for a minute."

"Well"—Stansbury thought—"General Clinton is in charge now. He is a great fan of entertainment. Much more so than Howe was. Clinton wants plays, and Masques, and music recitals constantly."

"How marvelous." Peggy imagined it.

"So it will be no surprise to hear that André has risen in the ranks and is a well-known favorite of Clinton's."

"No surprise at all." Peggy nodded, wistful in her remembering. "André could charm the boots off the devil if he wanted to." Peggy drained her wineglass, snapping her fingers to demand another refill. Clara poured her lady more wine and then chose a perch in the corner to take up a pile of Arnold's clothes. It seemed all his pants and jackets, patched so many times before, needed new mending. The corner was cold, being far from the fireplace. Clara's fingers felt brittle as she worked, but she knew her mistress would not want her too close when she had a visitor.

"And he's charmed his general, that's for sure," Stansbury said. "He's just recently been promoted, in fact."

"Oh? And what is André's new post?"

"Peggy." Stansbury paused, his face suddenly serious. "John André is now the chief of British Intelligence."

"Meaning?"

"Meaning, John André's job is to recruit spies," Stansbury said quietly.

"Spies?" Peggy's eyes narrowed. "How very dangerous."

"Indeed." Stansbury nodded.

"How does he find them?" Peggy asked.

"He has . . . sources . . . on the colonial side." The merchant paused, allowing Peggy to take another sip of her wine. "You know Peggy, I've been thinking."

"A dangerous pursuit. Why would you ever try such a thing?" Peggy giggled, hiccupping.

"No, I'm serious. You know how much I hate to see you suffering—in this tiny house, with no servants, no new clothing, no fun."

"Please, Stansbury, don't remind me. I'll cry."

"No, I simply mean to say that it's not right. Not after everything your husband has done. A woman like you should be glistening in jewels rather than shivering in calico. To see Reed slandering you both the way he has—spying on you while you shop and alleging that Arnold burned entire villages in Canada, killing everyone in sight."

"It's preposterous, I know." Peggy's volume increased with each sip of wine. "We Arnolds have been robbed of our fortune in this war, and have been called all sorts of names. And *these* are the men whom our so-called . . . revolution . . . has made into heroes."

"Peggy." Stansbury's voice was low. "If Washington doesn't appreciate your husband, there may be others who do." The windows beside them rattled in their frames, shaking against a violent gust of wind outside.

"But Stan, Washington is the head of the army. He must be the one to say—"

"I don't mean on this side." Stansbury held his thin hand out, like a seductive invitation to dance. "There *is* another way."

Peggy stared at her friend, her expression passing from confusion to understanding. And then to disbelief.

"Stan, surely you're not suggesting—" Peggy shook her head. She threw a glance in the corner toward her maid, but Clara had buried her face in the darning work and appeared not to have overheard.

"Stan, this is highly dangerous talk. To suggest that Benedict—" Peggy's voice remained low.

"I'm not suggesting anything, I'm merely stating a fact. Your husband is in debt and his name has been besmirched by the colonials. The . . . other . . . side might not treat him so roughly. No, they are much more genteel. They appreciate people like you. In fact, they'd likely give you both a hero's welcome."

Peggy cleared her throat, sitting in silence a moment before answering. "Stan, you know my husband; he's a man of character. He loves this country, he'd never—"

"Yes, but he's also a man who loves his wife. And with another mouth to feed soon." The merchant looked at her belly, causing her to cover it with her hand protectively. "He'd listen to you, Peggy."

"Stan, he would never speak to me again if I even breathed a word of this. You can't be serious."

"André is in charge of finding spies. It could be done. And it could be done quickly. Imagine . . . spending next winter in New York." Stansbury paused, leaning forward. "Or even better, *London*! Can you even imagine how much fun we'd have together at Christmastime at Court?" The merchant raised his eyebrows.

"Stansbury!" Peggy looked around the room, as if afraid that they would be heard. Clara, though her heart was hammering against her rib cage, still did not look up from her corner. Peggy, satisfied that her maid either did not hear or could not understand the nature of their discussion, continued in a low voice. "Stan, are you suggesting treachery? We could be hanged just for having this conversation."

The china merchant shrugged his shoulders. "Your husband once said there was nothing in the world he wouldn't do to make you happy, Peggy Shippen. Just . . . think about it, that's all I'm asking." Stansbury looked around the room, at the ragged curtains that shivered in the drafty air of the windows, at the threadbare carpet that covered only a fraction of the cold, rough floor planks. He turned back toward Peggy, allowing his eyes to linger on the faded collar of her too-tight dress. Finally he looked into Peggy's eyes, speaking in a suggestive, haughty tone. "That is, unless you're happy here."

"If we're to succeed," Peggy whispered, leaning her forehead against the cold windowpane, her breath clouding the glass as she exhaled, "we can't have him thinking that he's betraying his country. No, his character would never abide such a thing. But rather, we must convince him that it is his *country* that has already betrayed him. If the break has already been made, he commits no wrong."

Clara hesitated in the doorway, watching as her mistress spoke to herself, alone in the empty bedroom.

"Begging your pardon, Miss Peggy?" Clara knocked on the wooden door.

"Oh, Clara." Peggy turned to face her maid, her large belly protruding out from under the shape of her dressing gown. "I didn't see you there."

"The hot water is ready. Would you still like your bath?" Clara shifted her weight, struggling against the oppressive load of the pails of water.

"Yes, come in." Peggy opened the front of her gown and dropped it to the floor, standing before Clara in her brazen nakedness. Clara blushed at the immodesty, even after years with Peggy. "I'm so large I'll probably float in the water," Peggy grumbled as she stepped laboriously into the tub. "Hurry up and pour it in. I'm freezing."

Clara tipped the first bucket, splashing her mistress with the warm water she'd hauled from the kitchen fire. Then she poured the second bucket, and the third, and the fourth, hurrying up and down the stairs with the heavy loads that gave her an ache in her back.

"Now bring me my soaps," Peggy ordered once the tub was full, lapping the water onto her face.

"Which flavor would you like, miss? Bayberry? Lemon?"

"Wildflower." Peggy demanded the one bar that Clara didn't already have in her hands. Clara found the soap in Peggy's dresser and slid it into her mistress's wet hands.

"Ahhhh, this is nice." Peggy slipped down into the water, submerging her head under the surface. The room around them filled with the floral fragrance of the steamy tub—the bedroom windows fogged with condensation, and the air filled with the balminess of a Turkish bath. Clara had to admit it was a nice contrast to the rest of the drafty cottage.

She heard a stirring below, and the voice of Major Franks ordering the horses to halt. When the front door opened downstairs, Barley erupted in excited yelps.

"Hello? My Peg?" A familiar, thunderous voice rang out from below the floorboards.

"Benny's home," Peggy gasped, sitting upright in the bathtub. "Benny, I'll be right down," Peggy yelled. Then, turning to Clara, "No, I've got a better idea. Clara, go tell my husband that I'm in the bath and I'm waiting for him."

"Will you dress first, my lady?" Clara assumed, fetching the muslin dressing gown off the hook.

"No. Tell my husband that I would like him to join me in the bath."

"In the bath?" Clara did not attempt to mask her embarrassment.

"That's what I said, Clara."

Clara descended the stairs and entered the drawing room, where she found a red-faced, frozen Arnold poking the fire in a desperate attempt to coax some additional heat from its embers. "General Arnold, welcome home." Clara curtsied.

"Clara! It's good to see you." Arnold smacked his thick hands together and blew on them. His hair, Clara noticed, appeared entirely gray. "Where is the lady of the house?"

"Mrs. Arnold has asked me to tell you that she is in the bath." Clara cleared her throat, balling her fists by her side. "And she'd like you to join her."

Arnold raised his eyebrows, intrigued by the invitation, only prompting Clara's blush to turn a deeper shade of purple.

"Well, I suppose I should obey my wife." Arnold removed his dirty, snow-covered cloak and tossed it onto the chair. He limped to the stairs and pulled his way up with uncharacteristic agility.

"Benny, you're home." Peggy beamed as her husband entered the steamy room.

"And what a homecoming." He clapped his hands at the sight of his wife.

"My, you look frigid, Benny. Look at the tip of your nose, as red as a cherry," Peggy said from the bathtub.

"Look how big you've got while I was gone." Arnold stooped down, kissing his wife first, and then her belly, which protruded above the surface of the sudsy water.

"Clara?"

"Ma'am?"

"General Arnold is frozen from his travels. Fetch us some more hot water and two mugs of hot rum cider." Peggy turned back to her husband, her voice inviting now, like the balmy tub water. "Benny, why don't you get out of those weary travel clothes and join me? There's room for two in here, even if I am as large as a house."

"If you say so, my dear." Arnold kicked his boots off, landing them on the wooden floor with unceremonious thuds.

Clara knocked at the door, shifting her weight nervously. No response but the sound of Peggy's giggles from within. Clara knocked again. "I have the fresh bathwater, my lady."

"Yes, Clara, come in," Arnold answered her.

It was a staggering sight. Her mistress and Arnold, sitting opposite each other in the crowded, bubbly tub. Peggy, her breasts swollen from the pregnancy, swabbed warm, soapy water on her husband's scruffy neck and cheeks. He looked terrible—exhausted and cold, and as if he hadn't had a shave in weeks, but he seemed to be thawing under his wife's tender ministrations.

"Now, my darling husband, you must tell me how the court-martial went."

Clara poured the first bucket of steaming water over the tub, grateful for the heavy cover of the foamy, wildflower-scented bubbles.

"Oh, Peggy. My sweet Peggy. It was insufferable. The whole thing." Arnold waved his hands in defeat, splashing the sudsy water over the surface of the tub. "My leg ached after the journey. And to see Washington's face, Peggy. He looked at me, limping around, with such pity. It was just mortifying."

"So, what did he say?" Peggy picked up a sponge and began scrubbing her husband's thick arms.

"Well, first of all, Reed—for all his delaying and posturing, claiming he had damning evidence that would prove my corruption—the fool had absolutely no one to testify. And no proof," Arnold growled, pulling on the hairs of his beard.

"As we knew would be the case." Peggy ran her soapy fingers through the thick graying hairs on her husband's chest. "So they cleared your name?" She spoke slowly, languidly, as if to calm her husband's ire.

"On the contrary, my lady." Arnold's fist pounded the water again, this time splashing Clara's petticoat as she stood there, refilling the tub water. "They threw out all the charges but three. That . . . *court*"—Arnold could not hide the thick contempt in his voice—"found me guilty of making a personal gain from selling private goods, using the public wagons for my personal use, and . . ." His voice trailed off.

"And?" Peggy prodded, her jaw clenched tightly.

"Favoring loyalists."

Peggy nodded her head, absentmindedly weaving her finger through a loose curl. After a long pause, she asked, "The penalty?"

"Negligible. A light reprimand from Washington. But the indignity was enough to cause me to hate Reed and the entire Continental Congress forever; I might as well have been tarred and feathered. And by my own countrymen."

"It's not right." Peggy looked fixedly toward the steamy windows. "It's just not right. A reprimand from Washington, ha! You know how I feel about that tobacco planter."

"I know, Peg, I know," Arnold conceded. "But he is still our commander. And if I know Washington, he will refrain from issuing any reprimand. He will state publicly that he has, but he will not. He's an honorable man, even if no one else is, and he knows that all I have left to me are my character and good name. He did seem to sympathize with me throughout the entirety of the trial."

"Well, even so. You might think Washington has honor. But that damned Continental Congress. I'm guessing that they said nothing about reimbursing for you the thousands they still owe you?"

He looked down, silently shaking his head.

"How can we go on, then?"

They sat in brooding silence for several minutes. Eventually, Peggy spoke. "Benny, I know you still feel fidelity to Washington." She cocked her head. "Because you're a good and loyal man. But I think Reed and the Pennsylvania Council, along with the whole Continental Congress, are a pack of lying criminals."

"You'll hear no argument from me on that score, Peg."

"You know something, Benny?" Peggy took a long sip of rum. "The British have been offering peace since 1778. That's two years of fighting that we've been forced to endure now, patriots being forced to kill their own brothers. And why?" Peggy leaned in, whispering now. "Because the Continental Congress *wants* to prolong this war. All they care about is making a profit off this war. That is why they are coming after you like this—to distract the public. To make *you* the enemy, so that no one notices how corrupt *they* are!"

Clara bit her tongue at the statement. Never mind the fact that the Continental Congress, far from making a profit, had been driven to near bankruptcy funding the war. But she merely wished to dump in the last pails of water and leave this scene.

"Peggy." Arnold looked at his wife, his cheeks rosy now from the warmth of the bath. "I had no idea you were such a little conspirator."

"Benny, those are the facts, plain and simple." Peggy spoke with a carefully spun nonchalance, but Clara detected the intensity lurking beneath her words. Arnold sat opposite Peggy, uttering not a word as he stared at her—at her hair, which was even thicker with curls from the pregnancy, her cheeks flushed from the steam, the ripe and enchanting fullness of her face and figure. Peggy let him gawk, let the silence hang between them, heavy, like the fog of the steamy water.

After several minutes, Arnold spoke. "You know, I'm starting to believe that you may be right." Arnold stroked his beard as he thought.

"I know I'm right. Anyhow"—Peggy sighed, sliding her body

through the water to be nearer to her husband—"enough politics. I'm exhausted—it's tiring being this large with your baby." She smiled invitingly, caressing her swollen belly. "I think I'll have one more mug of rum cider and then get in bed, Benny. Will you join me? You must be fatigued from your journey."

"I'd love to join you in bed. Though I can't promise I'll want to sleep."

"Who said anything about sleeping?" Peggy giggled like her eighteen-year-old self, and whatever she did below the surface of the water caused Arnold to simper in boyish delight. He rose from the bath and Clara spun quickly so that she could avert her eyes before the image of her master's naked body was seared into her mind.

Clara missed Cal. Where was he on this cold December day? she wondered. Did he have a fire to keep him warm? Did he have shoes, or had they fallen apart during the grueling winter, like the shoes of so many of the other soldiers she'd heard of? She sat at the small table of the Arnolds' kitchen, alone in the world, with no one in whom she might confide. No creature who cared for her except perhaps Barley, the mutt. The only sound she heard was the crackling of the logs in the fire, the rattling of the windows against the bitter wind, and the giggling of her mistress from where she lay upstairs with Arnold.

Her mistress had complained of the boredom stretching out across the winter—but her mistress at least had some companionship. Her husband, her friend Stansbury. A baby growing inside of her to prepare for. And, if she chose to, Peggy could cross the garden and go see her parents. All Clara had were the other servants, and she only saw them for a few minutes at a time. And without Cal, it wasn't the same anyway. But perhaps they would have news from him over in the big house. Clara had an idea and grabbed her cloak. She would use this time while the Arnolds were enclosed in their bedroom to cross the yard to the Shippens' kitchen.

"Good afternoon, Hannah." Clara paused at the doorway, kicking her boots to dislodge the snow that had collected up to her ankles from the short walk. The cook was cutting into a thick side of salted pork, scraping off pieces of bacon for the family's dinner. The scent made Clara's mouth water.

"Ah, Clara Bell." Hannah looked up as she walked in. "You're a sight for sore eyes, and a welcome one at that. How are things going over in the Arnold household?"

"How shall I answer that?" Clara looked out the window through the darkening courtyard toward the little cottage.

"That good, eh?" Hannah offered her a sympathetic smirk. "There, there, let's see that smile we all miss so much, Clara."

Clara offered the old woman a feeble smile.

"Come in, stay awhile." Hannah waved her forward and Clara obeyed.

"It smells delicious in here, Hannah." Clara leaned over a cauldron that sat warming over the hearth.

"Carrot ginger soup," Hannah said. "You'll come over and fetch some at dinnertime for your mistress."

"Aye." Clara nodded, eyeing the warm concoction hungrily.

"So, she let you out?" Hannah asked, sampling the soup on the tip of the wooden spoon.

"She's napping." Clara slipped her cloak off and hung it on a hook, taking a seat at the table. "May I trouble you for a cup of tea, Hannah?"

"Certainly, my dear." Hannah reached for the pot heating over the flames and poured steaming water into a mug. "So, the general is home? I thought I saw the carriage dropping him off."

"Indeed, he just returned."

"His limp seems to be getting worse by the day."

"And the journey to New Jersey for the court-martial didn't help," Clara answered.

Hannah placed the tea before Clara. "How did it go? Was he cleared?"

"Of all but three charges." Clara blew on the scalding liquid. "Using the wagons, profiting from the goods, and favoring loyalists."

"You mean marrying a loyalist, right?" Hannah winked, slowly stirring the carrot soup. "Clara," she continued, "I don't mean to offend your lady, but, if you don't mind my asking—didn't he do those things? I heard you telling Caleb about the goods he had back at the Penn mansion." His name, spoken aloud, pulsed through Clara.

The old cook continued. "All the goods he'd taken from the shops and then sold through that merchant, Stansbury."

Clara cocked her head, focusing her attention on the question. "I think he's of the mind that the Congress owes him so much money, he is entitled to do a little profiteering on the side. That, and, he's made the case that it's what everyone in the army is doing, it's just that he's the only one getting punished."

"Ha! Everyone in the army doing it? I can guarantee you that General Washington is doing nothing of the sort. Why, he could be spending his winters in mansions or returning to Mount Vernon, but he sleeps out in the snow with his men just like he's one of them."

"Washington seems to be the one man my master still finds to be honorable," Clara agreed, taking a slow sip of her tea.

"Oh, Clara, hello." Mrs. Quigley entered the kitchen, carrying a bundle of papers. "How nice to have a visit from you. We miss you in this kitchen."

"I miss you too, more than you can know," Clara answered, warming her hands on the outside of her mug.

"It's so quiet with both you and Cal gone," Mrs. Quigley said distractedly, riffling through the papers she carried. Clara swallowed hard, lowering her eyes; the mere mention of his name quickened her pulse. She was about to ask Mrs. Quigley if she'd had any word from Cal, when the old woman continued. "When you go back over to the Arnolds' cottage, remember to take some fresh candles and firewood with you. You must be running low. The judge worries about you all in that drafty little cottage. Every time he sees me he asks me if I've made sure his daughter has enough food, firewood, tea, candles." The housekeeper poured herself a cup of tea.

"Well, we appreciate Judge Shippen's generosity, you can be sure of that." Clara did not want to imagine what the environment in the Arnold home would be like if not for the judge's generosity in feeding them and keeping them warm this winter.

"Is General Arnold still not getting wages?" Mrs. Quigley wore a look of concern.

"No. He got nothing for all the months while we were awaiting the trial, on account of his suspension." Clara took another sip of her tea, savoring the warmth it kindled in her belly.

"Oh dear. And with a baby on the way." Mrs. Quigley sighed. "How is Miss Peggy tolerating it?"

"She has her good days and her bad days," Clara answered.

"Look at you, Clara. You've become quite the diplomat!" Hannah laughed, turning to the housekeeper. "I don't think Mr. Benjamin Franklin could have answered that question with more grace."

Clara smiled as she continued. "Miss Peggy will be happier now that her husband is back and the trial is over."

"Let's hope, for your sake, Clara." Hannah nodded, stirring the soup.

Clara seized the lull in the conversation. "Mrs. Quigley, I don't suppose you've had any word from Caleb?"

"As a matter of fact, Clara, I'm happy you stopped in because I've just received a letter from my nephew and he asks after you specifically." Mrs. Quigley began once more to sort the pile of papers with which she'd entered. "Here it is. There's a parcel in his envelope, sealed, with your name on it."

"A letter from Cal?" Clara gripped her mug of tea to prevent her fingers from trembling.

"Yes, he mentions you several times in the letter to me. You can read it if you like. And here's the note especially for you." Mrs. Quigley slid two papers in front of Clara and rose from the table, as if to give her privacy to read them. Clara took the pages in her hands, elated. The first was the letter from Caleb to his aunt.

My Dear Aunt,

I write to let you know that I am well. I hope you and the entire household are as well. I've been assigned to Fort Verplanck, which is in New York on the Hudson River, approximately 30 miles north of New York City. We are in the southernmost fort of Colonial-occupied New York, while immediately to our south it is British territory. But do not let that give rise to concern—the two sides honor the battle lines with all proper respect and formality, with passes required to cross the lines, etc. etc.

As winter assignments go, I am one of the lucky ones, given that I am at a fort with a roof over my head and a fire to keep me warm. Washington and his men are down in Morristown, New Jersey, out in the open, so that their fiercest enemy this winter shall not be the one they meet in battle, but the cruel cold.

I will confess I think about Hannah's cooking often, and when I sleep, I dream sometimes that I'm back in the Shippens' kitchen, sitting at a full table of ham and sturgeon, potatoes and mushrooms, tarts and bread and jam. I grow hungry simply by penning this letter.

Please give my warmest affection to Uncle Quigley and the rest of the household, and especially the horses in the stables. I've included a separate note for Clara, which I ask that you give to her.

I look forward to the day when I shall be able to tell you more about my adventures in person. Until then, imagine me looking sharp and incredibly handsome in the soldier's uniform—for in your imagination, I can be so!

With affection, your nephew,
Caleb Little

Clara read the letter in its entirety twice, savoring each word and swallowing the admission of just how terribly she missed him. She imagined his smile and his voice. How his words teased her—this letter a mere shadow of the real person with whom she longed to share a conversation. When she had finished the letter, Clara sat in silence, making a plan to read his other letter alone.

"Keep it." Mrs. Quigley smiled at her, interrupting her thoughts.

"Pardon me?" Clara looked up.

"Keep that letter."

"No, I can't. It's yours."

"Oh, don't be a pest, child, I've read it through a hundred times—keep it. He'd want you to have it." Mrs. Quigley paused. "My nephew was always so fond of you."

"I miss him," Clara confessed, holding the paper a little tighter in her fingertips.

"He misses you as well." The housekeeper sipped her tea.

"You should write him," Hannah said.

Clara looked back at the letter, at Caleb's handwriting, and she imagined him working on it at night before the fire, up in Fort Verplanck.

"Of course you should. He would wish to hear from you," Mrs. Quigley agreed.

"Do you think that perhaps he might be too busy?" Clara wondered aloud.

"Not too busy to hear from home and a dear friend," Mrs. Quigley pressed. "Write him."

"All right, then. I will." Clara nodded, rising from the table.

"Before you go—there's a letter for your master in this pile. Where is it?" Mrs. Quigley riffled through her papers. "Ah! Here it is. Military business, from the looks of it."

"Thank you." Clara smiled at the housekeeper, her spirits lifted by this visit, by the news from Cal. "Thank you." She left the kitchen, stepping into the cold yard, and loped across the darkening orchard. Tonight, she would sit down and write to him. She had so much news for him. But first, she longed to hear what he had to say to her.

In the warmth and brightness of the Arnolds' empty kitchen, Clara opened Cal's second, private letter. The trembling of her fingers made it tedious to unfold the note.

His handwriting and manner of greeting were familiar, a salve to Clara's nerves.

Clara Bell,

A previous letter to my aunt contains many more details about my assignment, my daily life, and the rest of that news. But I needed a word with you in private, Clara Bell. Perhaps the war has made this soldier sentimental. Or perhaps having some distance and some space has allowed me to see things more clearly. Regardless, I've had a heavy heart since the day I left, knowing that you and I did not have the chance to bid one another a proper farewell. Yes, we said our goodbyes, but in a room crowded with our fellow servants. In any event, I'd like you to know that I think of you often, and I hold you to be one of my best friends in this world.

Heavens, that seems as if that were in another life, that day when I bid you farewell. How much has changed for me since then! The journey north, the assignment to my fort, the introduction to my fellow soldiers and patriots. Joining up was the best decision I could have made.

One of my fellow soldiers, a fellow by the name of John Williamson, has family in these parts. Next chance we have for furlough, we will travel to meet his cousins and uncle. I look forward to a home-cooked meal, though I'm certain the supper will be lacking when compared with Hannah's food. Did we not enjoy ourselves in the Shippen kitchen?

I hope you are well, Clara Bell, and I would welcome the chance to hear from you. I'd write more, but my candle wick is about to expire.

Your faithful friend,
Cal

Her hands trembled, forcing Clara to place the letter down on the table. As she read and reread his words, she saw him: blond hair, long and shaggy. His face soft with whiskers, lit up by the campfire as he sat, strumming on his guitar, pausing from his music to crack some joke. Perhaps even chewing on a piece of straw as he did. Taking her head in her hands, Clara wept.

How she missed him! Cal, the boy who had once sat beside her at every meal, was now a world away. He wrote of his fort in New York, but to Clara, it might as well have been England, it seemed so impossibly distant. And he was living a life about which she knew nothing. Yes, he still cared for her, of that she was certain. But nowhere in either letter did Cal speak of an emotion stronger than a deep friendship. The realization that she had missed her chance filled her with a regret so deep that she could have drowned in it. For how long she sobbed, she did not know. The fire had expired and the kitchen was dark, and she was certain that her face was patchy with tears when she heard the summons.

"Clara!"

Clara's shoulders dropped. She folded Cal's letter and tucked it alongside the other two in the folds of her petticoat.

"Clara!" Peggy had risen from her nap and seemed to be in the parlor. "Clara? Come at once!" Peggy's voice carried irritation, and Clara reluctantly rose from the kitchen table.

"Here I am, my lady." Clara hurried into the parlor.

"Clara, there you are. I had worried you'd gone deaf." Peggy sat, rubbing her bulging belly. "Where were you? There's a draft in here."

"I've just come in from the big house, Miss Peggy."

"Why did you go there?" Peggy looked at her maid, fresh-faced from her nap.

"To see whether there was mail for you and General Arnold," Clara lied.

"Oh, and was there?"

"Yes, in fact, there is a letter for the general." Clara slipped her hand into her skirt pocket and retrieved the letter Mrs. Quigley had given her.

"Good." Peggy took the letter. "Now light this fire; you've let out all the warm air on your walk outside."

"Yes, madame," Clara answered, but she was alarmed by how Peggy's face became pinched when she looked at the envelope in her hands. "Mrs. Arnold, is everything quite all right?" Clara asked.

"A letter from Washington." Peggy looked up, waving the letter. "It's from Washington! Benny! Oh, Clara, go wake my husband. Benny, wake up, come downstairs!"

Arnold rushed from bed and pulled himself down the stairs, tucking his linen shirt into his breeches as he entered the parlor. "Give it here." Arnold waved his wife toward him and propped himself up on the chair. The dog settled in at his feet. Arnold opened the letter.

With trembling hands, he held the note and read aloud. Clara, lighting the hearth before them, could not help but overhear its contents.

> *My dear friend, General Benedict Arnold: I would be much happier in an occasion of bestowing commendations on an officer who rendered such distinguished services to his country as Major General Arnold.*

"As he ought to," Peggy snarled, interrupting.

"Quiet!" Arnold showed rare frustration, and read on.

> *But, in the present case, a sense of duty and a regard for candor oblige me to declare that I consider some of this conduct imprudent and improper.*

Arnold read on with trembling hands as Washington commended the court for finding corruption and correcting it speedily during the recent trial.

> *Even the shadow of a fault tarnishes the luster of our finest achievements. I reprimand you for having forgotten that, in proportion as you have rendered yourself formidable to our enemies, you should have been guarded and temperate in your deportment toward your fellow citizens.*

Washington concluded this censure by sending his personal regards to the Arnolds. "Well, we do *not* return the warm feelings." Peggy spat.

Arnold summarized the remaining sentences: "And he expresses his hope that both I and the Pennsylvania Council will move forward without hard feelings. But, how is that even possible? And why doesn't he chastise Reed for his nastiness in the affair?"

"What is this? It looks like there is something more, at the bottom." Peggy pointed and Arnold looked down at the paper.

At the end of the letter, Washington had scrawled a postscript.

> *Postscript: Let General Arnold be made aware of the fact that I've sent a copy of this letter to the Continental Congress for their records as well, so that they may be assured that the punishment decided upon by the court was fully meted out.*

Arnold lifted his eyes from the letter, staring blankly into the room as if he saw nothing before him.

"He hasn't. He couldn't have . . ." Arnold stammered, hopeless. "The Congress will no doubt leak this letter, and news of my shame, to the papers." His face had drained of blood, his skin now paler than his white linen shirt.

"Ha! He is obligated by a sense of 'duty'? Does he even know what the word means?" Peggy's voice was thick with indignation. "It's an affront to your honor! After you've sacrificed so much. Here we are, living like servants. And with a child on the way."

Peggy looked to her husband, her eyes wild. But his silence only seemed to spur her to further outrage. "You know what I think? I think Washington is an impotent leader, just like he is an impotent husband! He's been married to that hag Martha for how long? Ten years? And yet they have no children!"

Peggy railed like a fury, pacing back and forth, while Arnold stood in a stunned silence.

"And he allows Martha's brats from her first marriage to keep the Custis name while they are living in his house. He's impotent! Weak! If he had any vigor, he'd order Congress to pay you back!"

Peggy stared at her husband, burning him with her gaze. "Well?" she shrieked. "What do you have to say, Benedict Arnold?"

If Peggy was growing louder with her frustration, Arnold had retreated into a still, stony silence. Finally, he spoke. "It would appear that no honor or loyalty remain, either in Congress or among the leaders of my beloved army."

"That's precisely what I have been telling you." Peggy fumed.

"Then, what is left for me? I wish they had simply ordered my execution, rather than have me live like this, with a blackened name. I cannot go back to an army that has labeled me corrupt."

"Nor should you," Peggy agreed, indignant.

"Then there's nothing left for me." Arnold practically collapsed into the armchair, stretching his injured leg out before him.

"There *is* another way . . ." Peggy glided toward him, balancing on the arm of his chair. "A way back to honor, and fame . . . and fortune." She ran her fingers through his hair. He looked up at her, questioning her with his expression.

"There is an army left in this world that still venerates honor. Still loves this land and the people of this land. And they would welcome you into the fold with open arms, rather than insult you."

Arnold's body moved back, away from his wife. "You cannot mean I should defect . . ."

"Benny." Peggy took her husband's hand in her own. "That is precisely what I mean."

In a harried whisper, almost as if he were afraid, Arnold leaned toward his wife. "Peggy, I will not hear this. And I'll ask that you never raise such a preposterous suggestion ever again!"

But Peggy's voice was perfectly calm, even soothing. "My darling, Benny. You haven't even heard what I have to say yet."

"B-but . . ." Arnold stammered, "but . . . it could never be done. We'd be hanged as traitors."

"What if I told you I could arrange it all?" Peggy spoke confidently, quietly.

"I'd say that you had gone mad. And I'd beseech you not to hazard our lives and the life of our child, Peggy."

"You think I'd risk my child's life?" Peggy pulled Arnold's hand onto her belly. "No, I wouldn't risk my child's life. After all, it is *for* my child that I'd even consider such an option."

"Peggy!" Arnold's hand recoiled from her belly, as if it were hot to the touch. "My darling wife." He paused, and Clara yearned for him to quiet her, to stop Peggy Shippen's scheming once and for all. Arnold studied his wife curiously, as if realizing in that moment that he'd never actually understood her true nature. Both Clara and Peggy held their breaths as they awaited his judgment.

And then, finally, Arnold spoke.

"Tell me more."

"I've thought it all through." The two aspiring traitors sat in their dark dining room, the light of a lone candle dancing off their faces as they ate the carrot soup and bacon provided by Peggy's father.

"Stansbury told me that a certain Major John André, with whom I used to be, er, friends, is now the chief of British intelligence. He enjoys a special closeness with General Clinton in New York City." Peggy refilled her husband's ale mug.

"Yes, I know of Clinton. And I've heard of André," Arnold said, scooping himself spoonful after spoonful of soup.

"Well, Stansbury sees Johnny, I mean Major André, all the time in New York. And Stansbury can be trusted."

"Yes, but can André be trusted?" Arnold took a gulp of his ale. "Who's to say he will protect our confidence if we approach him?"

Peggy paused for effect. A knowing grin took hold of her face, her features aglow in the dim candlelight as she slipped backward into some distant memory from an evening long past. "André knows me. He'd never betray his old friend Peggy Shippen."

It was decided on New Year's Eve. Arnold and Peggy ignored the noise outside Independence Hall, choosing instead to sit together by their fire to plot. Clara, ordered to stay indoors and tend to her pregnant mistress, strained her ears to hear the celebrations in the streets. She longed to hear the cheering of Mr. and Mrs. Quigley and Hannah, who had joined the revelry beneath the church tower. How much had changed in a year, she thought, remembering back to the night when she'd heard the "Liberty Song" and the ebullient wishes for victory. When Cal had told her he'd be enlisting. When Peggy had announced her engagement, then just a happy, hopeful bride with a doting groom. Clara willed her ears to hear, hoping at least to make out the cheers of all those strangers, their merry voices mingling with the church bells. But Clara heard nothing. Nothing but the low, determined voices of the two conspirators for whom she worked.

"That is the best way." Arnold agreed with his wife's suggestion that Stansbury could carry the note to André for them—if he agreed to the task.

"I'll ask him," Peggy answered her husband. "He won't disappoint us."

"I MUST look very fine today for my visit with Stansbury." Peggy found Clara in the kitchen on New Year's Day. The maid looked longingly at her warm bread, spread with the rare scrape of butter and a drizzle of honey in honor of the holiday. She had not yet had a chance to eat.

"Well? Come on," Peggy beckoned her maid, taking the piece of bread for herself and nibbling while she walked. "You must help me dress." Peggy trotted off toward the stairwell, her hungry maid following behind her.

Peggy selected a gown of rich purple velvet, which she wore without stays, and a matching cap trimmed with long black feathers. Her reflection took up more space in the mirror than it once had, but, Clara decided, her face still dazzled when she smiled, her curls still bounced when she cocked her head.

"How do I look? Can I still pass for someone who used to be the most popular belle in Philadelphia?" Peggy adjusted her cap.

"Of course, my lady," Clara answered dutifully.

"Thank goodness I still have you to help me." Peggy reached forward and took her maid's hand in her own soft white palm. "Now Clara, you shall be my special helper today."

This pronouncement kindled trepidation within Clara.

"You must go into town and pay a call to Stansbury." Peggy pulled on her cuffed sleeves so that they fanned out to their full width around her elbows. "The store won't be open on account of the holiday, but he'll be in his apartment above. He'll probably still be sleeping off his New Year's Eve wine, if I had to guess."

"I am to pay a visit to him?" Clara asked, confused.

"Yes, you," Peggy answered flatly. Clara knew precisely why her mistress wished to visit with the china merchant; she wanted to enlist him in her treachery. But how did she, Clara, fit in?

"But . . ." Clara knew better than to argue, but she was too confounded. "But, miss, I thought that it was *you* who had hoped to speak with the china merchant."

"I *do*!" Peggy sighed, exasperated. "But you think I'm going to go out in public like this?" She spread her palms over her belly. "No, the whole town would be scandalized, and everyone would be talking about how Benedict Arnold's expecting wife paid a visit to the china merchant. Reed would probably even have them print an article that I'm shopping again. No, this must be done in stealth." She leaned forward toward Clara. "That's why you shall go fetch him. No one knows or cares who *you* are. Tell Stan that Benny and I wish to meet with him in private, and bring him back here. Do not take no for an answer, and do not leave the shop until you have Stan in tow."

THE TASK did not prove to be difficult at all. Stansbury not only agreed to accompany Clara back to the Arnolds' cottage, he offered his coach to transport them. Whether it was to avoid the bitter winter weather, like he said, or to avoid the eager eyes of the town gossips who might see him walking with the Arnolds' maid, Clara could not decide. Either way, it seemed to Clara that the china merchant had been awaiting an invitation to such a meeting.

Clara led him into the house, lamenting the fact that she was now complicit in the nefarious plot. "General? Mrs. Arnold?" She scanned the empty drawing room. Mr. and Mrs. Arnold did not seem ready for the guest they had been expecting.

"Mr. Stansbury, please, take a seat by the fire. I shall fetch my masters and some tea." Clara ushered him to the chair closest to the blaze.

"Why, hello." Peggy appeared suddenly, as if she were a gowned apparition conjured from the air. "Joseph Stansbury."

"Peggy Shippen, you always did have a flair for the dramatic." The merchant rose and kissed her on both cheeks, pulling her hands aside. "Love the dress. You look divine."

"Thank you, Stan. You always look wonderful. Let me call that husband of mine in."

"Wait." Stansbury held stubbornly to Peggy's hands. "Does he know about . . . our idea?"

"He knows. I told him."

"And he supports us?" Stansbury's voice betrayed his hope.

"He does now." Peggy lifted a lone eyebrow, exchanging a knowing grin with her coconspirator.

"Excellent work, my dear. I knew you could pull it off."

"Joseph Stansbury!" Benedict Arnold limped into the room, extending his hand for a rough handshake that looked like it might snap the merchant's arm in half.

"General Arnold, an honor." The merchant doffed his cap and bent into a low, obsequious bow.

"Stansbury, sit down." Arnold limped over to a spot on the sofa beside him. Clara delivered their tea.

"You see how big my wife is?" Arnold handed his teacup back to Clara, asking the maid to bring him a mug of rum instead.

"She is radiant." Stansbury nodded, spooning sugar into his own drink. "The image of maternal bliss."

"Well, it's because I'm so fortunate in my choice of husband. That is what gives me my glow." Peggy nudged Arnold's shoulder.

A tense silence stretched between the trio, with none of them sure who should broach the purpose of their assembly. Peggy ran her fingers along the handle of her teacup but didn't touch her drink. Her husband gobbled down a mug of rum and asked Clara for a refill.

"Well," Peggy finally spoke. "Stansbury, thank you for coming here. We would have come to see you at the store, but, you see . . ." She pointed to her belly.

"It is my pleasure," the merchant answered. "I will admit I was hoping to get an invitation of this sort."

"Yes." Peggy nodded knowingly. "As you know, my husband and I have suffered a string of cruelties at the hands of certain people in positions of power. You know to whom we refer." Peggy looked at the merchant, who nodded his understanding.

Peggy continued. "We've suffered for such a long time, and for no good reason. We have come to the conclusion that there is no harm in reaching out to a certain . . . friend . . . you and I share. A friend who might be able to present us with a better situation."

"Your meaning is perfectly understood, madame." Stansbury nodded.

"It is my understanding that you see this . . . friend . . . quite frequently when you travel to New York for business?" Peggy raised her eyebrows, orchestrating this exchange purely for the benefit of her husband. Arnold listened.

"Our paths cross often, my lady." Stansbury nodded.

"Well then, if you would be willing, we ask that you would deliver to him a letter. It has been years, and I'd love to rekindle my friendship with the monsieur. Shall we call him—John Anderson?"

"He would answer to no other name." Stansbury grinned back at her.

"You understand," Peggy spoke, her voice lowered, "that if this plan works out, and we end up in the—er, situation we hope to, your reward would be handsome."

"I thank you." Another deep nod of Stansbury's head. "But you know that my . . . inclinations . . . have always been toward one side, the side I believe to be in the right. The side which I believe you, Peggy, have always felt a loyalty toward as well."

"My loyalty is to my husband alone. He may determine our politics," Peggy answered smoothly, eliciting a proud blush from her husband's whiskered cheeks. "Here." Peggy slid a letter across the table to Stansbury. "You have a right to know the contents of the letter you deliver. Read it aloud so that my husband may approve as well."

Stansbury retrieved from his pocket an oversized magnifying glass and unfolded the letter in his hands reverentially, as if he were handling some sacred text. In his nasal British accent, he read aloud.

> *My Dear Mr. Anderson,*
>
> *I am writing as an old friend—the lady with whom you danced after the Meshianza so many years ago. Not* <u>*at*</u> *the Meshianza, but* <u>*after*</u> *the Meshianza. You and I are alone in the world in knowing about that moment, so I trust by now you've understood whose hand pens this missive, and will react with appropriate discretion.*
>
> *As you have likely heard, since you've left my town, I've*

made a new friend. He is remarkably good—generous, honest, and heroic. And he is interested in meeting you. To be frank, we've learned that you have been promoted to a position of prominence in your trade. You sell lace, right? Well, we may have some very valuable lace which you may be interested in trading for.

You know how I always loved lace.

If you are interested in hearing more, you may write me.

Your dear friend,
Madame la Turque

"Bravo." Stansbury joined Peggy in chuckling as he folded the letter back up. "Splendid, Peggy, I especially love your signature: Madame la Turque. Oh, he will know for certain who you are!"

"Precisely," Peggy agreed.

You and I are alone in the world in knowing about that moment, Peggy had written, forgetting completely that Clara had been present.

"Isn't this fun?" Peggy's eyes sparkled with mischief. Arnold alone seemed to understand the gravity of their situation.

"Ahem!" Arnold cleared his throat. "Fun? We could all hang for this. Fun? I think not. Stansbury, when will you deliver this letter?"

"General"—Stansbury wiped the jollity from his face—"I can leave for New York tomorrow."

"Good, yes. The sooner the better. What we ask is that you bring us a response in return. Once this . . . Anderson . . . has proven he can be trusted, we shall begin to discuss more specifics."

"A very wise plan, sir," Stansbury agreed.

"Well then, we wish you a safe trip. And remember, whatever you do, you breathe a word of this to no one, you understand?" Arnold leaned forward, his eyes fierce. "If you fail in this mission, and give us away, we will all most certainly be hanging from the gallows by spring."

CLARA COULDN'T carry the burden alone. She had to share the news with someone. But who could she tell? Oma was gone; even the life she'd led with Oma seemed as if it had belonged to another girl, another Clara. Caleb was miles away. The thought of writing about a possible treason in a letter to a soldier was ludicrous; his letters were certain to be censored. The Quigleys and Hannah would never believe such a wild development, and even if they did, they'd most likely scold Clara and tell her to stay out of the Arnolds' affairs.

Betsy could stop it. Yes, Peggy's sister would feel bound to interfere, especially with her husband fighting for Washington. But Peggy had always overpowered her older sister; she'd do so this time as well. And Peggy would no doubt sack Clara for telling Betsy about the plot.

Clara was ruminating over this, seeking in vain the name of some confidante, when she nearly bumped into Mrs. Quigley. "Clara, girl, watch where you're going, would you?" Mrs. Quigley was out back, carrying a large sack from the direction of the barns. Clara had been on her way to the big house to send a letter to Cal along in the morning post.

"Oh, hello, Mrs. Quigley, I was just coming to see you. May I help you with that?"

"Please do, child." Mrs. Quigley handed the sack to Clara. "Goose down. It's time to restuff the quilts. The judge and the missus are always complaining of the cold nights, as if they don't realize it's winter." Mrs.

Quigley opened the back door and led Clara into the Shippens' kitchen.

"What brings you here, girl?"

Clara deposited the sack of goose down on the floor beside the table. "I've come with a letter for Cal, I mean, Caleb. Would you post it with the rest of the letters?"

"Certainly." Mrs. Quigley nodded, pouring two cups of tea for herself and Clara.

"Where's Hannah?" Clara asked, looking around the ordinarily bustling kitchen.

"She complained of some pains"—Mrs. Quigley creased her brow— "so Mr. Quigley and I have suggested that she spend the morning in bed."

"What kind of pains?" Clara asked, taking the mug of tea that Mrs. Quigley offered her.

"Just the aches and pains of growing old. Something you do not need to worry about." Mrs. Quigley smiled, her expression weary. She pointed at Clara's letter, which rested on the table between them, unclaimed. "I'm happy to see that you've written Caleb. He'll be glad to hear from you."

She'd written him the evening before. Her hand was nervous and untrained, and her cursive had looked untidy and juvenile compared to Peggy's. She'd read it through after it was complete, sealing it in the envelope before she could lose her resolve:

Caleb,

Hello. How strange it is to be writing you. It's less preferable than how it used to be, sitting beside you at the table, exchanging news. I did get the message from your aunt, and the separate note just to me. You should know that I think of you often and return the fond feelings.

It is heartening to hear you safe and so happily adjusted

to your new life as a soldier. It sounds as though you've made a handful of friends already. Why does this not come as a surprise? I hope you have some furlough to visit the home of the friend you mentioned, that John Williamson. I imagine some time away would come as a relief, even if you do seem to be enjoying your work very much.

Life goes on here as you knew it, and yet, much has changed. You'll have heard the outcome of the Master's Court Martial by now. And that Miss Peggy is set to have her baby in the early spring. The Christmas holiday had a very different feeling this year, but I thought of you and our times together often. In the meantime, I shall keep your letters close to me. Just promise you shall take good care of yourself, and do come back and visit us, should you ever have the chance.

Fondly,
Clara Bell

"Here is the letter." Now in the kitchen, Clara handed the parcel to Mrs. Quigley. "Thank you for sending it for me."

"Of course, dear." The housekeeper nodded. "Tell me, Clara, how are things going in the Arnold household?" Mrs. Quigley took a sip of tea. "They must be preparing for the wee one's arrival."

Now was her chance, Clara thought, her nerves coiling inside her like a ball of twine. They were alone in the kitchen, with no one to overhear, and perhaps Mrs. Quigley might offer sage advice.

"Mrs. Quigley, things are frightful. Miss Shippen, I mean, Mrs. Arnold, has begun corresponding with John André again."

Mrs. Quigley's eyes rounded into two vast orbs. "André, that English fellow from a while back?"

"The very same." Clara nodded.

"But that cannot be true. Miss Peggy is married now."

Clara spoke in a hushed tone, fearful that someone might overhear her confession. "Indeed, ma'am, but General Arnold knows all about it. In fact, he is party to their exchanges."

"But why on earth would the Arnolds be conferring with Major John André?"

The truth poured forth from Clara like a flood: Peggy's disgust with her current circumstances; Arnold's frustration with Reed and Washington; the bathtub conversation; the letters transmitted through the china merchant. Mrs. Quigley remained attentive, absorbing the news in stunned silence as their tea grew cold between them. When Clara had finished, several minutes passed before Mrs. Quigley could collect herself and form a reply.

"Well, Clara." The old woman shook her head, speaking in barely a whisper. "This is either the wildest mistruth a girl like you could ever concoct, or you seem to have found yourself in the thick of some terrible mischief."

"Mrs. Quigley," Clara stammered, stung. "I tell you no lie."

"But how could you possibly know all this?" Mrs. Quigley narrowed her eyes, and they singed with disbelief.

"They speak right in front of me, as if I were invisible." Clara felt a stinging frustration, threatening tears; how could the housekeeper accuse her of falsehoods? "Mrs. Quigley, you may believe me, I assure you. We all live under that same very small roof; you would not fathom how much I am forced to overhear."

"Well, you'll take my advice and you'll keep it at that: hearsay." Now Mrs. Quigley cast a leery glance over her shoulder before continuing. "You're not to repeat this, Clara, do you understand me? This sort of talk could cost you your neck."

Clara's frustration was mounting, spilling out in defiant words. "But Mrs. Quigley, don't you think we ought to alert—"

"Clara Bell, enough!" Mrs. Quigley spoke with a sharpness that shocked Clara, so unexpected and out of character was the censure. "I said: you are not to repeat this. It is for your own good. We cannot allow such dangerous rumors to be swirling like this. Especially when your employer is a man as powerful as General Arnold. I will not tolerate it, do you understand me?" Mrs. Quigley's cheeks smoldered a deep red. Her words were terse but her meaning was clear to Clara: speak about what she knew again, and she'd lose her job and her home.

"I understand, Mrs. Quigley."

THE WIND was so fierce that Clara didn't hear the visitor leave the package. It was not until she went outside to fetch a fresh load of firewood that she saw it: a parcel waiting in the snow outside the Arnolds' cottage.

"My lady." Clara reentered the parlor, handing the parcel to Miss Peggy. "Something's arrived for you and the general."

"What is it?" Peggy summoned Clara to her perch before the fire. She was making a rare attempt at knitting. The start of a pair of baby's booties sat in her lap.

"It's unmarked, ma'am." Clara studied the bulky package wrapped in brown paper. "Doesn't appear to have come via the post."

"Fetch my husband," Peggy replied, taking the package and turning it over in her hands.

Clara woke Arnold from his nap and told him that his wife requested his presence in the parlor, that a package had arrived for them. Arnold, groggy from sleep, limped down the stairs toward the armchair opposite his wife.

"A package, eh?" Arnold's breath, Clara noticed, was tinged with the sour smell of ale; he was drinking more these days.

"Shall I open it?" Peggy did not await a reply before she tore through the brown paper, easily rending it in two. "It's come from Stansbury." Arnold looked on in keen interest.

Clara hoped to slip from the room, having no interest in hearing any more of their plots or conspiracies. But Arnold called her back: "Clara, before you run away from us, fetch me some ale, won't you?"

"Make that two," Peggy added. "After all, we are celebrating, aren't we?" She winked at her husband.

When Clara returned to the parlor, carrying two mugs of ale, Peggy was reading Stansbury's note aloud to her husband.

I hand-delivered the letter to André myself. André was intrigued, particularly when he heard from whom the letter came. He sent me back to you with the item included herewith.

Peggy then reached back into the brown package and retrieved two items. The first was another letter on a flimsy piece of parchment.

"What does it say?"

"Nothing, it would seem," Peggy answered her husband. "It's a series of numbers—entirely devoid of meaning."

"Curious." Arnold creased his brow. "And what's that?" Arnold pointed at the second item retrieved from the package, which had the appearance of a thick book.

"He sent us a book?" Arnold asked, taking the mug of ale from Clara.

"It seems to be a dictionary," Peggy answered, thumbing

through the heavily bound volume. "Why would he send us a dictionary?" Peggy's face went sour, and she shook her head at the ale Clara offered her.

"Is this André fellow insulting me?" Arnold sat upright, indignant.

"What could he possibly mean, sending us a dictionary?" Peggy still studied the book, puzzled.

"He seems to imply, Mrs. Arnold"—Arnold's voice was forceful now, as it became when he demanded the respect he felt was so often denied him—"that we simple colonials cannot write in a manner worthy of your stylish British spy!"

PEGGY HOWLED and ranted so furiously that she tired herself out, and retired to her bedroom shortly after supper. The affront by André had been acute. More painful, Clara knew, than Arnold might even have guessed. She regretted ever initiating the communication, she yelled. Hadn't she risked her honor and the respect of her husband in order to reach out to her former friend? And he'd responded by mocking them. He'd always been dismissive, aloof, behaving as if he were too important for her, a simple colonial girl. Her temper was so aroused that it served to quiet her husband, whose own ego had been so bruised that he vowed never to receive Stansbury in their home again.

"Throw that dictionary in the fire, for all I care!" Peggy railed, as she marched upstairs and shut herself into her bedchamber.

Arnold didn't burn the volume, but he did give it to Clara to dispose of it with the remainder of the family's rubbish. Clara decided against tossing it. It seemed wasteful. And besides, now that she was planning to write regularly to Cal, a dictionary might be a handy book to keep nearby. She took it with her into the kitchen and began to flip through it. It was curious that a dictionary would be the weapon by which André had chosen to insult the Arnolds. Perhaps there was more to this book than the Arnolds had perceived.

It was the paper that accompanied the dictionary that struck Clara as especially odd: Why would André take the time to jot down a series of numbers if the message contained no purpose? His meaning must surely be hidden in the lines somewhere, as if there were some code that might be deciphered.

That's when the idea struck Clara. She turned her attention back to the thick dictionary. The first pair of numbers on the paper was written in André's long, narrow cursive: *100–36*. Clara opened the dictionary and fingered her way through the pages. When she arrived at page 100, it was as she had expected. And how about the second set of numbers? When she turned to the next number, she nearly dropped the dictionary. "Clara." She looked up, gasping when she saw Arnold at the door of the kitchen. She hadn't heard him enter.

"General Arnold," Clara stammered, fidgeting with the book.

Arnold noticed the dictionary and narrowed his eyes.

"I see someone is getting use out of that vile thing. What are you doing with that book?" Arnold limped toward the table, his empty mug in his hand—surely the reason he had come to the kitchen.

"Sir, this is no ordinary dictionary." Clara picked up the book, realizing for the first time the power held within its pages, should her suspicions prove correct. Oh how she wished now that she had burned the thing!

But it was too late—Arnold's interest had been aroused.

"Whatever can you mean, you strange girl?" Arnold looked from Clara to the dictionary with eyes wide and probing.

"You see, this dictionary is accompanied by this." Clara picked up the small piece of paper.

"That is just a bunch of nonsense"—Arnold scowled—"a series of numbers."

"It's far from nonsense. It's a code," Clara corrected him. "The key to reading the message is hidden within this dictionary."

"How does it work?" Arnold asked, taking a seat at the table. "Fetch us some ale." He gestured, urging Clara to sit beside him.

Clara poured him a mug of ale and sat beside him, finding it both strange and deeply troubling that she was suddenly abetting Arnold in the reading of his treasonous letter.

"How do you see a code in this, Clara?" Arnold asked, eyeing the letter over his full mug.

"Sir, this number refers to the page, and the second number refers to the word on that page. So, for instance"—Clara riffled through the pages, looking at the note as she scrolled—"page 100 is the letter *M*. And the thirty-sixth word on the page is *my*. So the letter begins with the word *My*." Clara stared at Arnold, a feeling of doom filling her gut when she saw understanding dawn across his features.

"So it's a letter, and not an insult after all?" Arnold asked, his eyebrows arcing in boyish hope. Clara nodded, stunned by how much this revered man craved respect.

"Quills and paper, Clara, now," Arnold barked, smiling fondly at his maid and, now, coconspirator. "Clara, you are brilliant."

Clara hated herself for blushing when her master offered this compliment.

They worked side by side at the kitchen table, muttering together and flipping from page to page. Clara was the faster of the two in locating the pages and words, so she navigated the dictionary, spelling out the words to Arnold. It took them close to an hour to finish decoding the letter; the whole time, the feeling of regret grew heavier within Clara, until a sense of dread seeped into her very bones.

"We have it." Arnold stared at the page, his eyes frantic after the effort. "I shall read it." He held the paper aloft and began to relay its contents.

"My Dear Lady,

You can be assured I remember the evening of the Meshianza vividly. I think of that night, and the other nights, often.

I am very happy to hear from you, and to hear the overtures you've made. As you know, any correspondence between us must be carried out with the utmost secrecy. It is best to communicate via this dictionary, a copy of which I keep in my possession.

As for your offer of sharing information that we might use to our advantage: we require more precise details as to what you can offer.

We cannot discuss monetary compensation until the exact arrangements have been made and we know what we stand to gain.

Fondly,
John Anderson
Postscript: The Lady may write me as often as she'd like."

Clara did not sleep that night. She was present when Arnold told his wife of his finding the next morning at breakfast. "So there

I was, sitting with the darned book in my lap, and I suspected that there had to be something more to this dictionary than initially met the eye."

Clara nearly dropped the coffeepot. Arnold shot her a pleading look, which seemed to beg the maid to protect his secret. Clara swallowed hard and assumed a mask of cool composure. She *wished* he had found it on his own, that she had not been the one to show him.

"Sugar, Clara?"

"We are out of sugar, my lady," Clara replied.

"Of course we are," Peggy sighed.

"The whole city is without sugar, Peg. Don't take it so hard," Arnold said.

"I bet they have sugar in London." Peggy leaned her head to the left. "But bravo, Benny, I'm astonished that you suspected such a thing. I will be sure to scold Stansbury for leaving us such little information with which to work." Peggy took a sip of her black coffee. "So? What did Monsieur André have to say for himself?"

Arnold handed Peggy the transcribed letter, which she read in silence.

Clara reentered the dining room, bearing a platter of eggs and ham, in time to hear her mistress's response.

"Is that it? It seems an awfully vague response," Peggy agreed. "That's all he has to say to our offer?"

"Do you think he shows me disrespect with a message of this brevity?" Arnold asked, scooping himself a pile of eggs.

"I think it more likely that André is being excessively cautious at this point. Perhaps trying to gauge how serious we are."

"So, you recommend we respond?" Arnold pulled on his whiskers as he always did when his mind was working quickly.

"Absolutely." Peggy nodded, stabbing a piece of ham from the platter Clara held.

Arnold gestured to his wife. "Fetch me a quill. I shall do it presently. If he wants to test our mettle, he shall see Benedict Arnold has no weak stomach for such correspondence."

"But wait, my darling Benny." Peggy's voice curled around the pet name. "We must first decide: What do we stand to gain? We have the high ground in the negotiations right now, as we have the goods he is intent on acquiring." Peggy was coy, always aware of how best to capitalize on her advantage.

"We will see what he offers." Arnold nodded.

"Not so fast." Peggy pressed her hand authoritatively into her husband's to stop him from reaching for the quill. "We have Mount Pleasant, and the land tract offered by New York. And you are a major general in the Continental Army. Are we expected to just throw that all away on some vague assurance that we'll be compensated? No, no, no. England must understand that the friendship of the Arnolds comes at a high price."

"Darling, you seemed so resolved. Are you wavering?" Arnold looked from his wife's face to her belly. "This must be exhausting for you. Why don't you take a rest?"

"Absolutely not." Peggy flatly rejected the suggestion. "I'm negotiating. André can be wily, so we must force him to give us specific guarantees."

"What would you have, Peggy?" Arnold asked.

Peggy cocked her head, deep in thought. "How do you think it sounds . . . *Lady* Margaret Arnold?"

"You mean, you'd like a title?" Arnold looked surprised.

Peggy's lips curled into a taut little smile.

"To be named an aristocrat?" her husband asked.

"I think the only thing that sounds better than *General* Benedict Arnold is *Lord* Benedict Arnold." Peggy turned to her husband, her face as serious as stone.

"Ha!" Arnold looked at her with undisguised wonder. "You know what, my brilliant little wife?"

"Hmmm?"

"I think we could do quite well as a pair of aristocrats."

Arnold agonized over the letter, and how best to respond to André. After a day of ruminating, Peggy convinced him to seek counsel from Stansbury.

"Clara, you are to deliver this to Joseph Stansbury in his shop on Market Square. You know the china merchant?"

Clara nodded her head. "Yes, General."

"See to it that nobody else is in the shop when you deliver it to him. Understood?"

"Aye, sir."

"Do not come back without a response, and see to it that he burns this paper before you leave his shop. Are you clear?"

Clara entered the shop and was relieved to find that she and the merchant were alone. She hoped for as brief an interview as possible. "Good day, Mr. Stansbury."

The merchant looked up as Clara walked in. He was impeccably dressed in a rose-colored suit and matching cravat. "The Arnolds' maid."

"Clara Bell, sir." Clara glanced around at the array of colorful plates and bowls that lined the walls of his shop. Did this man paint them all himself with those long, spindly fingers?

"What do you seek? Something for Miss Shippen, I mean, Mrs. Arnold?" Stansbury asked, coy, apparently enjoying his role as plotter even more than her lady was.

"I have a letter for you, sir." Clara spoke in a hushed tone, ill at ease in this shop.

A flick of Stansbury's long, ringed forefinger told Clara to hand the letter over. But he hesitated before reading. "Will that be all?"

Clara shifted her weight. "If you please, sir, I am to wait here until I may return with your response. The Arnolds wish for you to burn that letter once you've finished reading."

"Those Arnolds, they always have their demands." Stansbury smirked. He opened the letter, the contents of which Clara had already surmised: they wondered how much they needed to promise in order to gain a noble title.

The merchant scrawled off a quick note in reply, issuing no such demands of discretion as he sent it back with Clara. How incredibly reckless, Clara thought. Still, she could not help but resist peeking at his response as she rushed home.

My dear Arnolds—You demand too much. Money can be paid, but a title? That decision rests with the king alone. Better to take the money, then, perhaps you can buy a title?

Yours faithfully, J.S.

"Fine." Peggy read the letter alongside her husband. "Stansbury makes a good point. The money is the most important thing anyway, since all else issues from gold and silver. But we will do it for no less than ten thousand pounds. Plus a regular salary —you'll ask for a rank of general in the British Army."

"For a sum that large, we'll have to offer him something big." Arnold thought it over. "Like a port."

"Philadelphia?" Peggy suggested. "It's your city, after all. You could arrange it." How blasé she was, Clara marveled, bandying about the name of her city as if it were for sale.

Arnold made a face. "Too risky with Washington nearby. He'd come to the rescue of this city for certain."

"If you please, General and Mrs. Arnold, if there's no reply necessary at this time, perhaps I might be excused?" Clara looked down at the floorboards, anxious to retreat to the safety of the kitchen.

"We're done with you for now—you may go." Peggy waved her hand, and Clara willingly took her leave.

THAT NIGHT, after his wife had gone to bed, Arnold limped into the kitchen.

"Clara Bell." He rested his rusty cane on the edge of the table and seated himself opposite the maid. Clara, who had been in the midst of her evening prayers, stood up, rigid, at the sudden appearance of her master. "General Arnold."

"Please, sit, sit." He stretched his wounded leg out under the table.

"What can I do for you, sir? Perhaps some tea, or a mug of ale?"

Arnold put the heavy dictionary on the table between them, its appearance casting a pall over Clara's peaceful evening vigil. She hadn't noticed that he carried it.

"Clara, I was wondering if you could explain to me once more how to use André's code. I've got the book here, and the letter we've drafted, but I thought perhaps you might help me get it into those numbers he used."

Clara felt a panic at the realization that she was to be enlisted once more in this plot. She hesitated. She couldn't help but see the image of Oma's stern face in her mind. And Cal, somewhere north of here, fighting for the revolution. How was it that she could assist the Arnolds in this treason? She couldn't, she had to say no.

Sensing her apprehension, Arnold nudged her. "Come now, Clara Bell. I've always been good to you, have I not?" His taut face showed his own inner turmoil—balancing the awareness of his own treason with the demands of his wife and family.

"You must help me, Clara, so that I can keep you in my employ. If you don't help me, things will be very hard for Mrs. Arnold and me, and we may have to dismiss you."

Clara's shoulders sagged. "Give it here, sir." She sighed, her heart heavy. She'd help him tonight, and wrestle with the consequences alone, in private, later. Better to know what was being hatched, she consoled herself, if it was going to be happening around her. Using the code André had created for them, Clara translated Arnold's letter:

My Dear Mr. Anderson,

Thank you for your thoughtful reply.

As my life, my honor, and everything is at stake, I will expect some certainty before I commit. Are you interested in discussing the port at Charleston?

I would be amenable to the idea, not only of turning it over, but switching sides myself. My defection might create a movement to your cause. It would cost you ten thousand pounds sterling, and a comparable rank in your Army.

Your friend,
A

A,

We would be interested in discussing Charleston.

I understand that you have had some difficulties at your current post, and have expressed an interest in obtaining a new position. Perhaps if you were able to arrange it so that you could become commander at Charleston, and turn it over? I am certain that you know that the southern colonies are my general's priority of late.

That, or, if you can offer us some intelligence that leads to a specific victory at the Hudson River fort at West Point.

You will be rewarded beyond your highest expectations. No exact sum will be guaranteed at this time.

In response to your latter offer, no need for you to switch allegiances. It's better that you remain on the other side.

Anderson

"THE NERVE of that man!" Arnold spat in fury as he clutched André's response, freshly delivered from Stansbury to Clara. "Flat out refuses to name a sum, as if it's an unreasonable request!" Arnold read the letter again, massaging his wounded knee absentmindedly as he did so. The longer he stared at the letter, the more visibly agitated he grew.

"They don't want me on their side?" Arnold scoffed. "Don't they know who I am? My defection would cause an entire counter-revolution! It would practically hand them the victory!"

"Do not let them upset you." Peggy was the vision of calm as she sat, mountainous, in bed. Her belly looked like it weighed more than the entire rest of her frame—she was prepared to give birth any day now. Clara had helped her undress and was preparing their evening fire when Arnold had stormed into the bedchamber with the latest response.

"Let me handle this, Benny." Peggy waved her husband toward the bed. He handed her the letter.

"I shall reply, Benny. Sit down and rest. Have a drink." Peggy dipped a quill in the thick black ink and worked quickly, smiling as she wrote. When she had finished, she spoke aloud: "How does this sound?"

"Dearest Anderson,

You've written of a night, years ago, that seems to me now to be little more than a dream. I've worn many lovely dresses in my life, but none can compare to the white silk dress I had made for that evening. To think that I never got a chance to dance in it, it still brings a tear to my eye. Perhaps we will be reunited someday and we can throw another Grand Masque and I can have that dance I was denied.

You know how I love fine things. Dresses and ribbon and satin and shoes. I have so many fine things already. The only way I could give them all up is if you tell me what, in exact terms, I stand to gain.

Please, my old friend, we need specifics. Perhaps I should come to New York for a shopping trip? You can tell me all about the fine things you are willing to give me, and in return, we will offer you that information which we have that you could stand to benefit from. You understand my meaning?

I await your reply.

Fondly,
Madame la Turque"

Monsieur & Madame,

I am not in a position to offer money or a rank until I've gained a real advantage to which I can point.

An accurate plan of the fort at West Point would be one such piece. Or numbers of boats on the Hudson, and the plans for said vessels this spring and summer.

A face-to-face meeting with the lady is not necessary at this time, as I wish her not to burden herself by making the arduous journey. But I would like to meet her husband in person when the warmer spring weather arrives.

"VAGARIES, EVASIONS, and more insults." Arnold slumped over the most recent letter at the dinner table, allowing it to burn to ash in the candlelight. "And I don't like that you offered to go to New York to meet him. And I like even less that he denied you. Who does this André character think he is? I see no way of working with him."

"There is indeed a way." Peggy took the platter from Clara and served her husband a slice of mutton, pouring gravy over it. Then, with what sounded like admiration in her voice, she murmured, "I had forgotten how slippery Johnny . . . André . . . can be."

"As slippery as an eel, from the looks of his letters. Peggy, why did I let you convince me to begin these correspondences?" Arnold burned the last of the letter and ran his hands through his gray hair, ignoring his food.

"Excuse me?" Peggy stared him down, defiant, as she scooped them each potatoes.

"I don't like this so-called friend of yours. I plan to write him back and let him know just what I think of his sly tactics."

"Benny, you're being hasty. Perhaps if we—"

"They don't want me on their side, they won't name my reward. Am I to make a fool of myself dancing before them like some unwanted harlot? If they don't want me, damn them!" Arnold slammed his fist on the dinner table, sending the dinner plates an inch in the air before they settled back down. Clara jumped back in shock.

"Benny, you are being brutish." Peggy glowered at her husband but remained calm.

They sat opposite each other in silence. Arnold, at last, capitulated.

"I'm sorry, Peg." Arnold reached his hand toward hers, but she removed hers before he could touch it, lifting her wineglass to her lips.

Arnold continued. "But I am fed up. And there's no way I will hazard it all when they will give me no set reward."

"They will," Peggy answered tersely, confidently. She summoned Clara to refill her husband's empty wineglass.

"You've read the letters just like I have, Peggy." Arnold took the refilled wineglass in his huge hands and drained its contents with several gulps.

"Let's make them pursue us," Peggy suggested.

"How?" Arnold asked after several minutes, his lips stained red with wine.

Peggy smiled, a coy, ballroom smile: the dazzling look she saved for the man she most desired. "We shall withdraw our interest. Then they'll see what they have passed on."

Arnold stared back at his wife, his eyes twinkling. "You're right, my love."

"Of course I'm right." Peggy shrugged. Clara reached in front of Peggy to deposit a bowl of turnips, sliding her hand forward just as Peggy reached for the carafe of wine. Their hands collided, causing Peggy to drop the red wine.

"Oh!" Peggy screamed, turning from the spilling wine to her servant, her eyes furious. "Now, Clara, look what you've made me do."

"Mrs. Arnold, I do apologize, I'm so sorry." Clara's heart faltered as she reached for the overturned jug of wine and righted it. Peggy looked back at the table, where the wine had spread from the table linens now to her full, protruding belly, her cream-colored petticoat. Peggy lifted her hand, and before Clara knew what was happening, her mistress had landed a stinging slap across her face.

"Rags and water, now," Peggy spoke through a clenched jaw. "Or else I may lose my patience."

"Yes, ma'am." Clara dropped her gaze to the floor, her hand clutching her smarting cheek, and walked from the dining room.

"My darling." Arnold's face was tense—"I'm not sure such immoderation was necessary."

"Oh, honestly, Benny, it's like disciplining a child. You must be firm or they take advantage."

"Clara Bell is no child," Arnold retorted. "She's a perfectly able member of this household, and you ought to treat her with more respect."

"Careful now, Benny." Peggy's tone was icy. "Surely you don't mean to side with the maid against your own wife?"

Hearing this exchange, Clara did not return to the kitchen to fetch rags. No, Peggy could clean up her own spill. Instead, holding her face, her fingers wet from tears, she exited the kitchen and ran out into the yard. She picked up a fistful of snow and pressed it to her cheek. The tears that poured out against her will only made it sting worse.

Clara crumpled down into a humiliated mass in the snow and

cried. How dare Peggy blame Clara for her own spill, and then slap her like that? She never wanted to go back into that house—that miserable house where she was either utterly invisible or railed at for errors she didn't make. There was a limit to how much she could endure—being called lazy, and idiotic, and dishonest.

"Clara? Is that you?" Mrs. Quigley's figure appeared as a dark shadow in the yard. "Clara, what is the matter?" The woman hunched down over Clara, helping her up out of the snow.

"She . . . she hit me!" Clara stammered.

"Oh, no." Mrs. Quigley's face registered unmasked disapproval. "Now, let's have a look, there's a good girl." She gently lifted Clara's hand away to reveal the cheek, red and puffy. "Gracious."

Clara covered her face in humiliation.

"Well, what did you do?" Mrs. Quigley looked concerned as her tender fingers pressed snow onto Clara's cheek.

Clara broke out into fresh sobs. "She was pouring herself more wine and our hands collided on the table and she dropped the carafe."

"Oh, there, there." The woman pulled Clara forward into a gentle, warm hug. "Shhhh." She ran her hands through Clara's hair, and for a minute Clara imagined that she was a little girl again and Oma was soothing her in a strong, safe embrace.

"Well, you just try to stay away from her for a while, if you can. Give her time to collect herself. I imagine she will see the error in her ways."

"Mrs. Quigley, I hate her!" Clara confessed, feeling guilty for the words.

"Hush, Clara, hush. We don't want anyone hearing that kind of talk. I understand why you feel that way, of course." The old woman patted her back. "But we must remember our lot in life, Clara. We're servants. Without them we'd have no roof over our heads. No food. No clothing. Would you want to have to sleep out here on a night like this? With this war going on?"

Clara bristled from the injustice of it.

"My dear Clara." The old woman pulled away from Clara and held her eyes in an encouraging stare. "I was coming over here with something that might lift your spirits. I've got a letter for you from Caleb."

For days Peggy refused to rise from her bed, but stayed sunken in her feather mattress, bed curtains closed, and she complained that she could neither sleep nor eat. Clara kept trays stocked with food by her bedside, but other than that, she gave her mistress a wide berth.

Peggy's labor pains came in the middle of the night. At first, Clara had thought she was having a nightmare, given the shrill screams that permeated her dreams on her straw mat. But when she awoke, she saw that Barley had risen from the straw, and Arnold's panicked face was just inches from hers in the firelit room.

"Clara, run and fetch Mrs. Shippen now," Arnold ordered. "Hurry! Mrs. Arnold has broken her water."

Clara stood in the corner of the bedroom, staring in horror at a scene very different from what she'd imagined childbirth to be. Now she understand how her own birth had killed her mother all those years ago—it was impossible to see how any woman would survive this ordeal. What would happen to her if Peggy died in childbirth? she wondered. She wiped the thought away, praying for the life of the baby and the mother. All throughout the night, Clara kept a steady supply of clean rags and fresh pots of hot water at the ready while Mrs. Shippen and Hannah led the screaming Peggy through the birth.

The sound of Arnold's lopsided limping reverberated on the floors below. He paced from room to room, ale mug in hand, until the sun came up. Before the doctor had time to stir from his bed and arrive at the Arnolds' cottage, little Edward Shippen Arnold arrived, screaming less than his mother who delivered him.

"It's a boy." Mrs. Shippen handed the tightly bundled baby to Arnold, who entered the room only after he was assured that the labor was over.

"Good God, there's blood everywhere." Arnold stared at his wife on the bed, aghast.

"It's nothing but the normal birthing scene." Hannah shushed him, looking down at the baby. "Congratulations, General. Your son is beautiful."

"And . . . and my wife?" Arnold still had not looked at his son, but rather kept his gaze on Peggy, who seemed to have slipped into a fretful sleep.

"She'll be fine," Mrs. Shippen assured him, looking approvingly at her grandson. "She just needs rest. And a bath. Clara, will you strip the sheets and wash them?"

Little Eddy was a quiet, contented baby. He had his mother's blue eyes, but they lacked the calculating, restless expression that had seemed to settle permanently behind hers.

Hannah and Mrs. Quigley began to visit the Arnold cottage often, finding any excuse to stop by and take turns holding Little Eddy. The baby, like the first signs of the spring thaw, promised to breathe new life into the Shippen household, and Clara hoped that her domestic situation might finally begin to improve.

"Look at these legs." The housekeeper squeezed Little Eddy's chubby calves as she lingered in the kitchen after delivering Clara a fresh stack of firewood.

"You're so lucky to have a baby in the house, Clara." Hannah did not peel her eyes from the little boy as she spoke. "It's so quiet in the Shippen home these days."

"It's anything but quiet here," Clara said, smiling to herself as she spooned the baby a mouthful of warm milk. Even though Clara was finding her mistress more and more difficult, she couldn't help but fall in love with the sweet little baby she now had responsibility over—the baby who cooed as she fed him and dressed him. Who perched happily on her hip as she carried out her household tasks.

March brought with it longer days and the welcome signs of the coming spring—the faint warbles of birdsong; a lone bud poking out from the barren tree boughs; a breeze that felt docile and less like a biting wind. Nevertheless, spring also brought a sour thought: Clara knew that the approaching warmth would mean a resumption of fighting between the colonials and the British, and she hated to think of Caleb stepping out onto the battlefield.

Clara knew from his letters to her and his aunt that Caleb was still stationed on the Hudson at Fort Verplanck. He wrote her often, and though he never spoke of anything more than friendship, Clara found that he was still the only person in whom she felt comfortable confiding. In her letters she filled page after page discussing her work, her love for Little Eddy, her complaints against her mistress.

On one account, her situation with the Arnolds had improved that spring: Clara no longer fretted over the Arnolds' communication with André. Ever since his refusal to name a price or specific reward, the Arnolds had withdrawn their offer. André had not come calling, as they had expected him to. Finally, a man had resisted Peggy's bait.

THE VISITOR arrived on a pleasant morning, when the air was gentle and the sun was shining down on a lawn of new grass. Clara sat outside, bouncing Little Eddy on her knees, when a carriage rolled to a halt.

Joseph Stansbury appeared before her, a bored expression on his face. He ignored the baby on Clara's lap. "I'm here for General Arnold." He wore a suit of crimson silk and a pleated linen neckerchief around his collar. His powdered wig sat beneath a matching crimson hat.

Barley growled at the visitor, and Clara silently agreed with the mutt's sentiments.

"Well, are you going to let me in, or not?"

Clara reluctantly rose and led Stansbury into the house.

"Yoo-hoo, Peggy?" Stansbury marched into the front of the Arnolds' home. "Anybody at home?" The merchant made himself comfortable before the fire, removing his cap to reveal a head of tight curls.

"Oh, Stan, what a delightful surprise." Peggy hopped down the stairs, looking simple but fresh in a muslin gown of pale pink. She kissed her visitor on the cheek. "Stan, did you see my baby?" Peggy gestured toward her maid, who handed her the plump little bundle. Little Eddy began to cry, his arms reaching back toward Clara.

"Oh, it's yours? Goodness, I thought you were letting that maid answer the door with her bastard child on her hip." Stansbury tossed his head backward and erupted in laughter.

Peggy slapped the merchant on his shoulder and laughed. "Oh, Joseph Stansbury, you are *awful*!" She shuffled the baby awkwardly from one hip to the other, causing Little Eddy to cry louder. "No, this is my little Edward. You've been in New York for so long, you probably forgot I was expecting."

"I had to escape. Philadelphia is bad enough these days, let alone in the winter. New York was so much more fun." Stansbury stroked the baby's pudgy hand with a long, impeccably clean finger. "Nice to meet you, Edward." The baby erupted in fresh wails.

"Oh, he's giving me a headache with this howling." Peggy handed the baby back to the maid and sat. "Clara, get him to quiet down and behave, will you?"

Peggy turned back to her guest. "Are you hungry, Stan? Clara, bring a bowl of figs. And some almonds. Now, Stan, tell me why I shouldn't be mad at you—your spy has flatly refused our offer."

"You might feel differently when you see this." The merchant waved a piece of paper before Peggy. "I've carried it from New York, from a certain handsome major."

"Johnny?" Peggy ripped the paper from his hands and tore it open with unmasked relish. "I thought he had dropped us."

"Au contraire."

"It's short," she noted.

"But you will not be disappointed." The merchant leaned over Peggy's shoulder and read along with her.

> *Circumstances have changed. If you could attain the post at West Point, we would be willing to discuss exact compensation with you.*

Peggy gasped. Just then, Arnold limped into the room. "Benny, he's come crawling back. André is desperate for our help!"

"Is that so?" Arnold winced, clutching his left knee. "And what does he ask from us in return?"

"Something we can deliver," Peggy said confidently. "You must write to Washington immediately and ask to be made commander of West Point."

"WE DO not wish to raise any suspicions," Arnold mused, propping his chin on his hands.

"Why would you fear that asking for the post at West Point would raise suspicions?" Peggy sat down to breakfast beside her husband, fresh-faced and chipper. The dining room of their cottage was bright and warm, and it smelled of coffee and toast as she cracked open a soft-boiled egg.

"Well, look at Washington's reply to my initial query." Arnold passed a letter to Peggy, who put her fork down and took it in her hands. "This is his response to my request to be transferred to Charleston."

Clara rounded the table, shuffling Little Eddy to one hip as she leaned over and filled each of the Arnolds' coffee cups.

"There's my boy!" Arnold reached up for the baby, taking him onto his lap. The baby went to his father happily. "Aha! Look at how big he's getting. You're a strong one, aren't you, Little Eddy?" The little boy picked up his father's spoon and began banging it on the table.

"Quiet." Peggy snapped, looking up from the letter to her husband.

"There now, Peg, I want my son at my breakfast table with me. Isn't a man allowed that?"

"Benedict," Peggy softened her tone, "I'm trying to read."

"Well, Clara can keep him quiet." Arnold handed his son back to the maid. "Clara, take my boy in your lap and join us at the table."

Both Clara and Peggy turned on Arnold with expressions of

disbelief. "Why not? Clara's practically part of the family anyway. And I want my son here with me. This affects him, after all."

And me too, Clara thought, avoiding her mistress's smoldering eyes as she lowered herself into a chair, Little Eddy on her lap. Arnold leaned over to peruse the letter along with his wife.

"Ha! Listen to this line by Washington," Arnold scoffed, "'I refuse to accept the idea that your days of fighting under our flag on the battlefield are over. You are a true hero, a soldier, and a friend of mine.' So he thinks I'd still fight for him, the fool."

"Does he not realize that you are no longer able to fight?" Peggy's tone went sour.

Now Arnold became defensive. "Of course I *could* fight. If I wished to."

"But Benny, you just said . . ."

"I *would* not fight for Washington, or his rebel cause. But it's not because I can't, Peggy."

Peggy heaved a sigh. "Benedict, your injuries make it impossible," she mumbled, dipping a piece of bread in a soppy egg yolk.

"I *could* fight, if I wanted to," Arnold snapped, repeating himself.

"Very well, then you shall. But for the British." Peggy rubbed her hands together, dispersing a shower of bread crumbs before her. "Here's what you must do—you must guilt that tobacco planter into giving you the post at West Point. Tell him you deserve it. Remind him of how much you are owed for your service these years. Say: 'My wounds make it nearly impossible for me to walk or ride. As my leg disables me from being any use on the battlefield, but my heart refuses to stop serving, I write to ask to be put at the head of an outpost. West Point would be agreeable.'"

Arnold bristled at this. "You would have me plead like a cripple, Peg. Washington knows as well as anyone that I still crave the battlefield."

Clara could tell that Peggy was laboring to remain calm and sweet. "Yes, but in order to secure the role as commander at West Point, you must pursue this line of persuasion, my dear husband."

Arnold considered this. Finally, he answered. "All right. I'll write him that."

"Meantime, Benny, you'll write André and tell him that you've secured the post as commander of West Point. It's time we start discussing our . . ."—Peggy leaned forward toward her husband, her lips curling upward—"*. . . compensation.*"

IF THEY could secure the post at West Point, they held the trump card. That much Clara knew. The gossip she heard on Market Street, at the baker, in the Shippen kitchen, all led her to believe that both armies were turning their focus from the south onto New York City and the Hudson River. Whoever controlled that waterway had the key to either dividing or uniting the colonies.

"The British must be sick of sharing the Hudson with the ragtag colonials, no?" Peggy was strolling her father's gardens with Stansbury on a warm summer afternoon, twirling her parasol as she watched Clara and Little Eddy chase the birds on the lawn. "How is it possible that they both claim the Hudson?"

Stansbury spoke quietly. "The British control it from New York City up to about thirty miles north. And the colonials have it from West Point up."

"If Benny could deliver the fort at West Point, he would deliver the rest of the river?"

Stansbury nodded. "It would enable England to cut the colonies in half."

Peggy looked to her son, momentarily distracted by the sound of his laughter as Clara ran toward a bird, prompting it to fly before them.

Stansbury was not to be distracted. "André knows this, as does his general, Clinton. They are eager to reach an agreement with you both, madame."

"As are we. Benny has written Washington again, insisting that West Point is the only assignment he will accept."

"Will Washington oblige?"

"I think he will. He feels guilty about Benny's court-martial, and that rude letter he sent as punishment. He's always had a soft spot for my husband."

"And *you* have always had a soft spot for John André."

"Oh, Stan, you're naughty." Peggy chuckled.

"So are you." The merchant smirked. "So, what are you asking for as recompense, you delicious little spy?"

"The post of general in the British Army," Peggy answered boldly. "And twenty thousand pounds."

"Ha! Is that all?" Stansbury quipped. "So you've upped it from ten to twenty thousand."

"Well, we deserve it! Benny would be handing over the critical fort, and with it, thousands of American troops. And to whet André's appetite and let him know that we mean what we say, he told him a little secret."

"Which is?" Stansbury asked.

"Washington expects a fresh arrival of eight thousand troops for his northern campaigns in New England this summer. The French fleet will arrive off the east coast of Rhode Island by the end of the month."

"Well, that should get his attention." Stansbury hooked his hand under Peggy's. "I will be amazed, Peggy Shippen, if you pull this off."

"What's stopping me?" Peggy challenged him with a look. "My husband knows how to win on the battlefield. It's all brute strength and fighting. But spy work is different—it requires poise, and self-control, and grace. It's like a delicate dance. And if anyone knows how to dance, it's me."

Clara's face burned as she listened to the two of them burst out into laughter.

My Good Sir and Lady,

The General is much obliged to you for the useful intelligence regarding the French fleet and we are assured now, more so than ever, of your ardent desire to assist us in our cause. We are interested in being delivered West Point.

Mr. Anderson,

I am leaving for West Point, having secured the post. Now that I understand how crucial it is to my side, I feel compelled to raise my asking price to 20,000 pounds sterling.

I have a son now, and I must think about my family and my future. After all, the alternative is staying very comfortably on the current side, where I enjoy fame and high repute.

I will let you decide whether you deem my friendship worth the asking price.

Write your response to me at the post at West Point, where I am henceforth commander.

Mr. & Mrs.

"ALL THREE of you work for me now," Peggy said coolly, her voice devoid of emotion.

"Begging your pardon, my lady? Judge Shippen?" Mrs. Quigley stood between her husband and Hannah in the study of the Shippen mansion, looking back and forth from the judge to his daughter.

"What can you mean, sir?" Mr. Quigley's posture was erect, formal as always.

"What we mean," Judge Shippen began to speak, but his daughter cut him off before he could finish.

"My father has turned you three over to me. He and Mother shall be moving in with Betsy and Neddy and no longer have need of your services. The Burds have servants at their house. But my husband and I will need you at West Point."

"West Point—but isn't that in New York?" Hannah's voice betrayed terror. "And what about Brigitte? What's to become of my sister?"

"Your sister will move with my parents to Neddy and Betsy's," Peggy answered, looking to the door, bored of the conversation.

"You mean, Judge Shippen, that you are going to dismiss me after all these years and keep Brigitte?" Mr. Quigley looked stung.

"It's not that I would not wish to bring you, Quigley. You know how much I've valued your service all of these years," the judge spoke, his voice as flimsy as a reed. "It's just that . . . it suits our budget better if we keep only one servant." The judge now avoided looking at any of the servants he addressed. "I would not wish to split you from your wife. And Brigitte has become invaluable in tending to Mrs. Shippen, who, as you know, suffers gravely from her headaches these days."

"But you would split me from my sister?" Hannah looked as though she might cry.

"This home has become, well, overly burdensome." Judge Shippen apologized with his expression. "Mrs. Shippen and I no longer require all this space. And Betsy has been urging us to move in with her and Neddy for a while, but we didn't want to leave Peggy. Not while she still lived here."

"But now that Benny and I have been transferred to West Point, we're leaving Philadelphia," Peggy finished for her father. "Oh come on, Mr. and Mrs. Quigley, Hannah, how can you look so glum? Philadelphia has become so boring."

"Philadelphia is our home, Miss Peggy." Mrs. Quigley, usually so restrained, pushed back. "Has been for seventy years."

"Well, now your home will be West Point," Peggy said. "Besides, my husband and I have a post once more, and money. You'll get wages. My father cannot pay you. Right, Papa?" Peggy looked at her father, who was resting his head in his hands.

"Believe me, Constance and John," Judge Shippen looked up at the couple and then at the cook. "Hannah." He paused, his voice catching on their names. "If there was another way, believe me, I would have found it. This is the only solution we could find without turning you out on the streets."

The three servants stood silently, like thieves sentenced to the gallows. From her post in the corner, Clara watched the scene unfold, feeling a mixture of pity for the three of them who would be severed from their home, and relief that these three familiar people, the only family she had, would be traveling north with her to New York. She would not have to go with the Arnolds alone, and that fact gave her undeniable comfort.

"Well, I believe we've talked through all the messy issues. Everyone understands?" Peggy arched her eyebrows in a question.

"Believe me, if I could afford it, I'd keep you all until the day I died." Judge Shippen still looked pained. "But it's just, with the war showing no sign of ending . . ."

"Well, my husband and I will see what we can do about that," Peggy answered, and only Clara knew just what she meant by the clipped comment.

"Clara?" Peggy turned to her maid, acknowledging her presence in the corner for the first time in the conversation. "Prepare our things for the move to West Point."

Clara walked out, alone, into the dark corridor, hugging the baby in her arms. Inside, she was a swell of warring emotions. Her three friends would be coming with her, but at what cost to them? Together, the whole band was taking a step closer to fulfilling the Arnolds' planned treachery. And yet, in spite of these horrible facts, the news was not all bad to Clara. "Hear that, Little Eddy?" Clara whispered into his soft, squishy cheek. "We're moving to West Point." She'd finally be close to Caleb again.

VII.

She refuses to see anyone. Won't allow anyone in the room without wailing like a cornered animal. Except me. So I sit beside her on the bed, dabbing her face with a moist cloth and trying to reassure her that she's still alive, that her son is still alive.

"Clara, Clara, Clara. Don't leave me. Please don't leave me, Clara."

The day is growing warmer and the bedchamber is stifling, as she will not allow me to open any windows. Her face is flushed from the heat and the overstimulation, and the neckline of her sleeping gown is moist where it clings to her white skin.

She sings a childhood song, her voice sounding feeble and shaky. When I look into her eyes, she returns my gaze, but her glassy blue eyes do not see me, of that much I am certain. "Oh, Bets, Mother always takes your side," she says to me, mistaking me for her sister.

"There, there, Miss Peggy. It's me, Clara. Surely you remember me?" I dab her furrowed brow once more with the moist cloth.

"Clara? No, no." She smiles, correcting me.

"Shhh, Miss Peggy. It's best you get some rest." I reach behind her head and plump up a feather pillow for her, hoping that she will agree to sleep. But when I pull my hand back, she grabs me. Her grip is strong, and her eyes suddenly shine with a fierce blue lucidity, as if a veil had been lifted.

"They're going to kill me, Clara," Peggy says matter-of-factly.

I am not sure how to answer her. I don't know if they've found her husband yet. If they know that she was as involved in the plot as he was. "There, there, Miss Peggy." I dab her forehead once more.

"Ouch!" she screams, clutching her forehead.

"Have I hurt you, ma'am?"

"There is a scorching iron on my head," she mumbles, nonsensically.

"Pardon, my lady?"

"There is a scorching iron on my head." She points at her forehead, as if I might see the object she describes.

"My lady, there is nothing on your forehead except your own perspiration."

"No, no, no," she says, with the expression of someone half mad. "There is a scorching iron on my head, and only General Washington can remove it. Bring him here."

CHAPTER SEVEN

"Too Far Down This Path"

June 1780
West Point, New York

THEY MOVED in the full heat of summer, leaving the city of Philadelphia with its noise, its stink, and its swelling population, freshly arrived for the warm trading season. Peggy, so eager to leave, now claimed she could not bear to watch the receding images of the city she had loved. "Will I ever walk these streets again? Will I ever attend a party in the Penn mansion again?"

In the days before their journey, Clara thought she detected the signs of fraying patience in Arnold: an avoided embrace, a comment left unanswered, an excuse offered when his wife invited him to bed. And now, as his wife uttered these lamentations, he reminded her, his jaw tight: "Peg, it was your idea to leave."

"But I'm so sad." She sighed. "I shan't be able to look out the carriage window until we are gone from this city."

Though Peggy could not look, Clara found it thrilling to watch as the carriages pulled them north into the quiet greenery of rural Pennsylvania, where hundreds of miles of open farmland stretched out before them. They would know they had reached New York,

Clara was told, when they spotted the broad, curving outline of the Hudson River.

Escorted by General Arnold and his assistant, Major Franks, Peggy rode up front in Arnold's covered carriage with the baby for most of the journey, sprawling out and complaining of the heat as they pushed through the unshaded farmland. Clara followed behind in an open cart with the Quigleys, Hannah, Barley the dog, and the Arnolds' trunks. Even though the carriage was cramped and exposed to the strong sun, Clara was happy to enjoy the clean air and the long stretches of time away from her mistress. She was far enough away that she was spared most of Peggy's complaints about the rough road and wearying journey.

Other than Peggy, the member of their party who seemed to have the hardest time on the trip was Hannah; the old cook spent the endless hours alternating between staring out at the landscape in terror and breaking into inconsolable, silent tears. Each step the horse took, Hannah knew, she moved one step farther from her sister and home, on a journey that she knew would never be reversed.

The first few days of the trip, they passed an endless number of abandoned farms. Entire families had fled, leaving doors barred and fields fallow. "No one wants to bother farming anymore, as the British raiding parties just come through and steal everything anyway," Mr. Quigley explained. "There's no point in laboring all year only to be robbed by the so-called keepers of the king's peace."

"No farming. That's why Washington and his men are starving." Mrs. Quigley looked out over the rolling line of unsown fields.

"Are there loads of Indians in these parts?" Hannah eyed the distant tree line.

"Not to worry, sweet Hannah. The Indians have all switched

over to our General Washington's side at this point; they wouldn't attack an armed colonial officer. Besides, the Indians have always been fond of General Arnold."

"That so? Well, that's a relief to hear." Hannah nodded at the butler, but her expression showed no less terror, and she crossed herself just the same.

They stopped each day only for midday luncheon and at sundown. When they arrived at their nightly resting spots, Arnold, Peggy, Major Franks, and Little Eddy went into the tavern or pub to have their supper and find a warm, covered bed, while the servants slept in the carriages, amidst the neighing horses and the sounds of the country evening.

"It's so loud," Mrs. Quigley lamented, wrapping her cloak around her as she tried to find a comfortable position in the open carriage. "What is all that racket?"

"It's just the crickets," Clara answered, marveling at the fact that her three companions, lifelong city dwellers, found the countryside loud. She herself remembered how noisy she'd found the city at first.

"No, *that*! What was that? It was not a cricket." Mrs. Quigley pointed out into the unknown darkness beyond the carriage.

"An owl, Mrs. Quigley." Clara tried not to laugh at the old woman. It was the music of her childhood, the balmy evenings on the farm; with those familiar sounds as her backdrop, she'd close her eyes, thinking of Oma. And then, her thoughts would inevitably turn to Cal, her mind wondering if he was nearby as she drifted into sleep.

Aside from her happiness at being out in the open, in a familiar landscape, Clara's feelings on the Arnold household's move north were dreadfully mixed. Certainly, she was excited by the fact that they were moving deep into rebel territory—and very close to Cal.

Yet Clara was hauntingly aware of the reason for the relocation to West Point—a knowledge that she alone possessed among the Arnolds' servants. She could have shared her news with the Quigleys or Hannah—but they, like her, would not be able to take any steps to thwart the Arnolds' plot. Plus, Mrs. Quigley had threatened to sack her the one time Clara had tried to mention it, and she had no interest in risking unemployment this deep in the countryside.

She felt impotent; here she sat, saddled with the knowledge of the Arnolds' treasonous plot, but she could think of no way to stop them. How could a poor, uneducated maid hope to alter the course of events set forth by such powerful figures as Peggy and Benedict Arnold?

"Why do you fret so, my girl?" Mrs. Quigley had noticed Clara's bouts of troubled daydreaming as they traveled closer to their destination, and she looked at the girl now with a mixture of puzzlement and consternation.

"Do you . . . do you think this war will be over soon?" Clara asked. An end to the fighting was her best hope—it would mean that the Arnolds would not have time to follow through on their plans to cede West Point.

"I believe it will be," Mr. Quigley interjected. "Don't you trouble yourself, Miss Clara Bell. All will be well soon enough," the old man reassured her. How wrong he was, Clara could not yet tell.

On the sixth day of their journey, their pace quickened, and Clara could tell that they had almost reached their destination.

"Hurry on now, Franks. Almost to West Point!" General Arnold, whose leg had bothered him for much of the journey, was in visibly higher spirits as they moved north up the Hudson. "We should be there in time to take our midday dinner!"

Clara eyed the wooded land surrounding West Point with great interest. Unlike the abandoned fields of Pennsylvania, here the people were active and their farms were fertile. Clara watched as the scene outside her carriage flowed from green expanses of softly rolling hills to leafy copses filled with flowers and wild strawberries, to sunlit golden fields filled with lumpy haystacks and acres of freshly plowed earth. Being in the countryside felt freeing, like a homecoming after her years in the noisy city. As she stared out over the wide-open fields and green mountains, feeling the warm sun on her face, Clara could momentarily put aside her anxiety over the Arnolds' plotting and enjoy the country before her. But she could never forget for long.

Cal had written to Clara before about West Point, the location that he'd heard Washington describe as "the key to the continent." The fort of West Point was a series of rustic, hillside woodworks built high atop the western bank of the Hudson River. It occupied a strategic bend in the river, and was only a day's ride north of New York City. Because of this crucial position, it was an outpost frequently visited by Washington and the rest of the colonial high command. Did Caleb ride through these parts on missions from his nearby fort at Verplanck? Clara wondered. She'd have to write him immediately and find out. Perhaps he could manage a visit.

They finally arrived at a leafy riverside plot with a welcoming farmhouse, and the carriage rolled to a halt.

"Well, Mrs. Arnold, welcome home." Arnold looked approvingly at the generously proportioned wooden home. The farm had been left abandoned when the prominent local Tory leader, Beverley Robinson, had fled south to safety in British-held New York

City. What a shame to leave a home like this behind, Clara thought. The shuttered farmhouse sat on the east bank, tucked back from the river on a soft slope, shaded by ancient, leafy oak trees.

"How dreadful," Peggy scowled at the grand white structure, clutching her son in her sweaty arms as she hopped down from the carriage. She turned to her husband, who limped alongside Barley toward the front of the farmhouse. "Benny, is *this* the Beverley Robinson house? Why did they tell us that we would be comfortable here?" When Arnold didn't respond, Peggy sought her maid's agreement. "Clara, don't you find this home to be frightful?" Clara could not have felt less in agreement with her mistress, but that was the last thing she would have said.

"Course she doesn't, my Peg," Arnold interjected, revealing that in fact he had heard his wife. "Clara's got sense enough to appreciate a comfortable home." Arnold winked to soften the remark, but Peggy pursed her lips in a tight frown.

The horses were tied and members of the traveling group descended on the property in a hive of activity. Arnold and Peggy conducted a tour of the interior of the home and the exterior view of the fort on the opposite riverbank. Major Franks and Mr. Quigley hopped down and began unloading trunks, carpets, paintings, and stores of food that they'd brought from the now empty Shippen mansion. Clara picked up the baby and helped Mrs. Quigley and Hannah into the home through the back entrance, where the two older women found the kitchen and the servants' wing.

"Well, now, Hannah, look around at this kitchen. It should lift your spirits a bit." Mrs. Quigley eyed the large hearth, wide enough to fit four kettles over the fire. The thick wooden beams of the interior gave the home a more rustic appearance than the brick Shippen mansion, but the kitchen was clean and cozy, with a large storeroom, scullery, and larder abutting the cooking area.

"This'll do just fine." Mr. Quigley deposited a sack of potatoes in the storeroom and exited the kitchen.

The cook didn't appear particularly interested in her environs, but rather lowered herself onto the first wooden chair she could find, nearly collapsing onto the table like yet another sack of food.

"Hannah, are you all right?" Mrs. Quigley exchanged a concerned glance with Clara, who was transferring sacks of sugar into the storeroom.

"A little short of breath," the cook replied, massaging her chest in slow, labored movements.

Clara tried to comfort the old woman. "Well, you just stay put and rest. It's been a long journey, and it's taken its toll on all of us."

"Poor Brigitte. Always left behind, always forgotten. And now I'll never see my sister again." Hannah put her head into her cupped hands and wept, adding fresh tears to her already stained cheeks.

"What shall we do?" Clara whispered to Mrs. Quigley in the privacy of the cool storeroom.

"There's nothing we can do, dear. We must let Hannah grieve," the old woman answered.

"Mrs. Quigley, please don't misunderstand me, as you know I'm happy to have you, your husband, and Hannah here with me. But why didn't you put up a fight? Why didn't you three try to stay back in Philadelphia?"

Mrs. Quigley looked at Clara with patient exasperation. "Clara, what have I always told you? Don't forget your lot in life. We are servants. Without Peggy Shippen . . . I mean, Peggy *Arnold,* the likes of Hannah and me would be out on our bottoms. Without food, clothing, or a home. You think another household would hire us, at our ages? How long do you think we'd last in the city streets? Or the country? Lord knows if it wasn't the Indians who finished us off, it'd be the British. Or the highway bandits!" She cast a stern look of warning on Clara for emphasis. "Don't underestimate the desperation facing a servant who loses her post."

"I understand." Clara nodded, but inside she fumed. How was it possible for such a person as Peggy Arnold to hold people like the Quigleys, the Breunig sisters, even herself, hostage? It seemed the height of injustice, and her cheeks burned. But she checked her temper, nodding as she answered: "I'd best go help Major Franks with the rest of the unloading."

"Aye, you should. There's a good girl. Don't you worry about Little Eddy—Hannah and I will keep him in the kitchen."

It was a warm morning in early July, just days after their arrival. The rooster in the yard had not yet crowed, and no one in the house was stirring. Clara rose from the straw pallet, leaving Hannah snoring on her own pallet beside the fire, and wandered from the kitchen out into the north field. In the indigo predawn light, she walked past the one-room cottage the Quigleys occupied—a home originally built for the property's groundskeeper. Only Barley the dog heard her moving, and he joined her in the yard.

"Hi, mutt." Clara petted his ears, allowing Barley to amble along beside her.

The birds began to chirp, as if to coax the sun into rising and to welcome Clara into the peace of the field. It was the perfect solitude in which to pen a letter to Cal. She spread her apron down and sat in the cool grass, removing a paper and quill from her petticoat pocket. She hadn't had a moment alone since their arrival at the Robinson house, and solitude had proven hard to come by now that her sleeping arrangement involved sharing the kitchen with Hannah.

Nor had she received a letter from Cal in weeks, not since before she'd told him of their upcoming move. She wondered how he was doing, and how he would react to what she now had to say.

Clara believed she had found a way to tell Cal about the plot without the censors catching her meaning. Or, at least, that was what she hoped. At last, the thought of sharing her news with an ally filled her with relief. Mrs. Quigley had flatly refused to hear it, and had even forbidden Clara from speaking of it again. But Clara's knowledge of the scheme, along with her guilt at having unwittingly abetted the Arnolds, weighed too burdensome on her now. The sight of the fort across the river, waiting each day for its ignoble fate, was like a censure to her. Caleb would know what could be done.

Caleb,

Please tell me how you are doing. I think of you often and hope you are safe.

I write you this letter not from Philadelphia, but from much closer—our new home across the river from the post at West Point. As you might have heard, the master's assignment has recently changed. Is this close to where you are?

My feelings on this move are dreadfully mixed. I am thrilled to be here, in the beautiful country where I can roam the fields and smell the fresh, earthy scent of the river.

But I am saddened to tell you that some darker news also accompanies the relocation. Caleb, do you remember several Christmastimes past, when you claimed that you saw someone riding through Philadelphia in a carriage? You told us you had seen him, and none of us believed you (except me). You said he had a huge frame and he waved to the crowds. Do you now understand to whom I'm referring? Henceforth, let's refer to that figure as "Milk Cow."

Secondly, do you recall the person who often came visiting to the house? He was dark, and dashing, and he had a certain someone wrapped around his finger. He left in a great hurry, and we were not sorry to see him go. You now know to whom I refer. Let us call him the "Coq," as he was finely plumed and inspired such "coquetry" as I have ever seen.

And finally, there was the man who came after the Coq. He walks with a limp, and quickly became utterly besotted. We shall call him the "Bull."

Well, now I arrive at my point. My lady has never been fond of the Milk Cow. This, you know. She has now entered into an arrangement whereby she and the Bull intend to tell the Coq some invaluable information. Information which might be detrimental to the Milk Cow. You most likely find this too ludicrous to believe, especially if you remember the Bull as he used to be, years ago. But you must believe this: things have very much changed since your departure. The lady has a strong influence, stronger than you might have imagined possible.

I am at a loss as to what I should do—I would have brought this to you sooner, but I was frightened and unsure how to do so. But the situation is now too dire to sit silent with the news any longer, and I seek your counsel.

I shall end my letter here with one request: please help me. Tell me—what can be done?

—CB

As soon as the words had been scrawled on the parchment, Clara felt a lightening of the burden that she had carried alone for so long. She folded the letter neatly and tucked it into an envelope. She'd give it to Mrs. Quigley to mail with her other letters to her nephew.

The sun now peeked out over the eastern hill, casting slanted rays of orange and pink onto the river below. It would be a clear, hot day. Clara relished a few more minutes of peace—the cool of the dewy earth beneath her, the soft breeze that pulled wisps of hair loose from her bun, the delicate warble of a chickadee on some nearby bough. Her mind returned involuntarily to Cal—what was he doing at this moment? Was he, too, awake to witness this perfect sunrise?

"Claaaara!" A shrill cry arose from the farmhouse, silencing the nearby chickadee and interrupting her pleasant daydream. The maid turned her gaze, frustrated to be interrupted from her reverie. Peggy's summons persisted. *"Claaara!"*

Clara rose from the grass. "Yes, my lady, I'm coming!" she called out as she picked up her pace.

"Clara, where have you been? I've been scouring the house for you." Peggy stood outside on the front porch in nothing but her light summer shift, fixing her hands on her hips as Clara approached.

"I'm sorry, miss, I was just taking a walk." Clara stood far enough away that, should her mistress be moved by another urge to strike her, she'd be a safe distance from her hand.

"What are you, a field hand? Look at your feet, covered in mud."

"I'm sorry, my lady." Clara bit hard on her lower lip, subduing the desire to answer back.

"Come in. Eddy is awake and we have a crisis." Peggy turned and walked through the doorway, letting it close in her maid's face before Clara had reached the threshold.

"A crisis, miss? What sort?"

Peggy wheeled around, catching Clara off guard so that she was forced to stop midstride, her face just inches from her mistress's glower.

"My favorite brooch is missing, Clara. The ruby I wore when Benny first called on me."

Clara frowned, confused.

"Someone must have stolen it," Peggy said. That was a serious accusation, a charge that could cost someone their position in the household. But it was preposterous; Clara was confident that none of the servants would have taken anything from Peggy.

"Miss Peggy, are you certain that you've finished unpacking all of your jewelry? It could still be in one of the trunks."

"You were supposed to unpack everything," Peggy spat. "That's why, if anyone would know where it is, it's you."

Was Peggy accusing *her* of taking the ruby?

"I want you to solve this mystery, Clara. Find out who stole my brooch."

"Yes, ma'am." Clara curtsied, saddened that a morning which had begun so beautifully would turn into such a rotten day.

"Now, Clara, go change your dirty dress. We have luncheon with our new neighbor, a Mr. Joshua Smith, this afternoon, and my husband, for reasons entirely incomprehensible to me, wishes you to bring Little Eddy."

Clara made to leave, but the way her mistress still looked at her caused her to remain rooted in her place. Peggy's eyes burned Clara with their intensity, as if she were trying to sort out some riddle about her maid. "I'm not sure what you have done, Clara, but you seem to have made yourself a special favorite of my husband's." And now Peggy's tone became disarming—a calm, syrupy voice that seemed to mask a hidden fury beneath the words: "Be careful, Clara, or you might make me jealous."

★~~~★~~~★

Caleb's reply came quickly.

Clara,

I read your letter with great alarm. Not much time to respond at the present, but had to write to impress upon you the great urgency: you must do everything you can to protect the Milk Cow. That is from where all our future hopes come. More later.

—C

Clara sat alone at the long kitchen table, reading and rereading this brief letter. That was it? No advice? What was she supposed to do from her post as maid and baby nurse? Caleb asked too much of her. From his position on the battlefields he'd grown bold and accustomed to facing the enemy head-on; he'd forgotten that that was not how one would wage a war in Peggy Arnold's home. Clara looked up when she heard the sound of a cane rapping the wooden floorboards.

"General Arnold." She rose quickly as the unexpected visitor limped in.

"Hello, Clara." Arnold smiled at the startled maid, looking around at the kitchen. "How are you doing?"

"Fine, thank you, sir." Clara curtsied, still confused by his sudden appearance.

"Do I find you alone?"

"Yes, sir," Clara answered, still standing.

"Where is everyone?"

The hour was late in the afternoon, and she'd already put her mistress and Little Eddy to bed for their naps. "Your son sleeps, sir.

Hannah and Mrs. Quigley are in the garden, and Mr. Quigley has gone to the stables."

"I see." Arnold hovered opposite her, neither of them speaking. Finally, he broke the silence. "Do you like it in this kitchen, Clara?" Arnold studied the thick wooden beams that ran across the low ceiling.

"Yes, sir, it's very comfortable."

"It appears that way." He looked from the table to the hearth, but offered no further explanation for his visit. "Sometimes, at night, after my wife has gone to bed and I sit in the front of the house by the fire, alone, I imagine all of you in this kitchen together. I imagine it is quite merry in here."

Clara lowered her eyes. "Not quite as merry as you imagine, sir." At least, not since Cal had left and they'd all been separated. "We mostly retire to our beds early."

"I loved the nights with my men." Arnold's voice took on a nostalgic tenor. "Peggy says I ought not to fraternize with the servants, but when we were encamped, I always befriended my men. The evenings were often the best times. Sitting around the fire, passing around the jug, and sharing stories from home."

Clara nodded, sensing his loneliness. She, like him, knew that those scenes were unlikely ever to be repeated.

After a pause, Clara cleared her throat. "How can I help you, sir?"

He limped over to the table and lowered himself into a chair opposite Clara. "How about a cup of tea?" He smiled.

"Certainly." Clara curtsied and crossed the room to the hearth, where she removed the warming kettle. Had Arnold merely come wandering into the kitchen seeking companionship from his stunned maid? Clara wondered.

"You've been getting letters?" Arnold looked at the paper from Caleb that Clara had left out on the table.

"Oh, yes." Clara scooped up the paper, tucking it into her apron. Her heart lurched at the realization that she'd left it in plain sight, where he could have easily seen it, and possibly even guessed at its meaning.

But Arnold seemed not to have noticed its urgent content. "A sweetheart?" He lifted his eyebrows, causing a mortified Clara to flush a dark shade of crimson. "Now, now, no need to be bashful, Clara. We all fall victim to Cupid's arrows at some point." Arnold smiled amiably, taking the teacup from the maid.

"I certainly did," he continued. "Why, Clara, you know better than anyone else how embarrassingly hard I fell." Arnold pursed his lips, his expression turning serious.

"Yes, sir," was all Clara answered. *Oh, how well she knew.*

"I just hope he deserves you, that's all." Arnold looked back at Clara, disarming her with the directness of his gaze. "Does he treat you well?"

"Well, sir," Clara waffled, "he doesn't treat me in any way."

"What do you mean by that?"

"He's not my suitor. More like a friend." Clara averted her eyes and replaced the kettle over the stove.

"And you feel for him only as a friend?" Arnold probed.

Clara's silence seemed to be all the answer he needed.

"So then it is one-sided. You have feelings for him, which he does not return?"

"Sir, he doesn't know I feel this way for him." How was it that she was divulging her feelings this openly? She warned herself to bite her tongue.

"Then, you must tell him," Arnold insisted.

"I can't," Clara answered sheepishly, in spite of herself.

"Why not, Clara?"

"Well, you see, sir. He once made it plain how he felt for me.

But it was so long ago, and so much has changed. I fear that he no longer thinks of me that way."

Arnold considered this for a moment, weighing the dilemma with genuine thoughtfulness. "Well, Clara. I don't know the lad so I can't say for certain whether he still loves you or not. But I can say with absolute certainty that if he doesn't, he's a fool and he doesn't deserve you."

"You are too kind, sir." Clara wished her cheeks would stop burning.

"Not kind, just honest. I've always been an honest man. Even though it gets me into trouble." Arnold took another sip of his tea. Clara looked at him, finding it hard to understand how this sensitive, kindhearted man was the same person who fawned all over Peggy, even to the point of betrayal when she asked it of him.

"Clara, tell me something. Do you like being here?"

"Oh, very much," Clara answered, aware that in order to be polite, she had to also fib to her master. Which would be worse, she wondered, rudeness or falsehood?

"Please, Clara, sit down. You're making me nervous. I should be standing in a lady's presence but you'll excuse me." Arnold gestured to his left leg.

"Of course, sir." Clara smiled, sitting opposite Arnold. Never before had someone in his ranks called her a lady.

"Always so obedient." Arnold looked at her, his earnest expression rendering Clara slightly uneasy. "Never do I face an argument from Clara Bell."

She lowered her eyes.

"You like the countryside?" he asked.

"Oh, I love it." Clara looked up, beaming, and he smiled back at her.

"I can see that."

"Even more than the city, sir."

"I feel the same way." Arnold looked at her intently. "But I married a city girl. Do you like serving my wife?"

"Of course."

"Are you being honest?" He raised his eyebrows.

"I am grateful every day." Clara offered a half-truth, for she was indeed grateful to have a home and employment.

"Good." Arnold nodded.

"Is the tea satisfactory, sir?" Clara asked.

"Yes, of course." He looked once more around the room, eyeing the hearth. "It's a nice kitchen. Peggy told me I would like the rustic look of it."

That was odd, Clara thought to herself, that Peggy had urged her husband to come into the kitchen. Peggy never encouraged Arnold to mingle with the servants, and she herself had not ever been in the kitchen, as far as Clara knew. Arnold's gaze roved over the hearth to the corner and rested on the two straw pallets, Clara's and Hannah's.

"Clara?" Arnold's voice was suddenly alert, with an edge about it.

"Yes, sir." Clara looked at him. "More tea?"

"No." He shook his head, his eyes still fixed on the corner. "Clara, is that your bed? That straw pallet in the corner?"

Clara offered a perfunctory "Yes, sir," still looking at Arnold and wondering why he suddenly appeared so serious.

"Clara, why is my wife's ruby brooch on your bed?" He looked at his maid, his stare now rendering Clara very ill at ease.

"Pardon?" Clara turned her head to follow his eyes with her own. There, on top of the straw mattress from which she'd risen this morning, gleamed the brooch with the brilliant, red jewel. Her heart galloped as she looked back to Arnold.

"Sir, I have no idea. I haven't seen that brooch since it went missing, honestly. I have no idea how it came to be there on the mattress."

"Benny, oh, there you are!" Peggy bounded through the door. "I've been looking for you. I had hoped you would like to take a stroll with me and Little Eddy down to the river. That is, if you've had quite enough time alone with Clara." Peggy looked from her husband to the maid.

"Oh, no." Clara felt a panic swelling in her chest. She turned back to Arnold. "Sir, I have not seen that jewel since it went missing," Clara repeated, hoping he would sense the truth of her account.

"What is going on?" Peggy was the image of innocent confusion. "What jewel?" But she somehow knew to look straight to the straw mattress, where her eyes landed on her ruby. "My brooch!" Peggy exclaimed. "Oh, my beloved ruby!" She ran to the pallet, picking up the ruby. "Oh, Benny, I'm so happy! Look!" She flitted toward him, showing him the jewel.

Then her tone changed. "Clara." She looked at her maid with exaggerated suspicion. "Clara, why was my favorite piece of jewelry on your sleeping pad?"

Clara, mystified, knew not how to answer, but Peggy did not care.

"Why, you little thief!" Peggy raised her arm, charging the maid, but was stopped by her husband before she could land a blow.

"Peggy, no." Arnold stayed his wife's flailing arms. "Peggy, please, show some composure!"

"She stole it, Benny, she stole my favorite brooch, and then she lied to me! And yet, you side with her?" If this was a performance, it was so convincingly played that Clara found even her own mind running in circles.

"Please, Peggy." Arnold held on to his wife, trying to quell her temper. Just then Mrs. Quigley, Mr. Quigley, and Hannah entered the kitchen, responding to the commotion.

"I want her flogged for being a thief and a liar!"

The servants watched the scene, eyes widening with horror.

"I want her flogged!" Peggy continued to shriek, her cheeks red.

"General Arnold." Mr. Quigley stepped forward. "I can vouch for Clara's honesty."

"As can I," Mrs. Quigley added.

"She would never steal from you or Mrs. Arnold. This must be an unhappy coincidence." Mr. Quigley looked at the stunned maid, who had stood mute throughout this entire episode.

"Nonsense, it's right there. The proof is right there," Peggy snapped.

"Peggy, please, calm down. You will make yourself ill." Arnold looked at his wife beseechingly.

"What kind of man doesn't punish a servant who steals from his wife?" Peggy harangued him. "Our Lord received forty lashes for far less. I want that lying maid flogged!"

"All right, all right. But please, Peggy, you must calm down. Mrs. Quigley"—Arnold turned to the housekeeper—"please take my wife to bed. Hannah, help her."

He turned to Clara. "Clara, as the proof is right here in plain daylight for all to see—you were alone in the kitchen and the brooch visible on your bed—you will have to be punished. I am sorry."

Clara began to weep. She had never been flogged, and certainly not over a false accusation. And after the beating—then what? Would she be relieved of her post?

"Please, General, I would never . . ." Clara struggled to form some protest, to reiterate her innocence.

"Clara, come with me." Arnold was stern as he grabbed her arm and walked with her out the kitchen door. "Mr. Quigley, see to it that my wife is put in bed and that she stays there. That's an order." Arnold turned, escorting the maid out the door to the north side of the yard.

Arnold limped forward in silence, Clara running alongside him and begging, through her tears, to be pardoned. He paused under a thick oak tree. "Hush, Clara." He reached up and with his knife, clipped a small branch from overhead. He began to carve it into a switch.

"General Arnold, please, spare me! I would never steal from you or your wife!"

"I know." He looked at her, his eyes full of pity. He kept carving the switch.

"But . . ." Clara staggered. "I didn't do it."

"I know."

"Then why must I be flogged?" She looked at the switch, watching as his knife sliced it into a tool to inflict punishment.

"Do you think it escaped me that my wife asked me to go into the kitchen, for no apparent reason, as the brooch was lying visible? And if you *were* guilty, why would you not have hurried to hide the evidence of your crime as soon as I entered the kitchen? Instead, you sat with me, perfectly calm and polite, pouring me tea and talking about your sweetheart."

Clara stared at him, allowing her mouth to fall open. So then he knew she was telling the truth! "Then, sir, you believe me?"

"And, Clara Bell, if you *were* guilty, and my wife truly believed that you had stolen her favorite piece of jewelry, wouldn't she have demanded that we dismiss you? Throw you out into the woods? Instead, she accuses you of stealing her brooch, one worth your entire year's wages, and all she demands is that you be flogged?"

"But, then, General"—Clara's hopes lifted slightly at the realization that he knew her to be innocent, but her spirits sank lower when she noticed he was still fashioning the switch—"then why will you still beat me?"

"I don't intend to beat you, Clara," Arnold sighed, exasperated. "My wife has been put to bed in her bedchamber on the south side of the house. We are under a thick tree on the north side of the house. Completely concealed from her view."

"I don't understand, sir."

"Right now she's in bed, listening for the sound of the switch landing on your back, and your subsequent cries of pain. Let's just give her what she wants and we will all move forward." Arnold replaced the knife into his pocket and raised his switch. "There will be no peace in the house until the punishment is doled out."

"Please, no!" Clara screamed, bringing her hands protectively to her face.

"When I land this switch on the side of this oak tree, you will cry out as if it struck your backside. I will do it ten times. Do you understand?" Arnold looked at her, his face expressionless.

Understanding dawned on her. She could have collapsed in relief. "Yes," Clara answered quietly.

It was a humiliating charade—General Arnold beating a tree as Clara cried out in contrived pain. When it was over, Clara and Arnold turned, wordlessly, and walked back to the house. Arnold entered through the front door, Clara through the back. She found the Quigleys and Hannah in the kitchen.

"Clara." Mrs. Quigley ran to her. "Clara, my poor dear."

"Come here, love." Hannah rose from the table, her face twisted in empathy. "Clara, we heard the whole thing. What a brute."

"I'm fine." Clara slumped into a chair. "Can I have some tea?"

"Clara." Mrs. Quigley's eyebrows angled toward each other. "Aren't you hurt?"

"Let me see the wounds on your back. We need to put ointment on them right away. I've got some dandelion milk." Hannah fussed over her shirt.

"He didn't do it." Clara swatted the old cook's hands away.

"He didn't?" Mr. Quigley asked.

"But we heard it," Mrs. Quigley argued.

"No." Clara shook her head. "He hit the oak tree each time."

"Oh, thank heavens." Hannah crossed herself, as all three of them stooped in relief.

"So there is someone left in this house with a sense of decency." Mr. Quigley pounded the table with an angry fist.

"Why does she hate me so much?" Clara asked miserably, weeping as she took a fresh mug of peppermint tea from Hannah.

"She doesn't hate you, dear." Mrs. Quigley rubbed her back in a soothing gesture.

"She does," Clara moaned.

"She's threatened by you. She wants to make sure you stay in your place," Mr. Quigley answered.

"But how could I ever threaten her?" Clara demanded.

Mrs. Quigley thought about it, answering after a few moments. "Well, I suppose there are a couple reasons. Her husband is fond of you, firstly."

"He's fond of all of us. He's a kind man," Clara argued, but she couldn't help but notice the meaningful look that passed between the Quigleys and the cook.

"Her son prefers you to her," Mrs. Quigley continued.

"Her son cries out in terror every time he goes from your arms to hers," Hannah interjected.

"That's my fault?" Clara demanded defensively. "It's my fault that she has no interest in her child and he in turn fears her?"

"Of course not," Hannah answered.

"I don't understand," Clara continued. "She too used to be so fond of me, bringing me everywhere, confiding in me, giving me that fine gown for Christmas years ago."

"Yes, well, she's changed, there's no doubt about that." Mrs. Quigley nodded.

"Clara," Mr. Quigley said, pausing momentarily before he explained his thoughts. "Many things in Peggy's life have not turned out the way she had hoped they would."

Clara thought this over and knew it to be true. But still, it did not explain things. "Why does she blame me for that?" Hadn't everyone in that kitchen tasted bitter disappointment in their lives, as well?

"She doesn't blame you," Mr. Quigley explained. "But she takes it out on you, that much is apparent. You seem to occupy a unique role for her—she's reliant on you, and yet you are the one she punishes when she is dissatisfied with something."

"Why me?" Clara asked.

"Who else can she take it out on?" Mrs. Quigley answered. "Her family is gone. Her son is but a wee lad. And she can't alienate her husband—she needs to keep him charmed or he'll stop doing what she orders him to do. Apart from her family, you are the closest person to her on this earth."

Clara considered this, finding it odd to think that she, Clara Bell, played an important role in Miss Peggy's life: that Miss Peggy needed her and depended on her. All Clara had ever thought about before was the central role that Miss Peggy played in *her* life.

"My dear Clara." Hannah put a soothing hand on her. "I suppose the true test of character comes when facing life's harshest blows and disappointments. When things don't turn out how you had hoped they would, do you grow bitter? Spiteful? Blame others and spread your misery? Or do you keep your head high and walk with grace, meeting the struggles which God has placed in your path?"

Clara looked at Hannah, the kind, elderly cook, separated from her home and her sister, going about her work for a selfish mistress and never complaining: quite exactly the image of the suffering servant. Clara did not need help deciding which path the cook had taken. Or which path her mistress had taken.

"Here, here, we are a sorry lot." Mrs. Quigley placed her hands determinedly on the kitchen table. "I've got some good news that might cheer us a bit."

"Oh?" Mr. Quigley looked to his wife while Clara took a sip of tea.

"I've heard from my dear nephew, Caleb, and it seems that he's had some good luck as of late."

Clara's heart lurched.

"Has he now? So what news from our favorite soldier?" Hannah asked.

"Seems our young lad has been promoted to corporal."

"Well done, Caleb." Mr. Quigley beamed. Clara smiled into her teacup, feeling her spirits lift at the thought of Cal.

"And there's another piece of news," Mrs. Quigley continued.

Was Clara imagining it, or had the woman's tone shifted? Did the old woman now sound a bit hesitant?

"What else?" Hannah asked, refilling Clara's tea.

Mrs. Quigley paused a moment, her brow creased. When at last she spoke, her eyes landed on Clara. "Seems he's met a lady."

The news struck Clara like a blow, a blow worse than that from which Arnold had spared her. Mrs. Quigley still looked at Clara, and she was certain that the housekeeper studied her reaction. Clara swallowed hard, throwing her shoulders back.

"Oh?" Her voice was feeble, her effort at composure a failure. Now it was not only Mrs. Quigley, but both other servants who turned toward her as well.

"He's visited the home of a certain friend, a fellow named John Williamson. Seems as though Caleb met one of John's cousins there, a young lady named Sarah Williamson."

Clara's mouth was drier than if it had been stuffed with cotton.

"Is it serious?" Hannah asked.

"From the sound of it, yes. Serious enough for Cal to write me to tell me about her, which is a first. He's never spoken to me of a girl. Not even back when he had such a fancy for . . ." Mrs. Quigley looked up at Clara but let her words trail off, unfinished. "Clara dear, are you all right?" Mrs. Quigley put a hand on her shoulder.

Clara nodded, grasping for words. But none would come.

"Your cheeks are white as snow."

"If you'll excuse me, ma'am. I had better go and check on Little Eddy." Clara pushed herself away from the table, her legs feeling as if they might quake beneath her. She didn't walk toward the stairs, as she had said she would, but instead pushed her way through the door and into the yard. She just barely made it out into the blinding sunlight before her resolve gave way, and fresh sobs burst forth from her tightening chest like a flood overrunning a dam.

The one benefit of her alleged beating was that Clara was excused from her duties at that evening's dinner, as Peggy expected her to be in bed recovering. Clara accepted this reprieve willingly, wandering through the fields until well past sundown. At last her tears stopped, but her mind continued to race. The space within her, the space that had pulsed with joy and hope whenever she had thought of Cal, had been scorched. Replaced now by a leaden feeling of despair. Cal had a sweetheart. Cal now looked at another the way he had once looked at her. Those hazel eyes, once so full of longing, of earnest affection, now rested on another girl. A girl who would surely not be so foolish as to squander his love, as Clara had done. So, that was why Cal had written her so little of late. He was writing another girl, a girl who now occupied his attention and his thoughts.

It was dark when Clara wandered back into the home, having skipped the servants' supper. She did not speak to the others when she entered the kitchen, but rather she muttered something about feeling ill as she lowered herself onto her straw pallet, backside to them all. Though it was a warm evening, Clara pulled the blanket around her body and curled up, into a cocoon from which she wished she'd never have to stir. Hannah, sweet Hannah, was a small comfort as she rustled about the kitchen, replacing the dishes after the evening meal had been cleared. But the person she longed for, the only person whose face Clara wished to see, was Cal.

The next morning, Clara dressed and found the Arnolds in the dining room at breakfast, careful to move slowly as if her back were tender.

"Oh, good morning, Clara! How did you sleep?" Peggy looked up from her breakfast when the maid entered, in a rare acknowledgment of her servant's presence. She fed her baby a small bite of scrambled egg. "You stayed abed so late that I was forced to fetch Little Eddy myself."

"Not well, my lady," Clara answered, finding even the act of speaking to be exhausting.

"All these servants do is complain," Peggy muttered. "Well, Clara, Little Eddy's just finished eating. Why don't you take him so that my husband and I may speak with our guest here, Major Franks?" Peggy pointed to her dining companion on her left. Franks nodded politely at Clara.

"Yes, my lady." Clara took the baby and exited the dining room.

"So, Franks, you were telling us about your inspection of the defenses at West Point." Peggy resumed the conversation, and when Clara heard the topic she paused, just on the other side of the door.

"Are they in good condition?" Arnold asked.

Franks's nasally voice traveled to where Clara stood, just out of sight. "I am sorry to say, General Arnold, that after having completed a thorough investigation of the works there, I must report that the defenses at West Point are deplorably weak."

"How horrid!" Peggy said, with what sounded less like horror than delight.

"Yes, it's quite regrettable. The commander before you did not keep things up well."

"We shall have to rectify that situation, shan't we?" Arnold answered.

"Yes, and quite soon, sir. Especially now that we hear that General Washington is planning an offensive to take back New York City before the coming of winter."

"Yes, yes," Arnold said excitedly.

"We would not want anything to go wrong for General Washington," Peggy said.

"Precisely so, Mrs. Arnold. We would never want to do anything to diminish General Washington's chance of success." The aide finished his eggs and coffee, a placid smile on his face as he thanked the Arnolds for the generous meal.

Clara, meanwhile, felt frantic. There was only one other person who knew about the plot, but could she write Cal? Could she stand to speak to him, even now that she knew about his attachment to another girl? And did he even care to hear from her? But he had said he remained a faithful friend. Surely writing to him was better than taking no action. Still, her hands trembled as she penned her letter that night.

Caleb,

How can I intervene in this plot? Believe me, it gives me terrible pain to watch things unfolding and to be forced to sit back and not breathe a word to anyone.

It's all done so secretly, and with their belief that I know nothing, I see no way I can involve myself in their affairs. I have my place as a servant and they could easily throw me out, were I to overstep my place.

You would not believe how sad we are here. Mistress has been a fury lately. I have been warned that if I take one more step out of line, I shall be dismissed from the household.

It sounds as if things go very well for you. Your aunt has told us your happy news.

—CB

"FINALLY!" PEGGY ran into her bedroom, hopping on the feather mattress with a letter in her hand. Clara dared not look up from the floor, where she sat scrubbing the wooden planks.

"*BENNY*!" Peggy's call was answered by the familiar sound of her husband's limping stride as he climbed the steps.

"What is it, Peg?" Arnold lumbered into the bedroom.

"Oh, just a letter. From a certain . . . John Anderson!" Peggy waved the paper. "Fetch the wine from my table, Benny, this calls for a celebratory drink!"

"What does he say?" Arnold crossed the room quickly, carafe of wine in hand, and joined his wife on the bed. Clara must have been invisible on the floor, because Peggy did not ask her to leave before she blurted out the contents of the message she'd just read.

"It's settled," Peggy said, a grin pulling up the corners of her lips.

"Settled?" Arnold took a slurp of wine straight from the carafe before handing it to his wife.

"Settled." Peggy took a satisfied swig.

"What will we get?"

"Clinton has agreed to our conditions," Peggy answered.

"All of them?" Arnold asked, incredulous.

Peggy nodded slowly. "The British will pay twenty thousand pounds upon completion of the transaction. You, my husband, shall get a general's commission in the British Army in exchange for arranging the surrender of West Point to the British under General Henry Clinton."

Clara nearly overturned the bucket of sudsy water.

"Benny." Peggy reached for his thick, rough hand. "Benny, we did it!"

"Peggy." Arnold looked at his wife, bringing the wine to his lips but lowering the carafe without taking a sip.

"Yes, Benny? Why do you look at me like that?"

"Peggy, it's settled."

"It's settled!" She hugged him close and he kissed her. Clara rose to leave the room.

"But, Peg." Arnold pulled away. "I don't know. It feels . . ."

"What?" Peggy's voice was irritated. "It feels *what,* Benedict?"

"It feels wrong, somehow."

"We are not backing out now, Benedict Arnold."

Her husband turned away from Peggy's stare, stroking his whiskers.

"Benedict, we've gone too far down this path to lose our resolve now. Here, take some more wine, it will give you courage."

"Courage? Courage, you say? I've faced death itself on the battlefield. I've watched as a surgeon carved a bullet from my knee." Arnold turned to his wife, stung. "I don't need courage, Peggy."

"I know that, I know." Peggy ran her fingers through his graying hair in an effort to assuage him.

"It is a loss of honor that I worry about," Arnold fumed, shrugging off her attentions.

"It is not *you* who has surrendered honor, Benny." Peggy scooted her body closer and tugged on her husband so that he lay beside her on the bed. "Benny," she cooed, her tone more intoxicating than the wine they had nearly finished. "We must follow this through. We must do it—for our sons."

"Sons?" Arnold turned toward her, confused. "What do you mean? We only have one son."

"So, let's set about fixing that right now." Peggy sighed, kissing her husband's whiskered cheek. "And then, after we make our second son, we will figure out just how we plan to turn West Point over to Clinton." The two of them embraced now, Arnold surrendering to Peggy's seductive caresses.

"Do you love me, Benny?" Peggy asked, whispering into his ear.

"Oh, Peg, I love you," Arnold simpered, running his rough hands through her curls. "Anything you ask for, I'll do it."

"Shhh." Peggy kept kissing him, removing his coat before taking on the buttons of his cotton shirt.

Clara tiptoed across the creaky floor and shut the door quietly, even though she was certain that neither one of them had even noticed she was still in the room.

SHE SAT at the kitchen table, her legs giving out beneath her. The events unfolding around her were so much bigger than she was. How could she, Clara Bell, ever hope to thwart the plans of Benedict Arnold, one of the war's most powerful generals? Or even more difficult—his wife? On the kitchen table sat a pile of papers. She flipped through them—this morning's post. The same post that had carried John Anderson's message.

There was a letter for her. Caleb! Her heart soared for one brief moment, a habit that she had not yet lost. And then she remembered the truth. Slowly, she opened the letter.

> *Clara,*
>
> *Your last post fills me with worry. What is the latest, pray tell? Have you uncovered some way to foil this treachery? I pray that you write yes. Remember, if you allow this thing to happen, you are implicit in their scheme.*
>
> *We all are expected to hazard our lives for this cause. Freedom comes at a heavy toll.*

Stay safe, and I promise to do the same. My love to the Quigleys and Hannah.

Your faithful friend,
Caleb

That was all he had written. No advice, no counsel. Just his judgment, and his warning that, if she did not stop them, he would view her as a traitor. Never in her life had Clara felt so alone. How was she supposed to single-handedly stop the plot by one of the colonies' most powerful generals to hand over its most vital fortress?

It was too much.

"Emergency!" Mrs. Quigley ran into the room, her eyes bulging with panic.

"I know." Clara turned, wondering if the housekeeper had finally caught wind of the plot herself.

"Emergency! Clara, come quick, you must help me!" Mrs. Quigley was waving her hands and shouting indecipherable orders.

"What's the matter?" Clara rose from the table, her own pulse now racing from the housekeeper's visible distress.

"It's Hannah. Come to the larder at once, Clara!"

Clara followed the housekeeper into the small storeroom. There she found the cook lying motionless on the cold floor.

"Hannah." Clara knelt down beside the still woman. "What's happened?" She turned to the housekeeper.

"I don't know! She would come in here sometimes on hot days to keep cool. But when I walked in here just now, I found her lying on the ground, gurgling."

"Oh, Hannah." Clara pressed her cheek to the cook's. She was not sure how else she might check for a sign of life.

"Is she breathing?" Mrs. Quigley asked.

"Oh, Hannah, please wake up." Clara placed her hand first to the woman's chest, and then to her abdomen. "No sign of breathing." Clara looked back at the housekeeper in panic.

"Ladies, I'm looking for the general." Just then Major Franks appeared in the doorway of the larder, at the house on an errand with his arms heavy with papers. When he noticed the scene, his expression changed from one of business to concern. "Is everything all right?"

"No, Major Franks, look!" The housekeeper pointed at the lifeless cook on the floor beside Clara.

"Good God." The aide dropped his satchel of papers and knelt down beside Clara. He picked up Hannah's limp wrist and pressed his fingers to the flesh.

"What are you doing?" Clara asked.

"Checking to see if she has a pulse," Franks said.

"A what?" Mrs. Quigley questioned him.

"A heartbeat," Franks snapped. "That's the sign of whether a person is alive or not. Now please, let me focus." He screwed up his face in attention, his fingers digging around in the skin of the woman's pale wrist. Clara had a chilling feeling that the longer he poked and prodded, the worse a sign it was. He was most likely not finding whatever it was he was searching for.

Franks confirmed Clara's worst suspicion. "No pulse. My ladies, I am sorry to inform you that this person has expired."

"What can you mean?" Mrs. Quigley stared at Franks, dumbfounded.

"Dead," Franks said, with numb finality.

"Dead?" Mrs. Quigley gasped, incredulous. "Hannah Breunig, dead?" She fell to her knees, nestling her face into the cook's bosom as she began to sob. "The poor woman—died of a broken heart!"

THE AUGUST heat rolled into the Hudson Valley, bringing with it no comforting breeze. The air was so stifling that it was unpleasant to be indoors. The only cool room was the storeroom, which Clara and all the servants had been avoiding since they'd found Hannah's body there.

Major Franks had determined the cause of death to be a failure of the heart, based on the cook's shocked expression and Mrs. Quigley's description of her last few moments. This confirmed Mrs. Quigley's original theory, and the housekeeper maintained that the old German woman had died of heartbreak after removal from her home and sister.

"We will not tell Brigitte," Mrs. Quigley told Clara. "It won't do her any good to know that her sister is no longer on this earth."

"Yes, ma'am," Clara agreed, wondering with a pang of sadness how poor Brigitte Breunig fared these days. Most likely she would be very lonely in Neddy and Betsy Burd's household, and missing her sister.

"Clara, why don't you go outside? Let me finish up here." They were in the scullery, scrubbing the china and silver after luncheon. It was midafternoon and the small room felt like a hellish pit.

"But we've got all these dishes left," Clara objected, eyeing the dirty piles.

"Leave 'em to me," the housekeeper insisted. "It'll do you good to get outdoors for a bit. You're too young to be looking so old with worry all the time."

"It's really fine," Clara protested, continuing to scour a dirty bowl.

Mrs. Quigley sighed at Clara's stubbornness, and they continued to clean the china, side by side, in silence. Eventually, Mrs. Quigley spoke.

"You know, Clara, it was a long time ago. But would you believe me if I told you I remembered what it was like to be young like you?"

Clara looked up, a smile spreading across her face. "Of course, Mrs. Quigley. You're not so very old."

"I thought you didn't believe in lying, Clara Bell?" Mrs. Quigley leaned her head to the side, her eyes softening in good humor. "But it's true, I remember being young. I was like you. Hardworking. Serious. I wasn't in the Shippen home just yet, I was working for a family called the Dwights. That's where I met John . . . I mean, Mr. Quigley." The housekeeper giggled, her eyes alight—like a blushing girl. "I told Mr. Quigley—" and now her voice was laced with nostalgia, "that I couldn't marry him." She paused for effect, and it worked. Clara was listening. Never before had the housekeeper opened up about her past or her marriage.

"You see, Clara, I cared so deeply about my work, and the family I served back then, that I thought there was no time for romance. No place for love in the life of a servant." Again, she paused, leaving Clara eager to hear more. "But I was wrong. And Mr. Quigley made me see it. I had just as much a right to love as the ladies and gentlemen I tended to." Mrs. Quigley stared into Clara's eyes, allowing them to stand opposite each other in silence for several minutes, before turning back to the china dish in her hands.

Eventually the old woman spoke. "And thank goodness he did."

Clara thought of Cal, sweet on another girl, and did not quite know how to respond. She too resumed her scrubbing.

"I'm just telling you this, my dear, so that you know. Should it ever come up. No one here expects you to spend your days on this earth living someone else's life, never thinking about your own.

Well, maybe one person expects that. But none of the rest of us do. In fact, we hope that doesn't happen."

Clara nodded, suppressing the words: *but what if the one I love has found someone else?* Instead, she answered, "Thank you, Mrs. Quigley."

"I suppose that, after losing Hannah, I felt the need to tell you that, Clara. Life is short, and hard, but we're all entitled to our own little slice of happiness." The old woman paused, a sad smile on her lips. "And on that note, I *insist* you go out, Clara. Out with you. Go take a walk out of doors. Get some air, feel the sunshine, enjoy yourself for a little. You've been so very sad lately." The woman said it as though she were forcing Clara from the kitchen. But why the housekeeper was so eager to relieve Clara of her chores, she could not tell.

"Well, if you insist." Clara wiped her hands on her apron. "Would you like me to bring Little Eddy so you are free in the kitchen?" Clara looked at the little boy, sleeping on her straw pad.

"Leave him be. When he wakes up I'll get him."

"Are you certain, Mrs. Quigley?"

"Positive." The old woman nodded, smoothing Clara's unruly blond hair. "And take your apron off. This dress looks nice on you." Mrs. Quigley untied the linen apron so that Clara stood in her cotton dress, a calico print of blue and yellow with a white collar and cuff sleeves.

"Oh, and Clara?" Mrs. Quigley caught her before she left the room.

"Yes, ma'am?"

"Don't come back until supper."

Clara walked out of the kitchen, confused, as her light eyes blinked in the sunlight of the warm August day. She tied her straw hat into place and looked out over the yard, the distant wheat baking in the dry afternoon. Why had she been so uncharacteristically relieved of her chores? Why now, all of a sudden, was Mrs. Quigley eager to share advice on the matters of the heart? And what was she supposed to do outdoors in the heat of the day? Get out of the sun, that was the first thing. She walked to the large oak on the north side of the lawn—the tree that had so kindly suffered the beating in her stead.

She looked up at its leaves, watching as each one swayed in the breeze, dancing with a beauty far more effortless, far more natural than any waltz she'd seen at a British ball. Clara leaned her back against the cool, smooth trunk of the tree, and slid down it, resting on the grass.

She had forgotten how to occupy herself without work, without an endless list of chores, errands, orders. A crying baby, a plaintive mistress. She'd forgotten how to take refuge in her own mind, to allow her thoughts to glide effortlessly like a sweet scent on a breeze. These days, all her daydreams had turned sour.

She gently plucked a cluster of violet wildflowers that grew around the base of the oak. She'd bring them back for Mrs. Quigley, as thanks for this break. She brought them to her nose, breathing in their sweet, sun-kissed scent. Perhaps, she thought, there were still some joys to be taken from life. Even a penniless, heartbroken orphan like herself could still give thanks for the flowers from the earth, the gentle sunshine overhead. She had thought herself broken. Defeated. But she was strong, she always had been. She would continue on, cobbling together some form of a life even as the world seemed to crumble around her.

The sound of a steady clip-clopping interrupted Clara's reverie. A lone rider, from the sound of it, approaching the Arnold house by way of the narrow post road. Clara pulled herself up to a stand, clutching the nosegay of flowers to her waist.

It was a colonial rider, she saw, here on business with General Arnold.

"Poor gent thinks he's coming to meet with an American hero. Little does he know how wretched this hero and his household are." Clara twisted the flower stems in her fingers as she watched the rider. Barley ran out to greet the horse and its rider, tail wagging. Some guard dog he was.

Something about this man's mannerisms struck Clara as familiar, as he posted up and down on the trotting horse. His movements, his outline against the sun—they stirred some memory of hers that seemed just out of reach.

"Cal." Clara said it as a whisper at first, too terrified to breathe her thought lest it turn out not to be true. But it couldn't be Cal. She studied the man more closely now—his strong, narrow figure, his sand-colored hair. The whistle he let out to greet the dog.

"Cal!" she repeated, willing it to be true. She dropped the flowers and took off at a full run, bounding toward the approaching horse. The figure raised a hand to her in greeting.

He reined in the horse, coming to a halt a few feet before her. "Hello, Clara Bell." His face looked the same, only thinner. His skin had the glow of summer, darkened by long days spent outdoors. His light brown hair had grown longer but he still tied it loosely behind his head in the familiar fashion. A lone piece of straw dangled out of the side of his mouth, just as she remembered.

Clara stood before him, short of breath. "Is it really you?"

"It depends. Who do you think it is?" Cal cracked a grin, and everything about his face felt overwhelmingly familiar. A sensation of unadulterated happiness washed over Clara.

"I think I see Caleb Little," she answered, blinking against the sunlight as she stared up at him on the horse.

Cal doffed his tricornered hat to her. "It is I, Miss Bell. At your service."

"But Caleb Little wore stable clothes, and this man before me looks like a finely uniformed soldier."

"And the Clara Bell I left behind wore homespun and had a harried look on her face as she struggled to pour her lady's Champagne. But here is a young woman who looks as though she could be the lady of the house."

Clara nodded, reminding herself not to be bashful. Even if he looked at her as he used to, he no longer cared for her as he used to. Better not to think of him as anything more than a friend, she warned herself. "I guess we've both changed."

"Aye." He nodded.

And then a thought struck her. "Cal, did your aunt know you'd be arriving here today?"

"She did."

"That explains it," Clara said, reflecting on the uncustomary dismissal from her chores. But didn't the old woman know that the chance for Cal and Clara had passed?

Cal dismounted from his horse and Clara caught a whiff of his scent—a heady, familiar medley of horse, hay, and peppermint. She was struck by how strong her body's memory of him was.

"Hello, Clara Bell." He looked at her, his body just inches from hers. He still smiled with his hazel eyes, that lopsided grin just as she remembered it.

"Hello, Cal."

"It's been a while."

"Indeed it has." She swallowed hard. "It's good to see you."

"You as well, Clara Bell." He paused, shifting his weight from one boot to the other. Then, matter-of-factly, he spoke: "It's business that brings me here."

Clara nodded, even as her heart faltered. Of course it was business. Remember what you heard about that girl, Sarah Williamson, she reminded herself. Don't forget that Cal is nothing more than your friend.

Standing up straight, her voice clear, she looked up at him. "Nevertheless, everyone will be pleased to see you. Shall we tie up your horse so you can go inside to your aunt and uncle?"

"No." Cal shrugged his shoulders, looking down at the river. "I have an errand to see to first."

Clara nodded. "All right then."

And then, turning back to her, he asked, "Would you like to come with me?"

Her heart leapt, and she suppressed the smile that pulled at her lips. "Where to?" Clara asked, but she knew her answer would be yes.

"Just several miles up the post road. Old Buckwheat here knows the way." Cal rested a hand on the horse, a strong chestnut mare.

"Several miles away? But, I have work." She looked at the house with regret. "Mrs. Quigley—your aunt—might need me." But then she remembered the order: not to return until supper. Yes, Mrs. Quigley had most certainly hoped this would happen. "But then again . . ." Clara turned back toward Cal. "I've just been given my first afternoon off. I'd love to join you."

"Good." Caleb smiled at her, and she was struck by how close their bodies were. "Let's go."

"But, Cal, I don't think I can ask Miss Peggy for a horse. She would never let me borrow one."

"That's fine. Old Buckwheat will take us."

"Both of us?" Clara frowned, looking at the saddle on the horse.

"I promise, I'll hold on to you."

Clara hesitated.

"What is it?"

"I've only ever ridden sidesaddle."

Cal leaned close and grinned at her, his hazel eyes lighting up with mischief. It was not fair that he was so handsome, she thought to herself. "The war has made adventurers of us both."

"I shall not know what I'm doing."

"You won't fall off, I promise."

She protested a moment longer, more for propriety's sake, before she allowed him to help her onto the horse.

"See, that wasn't so difficult now, was it?" Cal directed her feet into the two stirrups.

"This saddle feels just big enough for me." Clara settled into the leather seat, looking down at him from astride the horse. "I'm not sure how you're planning on fitting both of us up here."

"You'll have to make room, because I can't keep up with Buckwheat when he runs." Cal hoisted himself up, positioning himself into the saddle snugly behind her. He threaded his arms around her waist and grabbed the reins. Again, his nearness overwhelmed her, and Clara was grateful that he could not see the rosy flush that colored her cheeks.

"You want to hold the reins, or shall I?" he whispered into her ear, and a shiver ran along her neck.

"I can," she answered, affecting a cool tone that did not at all reflect her inward state.

"I knew you'd say that." He clucked and Buckwheat started at a trot.

"Oh my," Clara exclaimed, startled. Her weight shifted back toward him as she struggled to regain her balance.

"It's not Miss Peggy's coach, but I hope you'll manage," Caleb teased. "Hold on tight, Clara Bell." Cal dug his boots into the horse's broad sides and Buckwheat picked up his pace—pulling them forward at an ever-increasing pace.

"Cal!" Clara squealed in delight. "This is too fast—slow us down!"

"Don't worry, I've got you." He wrapped his arms even tighter around her waist and she surrendered to the rhythmic forward movement of the horse. Effortlessly, their bodies slipped into a perfect harmony, rising and falling with each thunderous step of the hooves. The saddle suddenly felt like it was made for the two of them. She couldn't help but smile as she felt the wind whipping her hair; she saw the world gliding by beneath them as they galloped north.

"We're flying faster than the birds!" Clara lifted her arms and let out a laugh.

"I think old Buckwheat's got even more in him. What do you say, Clara Bell?" Cal shouted over the rush of the wind, spurring the horse faster.

Then they were weightless, and each time Clara let loose a peal of excitement, it only prompted Cal to answer her with a laugh of his own.

"Did I say we were going several miles? I meant we're going to Canada," Caleb shouted over the whir of the wind in their faces.

"That's fine with me," Clara answered him. She could have ridden like this for hours, days even.

After a journey that felt too short, Caleb slowed the horse. "Whoa, Buck." He calmed the animal, a thin sheen of sweat glistening on the surface of its backside. "Easy, boy."

Clara looked around. They had stopped in a small meadow dotted with wildflowers on the bank of the Hudson. The hill sloped gently to their right, the river's languid waters flowed to their left. She looked around her and saw no other sign of human life anywhere, just the birds that flitted about in the grass and a family of deer that grazed on the distant hill, unconcerned by the sudden intrusion.

"Where are we, Cal? This is beautiful," Clara exclaimed, giving him her hand as he helped her down from the horse.

"Well, we're at my home," Cal answered matter-of-factly.

"Pardon?" Clara was certain he was teasing her as he always did.

"This is Little Farm," he answered her and, for once, there was no humor in his face. "Or at least, it will be. Do you approve?"

Clara gazed back over the land, the soft slope of green that met the wide river, astonished anew by how beautiful this piece of earth was.

"This is your home, Cal?" Surely he was teasing her—how could a penniless orphan become owner of such a farm?

"Will be. When the war's over. Colonel Israel Putnam is giving out tracts of land to all of us who have served. The new country will need people to farm the land. I picked this one because I liked the view of the river." Caleb walked forward lazily toward the water. "What do you think?"

"It's . . . it's lovely." Clara fell into stride beside him.

"I was planning to build the house right over there"—he pointed to the crest of the gently sloping meadow—"about halfway between the river and the tree line, so the house would be bright and give a great view of sunset."

She closed her eyes, imagining the new cottage on the hilltop, Cal tying up his horse outside of it at suppertime. That lucky girl, Sarah Williamson, greeting him on the porch.

Clara closed her eyes and forced the image from her mind. She had had her chance with him, years ago. She'd squandered it, and so her present unhappiness was her own fault. She wouldn't be like Peggy, blaming others for her own misfortunes. She wouldn't hate a girl she'd never met, simply because that girl had been wise enough to accept Cal's love when it was offered. Regaining her composure, she asked, "And you'll work the fields?"

"Yes." He nodded. "Hopefully with the help of a few sons some day."

Clara lowered her eyes, wishing her heart would slow its pace. Once more, she willed herself not to hate Sarah Williamson. Not to envy her life because it was a life with Cal.

Cal still looked out over the land. "A place of my own. Not too bad for an orphaned stableboy, eh?" Cal sighed, lowering himself down onto the grass. Clara sat down beside him, and they looked out at the river in silence. A gust of wind stirred up the surface of the water, causing it to ripple like shards of glass.

"That's what this new country—this thing called America—is all about, Clara. It's a nation of people standing up and taking their own destinies in their hands. Saying, 'I can live my life better than some king can tell me how.'"

Clara thought about this. Caleb had always believed in the country—in America, in George Washington, in freedom. His was a patriotism that did not rise and fall with his own political fortunes; it was not a venture through which to gain fame or glory.

"You can do the same, Clara." Caleb nudged her. "You don't need to waste your life with Peggy Shippen. Aren't there things you want?"

I want to live here, with you, she thought, tortured by how immediately these words came to her. Their faces were close now, his honey-colored eyes just inches from her own. She longed to reach out and touch him, to stroke his cheek with her finger; to share a moment of tenderness that matched the warm feelings she felt for him inside. She remembered back to the evenings when he'd lingered in the kitchen, late at night, stealing the only opportunities he could find to be alone with her. How, years ago, it had made her uncomfortable. How young, how stupidly innocent she had been.

"Well?" He raised his eyebrows, his hazel eyes catching the light of the sun as he looked at her with genuine interest. He was the only person she knew who never made her feel as if she were invisible. The first person who'd ever even suggested that she ought to think about herself. Even Oma, who had clearly loved her and dedicated her years to giving Clara a life—a home, work, food—had always just told her to work hard and be a good servant. And she had been, she had served Peggy obediently every day.

She had to answer, so she did it with a half-truth. "I suppose I'd want to be my own master. To have my own family, my own home." Clara looked around. And then, she could not bite her tongue any longer. "I'm certain Sarah Williamson and you will be very happy here."

Now it was Cal's turn to be tongue-tied. "Sarah Williamson?" He repeated the name, confused.

"Yes." Clara nodded. "Your aunt told us about your new sweetheart." She tried to sound light. "We're all very happy for you, Cal. Even if you have yet to tell me."

There, she had done it. He knew that she knew. And she would be all right with it. They would be friends, just as they had always been. Perhaps some day she might even be able to be friends with this Sarah. Perhaps.

"Clara." Cal's voice was thoughtful. "Clara, you are mistaken. Sarah Williamson is not my sweetheart."

Her mind careened, and she was grateful to be sitting. "But your aunt told us. She is your friend's cousin, isn't she?"

"She is. And a very nice girl. For a while I thought that, perhaps, there was something there. . . ." His voice trailed off. Clara could not calm her frantic heart, or ignore the hope that had been kindled like a tiny flame within her.

Now Cal looked at her intently, those hazel eyes holding her in a steady gaze. "Clara, I don't love Sarah Williamson."

"Why not?" she asked, her voice barely a whisper.

Cal laughed, a short sigh of a laugh. And then he raised his eyebrows. "Because she is not you."

Clara was so delirious with joy that she suspected she might break out into laughter and tears at the same time. Did this mean Cal still loved *her*? But how could she have gotten so lucky as to have been given a second chance?

"Clara." Cal's voice was soft now. "Surely you must know . . ."

What she did know was that, if given this second chance, she would not squander it. "Cal, I love you." She had not expected to feel so light, so free, after finally saying those words. But then, she'd not expected to have the chance to say them, either. She laughed at herself, before continuing. "I've loved you for years. I only just realized it, when I thought I had lost you forever. Cal, please know—"

But before she finished her thought, his lips were on hers, silencing her excuses. Forgiving her for how long she had taken to see what was obvious. There, in the golden light of the midday sun, with the fields and the river as their only witnesses, Cal kissed her. It was only the second time in her nineteen years that she'd ever been kissed, and she felt shy at first. But as his lips touched hers, his hand moved to take hers in his, she softened into his touch. And now she kissed him with a fervor that made up for all the nights she'd imagined being kissed by Cal. It was even better than she had thought possible. It was the truth, what she was meant to be doing. Why had she waited so long to allow him to kiss her?

When he pulled his lips from hers, Clara had not yet had her fill, and she reached for him again. But he didn't allow her to kiss him. He raised a finger between their lips, asking: "What took you so long, Clara?"

Her mind was fuzzy, and she blinked, trying to answer the question. "I'm asking myself the same thing, Cal."

He took her fingers and threaded them through his own. "I had pretty much given up on you, Clara."

She didn't respond, but instead put her head on his shoulder.

Still looking out at the river, he said, "I'm glad that my aunt told you about Sarah Williamson."

Clara lifted her head, looking at him. "Cal, that's not why you wrote to Mrs. Quigley with your news, is it?"

A smirk tugged on his lips. "I must confess, I *was* sort of hoping that my aunt would share the news that I'd met a girl. That it might make you a little jealous. Perhaps get you to wake up, at last."

Clara smiled, kissing him on the cheek. "I should be mad at you for toying with me that way."

"I had grown impatient, Clara Bell."

She smiled. She deserved that. Leaning toward his ear, she whispered, "Thank you for waiting for me, Cal."

"You were worth it, Clara Bell." He kissed her again, his hand holding her cheek as he did so.

They sat beside each other for a long time, silently watching the current of the river as it meandered past. She felt warm from the sun and her love for Cal, so freshly declared. But her joy gave way to a darker, more practical concern. How would they ever be together? With him going back to his camp, and her returning to the Arnolds, a future with Cal seemed far from certain.

Caleb's thoughts seemed to have turned down a similar path. "We're getting close to the end of this war." Caleb's posture stiffened. "It won't be long now. And when it's over, I want to marry you."

Her heart leapt with joy. "Nothing would make me happier, Cal." She leaned forward to kiss him, but he quickly pulled his head back.

"But your letters have me very concerned."

Grinding her teeth, she thought, *Thank you, Miss Peggy, for ruining my engagement.* But it was so much bigger than that. The future with Cal, the future of the entire nation, was in peril—she understood the difficulties they faced better than anyone.

"Clara, it sounds an awful lot like treason, what you're describing to me."

She had been so happy a moment ago, so hopeful for the idea of a life with him. And now her stomach was twisted in knots. "It is," she said.

"What is the latest?"

"They are communicating with André."

"I gathered that from your messages. And?"

"I don't know what to do, Cal. I see no way of stopping it."

Caleb sat in thoughtful silence while Clara told him of all that she knew—of the correspondence the Arnolds had undertaken with Major André, of their efforts to get the assignment at West Point, of their plans to turn over the fort to André and Clinton.

"Just as Washington is planning to strike New York City too." Caleb grinded his teeth. "That snake. Sorry, Clara, I know he is still your employer."

"Don't be. I've thought far worse about her over the years," she said.

"If there was any way to prove that he was planning this, I'd shoot him myself," Caleb fumed.

"But that's the problem, Cal. There's no way to prove Arnold's plot. He burns all the letters once he's read them. And they never use one another's names. They could always just point to the names and say that clearly the letter wasn't intended for Arnold, but that he intercepted it to have it investigated."

"Yes." Caleb thought this through, his face pensive.

"I've been agonizing over this," Clara said.

"Have they met—Arnold and André?" Caleb asked.

"Not yet. But André did request a meeting with Arnold."

Caleb listened. "That's interesting. That would mean he'd have to come north to meet with Arnold. That could be our opportunity."

"You think so?" Clara considered it.

"Possibly. But there would have to be proof on André's person that linked him to Arnold. Or a signed letter. Otherwise he could just say he was traveling on official business on behalf of General Clinton. Crossing enemy lines on official orders is not in and of itself a war crime."

Clara thought this over.

"If André comes north to meet Arnold, tell me." Caleb looked at her intensely. "All right?"

"Yes." She nodded. "All right."

"Clara, we must stop it. It's our future together." He paused, looking out over the river, at the tiny gray speck that stood on the opposite hill, West Point. Lifting his hands, as if to hold all of this land in his arms, Caleb said: "The future of all of this."

VIII.

It is backbreaking work—rowing so hard, so long. His arms burn with the exertion, his brow grows moist with sweat.

But the other option is to have his neck broken at the gallows. To die a traitor. He would not have that. Not after all that he has sacrificed for this country, not after being insulted, cheated, and lied to. No, if anything, he *is the victim of untold treachery.*

Her face haunts him as he rows. The panic, the confusion. How could he have put her in such a dangerous position? How could he have left her to fend for herself among that pack of wolves? It was too much to think about.

Perhaps he should go back. Turn the boat around. Rescue her.

But they will have arrived by now. They are most likely stabling their horses at his barn this very moment. Do they know yet? he wonders.

He keeps his eyes fixed firmly down the river, where he hopes to spot the full sails of the Vulture *at any time. They will welcome him aboard as a hero. The hero's treatment he has so long deserved, so long been denied.*

He feels no remorse for John André; the man chose his own fate. Nor does the fault lie with him that the fool got himself caught. The man always seemed to walk with excessive swagger. And now he may hang. But that matters not. What he cares about is reaching the ship. That, and his wife. He grows sad as he thinks of her as he'd seen her this morning. Sleeping beside him, her blond curls giving her the cherubic appearance he'd always loved.

"Oh," he cries out, with nothing but the river to hear his doleful lamentation. Wouldn't it be better to die beside her than to live without her? Would she ever be reunited with him in this life?

CHAPTER EIGHT

"The Biggest Fish of Them All"

August 1780
West Point, New York

I SAW YOU riding away with that stableboy. The one that always smelled like horse filth." Peggy was in bed, watching Clara build her evening fire. Clara wanted to take one of the logs she was stacking and hurl it toward the bed. Instead, she bit her tongue and continued to unload the logs over the hearth. Nothing would quench the happy glow inside her, the one that burned ever since Cal's kiss had touched her lips.

"Oh my goodness. You . . . you are *attracted* to him?" Peggy pulled the feather quilt around her shoulders and Clara swore she overheard a titter of mocking laughter.

Clara's silence seemed only to propel Peggy to further taunts. "I always just figured he was trying to seduce you and that you, pure little Clara Bell, didn't understand what was going on. Like when Robert Balmor kissed you so brazenly and you allowed it."

Clara's face burned at the mention of that name—in shame, in embarrassment, in anger. How dare Miss Peggy compare the two?

"Oh, Clara, best not to get yourself attached." Peggy spoke with maternal care, a tone that Clara knew to be entirely conjured. "He's on the wrong side, which means he shall hang before this war is over. And besides, he's probably in bed with a different tavern wench every night."

Arnold opened the door just then, limping in without knocking. "Peggy." He moved toward the bed in several brisk strides. "André didn't await a reply. He's written again."

"Oh?" Peggy slid out from under the bedsheet, sitting upright. Clara's interest too was roused.

"He wants to meet." Arnold's face bore the signs of strain.

"To meet?" Peggy rose from the bed, walking to the mirror and studying her appearance as if her husband had told her eighteen-year-old self that John André stood outside the bedroom door. She turned from front to back, examining her curvy figure beneath the thin linen shift she wore. Clara knew Peggy well enough to know intuitively what her mistress was thinking: she was wondering if André would find her attractive after all this time.

"Well, Benny, invite him to meet."

Arnold was studying the letter and didn't seem to notice his wife's odd behavior. "We can't have him here, Peg." Arnold shook his head. "It's far too deep behind colonial lines. Someone will see him. It's not safe."

Peggy crossed her arms and thought about this.

Arnold continued. "I need to meet him somewhere in No Man's Land, right on the border of the two lines."

"Where is that?" Peggy asked.

"Tarrytown on this side of the river. Haverstraw on the other side."

Peggy answered, "How about that fellow we had luncheon with a few months ago? That Joshua Smith fellow? He fawned all over you, and he seemed thick-skulled enough to fall for the idea of hosting a meeting for you."

"Good idea," Arnold answered.

"When will it happen?"

"André has requested a meeting on the eleventh of September. I shall write to accept, and once I get an agreement from Smith, I'll write André back with directions. It'll have to be the middle of the night, so that André can slip over the line undetected. He'll most likely come by boat."

"Let's hope Smith agrees." Peggy faced her husband. "The man is clearly an admirer of yours, but will he ask too many questions?"

Arnold mulled this over. "The man is not particularly smart, and wants nothing more than to ingratiate himself with me. But perhaps not to the extent that he'd allow me to discuss treason with a British officer in front of his nose . . ."

"You shall have to lie," Peggy said. "Smith can't know that André is a British officer. Not while we still question where Smith's loyalty rests."

"André shall have to come in plain clothes," Arnold agreed.

Clara made a note in her mind of all the details of this treasonous meeting, determined to relay this information to Cal.

"That will work." Peggy nodded, hopping back into bed. "When shall we go?"

"'We'?" Arnold looked at his wife.

"I shall go with you, of course," Peggy answered, summoning him toward the bed, "seeing as I am the liaison."

"My dear lady." Arnold's voice betrayed incredulity. "I see no good reason why you should hazard your comfort, and more importantly, your safety, to attend this meeting. It is between John André and myself."

Clara braced herself for what was surely coming. When Peggy spoke, her tone was biting.

"And was it between you and André when I wrote the first letter initiating contact? And how about as you've negotiated the terms? And shall it be between you and André alone when the fate of our family, our child, is decided by this plot?" Peggy took her face in her hands and erupted in sobs, her eyes peeking through the spaces in between her fingers to ensure that her husband watched. "Benedict Arnold, you have hurt your dear wife deeply. Oh, Clara." Peggy summoned her maid away from the hearth. "Clara, run and fetch me a warm cloth, my head ails me so."

When Clara returned to the room, Arnold was perched beside his wife on the bed, his efforts at assuaging her grief proving futile.

"You would cut me out of these negotiations as if I were nothing more than a servant." Peggy sobbed, taking the cloth from Clara and dabbing her forehead. "Be gone from my sight, Benedict Arnold."

This distressed Arnold, who stayed beside his wife's bed. "My dear, of course you shall not be cut out—I shall return with a report, which I will share in full. I simply will not risk your safety on this excursion."

Peggy looked at her husband, her weepy eyes sharpening in focus. "But you overlook a key point, Benny." Clara sensed that Peggy was recalibrating her strategy, having failed at her first attempt.

"Smith shall be hosting this meeting, and he shall expect to be a participant. If you and Johnny, I mean, André, wish to speak in private without your host, Smith might take offense. Or worse, grow suspicious."

Arnold listened as his wife described this scenario, stroking the whiskers on his chin in thought. "If only there were a way to divert his attention for a few hours . . ." Peggy floated the words, without completing the suggestion. Arnold retreated into contemplative silence.

"We need to distract Smith, do we not?" Peggy watched as her husband paced the bedroom.

"Fine." Arnold nodded once, his jaw clenched. "You will come, to distract Smith."

Peggy's face brightened. "Indeed," she sighed, retreating into her own imagination to conjure up the scene. "I'll wear my finest gown and I will entertain Smith all night while you and Johnny discuss our plans in the other room."

"For heaven's sake, Peg." Arnold's ruddy cheeks flushed. "Why do you keep calling him *Johnny*?"

"JOHNNY'S FAVORITE dress." Peggy stood in her shift, staring into her wardrobe. She exhaled slowly, wistfully, eyeing the rose-colored gown she'd worn to the lawn soiree at Lord Rawdon's home years earlier. Clara remembered the gown and her first evening at her new job as if it had occurred just a month ago.

"He always loved this one." Peggy fingered the pink silk softly. "But I wonder if I can even fit into it now." She pulled the dress off its hook, turning determinedly to Clara. "You must squeeze me into it."

Wrapping her arms around a poster of her bed, Peggy braced herself. "Tie my stays as tight as they will go. I must fit into that dress," she demanded. Biting her lip, Peggy tolerated the pain as Clara stitched up the corset.

"Goodness, that baby ruined my waist." Peggy clutched her abdomen. "I don't think I'll be able to breathe." She moved slowly, pulling her hoopskirt up to hip-height. Clara unfastened the buttons on the back of the gown and slid it over the curves of Peggy's body.

"Well, can I pull it off?" Peggy waited until the buttons were fastened before walking to the mirror. The gown was more snug than it had been years earlier, but it fit.

"Oh." She performed a twirl for herself. "It's so tight. But it'll do. And he'll like this part." She pointed to her bosom, which was fuller than it had been, causing her fleshy breasts to spill out immodestly over the top of the gown.

"Yes, this will do just fine." Peggy clapped and performed a second spin before the mirror, apparently returning not only to her eighteen-year-old wardrobe, but also her eighteen-year-old personality.

She wore her hair in its highest, most vaulted *pouf*, and she coated her cheeks in rouge, her wrists in rose water. As Clara looked on at her fully dressed mistress, she felt that, but for the fuller breasts and the soft lines around her eyes, she could have been looking once more at the celebrated young belle Peggy Shippen.

"Clara, go and fetch Benny, tell him I'm ready." Peggy daubed another splash of perfume across her neckline. "Oh, yes, I've been ready for quite some time."

Clara and Little Eddy watched from the back garden as Arnold pushed them off, their small rowboat cutting silently through the glassy water at dusk, pointing south down the Hudson toward Haverstraw. Toward John André.

Clara ran to meet Peggy and Benedict the next morning when she spotted them rowing ashore outside the Robinson house. They had been out all night, and it seemed that they returned in a tense, fatigued silence.

"I want breakfast and then my feather bed." Peggy yawned, taking Clara's outstretched hand as she stepped out of the rowboat. She let the bottom hem of her pink dress drag carelessly across the mud, and Clara watched with resigned gloom, knowing she'd be tasked with removing those stains.

"You seem incredibly relaxed, considering we've just spent the entire night rowing, risking our own necks, to attend a meeting at which our counterparty never showed!" Arnold dislodged the oars from the rowboat and threw them on the ground. "I intend to write a furiously worded letter to Major André, telling him that we withdraw our entire offer." Arnold limped up to a stand, leaning on his cane as he wobbled out of the boat. As he thundered toward the house, he grumbled loud enough for Clara to overhear, "He disrespects me? I won't have it! I'll tell him so!"

"Benny, you will do no such thing." Peggy clutched her husband's arm and wheeled him around to face her, as she would a petulant child.

"Peggy," Arnold spoke quietly, like a teakettle moments before it erupts into a boil, "I will not negotiate with men who show me disrespect."

"There must be some good reason why André didn't show up at Smith's house last night. Trust me."

"A yellow liver?" Arnold spat, his features taut.

"Just give it a few days. We shall hear why," Peggy urged, turning toward the house before her husband could answer.

"Ale, now!" Arnold thundered into the bright dining room, where a breakfast table was set with a steaming spread of bacon, roast beef, smoked trout, eggs, fresh bread, butter and cheese, and peach cobbler.

"Look at this breakfast!" Peggy sat down, spearing herself a piece of bacon. "Clara, get me coffee. No, actually, make it wine."

Inside the kitchen, Mr. Quigley was polishing silver while his wife sat with Little Eddy on her lap. All three sets of eyes fixed on Clara when she entered, with Little Eddy laughing happily at the sight of her.

"Have they returned?" Mrs. Quigley asked.

"Indeed, they've just sat down to breakfast."

"Did they say what in the devil's name they have been up to, rowing down the river and staying out all night?" Mrs. Quigley continued.

Clara sat down opposite the old woman and the baby. She dropped her head into her hands. When she didn't answer the question, Mrs. Quigley spoke up.

"Well? Do you know something that we don't, child? Do you know where the mister and missus were last night?" Mrs. Quigley peppered her with questions before Clara could even figure out how to answer the old woman.

"If you know something, Clara, then out with it!" the housekeeper pressed her.

"Mr. Quigley, you might want to sit down for this." Clara sighed. The old man heeded her advice and lowered himself down beside his wife.

"I've heard them speaking enough to know with certainty where the Arnolds went last night . . ." Clara wavered. "General and Mrs. Arnold went south to meet Major John André."

The shock on their faces gave Clara some small comfort. It was a relief to know that she no longer carried this vile secret alone. That two others now shared her burden and perhaps might help her find a solution.

Mrs. Quigley shook her head, irritated. "No, Clara. Not this tale again. I told you never to mention it."

"Constance, please." Mr. Quigley overrode his wife, a rare display, which she heeded. "Clara." The butler looked back to the maid. "You mean . . . Major André . . . the former suitor of Miss Margaret Shippen?"

"The very same." Clara nodded.

"The Major André of the *British* Army?" Mr. Quigley asked, his facial features tight.

Clara nodded.

"But I don't understand." Mr. Quigley looked at Clara in confusion. Next he turned to his wife. "Constance, do you mean to tell me that you've had knowledge of this correspondence?"

"Clara mentioned something to me months ago, but I told her to keep out of the Arnolds' business. Besides, I was certain that she was mistaken. It can't be true."

"You never told me?" Mr. Quigley asked. "But never mind that, we shall discuss that later. Clara, please explain everything to me."

"They have been corresponding for quite some time now, you see." Clara felt her shoulders growing lighter as she released the news, as if she were shedding a heavy cloak.

"They have been? But how?" the butler asked.

"How many letters have been delivered from a John Anderson?" Clara looked back at them with an expressionless stare. "John Anderson is *John André.*"

Understanding crossed both their aged faces.

"And what sort of correspondence have they been conducting? To what purpose?" Mr. Quigley asked.

"Perhaps they are attempting to have André switch sides to the colonies," his wife chimed in.

"Quite the contrary," Clara answered, avoiding Eddy's pudgy

hands as they reached for her; his simple, childish sweetness seemed too far at odds with the conversation. "Major André is now the head of intelligence for General Clinton." Clara paused, unsure of whether or not to reveal the full extent of what she knew. Did they need to know how deep the Arnolds' treacherous plans extended?

"General and Mrs. Arnold are interested in selling André top-secret information on West Point. To allow for its seizure by the British."

"Treason?" Mr. Quigley gasped, putting a hand to his lips.

"Hush, John!" Mrs. Quigley scolded him, placing her palms protectively over Little Eddy's ears. "Lower your voice. They might hear!" She leaned toward Clara. "Is it true? They really intend to turn over West Point?"

"And they themselves would switch sides," Clara added.

"I don't want to believe that." Mrs. Quigley exhaled. As if sensing the mood of the room, Little Eddy began to wail.

"Nor did I, Mrs. Quigley." Clara looked at the old woman, sighing. "I know that you wish for no part in this." After a pause, Clara admitted: "I've told Caleb."

"Caleb knows? I bet he is fit to be tied over it." Mrs. Quigley began to bounce the crying baby on her knees.

"We are trying to figure out what we can do to stop them," Clara said.

"Stop them? Good heavens, child, have you gone mad? You two cannot involve yourselves in something this dangerous! Going up against a general as powerful and well-liked as Benedict Arnold? It'll be your word against his, and you and Caleb will both end up hanging." Mrs. Quigley's gaze was a stern warning, and it burned into Clara's face, causing her to shift in her chair.

"But we can't just sit back," Clara argued, stunned that the woman still advised against taking action, even after all that she had heard.

"Course you can! And that's precisely what you'll do!" Mrs. Quigley insisted. "What—you think that you, a lowly maid, will be able to thwart a plot between the highest ranks of both armies? The only thing we can do is hope it doesn't happen. Remember your place, girl. You're a servant. You serve them tea but you don't get involved in their dealings." Mrs. Quigley's harsh tone had further upset Little Eddy, who continued to cry.

"That's not what your nephew says." Clara pushed back, her throat burning. "It's a free country."

"Not yet it isn't," Mrs. Quigley said, her voice sharp. "And with talk such as this, neither one of you is likely to live to see the day."

"Enough." Mr. Quigley put his arms between them. "Constance, please." Then, turning to Clara, he said, "I don't like it any more than you do. But she's right, Clara."

"Mr. Quigley, please," Clara pleaded with him from across the table. "There's got to be something we can do."

Mr. Quigley rubbed his temples in a clockwise motion. And then, he reached for the pile of mail on the farm table. He thumbed through the papers and retrieved a small envelope. "A letter this morning in the post, from a Mr. John Anderson." He pulled the letter out of the pile, sighing. "I of course had no idea from whom it actually came."

Mr. Quigley slid the letter across the table to Clara. "You can deliver this to your mistress," he said, his face serious. "Or, you can forget you ever saw it." His eyes traced a line directly for the hearth, where a fire burned bright. A fire that could incinerate this piece of paper, removing it from sight forever.

This was her chance, her chance to atone for the aid she'd provided to this plot thus far. Clara picked up the treacherous letter.

Her heart beat faster. The Arnolds would think that André hadn't showed and he hadn't written. Perhaps General Arnold would in fact withdraw his offer, as he had threatened to do. She had the chance to thwart their plan entirely, and she would take it.

"There you are," Peggy turned the corner and appeared in the kitchen. She saw the scene—the three servants sitting at the table, and scowled. "Sorry to interrupt your leisurely morning chat. Where's my wine, Clara?" Peggy's eyes glared at the maid.

"Oh, yes, ma'am." Clara rose, keeping the letter from André in her hand as she moved toward the wine.

"What's that?" Peggy asked, crossing the kitchen in two quick strides.

"What's what?" Clara looked at her mistress, pulling her hand and the letter behind her back.

"That." Peggy reached around and snatched the paper from Clara's hand to look at the envelope. "This letter which you just attempted to conceal is intended for my husband." She fixed an accusatory glare on her maid.

"Yes, Miss Peggy. I was just delivering it." Clara averted her eyes to the floor, hoping her lady wouldn't be able to read the lies on her face.

Peggy studied her a minute, apparently undecided as to whether she might trust Clara. "Bring me my wine." She clutched the letter tightly, turning back toward the dining room. "And once we've finished breakfast, I want you to help me undress. I want this dress laundered and pressed and back in my closet. For the next meeting."

"Yes, ma'am." Clara nodded, grabbing the wine and ale from the counter.

Peggy turned on her heels, Clara following behind with the carafe of wine. "Benny"—Peggy waved the letter wildly as she entered the dining room—"look what I have: a letter from John Anderson!"

"Is that so?"

"I told you we'd hear from him—surely there's an excuse. Read it now." Peggy handed the parcel to him. Arnold tore it open and read aloud to his wife.

My Dear Sir and Lady,

You have no doubt heard by now that my ship was fired upon just south of our meeting spot.

My apologies for any concern or inconvenience this may have caused. Please be assured that I was thwarted not for a lack of will, but due to the unforeseen circumstances.

May I suggest the evening of September 22, around midnight when it turns over to the 23rd, for our next meeting? Same spot.

Neither our interests nor our offers have changed.

Your humble servant,
Anderson

"Well," Peggy said, self-satisfied, as she spread cheese on a piece of bread. "Didn't I say so?" She grinned. "I quite like him calling us 'Sir' and 'Lady.'"

Arnold studied the letter. "Well, no, Mr. Anderson. We had *not* heard that you were fired upon."

Peggy snatched the letter from her husband's hands and perused the message herself. "Well, Benny, everything looks to be in order. Thank God! The thought of returning to that tiny cottage in Philadelphia." Peggy shuddered. Just then, Clara heard footsteps.

"Someone's coming." Peggy pulled the letter onto her lap and out of sight as the door to the dining room opened.

"Franks!" Arnold rose, greeting his aide cordially as he entered the sunny room.

"General Arnold, Mrs. Arnold, good morning." The aide removed his cap and bowed to them.

"You always have a knack for showing up at breakfast time, my good man," Arnold roared. "I do not think it's coincidental. Please, join us." Arnold offered a chair to Franks. "Coffee?"

"If you please." The aide nodded, sitting down between them at the table. Clara poured him his coffee the way he always took it, black.

"We've just received news this morning from General Washington himself." Franks served himself a thick piece of smoked trout.

"Indeed? And how is the old giant?" Arnold rapped the table as if delighted to hear it.

"Very well, from the sound of it. He sends his regards to you, of course, Major General." Franks beamed with pride at being able to deliver such flattery to his superior. "General Washington plans to come here in a few weeks' time. Around the morning of the twenty-fourth. He's asked if he might stay with you while he visits West Point."

Peggy dropped her fork, causing it to clamor to the floor. Franks looked at her. "I'm sorry if I've upset you, Mrs. Arnold."

"No, no." Peggy reached down for her dropped silverware. When she came back up to the table, her face was a mask of composure. "No, you haven't at all, Major Franks. It's just that, well, I'm so delighted that the general wishes to stay with us."

"It's an honor indeed." Franks concurred, taking a satisfied slurp of his black coffee. "He intends to inspect West Point. So, General Arnold, you and I have our work cut out for us the next few weeks."

"We most certainly do," Peggy agreed.

Franks threw a quizzical glance in her direction before turning back to his plate. He did not notice that the Arnolds seemed to have lost their appetites, but Clara did. When he'd finished his meat and was serving himself seconds, Franks spoke.

"So, have you heard the big news this morning, General?" Franks wiped his mouth with the tablecloth. "A British warship by the name of the HMS *Vulture* was fired on overnight. Down around Tarrytown. They're not sure what it was doing venturing so close to our lines."

"Ah, yes, I did hear that." Arnold nodded, his face taking on a countenance of deep concern. "Damn redcoats, trying to test our mettle?"

"Appears so," Franks answered. "Who gave you the account? I wonder if it was similar to what I heard." Franks turned to his boss.

"Oh, I just heard from a source. I've got spies all through these woods working for us. I can't reveal their names. You understand, Franks." Arnold winked conspiratorially.

"Of course," the aide answered obsequiously.

"Good man." Arnold smiled at his attendant.

"Seems the *Vulture* slipped back behind British lines unscathed in the early morning," Franks continued. "Probably some of Clinton's men up from New York City."

"Aye, the sneaky lobsterbacks," Arnold agreed. "No matter. We'll get them next time, won't we, Franks?"

"We certainly will, sir," Franks agreed. "What a ghastly name for a ship carrying a bunch of redcoats, nay? The *Vulture*. I get chills just thinking about it."

They ate on in silence. Clara noticed that her mistress was merely moving the food around on her plate.

Franks broke the silence. "General Arnold, there's one more

thing. I am hesitant to raise the issue with you, but I do feel that you should know what is being said by some of the men."

Arnold ceased cutting his meat and looked at his aide. Clara's back stiffened, and she was certain that Peggy and Arnold felt panic.

"You'd like to hear what some people are claiming, would you not?" Franks asked again.

"Of course." Arnold lowered his silverware to the plate, his face ashen.

"It's some . . . complaint . . . that a number of the men around here are making about you." Franks looked down at his plate. Peggy reached for her husband's hand.

"What is it, Franks?" Arnold's voice was hoarse, quiet, as he took his wife's hand in his.

"They say that you—" Franks paused.

"Yes? Tell me, Franks."

"Well, they say that you . . ." Again the aide lost his resolve to make the accusation.

"Out with it, man!" Arnold roared. Peggy gasped, putting her hand over her heart.

Finally, Franks spoke. "They say that your eating habits are not what they should be."

Arnold and Peggy looked at each other, erupting in relieved laughter. "Is that all?" Arnold pounded the table with his fist. "My eating habits! That is what they are complaining about?"

"Well, yes." Franks looked on uneasily, apparently unsure of the comedy of his statement. "You see, your men are starving. And they hear that you and your"—he looked at Peggy—"family . . . are eating meat and potatoes and butter at every meal." The aide looked guiltily at the breakfast spread from which he had just partaken.

"They say that you should not be keeping an entire milk cow

for yourself. That the milk cow is intended to provide milk and cheese for the men over at the fort."

Clara tripped at the name. Milk Cow. Her code word with Caleb for George Washington. But then she calmed herself, believing that Franks merely meant the cow in the stable from where the Arnolds got their milk, butter, and cheese.

"It wouldn't be the Continental Army without some form of slander flying against my name." Arnold sloshed his coffee around in his cup. "What else do they say, Franks?"

"Well, it's quite serious, sir," Franks answered. "They say that your habits are causing some of the soldiers to go without."

"What do they expect me to do?"

Again Franks looked at the full table before them. "They say that a true officer should be eating salt cod and root vegetables at every meal. Like they are. Like . . . er, like General Washington does."

Arnold took his napkin out of his collar and slammed it on the table, causing his startled aide to jump back from the table. "Do they demand that General Washington and the others surrender the use of their legs, as I have? Or their personal fortunes?"

The aide offered no response to this.

"I am the general here, Franks, lest you forget. A rank which I have earned with my blood and my fortune. And if my wife wants fresh milk and cheese, she will have it."

"Thank you, Benny." Peggy glowered at Franks as she bit into her buttered bread.

"Do you understand?" Arnold leaned toward Franks, bellowing. "Do you understand?"

"I do, sir." The aide blanched.

"You may go now, Major Franks." The aide did not need to be

told twice. Franks hopped up from the table, leaving his plate full, and crossed the room in two strides.

Once the door had shut behind Franks, the two conspirators sat alone in silence. Peggy eyed her husband, waiting for him to speak. He did not, but simply turned his attention back to finishing off the last of his beef and ale. Peggy sipped her wine and Clara retreated farther into the corner of the room.

Finally, Arnold broke the silence. "Some nerve that man has, coming here and eating from my table."

"While insulting how your acquire the very same food you feed him." Peggy shook her head, sipping her wine.

"But did you hear what he said before that?" Arnold arched his brows. "It appears, my dear, that we may have just reeled in the biggest fish of them all." Arnold turned to his wife, his cheeks flushed and rosy.

Peggy turned to him, as if ready to burst. "Benny, you heard him. Washington wants to come *here*!"

"At last fate seems to smile upon us." Arnold stroked his gray whiskers.

"Benny." Peggy rose from her chair and moved to her husband's lap. "There will be no denying us a title when we deliver Washington!"

Arnold thought this over, eventually nodding. "You are quite right."

"André had asked us if our conditions had changed." Peggy gasped. "They have."

"Yes, I would say they have." Arnold gnawed on his lower lip, his face fixed with determination.

"Imagine us, turning over the leader of the Continental Army." Peggy's calm, cool tone caused the flesh on Clara's neck to prickle.

Arnold wrapped his arms tighter around his wife's waist, his eyes ablaze. "More milk in your coffee, Lady Arnold?"

Peggy looked back into her husband's eyes, her expression gloating. He *would* give her the life she had always longed for, after all. "Please, my Lord Benedict. Let's put that milk cow to work—otherwise, what would your men gossip about?"

"Oh, I think we'll give them something to gossip about soon enough, Peg."

Peggy giggled as her husband filled her cup to the brim, allowing it to spill over onto the white tablecloth.

CLARA WAS frantic. Still, she managed to work all day without her mistress noticing her distraction. When at last she had the kitchen to herself that evening, she wrote Cal.

Cal,

Much news to report. The meeting did not occur. The "coq" did not show, and you've likely deduced by now that his was the vessel spotted last night.

It's been rescheduled—down the river, just north of the line on the 22nd. Coq will come by water and they will rendezvous at the home of Joshua Hett Smith.

I will try my best to find an excuse to be included on this excursion, so that I may inform you of all the details. If I deem it safe, I will leave a note for you at the home.

Cal, can you take action with this news? If not, I fear that the milk cow might be in danger.

Clara Bell

Clara sent the letter the next day, handing it to Franks on his way out of the house without the Arnolds seeing. "If you could post this on my behalf." Clara leaned in, an exaggerated look of supplication on her face. "Please, Major Franks, it's for a gent." Clara lowered her eyes and a well-timed blush made the obsequious aide certain that the pretty maid's very happiness rested in his hands.

"I'd be happy to help you, Miss Bell. You can rest assured of my discretion."

All of that long, anxious week, she waited, seeking out the mail each morning, but no reply came. Meanwhile, it was perhaps her imagination, but Clara felt a gnawing suspicion that Miss Peggy was watching her even closer than usual. Her hawkish eyes seemed to keep Clara under their surveillance at all times. Did she suspect Clara? Would Clara be able to snatch away Cal's letter before Miss Peggy knew of its existence? But the week progressed, and still no letter came.

"Good gracious, girl, what are you waiting for?" Mrs. Quigley grew irritated at Clara as she lingered in the kitchen each morning, asking if that day's post had arrived. "You look as though you're expecting a letter from General George Washington himself."

No, Clara thought to herself. But nearly as important.

September marched on, and all around them it seemed that the world was preparing for the arrival of General Washington. Major Franks and a stream of officers rode in daily from West Point, carrying maps and lists of troop numbers and plans for the fortifications and improvements at the camp. Arnold no longer simply feigned interest as he pored over the documents and listened to the briefings. Now he spent his days studying maps, asking questions, dispatching messengers across the river. His men, delighted by their commander's heightened interest in the fort, dispatched every one of his orders dutifully.

Meanwhile, inside the Arnold home, Peggy was preparing for the meeting with André.

At the insistence of his wife, Arnold wrote André to tell him that their terms had in fact changed; the news of Washington's coming visit gave the Arnolds even greater power. At the meeting at Smith's, Arnold would turn over to André the plans and papers on West Point, which he had spent the month collecting. In return, André would deliver him a pouch of six thousand pounds. Once the fort was surrendered to the British, at the end of a highly unequal battle, Arnold would receive the remaining fourteen thousand pounds in silver he'd demanded. If Washington happened to be trapped in the battle, the Arnolds had every reason to expect an invitation into the ranks of the British nobility.

"If we can deliver the biggest fish of them all—" Arnold started, allowing his wife to finish his thought.

"Then this time next year, we shall be dining with King George the Third, as Lord and Lady Arnold."

Clara, having heard no reply from Caleb, still had to find a way to join the expedition. As the days dwindled, Clara struggled to plant this idea. Finally, on the eve of their trip, she tried her luck.

"Clara Bell." Arnold sat beside his wife on the porch, the two of them watching the sun slip behind West Point as dusk settled over the yard.

"Hello, General, Mrs. Arnold." Clara nodded to each one in turn, delivering the jug of ale that they had requested. "The river looks nice tonight, does it not?"

"Is Little Eddy asleep?" Peggy asked, ignoring her maid's small talk.

"Aye, ma'am."

"The river does look nice," Arnold replied more good-naturedly, accepting his mug.

"Let's hope that it stays calm." Clara kept her eyes only on Arnold.

"At least until tomorrow," he added, sipping his drink. "You know, Clara, that Mrs. Arnold and I will be setting off down the river tomorrow night? On business."

"Aye, sir." Clara nodded. Of course she knew. "Such a long journey to make twice in such a short time. The rowing must get very tiresome. I hope you know that if you require assistance, I would gladly come to help with the labor."

Clara floated the idea, knowing that Arnold would never accept the offer. But she hoped that it might give rise to another idea.

"Ha! Rowing? You?" Peggy reacted as Clara had guessed she would.

"It's kind of you, Clara." Arnold smiled. "But I can't ask you to row a boat."

"Understood." Clara nodded, looking down the river toward the south. "Besides, I'd just be a distraction once I got there. They'd probably wonder why General Arnold brought two women with him to the meeting."

Arnold looked up at her, his eyes alert. And then, looking out over the river, he began to stroke his whiskers. After several minutes, he spoke. "Perhaps it's not a bad idea that you join us, Clara."

Peggy turned, glancing at her husband in shock. "What are you saying, Benedict? Absolutely not."

"Perhaps Clara should accompany us down the river." Arnold still stared out at the Hudson.

"Why would she come? She has no cause joining us, Benedict."

"Peggy, you understand well the need to distract Smith. The last time around, he seemed adamant that he would join me when André arrived. I'll need to present a serious diversion to keep him occupied. The only thing more disarming than a beautiful woman," Arnold continued, looking between the two ladies, "is *two* beautiful women. We could dress Clara up as your sister."

"Absolutely not." Peggy shook her head in slow determination. "Have you gone mad?"

"Come now, Peg. Think about it: Smith is less likely to wander off with you if it means it's just him and another man's wife; he'd think it indecent. If we hope to lure him away from my meeting with André, it would be helpful to have the two of you."

"I won't have Clara masquerading as my sister."

"Why ever not?"

"Ha! Do you really think that Smith would believe the two of us could be sisters?"

Arnold looked from his wife to Clara. "Yes, I think it could be quite plausible indeed."

Peggy gestured between the two women. "Look at the difference between us—I'm a lady, she's a maid."

"But the only difference is in the clothing, really." Arnold ignored, or didn't notice, the irate look on his wife's face. "And we will do one of those hairstyles . . . puffs . . . or whatever you call them." Arnold waved his hands vaguely around his head.

"Poufs!" Peggy snapped.

"Right. Well, we shall dress her up like you. The two of you, side by side, will be the perfect duo to distract our oblivious host. You'll play cards, and dance with him, and ply him with wine. And once he's sufficiently enamored of you both, André and I will slip away to discuss the matters at hand."

"LET'S GET this over with." Peggy reluctantly marched Clara to her wardrobe and stared inside. "He wants us to look alike, so you'll need something pink." Peggy winced, putting her hand to her waist. Peggy was already dressed in her outfit for the evening's journey. "Goodness, these stays are tight." She looked through the parade of dresses. "You can't wear the magenta, because it's too nice. I don't want you wearing the silk one in light pink, it's too similar to mine. You'll wear this one." Peggy pulled out a dress of peach-colored taffeta. It may have been her least favorite gown in the pink hue, but it was likely the most beautiful dress Clara would ever wear.

It was strange. Dressing in this fine clothing after she'd spent years cleaning and mending these dresses. Clara obeyed, silently, as Peggy slid her into a shift, then a corset, followed by a wide hoopskirt, and finally the restrictive stays. How Peggy wore this bone corset every day, Clara could not understand, and it gave her some small insight into why Peggy was always so irritable. Clara had never been so immodestly poked, tugged, and yanked. Finally, once the undergarments were firmly in place, she slithered into the peach-colored taffeta. The gown felt like cool, smooth water running over her skin. As she watched the fabric sway, catching the light so that it reflected a faint shimmer of evening sunshine, Clara couldn't help but admire the figure she cut in the mirror.

"I suppose you can pass for a lady, after all." Peggy's mood had risen slightly as the hour for the visit approached. She gave Clara pearls to wear around her neck and hang from her ears. Clara lifted her own blond hair into the *pouf* she'd fashioned for Peggy so many times, even allowing Peggy to string a few strands of pearls through her curled tresses. It felt surreal, performing these duties on herself.

When she was done, Clara stood beside her mistress and looked in the mirror. The two of them did look like sisters, even twins. "Benny will be impressed with how I've been able to transform you." Peggy turned to the maid, her face growing stern as she said. "But do not get accustomed to this. This is the only time I will ever allow it, and it's only so that my husband can be successful in his conversation with Johnny."

"I understand, Miss Peggy." Clara nodded, suddenly feeling as though she were back in her calico gown with a low bun in her hair and an apron around her waist.

"Right then, go tell him we're ready. He can prepare the boat. I'll just finish up the last touches." Peggy turned to the mirror and scrutinized herself one final time.

Clara left the room, wobbling atop her high heels as she made her way down the hallway toward the staircase.

"Oh, Miss Peggy, there you are." Clara heard Mrs. Quigley calling out behind her.

"Miss Peggy?" But the housekeeper sounded as if she were right behind Clara. "Miss Peggy?" The housekeeper tapped Clara on the shoulder. Clara turned around.

"Good gracious!" the old woman screamed, as if she'd seen Hannah's ghost, clutching her hand to her heart. "*Clara!* Is that you? Good heavens, girl, what on earth are you doing dressed like Miss Peggy? You better change before the mistress sees you and demands that you be burned at the stake. Have you forgotten how she reacted when she thought you took her jewelry?"

"No, no, Mrs. Quigley. You don't understand." Clara reached for the housekeeper to try to calm her.

"Clearly I do not," the woman replied.

"They've ordered me to dress like this."

"Who has, child?" Mrs. Quigley looked at Clara incredulously.

"Miss Peggy has just dressed me herself."

The housekeeper ogled the peach-colored gown in disbelief, and Clara couldn't help but smile at the housekeeper's expression; she too found the recent events mystifying.

"What the devil is happening in this house?" Mrs. Quigley asked.

Before Clara had time to explain, Peggy was at the top of the stairs, fanning herself with a white silk fan. "Mrs. Quigley, you're in my way." Mrs. Quigley turned, doing a double take as she cast her gaze from Peggy to Clara and back to Peggy.

"My word, you two could be twins," the housekeeper stammered.

"Nonsense. We don't look anything alike," Peggy said.

"I am seeing double. But I still don't understand. Clara, why are you dressed like that?"

"That is none of your concern," Peggy answered, slamming the fan shut and descending the stairs. "She is coming with me as a guest and we don't want her looking like a maid, that's all." Peggy passed the housekeeper on the narrow staircase, her wide hoopskirt swooshing by the bewildered old woman in her descent.

"Now go fetch my husband and tell him we are ready for the boat."

TOGETHER, THEY watched as the sun sank behind the mountains on the west side of the Hudson, telling them it was time to set out. "Keep quiet now, ladies." Arnold helped them each step into the small rowboat. Before he pushed off, he wrapped the oars in sheepskin to muffle the sound of the splashing water. As he rowed determinedly down the river, an uneasy silence descended over them and the evening sky darkened.

Clara was grateful for the deepening veil of nighttime and the cover it allowed her as she sat across from the rowing Arnold in this immodest dress. She'd never been so exposed, and she hadn't liked the way he had looked at her, in much the same way he looked at Peggy, when he'd first seen her in the peach dress.

"Raiding parties all over these parts lately." Arnold cast a nervous glance toward the shoreline. "It's a good thing there's less moonlight tonight." It was now pitch dark and nearly impossible to see, but the shores groaned with late summer noises—bats, owls, bullfrogs. Clara's eyes darted back and forth between the eastern and western shores, scouring the woods for any sign of a patrol party. Had Caleb told his senior officers to look out for André wandering across their lines? Clara wondered.

Peggy fidgeted beside her, adjusting the neckline of her rose-colored gown. She smelled overripe with perfume. As the river widened the wind picked up, sending a ripple of waves across the surface, and a silver spray of water tickled Clara's skin. She shivered. The evening air had a chill, the hint of the coming autumn.

"Careful with those oars, Benedict, you've just splashed me!" Peggy smoothed the skirt of her dress for what felt like the hundredth time.

"Keep your voice down, Peg."

Clara knew her lady well enough to tell that she was not nervous about being intercepted by suspicious British search parties, or worse, suspicious colonial militiamen; Peggy was nervous about looking good for her former lover.

Clara saw through the milky moonlight that Arnold perspired

under the effort of rowing. Every few minutes, he'd throw a nervous glance over his shoulder in the direction of New York City, no doubt studying the dark horizon for patrols rowing the waters around No Man's Land. It took hours, but though his breathing grew labored, Arnold never slowed his pace. Clara watched moonlit forests and hills pass as they kept gliding determinedly toward Haverstraw.

"No need to be nervous, ladies," Arnold said. Clara suspected it was as much for his own comfort as it was for theirs. "It's a late summer evening, and I am a respected local commander with my wife and sister-in-law on a joy cruise to visit a friend, Joshua Smith. That is what we shall tell anyone who attempts to stop us."

The air had turned chillier. The night grew louder with the sound of crickets, the shrill call of an owl, the soft gurgle of the oars pulling them through the calm water down the river. "What's that noise?" Peggy jumped beside Clara, rocking the small boat as she ducked down in a rush of silk and hoopskirt.

"It's just a bat," Clara answered, attempting to quell her mistress's skittishness. She saw the creatures flying overhead erratically, their black outlines visible against the moonlit sky.

"It sounded like a ghost," Peggy said, peering out over the water.

"Perhaps you're right," Clara answered.

"Keep it down, girls," Arnold warned them. Since when did he refer to Clara as one of the "girls"?

They knew they were finally approaching Haverstraw when they spotted a flotilla of lights ahead, bobbing above the surface of the water. "Look!" Peggy gasped. The outline of a boat, blazing in candlelight, gave the appearance of a haunted mansion, its anchor dropped by its phantom crew.

"The *Vulture,*" Arnold said, eyeing the lights that pierced the dark night.

"André is here," Peggy said. Her bracelet jingled as her hands frantically adjusted her hairdo.

"He finally showed up," Arnold answered, a satisfied tenor in his voice. The lone candle on the bank signified the spot where their host, Joshua Smith, awaited them on the shore before his home. Arnold redirected the oars and guided their boat toward the western bank with renewed vigor.

"Ahoy! Visitors from up river?" A voice rang out from the shore, where a single lantern cast a foggy shroud of light.

"It is us!" Arnold growled back, maneuvering the boat to the west bank.

"You've reached your destination sir," Smith answered, evidently enjoying the practice of speaking in vague formalities, as if in code. He seemed to be taking this evening visit very seriously, having been told that he was to host General Arnold and a very high-ranking colonial spy.

"Smith, there you are." Arnold directed the boat ashore on the softly sloping bank. "What is the hour?" he asked, shaking his host's outstretched hand.

"It is approximately one hour until midnight," Smith bowed to Arnold, his nasally voice sounding very formal.

"Good to see you, Smith." Arnold slapped his host on the back, and Clara saw how the man's thin frame quaked under the rough handling.

"And you, sir," Smith answered.

"Thank you for hosting this meeting a second time, Smith. It's highly important to the colonial cause. The man is a top spy who has infiltrated the British ranks."

"It is my honor to host a meeting with two men of such import," Smith answered.

Arnold stepped back to help his wife out of the small rowboat, and then Clara, who accepted his outstretched hand with some surprise, slowly learning that the practice of dressing in fine clothing like this afforded her the solicitous hand of a man like Benedict Arnold.

"Smith, you are already acquainted with my wife." Arnold escorted Peggy forward.

"But of course. A lady of her beauty is impossible to forget. Charmed, Mrs. Arnold." Smith bowed low.

"And this is my wife's sister."

"Does she have a name, or shall I simply call her 'Sister'?"

Arnold faltered—they had not discussed what Clara's alias would be.

"I'm Clara." She stepped forward, offering her hand with an air of confidence that she hoped resembled Peggy's. "Clara Shippen."

"Clara Shippen, what a pleasant surprise." Smith held the lantern aloft as he kissed her hand. Clara smiled widely, curtsying as she'd seen her mistress do so many times. "I was not aware that Mrs. Arnold had a sister who was visiting, but I am delighted by the turn of events." Smith's smile was uninhibited as he stared at his two female visitors. "I can't decide which of the two is more beautiful."

Clara noted the quiver in Peggy's lip at this remark, but she kept her sweet smile fixed firmly on her face.

Smith continued, holding his lantern aloft so that its glow fell on the two women. "The family resemblance is really quite remarkable. What is clear to me is that you two ladies must have had quite the handsome set of parents." He seemed to take a particular interest in Clara, for he admired her unashamedly—his gaze roving over her hair, her face, her figure that was so clearly on display in this attire. This was what it was like, Clara realized, to have men constantly eyeing you. She didn't know that she liked it.

"Is Andrrr . . . Anderson . . . here yet?" Arnold asked, his voice with an edge to it.

"He is. Just arrived." Smith leaned close and whispered to Arnold. "He wanted to watch you disembark from a spot hidden from view. He seemed to have some last-minute suspicions as to who exactly he was meeting." Smith raised his voice now, apparently so that André could hear. "But now, he sees that General Arnold stands before me, along with his beautiful wife and sister-in-law, and he can have no doubts about the true attendees of the meeting."

All four of them stood in silence, awaiting André's response to this announcement. Peggy shifted restlessly beside Clara.

"You see that it is I, Benedict Arnold," Arnold roared into the dark evening. "Show yourself."

A shadowed figure slid out from behind a nearby sapling, the man's outline just barely visible in the velvety blackness. "Good evening." André, no more than a dark shape, spoke in a cool, calm drawl. Peggy inhaled a quick breath. Clara, too, recognized the voice and the clipped British accent, but none of them could see André beyond his shadow of an outline.

"Come closer," Arnold insisted. "Into the light, that I may see you."

"Well, well, well." The figure ambled toward them, his old swagger still evident in his gait. He walked into the feeble halo of light cast by Smith's lantern. On his face he wore a dashing, self-assured smile, like the one he'd worn to all of those Philadelphia balls years ago. Instead of his regimental uniform, he was bundled under a navy blue cloak over black breeches, a black tricornered hat on his head. He looked every inch the dashing colonial spy.

"If it isn't Peggy Shippen." André, his features now illuminated by the candlelight, inched up to his former paramour. Clara could feel her mistress trembling beside her as André lifted her hand to his lips and placed upon it a lingering kiss. "Hello, Peggy Shippen."

"It's Peggy Arnold now, Major André." Even though she pulled her hand back and straightened up as she spoke, Peggy's tone was as feeble as the candlelight in the evening breeze. "You forget that I'm married to General Benedict Arnold." Peggy cast her gaze sideways to her husband. "Soon to be . . . *Lord* Benedict Arnold."

Smith looked on, confused.

"That is, if you deliver on your promises, my good man," Arnold reached forward, taking André's hand from his wife's and shaking it roughly.

"I believe it is you who shall have to deliver . . . a certain someone," André nodded, returning the handshake.

"And we will." Arnold answered, defiant. "The name's General Arnold, happy to meet you, Major."

In every way, the men shaking hands before Clara were foils of each other. André was tall, slender, lithe in his movements, while Arnold stood before him stocky, rough-hewn, and less than graceful. The British officer's features were fine and delicate—almost as pretty as Peggy's—while Arnold's eyes were ruddy and round, his broad nose protruding from a whiskered face, his hair pulled back from his brow in an unruly gray ponytail.

Peggy too, stared on as the two men met—her former lover and her husband. It was clear to Clara, as she watched her mistress, that some of André's previous power over Peggy lingered still. She looked at him with all the yearning, all the desire, all the vulnerability with which she'd beheld him as a young debutante, tasting the sensuous pleasures of life for the first time at his hands. Her breath sounded uneven and labored, and even though it was dark, Clara was sure that Peggy's face was flushed by some distant memory.

"Now, General Arnold, you come with your wife as well as your sister-in-law?" André squinted through the candlelight. "Is it my old friend Betsy Shippen Burd I see before me?" André fixed his narrowed brown eyes on Clara, causing her to squirm.

"No," Peggy stepped forward, coming into the role she'd prepared for. "Major André . . . surely you remember my sister, *Clara* Shippen?" Peggy nodded at him with a meaningful expression, and a look of clarity came across André's face.

"Ah, of course," André played along, leaning in and kissing Clara's hand. "Of course I remember Clara! Your . . . *sister.* My man, Robert Balmor, will be quite disappointed that he didn't join me on this excursion." André grinned suggestively, and now Clara was appreciative of the dark night that concealed her reddening cheeks. She remembered back to the night in the Shippens' orchard, the kiss with Robert Balmor. How naïve, how foolish that Clara had been. It seemed as if it had occurred in another girl's lifetime.

"Miss Shippen . . ." André turned back to Peggy and took her hands in his. "I mean, Mrs. Arnold." His tone was flagrantly flirtatious as he looked from her face to her bosom, her bosom to her tiny waist. "My, how I would love to dance with you. For old times' sake."

Peggy stared back at him, her head falling sideways. "Oh?" She had no words to answer him, but her face made her desire embarrassingly evident. She stared at André as she would a piece of tender fillet after years of dining on salted river trout.

"Ahem." Arnold cleared his throat, his eyes darting between his wife and this British officer.

"But I fear that your husband and I have very important matters to discuss." André dropped Peggy's hands.

"That we do," Arnold piped up.

"Yes," Peggy sighed, poorly concealing her disappointment. André leaned forward, disregarding Arnold now as he whispered into Peggy's ear. Clara was close enough that she heard his words.

"We shall have to plan for a dance once you come over to my side. Shall we meet in New York City?"

"Anderson?" Arnold stepped forward, putting his arm proprietarily on his wife's lower back. Peggy didn't respond to André, but merely let out a low chuckle that told her seducer that she longed for such a reunion. In that instant Clara knew, without an inkling of doubt, that her mistress had not yet finished with John André. No, if Peggy Arnold were to successfully switch over to the British side, there would be dances, and dinners, and illicit late-night rendezvous just as there had been years earlier. Clara saw the scenes clearly before her. She felt a pang of pity for the husband who stood by, unknowing. It was not *yet* too late for him to renege, to save both his honor and his wife; after tonight, though, it would be.

Clara felt a leaden dread in her stomach for herself as well. She did not want to spend another day in the service of Peggy Shippen Arnold—dressing her, feeding her, covering for her nefarious schemes. Oh, how could she escape this life? Her mind wandered, unintentionally, to the life she'd allowed herself to hope for. A life of setting up a simple, comfortable home on a green hillside overlooking the Hudson. Of working—and working hard—but, working for herself. Of creating a garden and raising animals and welcoming Cal home to a dinner made from the foods they themselves had grown. Of tucking their children into bed each night and then spending the dark hours in Caleb's arms. A new start in a new country with the man she loved.

But, standing in the dark outside Joshua Smith's house, Clara saw that new country in peril. And she herself was complicit in a plot to betray the fight for freedom.

"Mr. Smith," Peggy spoke in her sweetest, most honey-smooth tone as she threaded her arm through her host's, remembering her purpose for attending the meeting. "I am so cold from the hours on the river. And I so regretted leaving last time without having requested a tour of your beautiful home. How about we go up together and you show me and my sister the inside of Smith House?"

"I, uh, well." Smith looked from Peggy to Arnold.

"Please, dear husband," Peggy crooned. "Won't you free Mr. Smith from your tiresome business talk and allow him to give me a tour of his lovely home?" Peggy sounded as if her entire life's hopes hung in the balance.

"I suppose I will allow it," Arnold sighed, turning to Smith.

"You're certain, Major General?" Smith asked.

"It's not easy to say no to her." Arnold elbowed his host.

"I imagine it's damn well impossible." Smith smiled back, as he thought a fraternal understanding passed between himself and Arnold. "Then it's settled. Miss Clara Shippen?" Smith offered his free arm to Clara, who took it without a sound. As they walked past the two men, Peggy leaned over to give her husband a kiss on the cheek. Was Clara imagining it, or did her lady look at André as she did so?

Smith led the ladies up the slope to his house. Once inside, Peggy wrapped her arms around herself. "Goodness, I've caught such a chill. How about some wine, Mr. Smith?"

"Of course." Smith smiled obligingly, crossing to the corner table to retrieve a glass carafe. "And Miss Clara? Some wine for you as well?"

"No, thank you," Clara answered, pretending to be mesmerized by the artwork on his walls. Smith poured just the one glass for Peggy.

"Won't you join me, Mr. Smith?" Peggy urged him. "So that we can make a toast?"

Again, Smith bashfully obeyed, pouring himself a generous serving of wine.

"To you." Peggy beamed at her host, raising her glass.

"No, no, to *you*, my lady." Smith clinked Peggy's glass as she giggled, and they both drained their drinks.

"Ahh, that is fine wine." Peggy wiped her mouth. "Shall we have one more glass?"

"I don't see why not." Smith refilled their glasses. A series of toasts followed, trailed shortly after by immediate refills and further toasting.

"To General Arnold." Smith offered a toast, his red-stained lips pulled in a relaxed smile.

"To victory in this war," Peggy countered at the next round.

After the two of them had finished the carafe, Smith commenced a very giggly tour, starting in the front hall and weaving his way through each individual room. Peggy listened with what appeared to be a keen interest, asking questions after every sentence. When had the Smith family come to America? How had they picked this location to erect their mansion? Was it awfully drafty in the winter? From where did they watch the sunset? And how about the sunrise?

Clara followed dutifully behind. Mr. Smith appeared bright-eyed and energetic, thanks to Peggy's jokes and constant chatter. When they arrived at the drawing room, Peggy gasped at the sight of the piano. She insisted on playing a song for her host, and one song stretched into three, and then six. Smith looked on, enchanted by this boisterous beauty who seemed to so thoroughly enjoy his company.

Clara used this distraction to slide noiselessly from the room back toward a study, where she found a piece of clean parchment and inkwell. There, heart racing, she sat in the dark and wondered how to pen her letter. She suspected that Smith might read it. And Cal hadn't guaranteed that he'd come retrieve it; she had to be certain that it would be opaque, should it fall into anyone else's hands.

She wrote the name.

Cal,

As she weighed how to continue, Clara heard laughter in the other room, followed by Smith's voice. "Where has your sister gone, Mrs. Arnold?"

"Good question. She's always up to something. *Clara!*" Peggy called to her, and Clara's nerves tightened. How could she convey this message?

Cal,

How is your new farm? Over here, the sum has been paid. The plan is to sell the milk cow and turn over the property. It will happen in two days. Plan accordingly.

—CB

Now she heard the sound of heavy boots on the wooden floor of Smith's front hall, and two new voices walking toward the drawing room. Clara folded the letter and tucked it into the folds of her dress. Rushing back into the drawing room, she arrived just a moment before Arnold and André entered. Peggy and Smith sat in the corner, engaged in what appeared to be a riveting game of cards.

"There you are, Miss Shippen." Smith looked at her through droopy eyes, and it took Clara a moment to remember her part.

"I wandered off, I'm afraid. I was just so intrigued by your paintings."

Smith beamed at this. Behind him, André entered the drawing room, Arnold limping in a moment later.

"Is the meeting concluded already?" Peggy rose from the card table. "And I was just about to lose to Mr. Smith in bridge. You saved me just in time, my gallant General Arnold." Peggy crossed the room to kiss her husband, and Clara seized her brief window of time to whisper to Smith.

"Mr. Smith, if you please." Clara took her host by the arm and directed him toward the far corner of the room. Behind them, Peggy was exchanging merry banter with her husband and André.

"Yes, Miss Shippen, what is it?" Smith leaned in toward Clara, his breath sour with wine.

"One of my former servants is in the colonial army, stationed nearby. I plan to sell some land I own, so I must tell him that he no longer has employment on our farm. Here, you may read the letter." Clara unfolded the terse note and Smith read the straightforward, innocuous words. "If you please, I've informed him that I was coming to his area, and that I'd leave a note for him at your home. The post is so unreliable these days. If he comes, might you deliver this note to him? His name is Caleb Little."

Smith nodded, ever the obliging host. "I shall be happy to be of service to you, Miss Shippen."

"You are so kind." Clara flashed what she hoped was her most beguiling smile, the one most resembling her mistress's expression, before she turned and walked back toward the center of the large room.

"My word, it's past five in the morning already." Mr. Smith scrutinized the small clock that dangled from a chain attached to his vest.

"Lose track of the time, good man?" Arnold sat down on a yellow silk settee.

"We must have played five games of bridge." Peggy perched on the armrest beside her husband.

"Indeed, I was so consumed by Mrs. Arnold's charms, I lost all track of time." Smith chortled.

"Not a bad way to spend the dark hours of the night, being distracted for hours by Peggy's . . . *charms* . . . is it?" André cracked a crooked grin. Arnold and Smith both shot him looks of disapproval.

"I know not what you suggest, but I assure you it was all quite aboveboard," Smith answered back defensively, looking to Arnold.

"I have no doubt of *your* honor, Smith." Arnold looked from his host to André, his expression turning sour.

"How did it go?" Peggy leaned over and placed a hand on her husband's shoulder, redirecting his attention.

Arnold exhaled, wincing as he extended his left knee. "We conducted our business satisfactorily, right, Mr. Anderson?"

"Quite," André answered, his eyes locking on Peggy with a hungry expression. She pretended not to notice.

"Tea, anyone? Please, Mr. Anderson," Smith entreated his guest, "remove your cloak and make yourself comfortable. I shall bring us all a warm drink." Smith tugged on André's wool cloak, and before André could stop him the navy overcoat had fallen to the floor, revealing the unmistakable red of André's uniform.

"Oh my!" Smith gasped, clutching his hand to his mouth. "What is the meaning of this?" He looked, eyes aghast, from André to Arnold.

"Now, now, now, Mr. Smith. It is not how it appears." Arnold raised his hands, reaching toward his host with a consoling gesture.

"I certainly hope not, for how it appears is that I've just unwittingly welcomed a redcoat into my drawing room!"

"You have not." Arnold looked to André for help. But André did not offer an excuse.

"Mr. Anderson is a spy, you see, for our side," Arnold spoke awkwardly, clearing his throat repeatedly as if to earn himself more time.

Peggy picked up the line of justification. "He has to wear the coat as part of . . . his spy charade."

"Be that as it may"—Smith looked back at André, still suspicious—"the cock is about to crow and the sun will rise in one hour, and I cannot have a man in a regimental uniform walking out from my house. He'd be apprehended immediately—they run patrols all through these woods. No, Mr. Anderson, you shall have to change."

"My boat is right there," André spoke up, pointing out the window to the river. "Just a brief walk down to the river, and they shall spot me and row to pick me up."

"It is close, I grant you that, but the militia might be closer. And already on the shore. I cannot have an English uniform walking out of my front door. You must change."

André sighed, his tone dismissive. "No need for that. All the men aboard that vessel believe me to be loyal to the English Crown. I shall stay in the uniform."

Smith cut him off. "I will not be accused of hosting a British officer, or someone who dresses like one." Smith now stared at André like he would a filthy dog. "On this matter, my good sirs, I will not yield."

The standoff ended with André nodding his consent. Arnold agreed that caution was prudent.

"I will give you plain clothes." Smith sighed, his look conveying to Arnold that this visit had become entirely inconvenient.

"Good man." Arnold nodded.

As he prepared to leave the room, Smith walked over to Arnold and whispered, loudly, "I wish you would have told me he was wearing the British uniform to my house!"

Before Arnold could answer, the sound of a thunderous explosion shook the room, causing the flowers to quiver in their vases. Peggy shrieked.

"God!" André braced himself against the back of a chair as a second roar sounded. Clara steadied herself on the back of the couch.

"What is happening?" Arnold looked around the room at the paintings on the walls, hanging lopsided after the blasts.

"My heavens!" Smith ran to the large drawing room window, looking out toward the river. There, in the feeble light of the predawn morning, they watched as a series of explosions sent ripples of orange light across the sky.

"They are attacking my ship," André exclaimed, losing his customary indifference.

"My heavens, they are firing on the *Vulture*," Arnold concurred.

Smith, seeing the vessel for the first time in the early light, turned from the warship to André, eyes narrowing in increased apprehension. "Why did you come on an imperial battleship? Who *are* you exactly?"

Neither André nor Arnold answered Smith, but they watched in dumbfounded silence as the *Vulture* hoisted its anchors and caught a gust of wind to fly south. Three small colonial gunships gave frantic chase in its wake.

André's expression was now one of unadulterated horror. "Where is my ship going? Wait! Wait!" He pounded at the window as the *Vulture*'s sails billowed in the wind, speeding the warship south.

The ship gone, a tension-fraught quiet remained in the room. Smith stared at André, while the rest of the company looked at the river, at the spot where the *Vulture* had bobbed just a moment earlier. Clara felt herself growing more uneasy with each minute, and she wanted nothing more than to be gone from this ill-fated meeting.

"Well, Mr. Anderson," Arnold spoke first. "You'll have to cut through the lines on horseback, I'm afraid. Best not to set out until the dark descends tonight." Arnold turned to Smith. "Smith, you are to convey Mr. Anderson safely across the lines. Row him across after sunset and take him as far as the British outpost at White Plains." A small gurgling sound indicated Smith's further irritation at the morning's strange turn of events. Then, turning to his wife, Arnold said, "Are you ready?"

"W-w-w-what? General Arnold, you're leaving?" Smith's mouth fell open. André, too, appeared uneasy.

"We must be off, Mr. Smith." Arnold patted his host on the shoulder, speaking close to him. "I trust you to convey this gentleman safely back to the line. Remember, he is a very important person, but his mission is of a most delicate and secretive nature. Only you and I are aware of it."

"You—you're going to leave me with this man?" Smith resisted, a look of incredulity on his face.

Arnold sought to sway him with bluster and flattery. "You're up to the task, Smith. Come now, we all must play our parts."

"But we will never be able to cross the lines unnoticed."

Arnold considered their dilemma. "Here, take this." Arnold quickly scrawled a message on a piece of paper. "If anyone stops you, or interrogates you, you just give them this pass signed by me. I am the commanding officer of these parts, and I say Mr. Anderson may have safe passage back to British lines."

André still stared out the window, his features taut. The river had settled back to a still calm surface, showing no sign that the *Vulture* had ever anchored on that spot.

"Cheer up, we'll have you back with them at nightfall." Arnold crossed the room to André, rapping him on the back. "Mr. Anderson, it was a pleasure. Thank you for your . . . payment." Arnold patted a small velvet pouch hanging from the belt around his breeches. "I will look forward to my next installment once the transaction has been completed." Arnold turned from André back to his host. "Mr. Smith, just make sure that Mr. Anderson makes it back across the line safely."

Smith shook his head, preparing to answer, but Arnold cut him off, turning to his wife.

"We best be off, my peach. We have an important visitor coming for breakfast tomorrow morning, and we must make sure that all is in order."

Peggy turned her face toward her husband, and Arnold thought that her broad, inviting smile was for him. What he did not realize was that his wife's eyes actually fell on the figure standing directly over his shoulder—the dark, handsome British officer whom she would look to once she made her grand reentry into the British ballroom.

IX.

I dig frantically, growing short of breath under the exertion.

The spade hits the dirt hard, slicing deeper into the soft earth with every strike. In front of me, the old oak tree still bears the scars of the switch, scars that my own skin would carry had Arnold not beaten it instead of me.

Now the oak tree will be the shelter of these crucial objects. Treasures which my lady will soon notice missing; will I be able to enact my plan before she does?

I glance over my shoulder to look once more at the house. It looks so calm from here. My lady is still sleeping, tossing fretfully in her troubled dreams. The men are in the house, busy with plans and impervious to the suspicion that the maid, an unnoticed little imp, could be playing such a crucial role in this battle.

I turn back to my digging. Time is running short and I must bury these items. Right here, in this hole, I will hide the evidence that comprises my sole chance at escape. What were the words I read in Oma's Bible? "The truth shall set you free."

The truth will be hidden in a hole in the ground beside the old oak tree. If revealed correctly, it will indeed set me free. And it could be the key to saving a nation.

CHAPTER NINE

"In Whom Can We Trust?"

September 24, 1780
West Point, New York

CLARA ROSE from bed. Sleep had eluded her the entire night. The sun hadn't yet appeared, but already the morning was warm. The predawn peace of the kitchen and the sleeping home mocked the rush of feelings Clara wrestled with as she lifted her weary body from her straw pallet. General Washington was coming today, along with his entire party, which included the man from the West Indies who had become a favorite, Alexander Hamilton, and the French nobleman, the Marquis de Lafayette. That alone would have sufficed to fray Clara's nerves; but then there was the Arnolds' plot, ripe and ready to be enacted.

Clara dressed in the faint glow of the kitchen fire's dying embers. How did one dress on a day like this? she wondered. Vanity felt absurd at such a time, when the world threatened to crumble around her. And besides, she knew perfectly well that no one would be looking at her when they had the option of staring at Mrs. Peggy Arnold.

Clara slid into a calico dress of white cotton with the pattern of blue and green flowers, tucking her hair under a mobcap and wrapping a fichu around her shoulders. Mrs. Quigley entered the kitchen just as Clara was coaxing a fresh fire from the hearth.

"Clara." The old housekeeper wore a disgruntled expression and had puffy eyes, and she too looked as if she had not enjoyed a good night's rest.

"Good morning, Mrs. Quigley." Clara replaced the fire poker and grabbed her apron from the hook.

"Not a good morning at all." Mrs. Quigley scowled, looking into the fire. "What I wouldn't give to have Hannah manning the kitchen on a day like this."

Clara fixed tea for them as the old housekeeper took out a mixing bowl and began slicing a bowl of peaches Clara had picked the previous day. "Lord, this cobbler will never be ready in time," the housekeeper lamented.

Clara placed a cup of tea in front of the housekeeper.

"Did you arrange the guest rooms upstairs?" Mrs. Quigley stopped her slicing momentarily and turned to Clara.

"Aye." Clara nodded. "Swapped the bed linens for fresh sheets. General Washington will be in the guest room upstairs on the north side, the French gentleman on the south side."

"That Markee bloke?"

"Yes, I believe he's called the Marquis de Lafayette."

"We'll just call him sir," Mrs. Quigley decided.

"Yes, of course." Clara nodded, rolling her sleeves up to her elbows. "And then for Mr. Hamilton and the rest of the aides we'll make beds on the sofa and the floor in the parlor."

"How terrible, asking these men to sleep on the floor." Mrs. Quigley sighed, shaking her head. "I suppose we could give the Hamilton gentleman the nursery and you could bring Little Eddy in here with you."

"Ma'am, they've slept on much worse, including the frozen ground of Valley Forge. I'd guess that a soft sofa under a wooden roof will be a welcome luxury."

"Fine." Mrs. Quigley nodded. "So the beds are set. You'll have to bring them each a pitcher of water, but you can do that later. And I'll have my husband make sure to stack the fireplaces with fresh logs. Though it's so warm I can't imagine they'll want a fire."

"Right," Clara agreed politely.

"And they'll all want fresh candles, and probably fresh paper and ink to write letters."

"I'll see to that." Clara made a mental note to pull these items from the storeroom.

Mrs. Quigley ran through her plans aloud. "My husband will handle their horses when they arrive."

"And General Arnold and Mrs. Arnold will be on hand to greet them. We will have breakfast ready for them," Clara concluded. *But who will be on hand to stop the treason?*

Mrs. Quigley's brow furrowed. "Lord help me, this meal will never be ready. And we need to help the missus dress, and feed Little Eddy."

"There now, Mrs. Quigley. I will help with the mistress and Little Eddy. Everything will be well."

But Clara was lying and she was certain her face said so. Everything was very far from well. These small worries like breakfast and clean bed linens would prove moot if the Arnolds had their way. Had Caleb even received her message about André's visit? If so, it was strange that he had not answered. Were men waiting down the river to apprehend Major André? The man was, at that very moment, somewhere in No Man's Land bearing the top-secret documents that General Arnold had given him. Each second that passed, the spy was closer to General Clinton and the British. In his possession, André had the means to capture not only West Point but also the three thousand colonial men currently stationed there. Also in André's possession was the knowledge that Washington, and his entire military party, were bearing down on the Arnolds' home, and that the commander of the entire army would be sleeping tonight within easy striking distance of British gunships and regiments that would soon be marching north to reclaim this stretch of the Hudson. Clara saw all of these pieces moving together and had no idea how they could possibly end in anything short of calamity.

"Clara, have you gone deaf?"

Clara snapped back to the present moment: the hot kitchen, the disgruntled housekeeper.

"I said your lady will want some of these peaches. Might want to take them up to Miss Peggy in bed."

Clara stared at the bowl of ripe fruit. "Ah, yes. Of course."

"Clara, you'll give yourself the brow of a woman with twice your years if you keep fretting so."

"Sorry, ma'am. Just a daydream," Clara responded, taking the small bowl from Mrs. Quigley.

"No time for a daydream on a day such as this. Now see if you can dress her as quickly as possible—we'll want her to be ready to greet them when they arrive."

"Yes, ma'am," Clara said. Walking up the stairs, she could not shake the feeling that her entire life, and the world around them, was about to crumble. She leaned against the wall of the narrow, dark stairway to steady herself. One thing and one thing only was for certain—today was the last day before everything changed; it was how that change would look that remained to be seen.

Clara knocked on the bedroom door, pressing her ear to the wood to listen for a stirring within. "Mrs. Arnold?"

"Come in," came a chirp from the other side of the door. Clara turned the knob and entered to find Peggy, fresh-faced and smiling, sitting upright in bed. Her room was warm with morning sunlight, but she still rested beneath the white bed linens.

"Good morning, Clara." Peggy tugged on her muslin nightcap and shook her head gaily, allowing her blond curls to come cascading around her rosy cheeks. "What a glorious day, nay?" Peggy looked out the window.

Clara entered the bedchamber.

"You brought me peaches?" Peggy eyed the fruit.

"I did, my lady."

Peggy yawned. "Is Little Eddy up yet?" She took the outstretched bowl of fruit in her hands.

"Not yet, ma'am." Clara pulled open the drapes and let the sunshine steep into the bedroom.

"That makes one Arnold man still in bed. My husband has been up since before dawn." Peggy nibbled on a peach, sucking the juices that slid down her fingers. "Didn't sleep a wink last night and rowed over this morning to examine West Point. He's nervous because Washington arrives this morning." Peggy spoke to her maid as if Clara were deaf, or dumb, and hadn't been privy to the planning and scheming of the past year. Even the past few days! Of course Clara knew why Benedict Arnold was nervous, and it didn't have to do with whether General Washington would be satisfied with the breakfast he was served at the Arnolds' home.

Just then a low, distant sound—like a faint heartbeat—began to hum its way through the bedroom windows. Horse hooves. Clara crossed the room to look out the window, seeing a lone rider emerge from the post road.

"What is it?" Peggy asked her maid.

"There's a rider approaching from the north," Clara answered, watching the horse as it galloped across the Arnolds' lawn. "The rider's horse looks to be bearing the livery of General Washington."

"Good gracious." Peggy fluttered her eyelashes. "Are they here already?"

"No, ma'am. Looks like it's just the one man," Clara answered, still staring out the window as a dark-haired figure came into view. "Must be an advance member of the party." She turned back to her mistress. "Mrs. Quigley is busy in the kitchen and Mr. Quigley is preparing the stables. I better go greet this visitor." Clara grabbed the chamber pot and left her lady still in bed.

Clara studied the man through the window before opening the front door. He was young, Clara noted, with a deep skin tone and a pleasing face. His wavy hair was pulled back in a loose ponytail. He stood on the porch, having tied his horse to the front post. Clara noted that the horse did in fact bear the Washington family crest of the griffin, indicating that this man outside the house enjoyed a close relationship with their commander in chief. She opened the door.

"Hello, miss." The visitor bowed deeply, allowing Clara a moment to take in his appearance from up close. He wore a navy blue coat, white breeches, buckled boots and gold epaulettes on his shoulders. Slung across his chest was a musket. "I come with a verbal message from General George Washington for General and Mrs. Benedict Arnold." The dark-haired man spoke with an accent altogether unfamiliar to Clara. It didn't sound as if it originated in either Britain or the colonies.

"Please, come inside, Mr.—"

"The name's Alexander Hamilton." He smiled, his features

bright from the exertion of the ride. This was the man from the West Indies, Clara realized. The young colonel who had won General Washington's respect after his fighting in New Jersey.

"Colonel Hamilton, it's an honor to meet you." Clara curtsied, her voice low.

"Are the Arnolds available for the message?" Hamilton arched his eyebrows.

"I'm afraid not at the moment, sir," Clara answered. "Mrs. Arnold is still abed, and General Arnold has gone across the river on an errand to West Point."

Hamilton cocked his head, looking out over the Arnolds' expansive lawn. "I'll give the message to you, then. The general sends word that he has been delayed this morning, as he has stopped to examine the fortifications at Mount Fishkill. He expects to be several hours late to breakfast. And here is where the message gets especially salacious . . ." Hamilton paused, his thin lips spreading into a smile. "His Excellency, General Washington, wishes me to tell you that his men send their special apologies to Mrs. Peggy Arnold. They are more upset at the prospect of distressing the lady than of being tardy. General Washington believes that the men are all half in love with her."

Clara had to quell the urge to scowl as Colonel Hamilton smiled at her. She curtsied politely. "Thank you, sir. I shall deliver the message." Hamilton nodded his thanks.

"Colonel Hamilton, may I invite you in for tea as you await the remainder of your party?"

"I thank you, but I am to ride back north to meet them." Hamilton slid his hands back into their riding gloves and made to return to his horse. Taking the reins in his hand, he turned to Clara once more. She felt her heart lurch, her lips parted in a gasp. She had Hamilton alone; couldn't she tell him all that she knew? Couldn't she spare Washington, and all of them, from their ill-fated trip to this home? But before she had the courage to deliver the words, Hamilton smiled and said: "I fear it will have to be several hours for me as well before I can lay eyes on the famous Mrs. Arnold."

"WELL, MRS. Quigley, your wish has been granted." Clara entered the kitchen. Her heart still racing from her failed attempt to warn Hamilton, she lowered herself into a chair. The housekeeper had been joined by her husband, and Mr. Quigley was rushing to load serving platters with cream, sliced peaches, sizzling bacon, and thick yellow butter. Mrs. Quigley stood beside her husband, kneading a mound of dough.

"How so, girl?" Mrs. Quigley barely looked at Clara, her cheeks smeared in flour.

"You have a couple hours longer to prepare. A gentleman from Washington's party has just sent word that they will be a few hours late."

"Late?" Mrs. Quigley lamented. "Now the loaf will burn, the tea will oversteep, and the peaches will start to attract the flies." Mrs. Quigley sulked under a cloud of flour but kept kneading the dough.

"He's the commander of the Continental Army." Mr. Quigley fidgeted with the pewter buttons of his coat as he checked his reflection in the silver teapot. "I am sure he will have no difficulty facing down a few flies."

"I'm sure he will!" Mrs. Quigley mumbled. "Clara, you best go and inform the missus of the delay."

"Clara, who was that at the door?" Peggy sat up in bed when she saw her maid reenter the bedroom.

"It was a Mr. Alexander Hamilton sending word that General Washington's party is to arrive late." Clara crossed the room and replaced the now emptied chamber pot. "Are you ready to dress, my lady?" Clara pulled the bedroom window open, letting in a breeze of fresh morning air.

"He's to arrive late? No bother," Peggy answered merrily, still nibbling on the peaches in her lap.

"Mr. Alexander Hamilton and General Washington both sent you their special apologies for the tardiness," Clara said, trying not to clench her teeth.

"Alexander Hamilton. I've heard of him," Peggy answered. "He's supposed to be quite handsome. Of course, no man looks truly dashing without the regimental redcoat of the . . .well, never mind." Peggy turned to Clara, her eyes glimmering with girlish mischief.

Clara averted her gaze, wishing Peggy would get out of bed so that she could change the linens while there was a lull in the morning's activities.

"Well, I suppose I shall dress," Peggy yawned, stretching her arms overhead.

There was a loud noise from downstairs as someone slammed the front door.

"Benny, is that you?" Peggy slid out of the large bed and called out her bedroom door.

"I'm back!" Arnold hollered up the stairs.

"Where have you been?" Peggy called back to him.

"Out on the river," he answered her through the floorboards. "West Point is ready."

"But for what?" Peggy lifted an eyebrow and sniggered. Then, calling back to her husband, she answered: "I'm just finishing up dressing. Be right down."

Clara was staring into the wardrobe, helping her mistress determine which dress to wear, when she detected the second set of hooves. Barley heard it too, and began a round of wild barking. The window-rattling noise started faint but grew louder, more urgent, its tempo signaling a rapid approach. Peggy and Clara turned to each other, listening to the frenzied pace of the horse hooves clamoring like a drumbeat outside the open window.

"Is Hamilton back? Did he forget something?" Peggy asked her maid. Clara crossed the room and looked through the open window. But this was not Hamilton returning.

"No, my lady," Clara answered, studying the small, hunched figure that approached, clinging to a black steed that looked as if it were racing to outrun the Apocalypse. "This is a new rider," Clara said.

"Another messenger? Goodness, we must be the busiest home on the Hudson this morning." Peggy chuckled, tugging at the loose sleeves of her white linen nightdress. "Don't they know we are set to receive Washington and his party for breakfast this morning? You'd think they could withhold these tedious errands for at least one day." Peggy sighed, her face beautiful beneath the frame of her loose blond curls. "Better go see what they want." Peggy gave Clara a nod, and her maid obeyed, leaving the bedroom to make her way down the narrow wooden staircase.

"Scoot, Barley dog." Clara edged the barking dog gently aside from the front door. From her perch on the front step, she shaded her eyes and stared up the road. The rider was not liveried in the general's crest, and therefore not from Washington's camp. He approached the house at alarming speed, urging his weary horse forward with the spurs of his dusty boots. Halting just feet in front of

Clara, uniform filthy and hair matted with sweat, the man hopped down from the horse.

"Can I help you?" Clara stood, sentry-like, before the front door to the farmhouse.

"I need to speak with Major General Benedict Arnold." The man, breathless, careened toward the house, the cloud of dust his horse had kicked up surrounding him like a shroud. "Take my horse, I must speak to the general!" Alarmed, Clara stepped down toward the horse, and the messenger did not wait for an invitation before he pushed his way through the door.

Clara tied the horse quickly, listening to the commotion in the front of the house as the new visitor hollered Arnold's name. "Where is Major General Benedict Arnold? Urgent message for Benedict Arnold from the south Hudson!"

The south Hudson. Where André had been traveling. With her heart in her throat, Clara entered the home and waited at the threshold of the small parlor. She heard Arnold approaching, his telltale plodding on the wooden floor—lopsided, uneven—followed by a curt nod in her direction. "Thank you, Clara." Then Arnold greeted the messenger, his gravelly voice courteous but stern with his subordinate.

"What is your aim, man?" Arnold demanded. "Barging in on us like this on the morning we are to receive His Excellency George Washington, and with the lady of the house not yet arisen and dressed?"

The dusty messenger made no apologies as he answered quickly.

"I assure you, Major General, you will pardon my urgency when you see the message I'm now delivering to you. I was told to deliver it posthaste." Arnold turned to Clara and she saw the concern rippling across his features.

"Good heavens, where are you coming from?" Arnold asked.

"North Castle Fort, down the Hudson. A day's ride. I was dispatched two days ago by a Colonel John Jameson."

"And what is the crisis down there?" The alarm in Arnold's voice was noticeable, even as Clara heard him endeavoring to remain calm.

"A certain John Anderson has been apprehended while en route to New York. He had a pass signed in your name and a parcel of papers taken from under his stockings, which I think are of a very dangerous tendency." The messenger struggled to calm his breath.

When Arnold answered, his voice had a quiver that Clara had never before heard. "Papers? Well, where are the papers?"

"The papers have been sent to General Washington," the messenger answered.

Arnold took the smaller man by the collar, nearly lifting him from the floor as he growled into his face. "Washington?"

"Aye." The messenger hung like a limp fish on the end of the line, dangling a few inches off the ground.

"Why did they not come to me?" Arnold demanded. "*I* am the commanding officer in these parts!"

"Colonel Jameson's orders, sir, are that they be sent directly to General Washington. We heard that he was in the area. I . . . I . . . can't breathe. Please, sir!"

Arnold dropped the man, allowing him to crumple into an unhappy heap on the wooden floor. But Arnold wasn't done questioning him. "And does Washington have the papers yet?"

"I do not know, sir." The messenger pulled himself to his feet, his face still aggrieved from the rough treatment. "Another rider departed from Colonel Jameson's command post at the same time I set out. I was to ride directly to you to give you word of the apprehension. The other rider was to give word to Washington and to deliver the papers to him, so that the general might find out from where the treachery originates."

After a long pause, her master spoke. "Give it here then."

The messenger transferred the letter to Arnold. A long, excruciating silence followed. Clara struggled to quiet her breath, her pounding heart, as Arnold read the message. Had Peggy overhead any of this? Clara wondered.

"Somehow, sir, the spy obtained a pass with your signature on it." The messenger broke the silence. Was he implying anything?

Looking up from the paper, Arnold addressed the messenger. "This is high treason, and we will react immediately. Clara, run upstairs and fetch my quill and parchment. In fact, on second thought, I shall come with you. You, man, let me prepare my answer to your colonel. Meantime, go into the pantry for some water and bread. My servants will see to it that you are taken care of." Arnold began limping away from the messenger before he'd completed his sentence.

Clara turned and fled back up the stairwell, certain now that Arnold was right behind her. She heard her master's gait, with its familiar lopsidedness, but with an urgency she hadn't heard in years. She flew up the steps as he labored behind her, pulling his thick frame up the stairwell.

Clara charged into Peggy's bedroom, where her mistress stood before the mirror, holding up a cream-colored gown. "What is it?" Her mistress's eyes widened when she spotted Clara hovering on the threshold of her merry, sunlit chamber.

"Master's coming!" It was all Clara had time to say. The two ladies heard him close by now, using his impressive upper body strength to pull himself up the stairs. The floorboards groaned beneath his boots as he lurched upward. Clara looked to Peggy and watched as her features turned horror-struck. She understood her thoughts; no words were needed between them after all these years.

"But surely it's not . . . it can't be?" Peggy let the cream-colored gown slip from her hands to the floor.

"Peggy." Arnold bounded through the door, his thick, hulking frame atremble in the doorway. Breathless, he gasped, "They've found us out. All is lost!" And then, as quickly as he had entered, General Arnold exited back out the bedroom doorway.

Peggy was left alone with Clara, struggling to make sense of the announcement.

"What did he say?" Peggy's face was drained of color. Clara knew what was coming: it was a scene she had seen numberless times—a tantrum, a litany of shrieks and sobs—but with a newfound hysteria beneath it. *"Benedict!"* Peggy shouted at the empty space in the doorway where her husband had just stood. *"Benedict Arnold!"* But Arnold didn't answer, and he didn't return her cries. Peggy turned to her maid, her face ashen. "How can this be, Clara? He says we are ruined!" Clara was silent.

"All is lost, he says." Peggy repeated her husband's words aloud in the abandoned bedroom, as if through repetition she would find sense. "But I don't understand how."

Downstairs, Clara heard Arnold once again conversing with the bewildered messenger. Arnold was peppering him with questions faster than the man could answer.

"Did they ascertain with whom this spy had had his rendezvous? Did the spy talk? Did he offer up the name of his fellow conspirator?" Arnold demanded. The messenger, bewildered, answered that he knew nothing of the matter, simply that he had been ordered to deliver this letter with haste.

"But did you hear anything more, man? Anything at all?" Arnold probed. "The letter says the spy was apprehended with secret documents. Documents intended to give over the fort at West Point, and the body of our Commander Washington. Who gave him these documents?" Arnold's voice boomed down at the messenger from the deep recesses of his stocky frame.

The messenger spoke quietly, apologetically. "Sorry, sir, I don't think they know yet. At least they did not yet know at the time I set out with this message."

This answer must have satisfied Arnold, must have convinced him that there was still time. Very little, but it might be enough.

"All right, man." Arnold nodded. "Here is my reply." Putting a sealed paper in the messenger's palm, Arnold continued, "Ride back to Colonel Jameson with this at once. And do not stop on the road to speak to anyone—do you hear me? That is an order. Even if you pass General Washington's party along the way. You ride south and do not stop or turn back here for any purpose."

"Yes, sir." The bewildered messenger took Arnold's note and set out.

The dust kicked up from the rider's horse had not yet settled when another knock rapped on the front door below. "Good heavens." Clara looked out Peggy's bedroom window toward the front yard and saw the familiar figure of Major David Franks. Behind her now, Peggy was wailing like a menacing banshee.

"Hello?" Franks knocked on the front door again.

"Oh, what does *he* want?" Clara muttered, trying to think amid her mistress's bloodcurdling cries.

"Hello, General Arnold? Mrs. Arnold?" The aide let himself in through the front door, so that now he called into the interior of their home. "Hello? Are you at home?"

"What is it, Franks?" Clara paused at the top of the stairs. She was certain that the aide could now hear the wails of Peggy from the bedroom.

"Oh, hello, Clara. Is something amiss?"

"Nothing to concern yourself with," Clara answered shortly. "How may I help you?"

"I've come to tell the Arnolds that His Excellency General George Washington approaches. I've just seen his party riding south on the post road." Franks adjusted his vest in a self-satisfied way.

"General Arnold is in the parlor. Please see yourself in," Clara called back.

"Greetings, General Arnold." The aide entered to find his harried boss pacing and seemingly deep in thought. "I've come with the news, sir, that the General George Washington, accompanied by the honorable Marquis de Lafayette, Colonel Alexander Hamilton, and the rest of his staff, shall be arriving in just a matter of minutes."

Arnold looked to his aide, clearly laboring to keep his face from reflecting panic. Managing some quick, mumbled statement about needing to go to West Point immediately, to "prepare the welcome reception for General Washington," Arnold tapped the aide on the shoulders in a gesture of forced camaraderie.

"A welcome reception? I was unaware of any welcome reception. I thought the entire group was to breakfast here with Mrs. Arnold?"

Arnold did not offer a reply, but quit the room and loped quickly into the dining room, from where he cut into the buttery.

Through the window in Miss Peggy's room, Clara spotted a navy blue blur running to the stables, with a vigor uncharacteristic of Arnold's wounded legs. Just minutes later, the figure of Arnold emerged from the stables, atop a hastily saddled Hickory. The horse galloped across the yard and down the sloped incline to the river, Arnold now just a faint speck of navy blue atop the shrub-line. It looked to Clara like her master was in flight, soaring to the river, to the ship called *Vulture*.

FOR HIS part, Franks remained alone in the parlor, muttering aloud as he tried to make sense of his general's swift and inexplicable departure. "I pass a uniformed rider flying in the opposite direction and he does not stop to speak. Then Arnold sets out onto the river. Something very odd is going on, very odd indeed."

The thundering of the lone rider's horse hooves was nothing compared to the clamor that shook the house when Washington's party arrived.

"They're here!" Peggy hissed, running into bed and burrowing under her bedcovers. Barley the dog barked below as they approached, setting the horses to neighing.

"I can't go, I can't do it!" Peggy buried her head in her pillows.

The two women heard them arriving with all the noise one would expect from a military party. Clara could not resist looking out the window.

"Whoa!" The party halted before the farmhouse. Each man alighted from his horse and handed his reins over to Mr. Quigley. Barley circled the group, barking and wagging his tail.

"Come to me, Clara!" Peggy ordered her maid from bed. "Away from that window. Come hold my hand."

Clara, mesmerized with the scene of their arrival, barely heard the order, and stayed perched at the window until the last of the men had entered the front door and slipped from her sight.

A rowdy chorus of sturdy boots fell on the wooden floorboards below. She heard the slamming front door, luggage being dropped, and jovial laughter of comrades-in-arms who had long ago become friends. It was clear that these men thought they had nothing more planned for this morning than a hearty breakfast with a top general and his charming young wife.

"Careful, men." Above the chatter rose one voice—one voice that, when speaking, quieted all the others. "We are now in civilized society. Let's behave accordingly." Washington's calm, deep voice was muffled yet commanding from his place in the drawing room below them. When he spoke, the others listened. When he laughed, the others laughed. Clara could sense the authority of the commander-in-chief even from the second floor; it permeated the very wooden structure of the farmhouse.

"General Washington, what an honor!" The ladies heard Franks walk into the drawing room and introduce himself to Washington.

"Ma'am, hadn't you better go down and welcome them?" Clara suggested, looking at her mistress's stricken face.

"Must I go?" Peggy was a shadow of her former self.

"Yes, you must," Clara answered. *If not you, then who else? There is no longer a master in this home.* "My lady, think of Little Eddy."

Peggy burrowed deeper into her bed, covering her face with a wall of downy pillows. Clara watched in horror, wondering whether her mistress was trying to suffocate herself. Peggy emerged after several moments, her face as white as the pillows, but set like clay. But still, she did not speak.

"I shall go, Miss Peggy, to tell them of breakfast." Clara's heart raced at the thought of beholding General George Washington. "Come down when you are ready, my lady."

Peggy sighed, and when she spoke to her maid it was barely a whisper. "Seat them at the dining room table. I shall be down."

Peggy wanted to rail, Clara knew. To erupt as she had so many times before over problems far less grave than this. But she was a tried and tested performer, Peggy Shippen Arnold. She knew how to distract men, how to allure men, how to manipulate them so that they saw only what she wanted them to see. Hadn't she been preparing for this moment her whole life?

"I have to do this," Peggy said to herself. "I must do this."

Clara descended the stairs and found the party in the drawing room, encircling General Washington as he looked out the window toward West Point. "You see how well protected it is by its position atop that cliff?" Washington was speaking to Hamilton and a red-haired companion, pointing toward the fort. "I shall say it again: the key to the continent sits atop that granite cliff."

"Begging your pardon, sirs." Clara hovered in the doorway, lowering her eyes as she curtsied. The entire company of men turned their eyes suddenly to her, and she could do nothing to stop the crimson flush that tinted her face.

"Hello, miss." General Washington bowed in her presence, even though it was a courtesy he did not need to show a poor servant girl. The others, including Franks and the man she recognized as Alexander Hamilton, followed his lead. The red-haired man in a light-colored suit, surely the Marquis de Lafayette, smiled at Clara.

"Mrs. Arnold has asked me to inform you that she will be right down." Clara finished with a quick curtsy.

"Thank you, young lady," Washington replied, his words strong like cannon fire after the timidity of her own announcement. He had a kind smile and an open, friendly manner about him that softened the impact made by his imposing figure and military regalia. He was dressed as they always described him in the newspapers: a uniform coat of a deep navy blue with gold buttons and cuffs. Epaulets of gold satin and fringe sat atop his broad shoulders, enhancing their already wide appearance. He seemed to take up half of the space in the drawing room.

"I hope your master and mistress will not mind that we've let ourselves in and, I'm afraid, made ourselves quite at home," Washington said.

"My lady will not mind in the slightest," Clara answered. "In the meantime, may I show Your Excellency to the dining room?"

"Please, just call me 'General.'" Washington smiled gently at Clara. "What is it with this 'Excellency' nonsense?" Washington turned to Hamilton, erupting in amicable laughter. "I'm not a king, nor do I wish to be."

The men rose at Washington's direction, the floorboards creaking under the dozens of boots and heavy legs. Clara led them out of the room.

"Hello."

They all heard the light footsteps at the same time and turned. Peggy stood at the top of the dark stairwell, the light of the second-floor windows illuminating her from behind so that she was bathed in a white glow. "General Washington, even more handsome in person." Her voice was laced with a girlish sweetness, as if the sight of Washington filled her with delight. How many times had Clara heard Peggy Arnold rail against this man—calling him an impotent tobacco farmer, faulting him for her husband's disappointing military career, blaming him for ruining their lives? Yet here she stood, beaming at Washington as if he were a suitor at a ball and she wanted nothing more than to dance with him.

"Mrs. Arnold!" Washington seemed to grow even taller under her admiring gaze. He walked to the bottom of the stairs and bowed, his towering frame poised to greet her. "What a delight to finally meet you."

The men stood in rapt silence as Peggy clutched the wall and descended, dressed in a cool dress of white linen with lace detailing at the sleeves and collar. A sash of light blue with pink and yellow stitched flowers was tied tightly around her waist, showcasing her famous figure. Clara noticed how Hamilton and Lafayette exchanged a knowing glance before looking back toward Peggy. Her blond hair was not swept high above her head, but in a loose chignon on the nape of her neck. Her face had regained its color and she looked early-morning fresh, unblemished, excruciatingly beautiful. Clara alone knew that her insides coiled with anxiety and anger.

"At last, I meet the legendary Mrs. Arnold." Washington bowed deeply before taking her tiny hand in his for a kiss.

"I must confess, my lady, my men were worried about being late this morning only because they didn't want to keep the charming Mrs. Arnold waiting."

Peggy laughed, and for the first time Clara noted that her gestures were labored, forced. But Washington suspected nothing; he, after all, had only heard of her radiance but had never seen it to its full effect.

"I think they are all half in love with you." Washington winked and offered his arm to escort her into the dining room. "Shall we?"

"Oh, I'm sure it's not true." Peggy clutched her side, and then took the offered arm to be escorted by Washington. The rest of the men followed in their wake. Washington ducked as he crossed over from the drawing room to the dining room.

"You're too tall for our home?" Peggy glanced sideways at him.

"I'm too tall for most of the buildings I enter," the general answered. "Probably why I prefer to sleep outdoors."

"General Washington, Excellency, I must make apologies for my husband." Peggy cocked her head and looked up at the white-haired commander. Washington did not correct Peggy's choice of title for him, but rather stared down at her with fixed attention.

"You, my lady, need not apologize for anything." Washington leaned toward her.

"You are too kind, sir. But I must tell you that my husband, General Arnold, is not here this morning because he is preparing a grand reception for you over at West Point."

"Is that right? It's very kind of your husband, but surely not necessary. His presence at breakfast would have been all the reception I needed," Washington answered good-naturedly.

"Yes, well, you know how deeply my husband admires you. He said—" Peggy smiled, but did not finish her thought. Her frailty seemed glaringly obvious to Clara, and now even General Washington seemed to take note.

"My lady, are you well?" Washington's brow furrowed in genuine concern.

"Oh." Peggy managed a smile, cocking her head. "I am a new mother, General Washington. With little Edward consuming all of my energy . . . I'm afraid there's very little with which to entertain. It's nothing, simply what ails all young mothers." Peggy smiled at him and then directed the men around the dining room table.

Peggy seated Washington in Arnold's usual seat at the head of the table opposite her. To her left she sat Hamilton, to her right she sat Lafayette. The rest of the men filled out the remaining chairs and momentarily turned their attention from their hostess to admire the spread before them—two warm loaves of bread, slices of ham, bowls of fresh cream, sliced peaches, a pot of tea, and a pitcher of ale.

"Our spread is humble, but sufficient, we hope." Peggy accepted Washington's help into her chair. "We all must cut back on our portions on account of the war." She sighed.

"It is a feast and we are not worthy to partake of it in your presence." Washington smiled earnestly before crossing the table to take his place.

"Now, my guess is that if you men are anything like my husband, you'll take your breakfast with ale?" Peggy raised her eyebrows at Washington across the table.

"That would be splendid." Washington agreed, his men murmuring their assent.

"Clara, tea for me, and ale for the men," Peggy spoke to her maid. "Please."

Clara left the room, running to the kitchen to grab several more pitchers of ale. When she returned, her mistress was serving large slices of ham to the French gentleman beside her.

"Marquis, I fear that my table cannot compare to the feasts you must have enjoyed at Versailles." Peggy leaned close to the red-haired nobleman.

"But my lady," Lafayette answered in his thick French accent, "it is Versailles which cannot compare to your charming home."

"Do you find yourself longing for the comforts of the court, Marquis?" As Peggy chatted with the Frenchman, she turned to her left and offered Hamilton several large slices of ham.

"Quite the contrary, madame. I feel as though, at last, I am in the country that feels like home. What an idea—a new country based on the idea that all men are equal! The fight for liberty seemed to call out to me in the very deepest place in my bones." Lafayette broke off a small piece of bread for himself and bit into it.

"And how appreciative we are that he has answered the call," Washington answered, offering his empty mug to Clara for filling.

"Indeed," Peggy answered, lifting her teacup as if to toast the Marquis. "We have been reading of your military skill and your dedication to our cause, Marquis. It is an inspiration to us all."

"The Marquis is noble enough to avoid the opportunity for complaining," Washington said, loading his spoon with a serving of peaches and fresh cream, "but the battlefield will take its toll on a man's morale. Being in the society of a lady is refreshing." Washington smiled at his hostess, spooning the fruit into his mouth. "My word, Mrs. Arnold, I understand why your beauty is legendary. But why are your peaches not more famous? They also deserve much praise."

"You are too liberal with your compliments, sir." Peggy smiled at the compliment and managed a perfectly timed blush.

"Not so, Mrs. Arnold. Am I not correct, lads? Are not these peaches delectable?" Washington looked around at his men, inspiring a chorus of agreement. "Or perhaps our meal is sweetened by the company."

"General Washington, I had no idea you were a flirt." Peggy spoke to him as if it were just the two of them, and Clara could see that her lady's spirits had lifted noticeably under his attentions.

"Oh, terrible flirt," Washington answered, mouth full. "I love the society of women, love to dance, love to play jokes. It is the only diversion that can truly soften a man after the sights of war." Washington winked at Peggy, a boyish mischief glimmering in his pale blue eyes.

"In that case, you must find the separation from Mrs. Washington very taxing?" Peggy was moving her food around on her plate but barely eating.

"Indeed." Washington rested his fork on his plate and took his chin in his hands, thinking his answer over. "I miss my wife dearly.

She is my best friend and closest confidante. I urge Martha to join us at camp whenever it's possible."

"I read that she's spent every winter with you since the war broke out. What a strong woman she must be," Peggy said, sipping her tea. "To pass on the comforts of Mount Vernon to encamp with you and your men."

"She is a strong little lady." Washington smiled. "Though I suppose she'd have to be, putting up with me. But it's the Marquis here who is farthest from his wife." Washington pointed with his fork at his aide. "And Hamilton is engaged."

"Is that so?" Peggy turned to Hamilton, who nodded. "Well, congratulations, Mr. Hamilton."

"If I may be so bold"—Hamilton straightened his posture—"Mrs. Arnold, your husband has the best post in the army, because it allows him to carry out his duties while also remaining with you."

"Well, Mr. Hamilton, my husband would gladly give up this comfortable post for one that drew him out to the battlefield with the rest of you, but his leg injuries suffered at Saratoga and the Canadian campaign make that impossible," Peggy said, an edge now apparent in her voice.

Hamilton's face flushed a deep shade of crimson. "Of course, I meant no disrespect to General Arnold. I simply meant to say—"

Washington interjected. "I know that Alexander, like all of us, appreciates the heavy sacrifice which your husband so selflessly made on behalf of these colonies."

Peggy nodded. "Yes, I'm sure he does."

"Why, Arnold once shot his own horse out from under him in retreat to prevent the Brits from getting the beast," Washington spoke, before erupting into appreciative laughter. "What a man Benedict Arnold is!"

"After the Battle of Norwalk, that's right." Peggy nodded, smiling with tight lips.

"No one questions your husband's valor," Hamilton insisted. "I simply meant that, any man who lives with you, occupies a most fortunate post."

"I understand your point now, Mr. Hamilton." Peggy looked at the dark-haired man. "Now, who needs more ale?"

Clara rounded the table, refilling each ale mug that was offered to her. As they grew full on food and beer, their chatter grew boisterous and merry, each of them vying for their hostess's attention. Peggy managed to dole out her charms liberally, blossoming like a tulip under the sunshine of male flattery. Washington, it seemed to Clara, liked to laugh loudly and often, and his aide Alexander Hamilton appeared well-practiced in provoking his good cheer.

When the platters of food had been scraped of their last morsels, Clara returned to the kitchen. "Mrs. Quigley, they need more ale—" Clara rounded the corner into the kitchen, but stopped short when she saw them. A man Clara had never seen before sat at the table, struggling through labored breath to drain a mug himself. Mr. and Mrs. Quigley looked down at the man, their faces white. The man was dressed in the colonial military uniform, with a tricornered hat, a musket around his midsection and a tattered, navy coat. He did not look up when Clara entered the kitchen.

"Clara." Mrs. Quigley looked to her, shifting the baby on her hip. "Here's a messenger come for General Washington. From south of the river."

Clara's heartbeat hammered in her throat at the announcement. "Are you from North Castle Fort?" she asked, but she already knew his answer.

"Aye." The messenger drained his final sips of ale and looked up at Clara for the first time. His face was rosy and rutted with a travel-weary expression. "Hell of a time finding General Washington, if you don't mind my saying so." He spoke like a backwoodsman. "They sent me up from North Castle to find him in Danbury, Connecticut. Only, by the time I got there, Washington had departed for West Point. I took the low road, thinking I'd catch up to him on his way 'ere, but he came by the upper road, through Fishkill."

"They have just finished breakfast," Clara told Mrs. Quigley. Turning back to the messenger, she said, "I'll take you in to see him." Clara left the kitchen with this windswept man on her heels. So, the hour had come.

In the dining room, the Marquis de Lafayette was making a joke about Mother Nature's gift for forming perfect, round circles, and it wasn't clear whether he was talking about Mrs. Arnold's peaches or her famous figure. Washington roared with laughter while Peggy feigned modest embarrassment. Her smile, however, told the men that they had not offended her in the slightest.

Clara stood at the threshold of the dining room. "Mrs. Arnold." She looked to her mistress. "Begging your pardon, ma'am, there's a messenger here for General Washington." Clara could have told her mistress in private, thereby delaying—or even thwarting—the messenger and his news, but she was certain to speak loud enough so that Washington himself would hear.

Peggy, who had been serving spoonfuls of peaches, could have seared a coal-hot scar into Clara's skin with the intensity of her gaze. "Not now, Clara, the general is enjoying breakfast. All correspondences shall wait until we've finished." Peggy turned from Clara and resumed scooping the peaches, as if to put the matter to rest.

"If you please, ma'am." Clara remained in the room. "This messenger says it is of a very urgent nature."

Peggy fixed her eyes on Clara and the maid detected a momentary, barely perceptible look of panic. But, aware that the whole party was watching, Peggy simply smiled and nodded her head. "Thank you, Clara." Her eyes said: you shall pay for this later. But Peggy continued: "Tell this messenger to come in, please. If there's an urgent message for General Washington, then of course he must have it." Peggy's voice was smooth like syrup, her face now betraying not the slightest concern. "More perfectly round peaches, Monsieur le Marquis?" Peggy cooed, and the men laughed.

Clara stepped aside to allow the entry of the ragged messenger. The men, accustomed to soldiers like him, took little note of his untidy uniform. It was Peggy who seemed to study his appearance with special interest—his jacket had the same dusty and mud-matted look of the earlier messenger from North Castle. On his face he wore the harried and exhausted expression worn by the man who had delivered the fateful message to Arnold hours earlier.

"More ale for the men, Clara," Peggy said, averting her eyes as the messenger hurried to Washington with a packet of parcels. Her heart must have been beating as quickly as Clara's was, but her pale face was as calm as a pool of still water.

"Where do you come from?" Washington turned to the man, pushing his massive frame back from the table.

"North Castle, sir," the messenger replied. "On an urgent errand from Colonel Jameson, Your Excellency."

"What is Jameson up to that can't wait until I've finished savoring Mrs. Arnold's peaches?" Washington quipped good-naturedly, but he took the envelope from the man's hands.

It seemed as though Washington held the sealed envelope for an eternity. "Really, though, Mrs. Arnold, I shall have to tell Thomas Jefferson that he could learn a thing from you. He fancies himself quite a farmer."

Clara swallowed hard as Peggy forced out a short snap of a laugh. At last Washington broke the seal and pried open the fold, turning to Peggy. "You and your husband shall have to come visit me in Virginia. I have my own orchard as well."

Peggy let out another short, labored laugh, trying not to look at the letter, now resting open in Washington's hands. The general took a slow sip of tea before he lowered his eyes and focused on the cache of papers.

"Let's see what we have here." He lifted the parchment in front of him. The room was silent, all conversations put on hold until the senior commander finished reading. The paper concealed Washington's face from view, so that none of them could gauge his reaction to the words he was reading—words that both Clara and Peggy already guessed. Clara noticed how the letter began to quaver like a windblown leaf in Washington's large, strong hands. Then the paper lowered. Washington lifted his eyes, peering over the top edge of the parchment, his face drained of color.

Ignoring Peggy for the first time all morning, Washington stared into the eyes of Hamilton. "He has betrayed us. Benedict Arnold has betrayed us." He said it with quiet incredulity.

No one in the room spoke, but they all stared at Washington with questioning silence.

Washington looked once more at the letter. "If not him, then in whom can we trust?"

Clara's eyes joined the gaze of all the others in the room as she turned to stare intently into the beautiful face of her mistress.

"It can't be! How could he have done this to me?"

Clara watched, horror-struck, as Peggy shrieked these words

over and over again. Around the table, the men rose to their feet, their gazes alert as they awaited Washington's orders.

"How could he have done this to me?" Peggy was flailing her arms wildly, tearing at her hair as she sobbed. "He might as well have killed me." Peggy pulled on the collar of her soft linen dress, tugging at it as if she had difficulty breathing. She pawed it so wildly that Clara watched, in horror, as she shredded her gown down the middle.

Washington looked from Peggy to Hamilton in dismay as Peggy's body slid from her chair and she collapsed into a sobbing heap on the floor. Clara could do nothing but stare at the scene in paralyzed bewilderment, wondering if this was genuine hysteria or Peggy's best performance yet.

"How could he do this to me?" Peggy's whole body quaked as a stream of tears ran down her red cheeks. "I will be hanged now, simply for being the traitor's wife!"

"Please, Mrs. Arnold." Washington's face was stricken. He walked toward her, but she began to swing her hands violently so that he looked afraid to move any closer.

"It can't be!" Peggy's hair had come loose now, and it flew around her face as she wrung her arms, tugging on the fraying fabric of her gown.

"Alexander, please, help me." Washington approached Peggy from the right, Hamilton from the left, and the two of them gripped her arms as she struggled, in vain, to wrestle them off.

"I won't let you kill my child," Peggy snarled, raising two fists into the air as if she would fight. She swung one threateningly toward Hamilton's face, but the Marquis stepped in and helped them stay her hands.

"Please, Mrs. Arnold, you have gone mad!" Washington spoke firmly, but to no avail. After several minutes of struggling against the strength of the three men, Peggy gave up, surrendering into an unresponsive, sobbing heap.

"I am ruined," she whimpered. Washington patted her head in a paternal gesture as she cried into his broad chest. Had the men not been propping her up, she would have fallen backward on the floor, but instead she fell into Hamilton's arms.

"Oh." Peggy's body shook under the exertion of one final sob before her eyes shut.

"Good gracious." Hamilton looked down at Peggy. "Is . . . is she dead?" Hamilton turned to Washington, his mouth agape.

"No, fainted," Washington answered, removing his coat to cover Peggy's torn dress. "Hamilton, take Mrs. Arnold upstairs and put her in bed. You, miss"—Washington looked directly at Clara—"will you please sit with Mrs. Arnold until she wakes? When she does, tell me immediately. The rest of you men, outside with me, now. We will discuss our plans for Arnold."

Hamilton scooped Peggy up and climbed the stairs with Clara following behind. "Please, direct my way," Hamilton called back to Clara, who pointed him toward the Arnolds' bedroom. As Hamilton reached the top of the stairs, Peggy's head fell back. For just an instant, Peggy's eyes opened, and Clara would have sworn that her mistress flashed a devilish glance at her maid. But before Clara could be certain, Peggy's eyes were shut again.

Hamilton entered the bedchamber and eased his hostess onto the bed. Peggy awoke almost as soon as she was deposited there, and immediately resumed her protestations. She saw Hamilton and Clara hovering over her bedside and looked at them, her eyes narrowed. "Stay back, you demons," Peggy shrieked, peeling Washington's coat off her as if it bore a contagious plague in its threads. Hurling it at Hamilton, she continued her tirade: "They are going to kill me and my son." Peggy kicked off the bedsheet that Hamilton had placed over her. "I will not let you kill my son," she hissed.

"Please, Mrs. Arnold . . ." Hamilton looked helplessly at Clara, who had no answer for him.

"Do not come any closer to me, you murderer!" Peggy fumed, her eyes listless as she glanced around the room.

"No one seeks to do you any harm, Mrs. Arnold." Alexander stood a ways back from the bed. "Please, it is I, Alexander Hamilton. And—" Hamilton turned to Clara.

"And Clara," the maid answered.

"I won't speak to either of you," Peggy cried. "I want to speak to Washington!"

Hamilton sighed. "Better go get him," Hamilton turned to Clara. The maid nodded and descended the stairs. As she walked, she heard Hamilton endeavoring unsuccessfully to calm his hysterical hostess.

Clara found Washington outside, encircled by his men as he delivered orders.

"General Washington, sir." Clara hovered on the porch. "Mrs. Arnold is awake, and is requesting you."

"Take me to her." Washington told his men to await his further instructions and followed Clara back up to the bedroom.

"Here he comes. I can hear him now. Listen." Hamilton was still at Peggy's bedside, attempting to mollify her.

Washington followed Clara. "Mrs. Arnold." He paused in her doorway. Peggy, seeing Washington's frame upon her threshold, let out a wail and devolved into fresh hysterics.

"No! That is not Washington! That is the man who is going to help them murder my child," Peggy screamed, kicking her legs furiously in the bed.

"You'd better go, sir." Hamilton rushed at Washington, ushering him out of the room. "She is possessed of a fury!"

"We mustn't let her harm herself." Washington stared at Peggy with a look of genuine pity. "She is clearly a victim in all of this, more distressed than even we are."

"Of course, sir," Hamilton agreed. Lowering his voice, he addressed his commander. "Sir, if you don't mind my asking, how do you know that Arnold has betrayed us?"

Washington hunched over, beckoning Hamilton close. Leaning toward his aide, Washington whispered so that Peggy would not hear from the bed. "They've found a redcoat spy, a Major John Anderson, trying to cross over into British lines near Tarrytown. He was picked up by some colonial men. Anderson was carrying maps, troop lists, and top-secret information in his boot. Who could have possibly given him that?"

Hamilton stammered. "Arnold was planning to give him—this Anderson fellow—control of West Point?"

Washington's face was heavy with grief. "What's worse—this Anderson carried a pass signed by Arnold, granting him access back over into British lines. He was dressed in plain clothes, and he came damn close to slipping back out, but there was an informal patrol waiting for him. It was miraculous that these men happened to be out and had the wit to question Anderson."

Clara's heart leapt with joy. Caleb! He had received her messages after all.

"Benedict Arnold is not at West Point preparing a reception for us—Benedict Arnold is fleeing down the river to the British," Washington said, his earlier good humor gone.

Hamilton's eyes burned in anger as he understood the situation. "We must catch him." The aide stood up straight. "We must ride south and catch him before he can reach safety, that traitor."

"Lower your voice, Hamilton," Washington placed a paternal arm on his aide's shoulder. "We don't want Mrs. Arnold to hear this. She already suffers enough. She need not know the full extent of her husband's villainy."

"That is right, sir," Hamilton nodded. "We should shield her however we can. Lord knows she's been through enough, and will go through even more if her spy of a husband is apprehended."

"That is the matter at hand right now. We must apprehend Arnold," Washington spoke with determination in his voice. "You and Lafayette, saddle up and ride south. Bring however many men you need to take Arnold down. I will go with the rest of the men across the river to ensure that West Point is prepared. If Arnold intends to lead the British up the river to attack West Point, we will be ready for him."

THE ARNOLD home had been transformed from the site of a cordial country breakfast party to a military headquarters, and the base for Washington's defense of West Point. Having the colonial commander under the same roof was both a thrill and an unaccustomed comfort for Clara—no matter what happened now, she knew that Washington was in charge. The tyranny of Peggy Arnold had ceased. Nevertheless, Clara spent most of the following day with her mistress, sitting beside her bed as Washington had ordered. Peggy was still too distressed, she said, to rise from bed, and would see no visitors. Except Clara. So, Clara was forced to remain in the secluded bedroom.

From her post, Clara heard doors opening and horses running to and from the house. She longed to see what was occurring. Had Arnold been caught? And what was to happen to West Point?

When the sun had dropped from its perch high in the sky, Clara decided that it was safe to take a break from her bedside vigil. Mrs. Quigley would likely be preparing supper for the men, and Clara would go seek out some food for herself and Miss Peggy.

"Miss Peggy," Clara whispered into the bedroom, its corners illuminated by the sun's slanted rays, "I shall go see about supper."

"What is the point?" Peggy asked, surprising Clara with the crystalline clarity of her voice. "Why eat? Why live? We've failed."

"Plenty to live for, madame. Perhaps you'd like me to bring Little Eddy up to you?" Clara suggested.

"I can't bear to see the child. Not when his father has abandoned us like this." Peggy turned her head, closing her eyes against the orange sun shining sideways into her bedchamber.

"Very well. I'll still go and see about that food, nevertheless." Clara rose and quit the room.

She slipped past the officers in the parlor and pushed the front door ajar, stepping out into the dusky yard for her first gasp of fresh air all day. To her left, the river was a placid ribbon of slow-flowing silver, emblazoned by the sun sinking behind the mountains of West Point.

Barley, having heard Clara exit the farmhouse, ran to her from the direction of the post road, tail wagging. "Poor pup." Clara leaned down and stroked the coarse fur behind the animal's ears. "You keep watch for your master, Barley, but he will not return." The dog lapped a slobbery kiss onto the top of her hand as she pet him. "What shall become of you, Barley pup?"

Clara wondered the same for herself, for the Quigleys, for Little Eddy, for the whole household. How long would it be before Washington and his men departed? If they left having failed to apprehend Arnold, would they allow the traitor's servants to make their own ways? But Peggy would never allow it. Which was precisely why Clara had taken steps to secure her own future.

She thought about Cal, guarding the woods, waiting for André to come out, and her loneliness began to gnaw at her, aching from within. She longed for him so deeply that she began to imagine him before her: there he was, crossing the yard, his right hand removing his tricornered hat to reveal his wavy, honey-colored hair. In the other hand rested the bridle leading old Buckwheat, the two of them walking beside each other in a lazy saunter. A lone piece of straw hung from his lips, disrupting that casual, familiar smile. This imagined Cal was so solid, so real, that Clara felt certain that if she reached forward, she'd be able to run her fingers through that tussled mane of golden hair.

Surely her eyes deceived her, for she could not actually be seeing Cal. But then, he spoke.

"Clara Bell."

She shook her head in disbelief, blinking. "Cal?"

"Aye." He cocked his head, making an odd face at her. Beside him, Buckwheat whinnied. "You are as white as snow, Clara Bell. Are you ill?"

"Cal, I'm so happy to see you." She collapsed into him, pulling him close to her in a hug. Neither of them spoke for several minutes as he lifted his arms and returned the embrace, wrapping her up in him. She breathed him in, breathed in his familiar Cal scent, his nearness, the thick strength of his arms. She could have cried, she was so overjoyed.

"How about a kiss for a poor soldier?" He put his forefinger under her chin and lifted her lips to his. She happily obliged.

When she reopened her eyes, she looked up into the familiar hazel of his own. "How is it possible that you are here, Cal?"

"Message." Cal retrieved a sealed paper from a pocket in his uniform. "From down the river for General Washington. You can imagine I was all too eager for the task when I heard a letter had to be delivered to this home."

"What does it say? Have you any idea?" Clara walked beside him as he tied his horse to the front post. "Have they caught Arnold?"

"They didn't say one way or the other. This note pertains to the prisoner, Mr. John André. Seems the British are already offering a huge sum to buy his freedom."

"Washington will never accept," Clara answered.

"And yet the letter had to be delivered anyway, did it not?" Cal grinned at her, and she felt overwhelmed. She leaned forward and stole another kiss.

"Cal, can you believe it? They stopped André. *You* stopped André."

"No, Clara." Cal shook his head. "*You* stopped André. You ought to feel very proud."

She felt many things, too many to explain aloud. Too many to even understand just yet. Rather than try, she took a deep breath, her eyes still fixing on Cal. He was the one thing that felt safe, certain to her. And then she asked, "I wasn't sure whether you got my message."

"I did. But I didn't want to write back. Too risky. Just in case Arnold or the missus had seen it first. I figured I'd find a chance to slip away and come see you in person, once everything was settled."

"I'm glad you did," Clara said, taking his hand in hers.

They stood opposite each other a moment, no words passing between them. Eventually, Cal sighed. "He really did it. Or tried to, at least."

"*They* really did it," Clara corrected Cal. "Only he ran, and she remains."

Cal followed her eyes as Clara looked up at the house, toward the bedroom window that sat, darkening, with Miss Peggy on the other side of it. "I have to admit, I held out hope until the last that Arnold would change his mind." Cal ran his fingers through his hair, tussling several waves loose. "He was a good man, once. A great man."

Clara nodded but said nothing. She knew too well, had seen too close, to imagine that a change had been possible in the end.

"Clara?"

"Yes, Cal?"

"Are my aunt and uncle all right?"

Clara nodded. "They bear no guilt, Cal. They never even allowed me to tell them fully of the plot." Clara paused. "They are remarkably strong, considering what they've weathered."

"You all are."

Clara shrugged her shoulders. "They're inside. They will be happy to see you."

"Aye." Cal nodded. "Well, let me go in and deliver this to General Washington. But first, I need one more kiss."

CAL LATER found Clara by the river, where she sat, awash in the last few minutes of sunlight. As the golden disc slid behind the western mountains, a tattered colonial flag cut a silhouette against the sky over West Point. The fort remained in American hands.

Cal sat down beside her on the shore of the river. For several minutes they stared at the fort, but neither of them spoke. "So, Clara Bell, here we are."

"Here we are." Clara nodded, turning to him. "When must you go?"

"Not tonight. I've been given some time off. When Colonel Putnam heard that my farm was just adjacent to this home, he told me I may have a few days up here to see my family and settle some matters."

Clara could have leapt with joy, and she was certain her face betrayed that. "How very important you are, Cal," Clara teased. He smiled back at her.

"I suppose, Cal, if you have the night off, then you have time for another kiss?"

"I have nothing else planned."

"Good." She put her palm to his cheek, savoring the feel of his skin. "Then you had better kiss me."

"If you say so, Clara Bell." They stayed on the hillside as the sun dipped below the horizon, the last rays of light filling the yard. Clara felt as though they had years of lost time for which to atone, years in which she should have been telling Cal of her love for him. She looked forward to making it up to him, to showing him how deeply she loved him every day for the rest of her life.

Clara could have happily remained out there all night, but Cal pulled away from her before she was ready, his face suddenly serious. Tucking a loose curl behind her ear, he asked: "But what about you, Clara Bell? How will we get you away from this home? Do you think Miss Peggy will allow you to just get up and leave?"

"No," Clara answered, looking out over the river with a determined gaze. She was certain Peggy would not let her go. "But I have a plan that will give her very little choice."

When Clara returned to Peggy, having made a plan to meet Cal the next day, the bedchamber was dark and her mistress had slipped into a fretful sleep. Clara lit the candles around the room, her heart glowing even in the shadows of this darkness. Nothing would dampen her spirits now.

"No! No! Johnny, don't leave me!"

Clara looked upon her mistress, her expression tormented even as she slept. The beautiful woman moaned in the throes of a nightmare that had now come true. And it was only Clara who knew, fully, the nightmares that haunted Peggy.

Peggy, who had always thought of her maid as invisible. This woman who had alternately spoiled and abused Clara for years, taking her for a simple, timid extension of her own life and plans; taking her maid's blind, stupid obedience for granted, even to the point of bringing her along to plot treason. Clara had been so invisible to this woman that Peggy had allowed her to sit by, watching plans of treachery unfold, never guessing that Clara herself could play a part. Never guessing that Clara had a mind and a heart of her own, her own desires for a life and for love.

Peggy wouldn't let Clara go without a fight. No, she'd resist Clara's departure; and Peggy knew how to get her own way, of that, Clara was all too certain. But hadn't Clara been learning from her mistress all this time? Observing, obeying, taking it all in with perfectly polite silence? Wasn't she finally prepared to stand up for herself, even if it meant going against Peggy Shippen Arnold?

As the house darkened, the Quigleys lit candles and fireplaces, and a loud commotion downstairs told Clara that Hamilton and Lafayette had returned from their ride south. She ran down the stairs to hear their news with the rest of the crowd.

"Any news?" someone asked as the door slammed.

"Where's Arnold?" another soldier demanded. The men showered the two new arrivals with questions while Barley the dog barked, confused by the frenzy of activity as he sought out his master in the crowd.

"He slipped away," Lafayette said, his French accent exacerbated by fatigue. "Arnold has escaped the hangman's noose." The muffled sounds of swears and chatter filled up the room, but Clara didn't hear the rest. She had her hand over her heart, overcome by her relief that Arnold would not hang.

SEVERAL MINUTES later, someone knocked quietly outside Peggy's bedchamber. Clara walked toward the door while her mistress stirred, sitting upright in bed.

"Who is it?" Peggy asked, rubbing her puffy eyes.

"It is I, my lady, George Washington." He remained on the threshold, hesitant to enter.

"Come in," Peggy answered.

Two men, Washington and Hamilton, peeked their heads into Peggy's bedroom. They each held candles, casting a dim light across the room.

"Mrs. Arnold?" Washington refrained from pointing his eyes toward the bed. "Are you well?"

"General Washington, Colonel Hamilton." Peggy's face was splotchy and her hair disheveled, but she had regained composure, and she even conjured a smile when she saw the men. "Please, please come closer. You will see that I am much recovered." She adjusted the nightdress that Clara had slid her into.

The two men approached cautiously. "Mrs. Arnold, I cannot tell you how relieved we are to see that you've recovered," Washington now looked at the resting woman with paternal sympathy.

"These are for the lovely lady." Hamilton tiptoed behind Washington. Clara had to steady herself when she saw, to her utter shock, that Hamilton carried in his arms a bouquet of flowers. "From your garden, Mrs. Arnold." Hamilton smiled sheepishly. "We hoped they might lift your spirits."

So this was the punishment for orchestrating the worst treason of the war—a bedside visit from George Washington and freshly picked flowers from Alexander Hamilton?

"You are too kind, Mr. Hamilton. Clara shall put those in water for me."

"May I?" Washington approached the bed.

"Please." Peggy urged both men forward. "You are so good to visit me in this state. I must confess, I remember very little from yesterday morning's events."

"We are just happy to see you revived, my lady." Washington pulled a chair up to the bed and sat beside Peggy. Hamilton stood behind him. "Mrs. Arnold," Washington continued. "Hamilton and Lafayette have just returned from south of the river. The bad news, from my point of view, is that your husband has escaped us. He has slipped past the lines and is in New York City this evening. We will be unable to capture him and send him to the same fate as that of John André."

Peggy exhaled a long, deep sigh. Taking her face in her hands, she concealed her expression and began to weep, quietly, into her palms. Whether she wept for her husband's deliverance or André's death sentence, Clara did not know.

"Mrs. Arnold," Washington continued, "we would have liked to have had justice, of course. The only positive I see in the present situation, however, is that your husband will survive. And knowing that that is a comfort to you, helps me to accept the outcome more easily."

Peggy dropped her hands, still tearful. "Oh, General Washington," she choked out through her sobs. "You must think I'm so terrible, being happy that he survived. But he's my husband. The father of my son. Surely you understand that this is a tremendous relief to me?" Peggy reached for Washington's hands, and he took hers in his and kissed them in a tender gesture. Clara looked on, marveling at the scene. So André would hang while Arnold would join the British ranks. Peggy, the woman who had arranged the whole plot, would be allowed to go, untarnished, to her husband. Who had come out of this with the worse punishment, Clara wondered, André or Arnold?

"There is but one small consolation in this whole terrible drama, Mrs. Arnold." Washington gazed at her, his eyes sad. "And that is seeing you smile right now. It makes me happy to see you recovered."

Peggy sighed. "How will I ever recover? When I'm abandoned by a husband such as the one I have? But relieved, yes."

"Mrs. Arnold." Hamilton edged closer to the bed. "May we be so bold as to make the suggestion that you go stay with family in Philadelphia rather than trying to reunite with your husband?"

Peggy shut her eyes and released a slow exhale.

"It is wrong of us to speak of a man thusly to his own wife, but such a man as Benedict Arnold has proven himself a traitor," Washington agreed with his aide.

"Yes, you're right," Peggy conceded, fidgeting with the bedsheets. "I should go to my parents." She paused. "But eventually I must go to my husband."

"But he has betrayed you." Hamilton's voice had a hard edge. "He does not deserve you in any way."

"It's my duty though," Peggy sighed. "My duty as a wife and a mother to go to him. Even if it means crossing over to the British." She sunk her face into her hands and began to cry, now with exaggerated, theatrical sobs that Clara knew to be disingenuous.

Hamilton and Washington exchanged a forlorn glance. "Well,

we will not stand in your way." Washington looked at Peggy admiringly. "But Hamilton is right to say that Arnold does not deserve you."

They were correct, Clara thought to herself. Arnold did not deserve her. No one deserved her.

WASHINGTON AND his men were gone in the morning—gone across the river to West Point to prepare the defense plans. Knowing that Arnold had slipped into British hands, Washington ordered them all to brace for an assault. The commander had promised Peggy the night before that she, her son, and her servants would receive a full military escort to Philadelphia, the treatment an officer's widow could expect when crossing military lines to be reunited with her parents.

Peggy did not see the men off the next morning, but rather stayed in bed. She rose in the late morning, having slept the deep, undisturbed sleep of a child. When she awoke, she summoned Clara.

"Clara, aren't my flowers from Mr. Hamilton lovely?" Peggy said, her eyes restless as she looked around the room. "What a romantic fool that man was. I suppose I quite liked him."

Clara did not answer, but rather swallowed hard as she slid the curtains open.

"Well, win or lose, at least we'll get to go to England once this awful war is over," Peggy mused, stirring milk into a cup of tea her maid had brought. "We won't get the title," she thought aloud. "That is a shame."

Clara turned to her mistress now with unmasked disgust.

"But London *will* be so much more merry than this drab countryside. And we'll have the money, at the very least. Perhaps Benny will take Eddy and me to meet the king, how lovely that would be! I suppose things didn't turn out so rotten for us Arnolds after all." Peggy splayed her arms overhead, stretching into a languid movement as she yawned out her next order: "You might as well begin packing our things, Clara. We shall leave as soon as Washington has arranged our escort."

Clara decided that this was her time. She wouldn't wait any longer.

"I'm not going, ma'am."

"What did you say?" Peggy's arms dropped from overhead, landing on her breakfast tray with a hard thump.

"I said I'm not going." Clara shook out the bedding as she did on every morning, not bothering to look at her mistress.

"Of course you are coming to England. Where else would you go?"

"I'm going to stay here."

Peggy laughed, certain this was a joke. "Stay here and do what?"

"Marry that stableboy. Remember Caleb, the one who . . . how did you refer to him? . . . *the one who always smelled like horse filth*?" Clara turned now and stared into her mistress's cold blue eyes.

"Ha!" Apparently Peggy still believed her maid to be joking. Clara did not return the smile.

"You can't be serious, Clara?" But when her maid did not answer, Peggy continued. "Sorry, Clara, but you're not marrying anyone. You're coming with me to London. Don't you want to be the lady's maid to an aristocrat?"

"You're not going to get the title, especially now that the plot failed and your husband didn't deliver General Washington."

Peggy was momentarily beaten back to silence. Clara seized

this pause: "Your failed plot, Miss Peggy, cost General Clinton one of his favorite men. John André will hang for this."

Peggy winced. Sensing the opening in her momentum, Clara continued. "You failed. West Point will not fall. You will not be paid any additional money. You and your husband have earned yourself no prime spot in the British military." Clara spoke with a frankness that her mistress had never witnessed in her. Never witnessed, perhaps, in anyone. The stunning outrage of such bold opposition served to fortify Peggy.

"You listen here, Clara." Peggy placed the teacup down on the tray. "It's been a trying few days, and I'll allow that you have been upset by these events, as we all have, but this sort of behavior . . ."

"No, you listen," Clara interrupted. "I'm not going to England. I resign my post as maid. Today shall be my last day in your employment."

"Well, I don't accept your resignation," Peggy retorted, defiant.

"It doesn't matter, ma'am." Clara shrugged her shoulders.

"You insolent little wretch, what has gotten into you?" Peggy picked up her teapot and refilled her cup, shaking her head at Clara. "Who do you think you are, telling me no?"

"I'm no one special. Just Clara Bell. But the beauty of this country is that, no matter how insignificant I am, I'm free to plan my future how I see fit."

"You dare defy me?" Peggy's face was flushed now. "Watch yourself, Clara Bell. Or have you forgotten who you are up against? I arranged a conspiracy with my former lover, John André. I convinced my husband to abandon the country he loved, and conspire with André, without ever knowing I intended to cuckold him. And, perhaps best of all, I had the chief victim of the treachery, George Washington, sitting at my bedside, comforting me and bringing me flowers. André will end on the gallows, my husband will be smeared as a traitor, and Washington carries the sadness of betrayal with him. But me? I make it out with my reputation only enhanced." Peggy rose from her bed, walking menacingly toward her maid. "You see, Clara, I always get my way." She pressed her pointer finger strongly into Clara's breastbone, striking on each word for emphasis. "And so do you really think, after all that I have endured, that I intend to take orders from my maid?"

Clara stared back at her employer, her expression blank. "Yes, my lady, I do."

Peggy released a round of erratic laughter, as jumpy as musket fire. "And how is it that you can have that illusion?"

And here, Clara knew she must perform as she'd been taught by her mistress. She would play a part. Even as her heart clamored within her, she conjured a facial expression of serene calm and authority. "Because I possess all the means to undo your triumph, Peggy Arnold. To expose you for the traitor that you are." It was a direct challenge, but if she delivered it correctly, it would work. It was Clara's only chance to break free.

"Ha! And how is that?"

"By telling the truth. The truth that only you and I know."

"You think anyone would believe *you* over *me*?"

"At this moment, your former servant, Caleb Little, the one who smelled like horse filth, is waiting nearby. Caleb knows where to find a few *implicating* items."

"What are you talking about?" Peggy hissed, drawing back from Clara.

"Certain items you've kept over the years. Damning evidence. Check your jewelry box and you'll note a few items missing." Clara ticked the items off on her finger for dramatic effect. "The lock of André's hair you kept when he fled Philadelphia, the drawing of André you still keep, and, most disastrously, the letters. Letters from André penned back in Philadelphia, reassuring you of his affection. How do you think Master Arnold might feel, finding out that these existed? And of course, more recently, André's letter promising to make you a

Lady in the British court in exchange for Washington's head. How do you think Washington will respond to these keepsakes?"

Clara let the damning news sink in. "You've slept quite a bit the past few days, Miss Peggy. Worn out from your plotting and tantrums. Lots of time for me to safely stow the evidence." Peggy ran to her jewelry box and dug frantically in search of these treasures only she and Clara knew about. But as she realized they were gone, she turned to her maid, quivering with fury.

"Where are my things, you vile little thief?"

"I alone know. And my fiancé, Caleb." She'd told Caleb where she had hidden them beneath the oak tree, the site where she had once pretended to endure a beating at the hands of Arnold.

"So, Peggy." Clara paused. "If, by this evening, I have not met Caleb on his farm by the banks of the Hudson, he will know where to find all of these items so that he may deliver them to the general. Do you have an escape plan ready, in case you, like your husband, must flee?"

Peggy stared at her maid with panic in her eyes, pondering how to make a counterattack.

Clara continued. "However, if I do go meet him, we will never breathe a word of your treachery. You see I, unlike you, feel loyalty. And even though I despise you, I love your son and I pity your husband. I do not wish to bring about your trial and murder as a traitor, Peggy Arnold. Not after you have fed and sheltered me all these years. I will let you go to your husband, your reputation unsullied. All I ask is that you let me walk out that door a free woman, and I wish to never hear from you again."

Clara let the offer hang in the air between them, her heart clamoring against her ribs as she awaited a reply. But Peggy seemed reluctant to take Clara's offer.

"As if I could believe you now."

Clara shrugged. "All I want, my lady, is to leave this place."

"And why should I believe a word of what you say, when you've just deceived me?" Peggy clipped toward her maid.

"Because you know that I love your son. And I would never want him to grow up motherless, as I have." And it was the truth; she felt no need to condemn Peggy Arnold and bring further ruin on the household in which she'd been welcomed. Her mistress, like all the rest of them, would have to atone for her own sins, but it was not before Clara that she would face her reckoning.

But Peggy appeared even more distrusting of this offered magnanimity. "You . . . little . . . schemer! How dare you abuse me like this?" Peggy roared, incredulous, hating her maid for having defeated her.

"I have no interest in exacting any abuse on you, Miss Peggy. Or even in ever speaking to you again after today. I hope you find happiness, and even peace. All I ask is that you let me go."

"Out of my sight." Peggy spit at her. "Be gone before I get my husband's musket and shoot you, you wretched little *traitor*. Turning on me like this—after I've fed you, and clothed you, and treated you as my very sister," Peggy growled. "Get out!"

It would be the last order Clara ever took from Peggy Arnold. "As you wish, my lady. Oh, and, you might notice before too long—Mr. and Mrs. Quigley have resigned as well. You have the place to yourself." With that, Clara curtsied one last time to Mrs. Arnold, and turned on her heels. As she descended the staircase, Clara heard the screams. Filthy words and insulting names being shouted out by her mistress, who seemed as if she had gone mad with rage. This time, her hysterics were genuine. She was truly undone by the fact that she could not control Clara, could not control this situation to her own benefit. Peggy, for perhaps the first time in her life, was at the mercy of another, and it drove her mad.

But Clara did not let the accusations slow her down. She ambled out the door, out the same door through which George Washington had entered and Benedict Arnold had fled, three days before.

The morning was sunny and bright. It would be a beautiful day on Little Farm, Clara thought, as she looked toward the river. She picked up her pace, following the same path Arnold's frantic horse hooves had torn up on his flight to the *Vulture*. Soon, she could no longer hear Peggy's shrill wailing, the sound replaced by the gentle footsteps of someone, or something, behind her. Clara turned. "Barley pup!" The dog ran toward her, his shabby tail wagging. Clara paused to stroke him. "The most loyal of the bunch." She petted his tawny fur. "Since you've come all this way, I suppose I can't very well make you turn back now. All right, Barley, might as well come along. We'll have need for a dog on the farm."

With her furry companion beside her, Clara continued her walk, her heart brimming with hope, her mood as placid as the Hudson before her. The river guided her north—toward Caleb, toward her new home, toward freedom.

Clara looked across the Hudson, toward the rugged, hilltop fort at West Point. The fort that she, an invisible spy, had helped to save. West Point would stand ready for the attack. The colonial army under George Washington would stand ready for the attack. They would not be defeated by the treason of a fallen hero and his scheming wife. The British Army would abandon its quest to suppress a people crying out for liberty, and the entire nation would be free.

It wasn't until she reached the border of Little Farm, her breath heavy from the rapid pace she'd maintained, that she peeled her eyes from the opposite side of the river and looked at what was right in front of her. There, in the full splendor of the afternoon sunlight, stood Cal. His familiar silhouette was framed against the backdrop of the golden field, a piece of straw poking out from the corner of his mouth. Seeing her approach, he removed his tricornered hat and doffed it before him, greeting her with a playful bow.

"Cal!" Clara ran the final distance between them, her breath uneven, her heart brimming over with joy. How happy she felt every time she saw him. "Cal." She ran into his arms, savoring the safety of his strong embrace; he stood right before her, the man she would love for the rest of her life.

"Clara Bell, you made it."

"I made it."

"I suspect she was not too happy to let you go?"

Clara shook her head, her breath still uneven. "Did the others make it?" Clara looked over the field, scanning the area near Cal's makeshift camp for the sight of Mr. and Mrs. Quigley.

"They did make it. But they've gone to fetch the preacher." Cal handed her a bouquet of flowers, which she took in one hand, the other reaching for him. "Seems they heard that there was going to be a wedding around here today."

"Well, then, Cal, it seems I'm just in time."

Without another word, Cal reached for her and wrapped his hands around her waist, pulling her toward him in an eager embrace. When he kissed her, Clara knew that all the waiting had been worth it—the present moment soared to unimaginable heights precisely because of the treacherous road she had run to get here.

She kissed him back, savoring the knowledge that in him she had finally found her home. A home that they would build together, in a country that, like them, was just starting out. Clara was, at last, free.

EPILOGUE

MAJOR JOHN André was found guilty of spying by a military court convened by General George Washington. Because André had been apprehended behind military lines using an alias, and dressed in civilian clothing (as had been insisted upon by his host, Joshua Smith), his appeal that he be tried as an officer and a prisoner of war was rejected by Washington. For him, it would be the fate of the spy. André was executed by hanging in Tappan, New York, on October 2, 1780. But not, it seems, without winning a few more hearts. Several of his American captors expressed grief over André's death, referring to him as a likable and talented man. Upon André's death, Alexander Hamilton wrote: "Never perhaps did any man suffer death with more justice, or deserve it less."

Once aboard the HMS *Vulture,* Benedict Arnold officially declared his allegiance to the British Empire. In New York City Arnold was commissioned as a brigadier general in the British Army, a demotion from his colonial rank of major general. Aside from the £6,000 pounds he received at his first midnight meeting with André,

Arnold received no further compensation for the failed plot, nor was he granted the noble title he had coveted. In the days following his escape, Arnold proposed a prisoner swap that would have changed his place with the doomed André, but the rules of warfare prevented such an exchange. Arnold wrote to his former friend and mentor George Washington, defending his decision to join the British and pleading that his wife be allowed to return to Philadelphia. Washington granted this request but never responded to Arnold's letter.

After the revolution, Arnold moved with his wife and children to London, where he struggled to find regular employment and earn a living for his family. Arnold worked for a period as a merchant in the West Indies. There he tried his hand at business, but he argued with his partners, became embroiled in a series of lawsuits, and he returned to England having gained little monetary success. Later in his life Arnold was granted a large property in a remote region in northern Canada as a reward for his service in the British ranks. Due to his failing health, Arnold never made a home there for his wife and children.

As had been the case earlier in life, Arnold faced no shortage of critics and rivals in England; Arnold feuded with colleagues in the British Army, members of the British government, and his business partners. He struggled with debt and physical maladies for the remainder of his life. The gout infecting his earlier war injuries spread, causing Arnold lifelong pain. He also suffered from dropsy, which is a buildup of fluids in the body's tissue, as well as asthma.

On June 14, 1801, Benedict Arnold died in London. His wife labeled the cause of death "a perturbed mind." Legends surrounding the war hero and traitor allege that during his last moments of life, Arnold recalled his days in the American Revolution, and asked God to forgive him for ever trading in his first uniform.

Peggy Arnold returned to her parents' home in Philadelphia

immediately following her husband's defection. She remained there for a time, but faced some hostility from the patriotic population in her hometown. Peggy eventually left Philadelphia and she and her son were reunited with Arnold in New York City. They had a second son in August 1781.

After the war, Peggy sailed for England with her husband. At first, the Arnolds enjoyed substantial popularity, and Peggy even realized her dream of meeting the royal family at court. But her happiness in England was not to be long-lasting; as her family's economic situation worsened, Peggy settled with her husband and five surviving children in a poor neighborhood in London.

Though much younger than her husband, Peggy Shippen Arnold outlived Benedict Arnold by only three years. Her husband's death left Peggy strapped with financial debt and anxiety over how she and her five children would provide for themselves. Peggy died from cancer in 1804 at the age of forty-four and was buried next to her husband in a London cemetery. Those who knew her in England remembered her as a loving and devoted mother. It was rumored that Peggy Shippen Arnold kept a lock of John André's hair until the day she died.

A NOTE ON HISTORY AND SOURCES

THE INSPIRATION to write this novel came from a New York State Historic Marker in my hometown in the Hudson Valley. I happened upon the spot a few years ago while walking my dogs in the woods across the river from West Point. My mother and I paused to read the post, which describes "Arnold's Flight" and the conspiracy to sell West Point.

A few paragraphs told me what I, as a local to the area, already knew: that I walked the same trail traveled by General Benedict Arnold, centuries earlier, as he fled from George Washington to the British warship *Vulture*. Many American schoolchildren grow up learning the history of this notorious traitor and his coconspirator, John André, and I had grown up knowing that I lived near where Arnold and his family had once lived.

What I had *not* known, however, was whose face belonged to the portrait of the beautiful young woman beside Benedict Arnold's. I stared at the image of the fine-featured woman, her hair piled high atop her head, a quizzical smile on her face. She was described as a devoted wife, a loving mother, and a popular socialite who, with suspected fealty to the English Crown, might have incited Benedict Arnold to his infamous treachery. As I continued my walk on that cold, clear morning, I could not stop thinking about this figure, largely obscured in history's forward march. Who was Peggy Shippen Arnold? How must she have felt about the events that unraveled around her? And what role, if any, did she play in this mesmeric plot?

As I began to dig deeper into the history, I uncovered a tale and a cast of characters that proved truly Shakespearean in its scope and drama. Peggy Arnold is a confounding character—charming yet dangerous, loyal yet duplicitous, cunning yet reckless.

This novel is a work of fiction, but many of the characters and events depicted in *The Traitor's Wife* are based on the historical record. How could they not be, when history had provided me with such a salacious and intriguing framework?

Margaret "Peggy" Shippen did in fact preside over Philadelphia society during the social seasons of 1777–1778, during which time the British occupied the city and a certain Major John André caught the eye of the popular young socialite. Peggy did in fact wear dresses made at Coffin and Anderson dress shop and sip Champagne with the likes of General William Howe and Lord Rawdon. She did in fact exchange love letters and poetry with the dashing Major André; she did in fact compete with fellow socialite Margaret Chew for his attention; and she was in fact thwarted from attending the Meshianza Masque by her parents, who were becoming increasingly concerned with their daughter's very high-profile social life and the Turkish harem theme of General Howe's farewell party.

Major General Benedict Arnold, on the heels of his heroic military feats at Saratoga; Fort Ticonderoga; Valcour Island; and

Ridgefield, Connecticut, did in fact march into Philadelphia and take control of the city to the backdrop of a grand parade. With Washington as his staunchest supporter, Arnold imposed martial law. What happened next was what got him into trouble. Arnold closed the shops and began a black market trade with the help of a local merchant, Joseph Stansbury.

Details relating to Arnold's crippling injury, his military accolades, and his worsening financial situation are factually based. So too are the details related to his lavish spending, at times abrasive personality, and increasing bitterness toward the colonial cause. This bitterness was only exacerbated when Arnold found a vocal critic in the leader of Pennsylvania's Executive Council, Joseph Reed. The acrimony that developed between Arnold and Reed did in fact culminate with Arnold demanding a court-martial to clear his name, and Washington reluctantly issuing a public reprimand to the junior officer for whom he'd had such high hopes.

Arnold and Peggy did in fact meet at a reception at the Penn mansion, given by its new tenant, Benedict Arnold, in honor of the French ambassador, the Count Conrad Alexandre Gérard. During their courtship, Arnold was in fact turned down by Judge Edward Shippen in his suit for Peggy Shippen's hand. Arnold did rehabilitate his injured leg in order to win over the much younger and more attractive Peggy Shippen. And he did buy Mount Pleasant for his bride, though he never could afford to occupy it.

Clara Bell and Caleb Little, as well as the Quigleys, the Breunig sisters, and Robert Balmor, are all fictional, and so are all of the plot developments relating to them. In order for the reader to be able to witness the events from an outsider's perspective, I felt that the narrator had to be similarly situated. The historical record refers to Peggy Arnold as having a lady's maid with whom she traveled, and so Clara was created.

This is a work of fiction, but the remaining cast of supporting characters: Little Eddy Arnold, Major David Franks, Joshua Hett Smith, Joseph Stansbury, Neddy and Betsy Burd, Judge and Mrs. Edward Shippen, Dr. William Shippen, Margaret Chew, Christianne Amile, Becky Redman, Lord Rawdon, General William Howe, the Marquis de Lafayette, Alexander Hamilton, and of course George Washington, are all characters plucked from history who did in fact inhabit roles similar to those developed throughout *The Traitor's Wife*.

George Washington was indeed at Benedict Arnold's home on the morning of September 24, 1780, when he received word of John André's apprehension. Peggy Arnold did feign a hysterical fit during which she tore at her gown and screamed some of the incoherent quotes and accusations that I've included in this novel. Her fit, whether genuine or conjured, served to distract the men and convinced them of her innocence. Believed by Washington to be a victim in the entire affair, Peggy was nursed back to health, brought flowers in bed, and eventually allowed to return to her husband. Throughout her life, Peggy remained largely shielded from the enmity and ridicule that haunted her husband. It wasn't until after her death that historians discovered the significant role Peggy played in her husband's treason.

The meetings between Arnold and André did in fact occur at the home of Joshua Hett Smith in Haverstraw, New York, in the weeks leading up to André's arrest. Though Peggy Arnold was not actually in attendance at those rendezvous, she was the integral figure who initiated the written correspondence between Arnold and André. Letters remain to this day showing her handwriting in the messages passed between her husband and her former suitor. After André was captured out of uniform and charged as a spy, Arnold did attempt to swap places with André to save his coconspirator from the gallows. That offer, like his letter explaining his motives to Washington, went unanswered.

Though I've tried to weave this story with as much historical fact as possible, this novel is historical fiction, and there were points at which I took license to alter what is in the historical record. A few points of note are included here:

Prior to meeting and marrying Peggy Shippen, Benedict Arnold had been married once before, to Margaret Mansfield Arnold. The first Mrs. Arnold died in 1775, leaving Benedict Arnold a widower and the father to three sons. All accounts point to the fact that Peggy Shippen Arnold was a loving and caring figure in the lives of her stepchildren, none of whom lived with their father and his new bride.

Since Caleb Little is a fictional character, so too is the role he played in the apprehension of John André following his meeting with Benedict Arnold. The true credit goes to militiamen John Paulding, David Williams, and Isaac Van Wart. I apologize for omitting them and not giving them their proper due for the role they played in saving the American Revolution.

Peggy Shippen was the youngest in a family of five surviving children born to Judge Edward Shippen and his wife, Margaret. For the purpose of the plot, I've written about only one sister, Elizabeth, in my novel. But Peggy's additional older siblings included sisters Sarah and Mary, as well as a brother, Edward. Elizabeth did in fact marry Edward Burd, and Peggy was described by many as her father's favorite daughter.

I began my research where the plot itself began—Philadelphia. The city's old quarter, specifically Society Hill, is remarkably well preserved, and one can walk through the Shippens' former neighborhood and imagine briefly that they have stepped back in time; at any moment, Peggy Shippen's carriage might roll by. Other locales along the way included Williamsburg, Virginia, where General Washington was in residence during some of the years covered in this novel, as well as Manhattan, Garrison, and of course West Point, New York.

The New York Public Library has countless archives on colonial history. Of special interest was its collection on antique maps from the period of the Revolutionary War. The Metropolitan Museum of Art was invaluable in helping me to learn about early American architecture, clothing, and furniture. Similarly, the New-York Historical Society is a trove of not only colonial history but the furniture, history, literature, and art of the period as well.

Books read for research include: *The Traitor and the Spy* by James Thomas Flexner; *Patriot John, The Man Who Saved America* by Philip B. Secor; *Washington: A Life,* by Ron Chernow; *Benedict Arnold: Traitor of the Revolution* by Ronald Syme; *Benedict Arnold: Patriot and Traitor* by Willard Sterne Randall; *West Point: Legend on the Hudson* published by the *Poughkeepsie Journal;* and *1776* and *John Adams,* both by David McCullough.

Other thanks go to the Federal Museum in New York City; the West Point Foundry in Cold Spring, New York; the Fort Montgomery State Historic Site; and the Putnam County Tourism Department.

ACKNOWLEDGMENTS

I WANT TO thank the friends, colleagues, and family members who have supported me while writing *The Traitor's Wife* and who made its publication possible.

Mom, you are the reason I found and wrote this story. Dad, you are the reason I love history. I was able to write this novel because the two of you have encouraged me and loved me and taught me that no dream or aspiration should be considered out of reach. I will never be able to properly thank the two of you, but I hope you know how much I love you.

Dave: my husband, best friend, and the most reliable grammarian and editor I know. Thank you for being my partner in every way.

My siblings: Owen, thank you for always knowing the answer to any historical question I ever ask. Teddy and Emled, thank you for inspiring me to look deeply into questions and to pursue dreams passionately. Emily, thank you for telling me, years ago when I first set out on this journey, to look for the conflict that makes characters compelling, and for encouraging me at every step since then.

Nelson and Louisa: thank you for believing in me even before I knew this was something worth believing in. I'll never forget the moment when you offered your initial feedback for my very first (and very "rough") manuscript. Your belief in me meant more than you know. And to all the Levys: my second family, I have learned so much from you on how a family ought to love and support one another.

To Jan Miller and the entire team at Dupree Miller & Associates: thank you for your faith and for taking a chance on me, years ago, when there was still much work ahead. To my agent and friend, the tireless Lacy Lynch: you are truly talented at what you do and there's no one I'd rather have championing my work.

To Jonathan Merkh, Beth Adams, Amanda Demastus, and the entire team at Howard Books and Simon & Schuster: thank you for sharing my vision and helping me to make it a reality. To my editor, Beth Adams: somehow you managed to make the editing process fun. Thank you for your diligence and your dogged devotion to *The Traitor's Wife.*

To the earliest readers and editors: Marya Myers, my first guinea pig and constant cheerleader, thank you for your contagious enthusiasm; Charlotte d'Orchimont, my sounding board and soul sister, thank you for always understanding what I'm trying to say; Margaret, my cover model and favorite playmate with whom to explore our beloved jungle gym—the imagination; Carolyn Rossi Copeland, Jamie Copeland, and the Copeland girls—my home away from home and the first people with whom I discovered the joys of creating; Liz Steinberg: my Philadelphia tour-guide and constant confidante. Other dear friends have helped by reading, editing, and encouraging me throughout the process: Cristina Corbin and

Jonathan Corbin, Kasdin Miller, Cristina Scudder, Shannon Farrell, Alyssa Oakley, Emily Shuey, Dana Schuster, and Jackie Carter.

And to the many others who have helped me on this journey: Zenia Mucha, thank you for your belief in me and my work; Allison McCabe, your early editorial expertise taught me how to develop a manuscript; Philip Rowland, thank you for my website and for your enthusiastic support; and to Tessa and Andrew Farnsworth, Sheila Weber, Fred Newman, and Earle and Carol Mack, thank you.

Reading Group Guide

THE TRAITOR'S WIFE

A Novel

Allison Pataki

Introduction

When turncoat Benedict Arnold aided the British during the Revolutionary War, he wasn't acting alone. Orchestrating the espionage was his spouse, the beautiful socialite Peggy Shippen, whose treachery nearly cost the fledgling nation its fight for freedom. In *The Traitor's Wife,* Allison Pataki brings to life an intriguing slice of American history, told from the perspective of Peggy's lady's maid, Clara Bell, who must decide where her own loyalties lie.

Topics and Questions for Discussion

1. Before moving to Philadelphia, Clara spent her entire life on a farm in the Pennsylvania countryside. How does Clara's identity evolve throughout her years of service to Peggy and Benedict Arnold? What character traits does Clara retain? Discuss which characters have the greatest impact on Clara's growth and development.

2. Why does Clara take a nearly instant dislike to Major John André? Why is she relieved when Judge and Mrs. Shippen refuse to allow Peggy to attend the Meshianza Masque? Compare the way André treats Peggy with how Caleb treats Clara.

3. Clara is flattered at "having so quickly become her lady's confidante and friend" (page 108). Does Peggy sincerely consider Clara a friend, or is Clara misreading her mistress? Why does Clara so desperately crave Peggy's approval, and even friendship? At what point does this begin to shift?

4. Discuss the theme of loyalty in the novel. What drives the different characters' allegiances? Who is the most loyal character?

5. “I hate the man, and I always will,” says Peggy of Benedict Arnold (page 135). Why then does she begin pursuing him the first time they meet? Does she truly come to care about him, or is it all an act?

6. What is your view of Benedict Arnold? Trace his evolution from ardent patriot to turncoat. Do you think he would have committed treason without Peggy’s influence? Why or why not? Discuss both his and Peggy’s motivations for aiding the British.

7. “My husband knows how to win on the battlefield. It’s all brute strength and fighting. But spy work is different—it requires poise, and self-control, and grace. It’s like a delicate dance. And if anyone knows how to dance, it’s me,” says Peggy (page 303). Which traits make Peggy better suited for espionage than Arnold? Why does the couple freely discuss their plans in front of Clara? Is it because they trust her not to reveal their secrets or, as Clara believes, because they find her invisible?

8. When Arnold’s treachery is revealed, he immediately flees and leaves Peggy behind. Given the circumstances, are his actions justifiable in any way? Why doesn’t Peggy hold it against him? Share whether or not you were surprised that Peggy was able to so easily convince George Washington and his companions of her innocence.

9. Does Clara intentionally or unintentionally help the Arnolds commit treason by cracking André’s code and translating the clandestine correspondence? Does her role make Clara partly to blame? What would you have done if you were in her position?

10. At one point in the story, Clara laments that she is not the master of her own fate. How do she and Caleb take charge of their future, both individually and as a couple? Discuss Clara’s warring emotions of impotency and desperation to intervene in the Arnolds’ plot.

11. When Clara confides in Mrs. Quigley about the Arnolds’ plotting, why is the older woman so quick to dismiss her claims? When Mrs. Quigley later understands exactly what’s happening, why does she still advise against Clara and Caleb taking action to stop the Arnolds?

Explore how Mrs. Quigley's response to the news differs from Caleb's response to the news. Does either of them understand Clara's position and perspective?

12. Examine the character of George Washington. Why does the novel open on the morning of his visit? What does George Washington mean to Benedict Arnold? To Peggy Arnold? To the servants like Hannah, Caleb, Clara, or the Quigleys? Discuss whether George Washington's disapproval was the impetus for Arnold to agree to treason.

13. How does Clara use tactics she learned from observing her mistress to achieve her freedom from Peggy? What gives Clara the strength and courage to stand up to the imposing Peggy? Would Clara actually have reported Peggy's guilt, or was it a bluff?

14. When news comes that Arnold successfully escaped, why is Clara relieved he won't hang for his crimes? Why does she promise to keep quiet about Peggy's role in the plot?

15. In what ways did *The Traitor's Wife* give you new insights into the Revolutionary War? What, if anything, did you learn that surprised you?

A Conversation with Allison Pataki

Q: It seems remarkable that one woman might have come so close to single-handedly turning the tide of the Revolutionary War. Why do you suppose Peggy's part in the treasonous plot didn't come to light sooner?

A: My thoughts exactly! And why don't more people know about the role Peggy Arnold played in her husband's life and career? That was how I felt when I came across the story, and that's been the consistent reaction I've gotten as I've told people about *The Traitor's Wife.* People find it hard to believe the story is true, because if it was, why hadn't they heard about it?

According to Arnold biographers, people didn't learn of Peggy's role in the plot until the nineteenth century, after all of the principle players in the plot were deceased. Apparently Aaron Burr (the man responsible for Alexander Hamilton's death—of all people!) confessed what he knew of Peggy's role on his deathbed, based on Peggy's own confessions while she was alive. Whether or not the Burr deathbed confession is credible (though many historians have debated that point and assert that it is), there is plenty of other proof of her involvement. The New York Public Library has letters exchanged between Arnold and André, on which you can see Peggy's handwriting. And, how else would her former suitor have come into contact with her husband?

I think Peggy understood and skillfully harnessed the belief of the time—the flawed supposition that women were much less intelligent or capable than men. Boy, did she use that to her advantage!

Q: As an epigraph to *The Traitor's Wife* you selected a quotation by Lady Macbeth, and another from Benedict Arnold's own letter. Why did you select these quotations?

A: I love epigraphs and I'm always intrigued by which quotations writers choose to begin their books with, and why. The Lady Macbeth quotation was on my mind from the beginning. I went back and reread *Macbeth* before I began writing *The Traitor's Wife* because I wanted to revisit some of the themes of the play. I especially wanted to read Lady Macbeth's speeches to her husband. Lady Macbeth is literature's consummate double-dealer. She charms the men and welcomes them into her home, all the while she's whispering into her husband's ear to kill the king and take his crown. She uses soft, beautiful words to incite gruesome and treacherous actions.

I was intrigued by the similarities between Lady Macbeth's style and how Peggy Arnold enacted her plot. Peggy, like Lady Macbeth, believed in her husband. She felt that he had been denied the glory he deserved. She was patient and strategic and bitter and ruthless. She knew how to charm and coax and manipulate people with her words. And she welcomed the leader, George Washington, into her home with a smile, all the while intending to betray him and quite possibly cost him his life.

The whole thing just felt so Shakespearean, with all the plotting, the human foibles, and the drama. I kept telling people as I was working on it: the Arnolds' story is so salacious, you really cannot make this stuff up! And it's true. One difference, however, is that Lady Macbeth gets her comeuppance in the end, whereas Peggy Shippen Arnold makes it out unscathed. Maybe Peggy was the greater wit, even more cunning than Lady Macbeth!

And then the Benedict Arnold quotation just makes me sad every time

I read it. In that letter, you are seeing Arnold attempt to exculpate himself in the hours after his plot had failed. He wrote it knowing that all ties to the country he had once served and loved were irreparably severed. Knowing that his greatest hero, George Washington, now wished him dead. It's tough to imagine how Arnold must have felt while writing that letter. Did he truly believe that what he had done had been in the best interest of the country, or was he simply making a justification? And, if it *was* just a justification, to whom was he speaking? To himself? To Washington? To history and the crafters of his legacy? It's hard to know. But I do think it's true what he says—that the world "*very seldom judge(s) right of any man's actions.*" The truth is always more complicated than it appears.

Q: Peggy and Clara are on opposite ends of the social spectrum, one born into a wealthy family and the other a servant and orphan. Did you find it challenging, energizing, or both to write about these two very different main characters?

A: I found it exciting. It was fun to explore the ways in which these two women, with their different resources and perspectives, would have navigated the events into which they were thrust. In some ways, Clara and Peggy are similar. They are both young women of pretty much the same age (Peggy is one year older). Both of their fates are inextricably tied to the fate of not only the Arnold family, but also the new country. They resemble one another physically. Look how easy it is for Clara to masquerade as Peggy's sister once she has the right hairdo and the right dress.

And yet they occupy completely different worlds. Clara begins the novel as a naïve, friendless servant who has never known anyone so sophisticated and worldly and charming. Clara has never had fancy dresses, or gentleman suitors, or even her own bed. That is why, at first, Clara is so enamored of Peggy Shippen. Clara's new mistress is this popular, witty, fashionable force who has all of Philadelphia society at her feet, and Peggy not only wants Clara to work for her, but seems to want Clara as a *friend*. Clara is, in her own way, just as seduced by Peggy as many of the other characters in the novel are. Given the social and economic disparities between the two of them, it's clear why Clara becomes pretty much entirely dependent on Peggy.

But just as Clara is reliant on her mistress, so too is Peggy dependent on Clara. She invites Clara out with her; she asks for Clara on her wedding day; she moves Clara with her to set up her new home. You see time and again that when Peggy is in a particularly tough spot, it's Clara whom she asks for. But then, as Peggy's luck worsens, it's Clara who suffers. It's the classic case of someone venting their anger on the person nearest to them, the person they trust so implicitly that they take his or her presence entirely for granted. That's why, even after everything devolves with the plot to turn over West Point, Peggy reacts so violently to the idea of Clara leaving her employ. She can't fathom the possibility of Clara not always being there.

Q: How would it have been different had you written this novel from Peggy's perspective?

A: The novel would have been entirely different had I written it from Peggy's perspective—both for the reader, and also for me as the writer. I think introducing Clara's perspective allowed it to be a more well-rounded story.

Writing from Clara's perspective allowed me to interject feelings like hope, optimism, insecurity, and idealism into the novel. All of the feelings that one might have felt as they witnessed a new nation's fight for independence. Clara and Caleb are the consummate idealists—they completely believe in what the fight for American freedom would have been at its best. They believe in the new country, and in George Washington, and in the futures they see as possible. And they, like the new country, are young and naïve and incredibly vulnerable to forces that seem more powerful than they are.

Written from Peggy's perspective, the book would have been a much more tense, much more uncomfortable experience, I think. With Clara as the protagonist, the reader can be introduced to Peggy, just as Clara is. The reader can be seduced by Peggy, but also repulsed by her. I hope that Peggy is the woman that you love to hate. Seeing it through Clara's eyes, the reader has a front-row view to the scheming and the double-dealing (which can be really fun to witness), but also enjoy a refreshing dose of sincerity and guilelessness. Peggy is anything but guileless!

Q: The upstairs/downstairs aspect of the novel is intriguing. Did you intend from the start to juxtapose the lives of a well-to-do family with those of their servants, or is it something that developed during the writing process? What kind of a shift is there between older servants like the Quigleys and younger ones like Caleb and Clara?

A: I absolutely set out with the intention of weaving those two different worlds together. So many of the old Colonial era homes I've seen have the front half of the house, and the servants' half of the house. There are separate doors, separate stairways, separate bedrooms. A "servants' wing" seems like such an antiquated architectural feature now, doesn't it? But I was always fascinated by the upstairs/downstairs dynamic, and how these households must have felt so differently depending on which side of the door you lived on. I think, in many ways, the dramas and perspectives that play out in the servants' wings of this book are even more exciting than what is going on on the other side of the house. And, like I mentioned above, the fates and futures of the servants would have been just as tied to the outcome of the American Revolution as were the fates of families like the Shippens or Arnolds.

Benedict Arnold is a figure who could have easily moved back and forth between these two realms. He was always so beloved by his men, and was really known as a man of the people. I tried to illustrate that, and to show his longing, at times, to be able to shed the pressures and burdens of his upper-class lifestyle in order to share in the camaraderie and companionship of people like Clara or the Quigleys.

I imagined the shift between the older servants and the younger ones as I would describe it today, even if that is slightly anachronistic. I'm not sure whether it is or not. Caleb and Clara are young and healthy and strong—and naïve. Of course they are going to be more willing to take risks. They might even be, at times, reckless, as young people are more wont to be. The Quigleys, I imagined, would be much more risk averse. They have known nothing their entire lives but the life of the servant, and they are content. Why tamper with that? Why hazard everything, including your life? But yet, that can be naïve too, because if you fail to take action, you make yourself powerless to the events around you. Both perspectives benefit from hearing the other one. That was how I saw it.

Q: While others around Judge Shippen, including his brother and Peggy, are vocal about supporting one side or the other during the Revolutionary War, he refuses to align himself with either. How unusual was his decision to remain neutral and not take sides?

A: Not unusual at all. John Adams wrote that one third of the population supported independence, one third remained loyal to England, and one third remained neutral. Historians aren't unanimously agreed on the percentages, but it was by no means a universal sentiment that the colonies should break from England. Judge Shippen probably felt a personal allegiance to the British, but publicly he remained neutral.

Q: Could something like this happen today?

A: Espionage obviously persists to this day, but I don't think it could happen like this. What struck me was how much longer it took for information to be transmitted. News could only spread as quickly as a horse could carry a messenger. Or, more often, as quickly as a person could walk a letter from point A to point B. The fact that Washington didn't hear of Arnold's treachery because the messenger took the wrong road and didn't deliver the letter in time astounds me. Especially when Arnold escaped by only a matter of minutes. Nowadays, it would have been a text message or a cell phone call and the plot would have been known in seconds.

That's why I had so much fun with the theme of writing and reporting. Everyone in this book is always writing and reading letters and reports. There are the love letters to Peggy, then the newspaper reports about Arnold, then the damning letter of censure from Washington to Arnold. There are the secret spy letters to André, there are the letters between Clara and Cal, and of course you have the fatal documents found in André's boots. All of this news was flying back and forth all the time, and so much of it got redirected or misinterpreted or apprehended. It made for so much confusion and so much drama.

Q: "But when you're in a position of power, your friends can become more dangerous than your enemies," says Caleb in *The Traitor's Wife* (page 174). Arnold certainly faced a number of critics from his own side. Why do you think that was? And how did those soured relationships impact his fate?

A: "Poor Benedict Arnold" was how I felt, time and again, while researching his life. As strange as that may sound, he really did face a legion of critics on the colonial side, and I do believe he was treated unfairly at times. His internecine rivalries and feuds began in the very first days of the Revolutionary War. When both Arnold and Ethan Allen led the joint mission to take Fort Ticonderoga from the British, Ethan Allen and his Green Mountain Men enjoyed all of the credit. Some of Allen's men, drunk after the victory, reportedly held a pistol to Arnold's chest when Arnold demanded that they stop looting and drinking. The men taunted Arnold and threatened "another war inside the fort."

During the Battle of Quebec, when he was first shot in the left leg, Arnold held out with just his ragtag team of men for the entire winter of 1776. They were frozen and starving. Arnold paid his men and fed his men with his own fortune during the entire siege, and wrote on multiple occasions that he was fully prepared to die for the Revolution.

Arnold was fighting on Lake Champlain, preventing a British invasion, when his colleagues were in Philadelphia during the summer of 1776, signing their names to the immortal Declaration of Independence. Arnold fought the British in Norwalk, Connecticut, famously shooting his own horse out from under himself in order to prevent it from falling into British hands. Arnold was with George Washington just four days before Washington famously crossed the Delaware to victory in Trenton. Again, had Arnold been there just four days later, he might have been able to share in some of that glory.

The one battle where Arnold finally earned the recognition that was due to him was the Battle of Saratoga, the undisputed turning point of the war. It would have been a British victory, if not for Benedict Arnold. Arnold repelled the British attack, and then defied the orders of his commander, General Horatio Gates, to lead the crushing attack on the British. It was during this battle that Arnold was shot a second time in his left leg. He did in fact refuse a surgeon's orders for amputation, and suffered severe pain from then on.

In spite of his skill in battle, Arnold seemed to make enemies at every turn. He was passed over for promotions constantly; he was never reimbursed by the Continental Congress for the thousands of dollars he had spent; and he was never again able to walk without pain. And in spite of this, he saw himself constantly mocked and delegitimized by his colleagues. Throughout the early years of war, though the American people absolutely adored him, it seemed that Arnold's only ally in the army was General George Washington.

It was after all of these battles and feuds had occurred that Arnold assumed his role as military commander in Philadelphia. In that city, Arnold faced his greatest nemesis yet: Joseph Reed. Reed was a man who got along with no one. Reed even disliked Washington, whom everyone admired and loved. But Reed turned the majority of his vitriol on Arnold, slandering him to the press and deriding him to the Continental Congress.

This maddened Arnold, who wrote to Washington: *"I have nothing left but the little reputation I have gained in the army."* In Arnold's defense, much of the back-alley trading that he conducted in the city was a fairly common practice. And many American generals at the time butted heads with their civilian counterparts. But Arnold's critics always seemed to win the public relations campaign, and he was time and again painted as a very ornery, apish, questionable figure.

If you use George Washington as the gold standard of how a leader at that time should have behaved, you see that even Washington was disappointed to see some of Arnold's behavior in Philadelphia. And, perhaps, rightly so. Washington was a man whose own personal conduct was above reproach. It was at this time that Washington, who had been his advocate in every single previous internecine dispute, did show some frustration with the constantly beleaguered Arnold. But some historians assert that Washington *had* to issue his censure (which is actually relatively light). Reed had allegedly threatened to pull the Pennsylvania militia if Washington did not censure Arnold. In the letter Washington wrote after the court-martial, the high commander states: *"Even the shadow of a fault tarnishes the luster of our finest achievements. I reprimand you for having forgotten that, in proportion as you have rendered yourself formidable to our enemies you should have been guarded and temperate in your deportment towards your fellow citizens."*

These words, however measured they may seem, crushed Arnold. So, it's hard to exactly know how it all evolved. Was Arnold treated so unfairly, time and again, that he became bitter? Or was Arnold a difficult personality who invited all of this criticism and enmity? Perhaps it's not black and white, and perhaps it's some combination. I guess we will never know. But, unfortunately for Arnold, he got one big decision wrong. And that decision, to turn to the British, is how history has remembered him.

Q: In the afterword, you mention that your family's home is near West Point, New York, and the former Arnold residence. Did growing up in such a storied place influence your decision to write historical fiction?

A: *This* historical fiction in particular. West Point is right across the river, so we grew up looking at it every day and learning about the role it and the Hudson River Valley played in the American Revolution. And George Washington spent a lot of time in our area during the Revolutionary War, as a result. I have many memories of playing in the yard that was once Benedict Arnold's yard. It made that portion of the story that much more fun to write—I had major home court advantage!

But yes, growing up in a place where history is so alive and accessible and ubiquitous definitely contributed to my love of historical fiction. My parents always stopped to read the historical markers, and we were always getting impromptu history lessons. In fact, I think it's rare that a family dinner doesn't turn to a history lesson—someone always has some fascinating historical nugget that he/she wants to share.

Historical fiction is without a doubt my favorite genre to read. It was a no-brainer that it was also what I wanted to write. In college, I had a really hard time deciding whether to major in English or history. I went with English, but now, I don't have to make that choice. I get to blend my two favorite dorky pastimes—reading/writing with history. Yes, please!

Q: When writing a historical fiction, what role does the research play? How do you decide when to deviate from the facts and when to stick to them? Discuss your process.

A: I hadn't intended to rely as heavily as I did on the historical list of characters and events. However, it wasn't long into my research that I realized I was dealing with some *very* intriguing material, and that the cast of characters I found, along with the events that unfolded around them, had the potential to inspire a very salacious plot. Obviously the servant characters—Clara, Caleb, the Quigleys, etc.—are entirely fictional, so that half of the plot is not based on any historical figures. But I would have been crazy *not* to rely heavily on the real facts!

In terms of the process, I definitely do most of the research before I begin writing anything. This allows me to map out the framework of the plot—dates, locations, characters, etc. So for this novel, I read as many biographies and historical sources as I could find. I visited the places where the action occurred. I visited museums and libraries in Philadelphia and New York. All of this was helpful in learning about the historical context and the events that made up the story. And then once I have the historical skeleton in place, I get to make up the rest.

While writing, I'll come across moments when I realize I need to go back and do some more research. I'll be writing and I'll realize I don't know what Peggy's dress would have looked like, or what sort of furniture they would have sat on, or what sort of music they would have been listening to. It's all very fun.

Q: What advice would you give to someone who wants to write a first novel?

A: Do it! Write the novel. People are always telling me that they have a book idea and that they want to write. To which I always say: do it! This started out as a guilty pleasure for me—something I would do to unwind at the end of a workday or work week. I had no idea that it would turn into something real. You never know until you try. If you're inspired to write a novel or a poem or a screenplay, you are lucky. Inspiration in any context is an incredible blessing.

Oh, and, the other thing I would say: be kind to yourself along the way. Don't expect yourself to bang out a polished manuscript on the first try. If you do, then more power to you. But a first draft should be treated as a first draft, not a glossy, finished novel.

Q: Are you currently working on another book? If so, what details can you share about the story?

A: Absolutely! I've got several books in the works, at various stages of completion. They are all in the historical fiction genre. And I hope that they, like *The Traitor's Wife*, will shine a light on a well-known, fascinating moment in time—but from a new angle or different perspective. The best part of reading a book, in my opinion, is being transported to another time period. You get to see that world through another set of eyes. If I can give that experience to readers, then I will feel like I have accomplished my goal.

Enhance Your Book Club

Learn more about the Revolutionary War, including its major figures and decisive battles, at www.history.com/topics/american-revolution and www.pbs.org/ktca/liberty. On the latter website, you'll find the Road to Revolution trivia game to add some friendly competition to your book club gathering.

Hit the road on a historically themed outing. The interactive guide at www.nps.gov/revwar features places related to the Revolutionary War, which took place from Maine to Florida and as far west as Arkansas and Louisiana. Consider visiting Philadelphia, where Peggy Shippen met both Benedict Arnold and John André.

Peggy Shippen Arnold was renowned for her beauty. View a portrait of her at www.explorepahistory.com//displayimage.php?imgId=1-2-2E4, or search the website for "Mrs. Benedict Arnold and daughter."

Show your patriotic pride by having book club members dress in red, white, and blue, as Peggy did when Benedict Arnold came to call on her. If your loyalties lie with the British, stick with red attire.